"John Weisman redefines high-impact, action-adventure suspense novels for the decade."
James Grady, author of *Six Days of the Condor* and *River of Darkness*

Former CIA Moscow station chief Sam Waterman left his post in disgrace, damned for a deadly foul-up not of his doing. But now the return of a legendary traitor to America's shores is pulling Waterman back into the lethal shadow world he left behind—because his nation's very survival depends upon it.

Despised defector Edward Lee Howard has come home bearing dangerous secrets and a stunning allegation: the U.S. intelligence community has been infiltrated by moles at the highest levels, their influence spreading into the White House itself. Their secret agendas already helped to bring about the most horrific terrorist attack the world has ever seen. And their treachery is paving the way for more.

"The kind of truth you can only tell in fiction, otherwise lives would be lost. John Weisman takes the reader into the very heart of the CIA and its special operations."
Robert Baer, author of *Sleeping with the Devil*

More resounding acclaim for
John Weisman and
JACK IN THE BOX

"There are only a few authors who are able to climb inside the culture, mindset, and passions of the people who conduct covert and special operations . . . John Weisman is the best in the business at writing about it."

William S. Cohen, former U.S. Secretary of Defense

"One of the best in the thriller business . . . It is refreshing to spend an afternoon with an author who writes intelligently about the new focus of intelligence—counterterrorism . . . A mole chase made all the more interesting by Mr. Weisman's wide use of spy lore, references to actual cases, and detailed tradecraft."

Washington Times

"Engrossing . . . Lavishly sprinkled with scenes and details of state-of-the-art tradecraft."

Alan Cheuse, NPR "All Things Considered"

Books by John Weisman

JACK IN THE BOX
SOAR: A BLACK OPS MISSION
BLOOD CRIES
WATCHDOGS
EVIDENCE

The Rogue Warrior series
(with Richard Marcinko)

DETACHMENT BRAVO	ECHO PLATOON
SEAL FORCE ALPHA	OPTION DELTA
DESIGNATION GOLD	TASK FORCE BLUE
GREEN TEAM	RED CELL

NONFICTION
ROGUE WARRIOR *(with Richard Marcinko)*
SHADOW WARRIOR *(with Felix Rodriguez)*

ANTHOLOGIES
THE BEST AMERICAN MYSTERY STORIES OF 1997
(edited by Robert B. Parker)
UNUSUAL SUSPECTS
(edited by James Grady)

JACK IN THE BOX

A SHADOW WAR THRILLER

JOHN WEISMAN

AVON BOOKS

An Imprint of HarperCollins*Publishers*

The first two chapters of *Jack in the Box* appeared in the August 2002 *Playboy* magazine in a slightly different form under the title "A Day in the Country."

"A Day in the Country" was selected by the editors of *The Best American Mystery Stories of 2003* as one of the most distinguished mystery stories of 2002.

This is a work of fiction. Names, characters, places, and incidents are products of the author's imagination or are used fictitiously and are not to be construed as real. Any resemblance to actual events, locales, organizations, or persons, living or dead, is entirely coincidental. However, voluntary redactions of sensitive materials, sources, and methods have been made in accordance with current CIA Publications Review Board standards and practices.

AVON BOOKS
An Imprint of HarperCollins*Publishers*
10 East 53rd Street
New York, New York 10022-5299

Copyright © 2004 by John Weisman
Excerpt from *Direct Action* copyright © 2005 by John Weisman
Author photo by S.P. Weisman
ISBN 0-06-057069-5
www.avonbooks.com

First Avon Books paperback printing: May 2005
First William Morrow hardcover printing: June 2004

Avon Trademark Reg. U.S. Pat. Off. and in Other Countries, Marca Registrada, Hecho en U.S.A.
HarperCollins® is a registered trademark of HarperCollins Publishers Inc.

Printed in the U.S.A.

10 9 8 7 6 5 4 3 2 1

Three may keep a secret, if two of them are dead.

—Benjamin Franklin,
Poor Richard's Almanac, July 1735

CONTENTS

JACK-IN-THE-BOX

Jack-in-the-Box (JIB): CIA-devised automobile pop-up dummy used to deceive, mislead, and foil hostile surveillance during denied area operations.

14.00 JIP Technique (from the Central Intelligence Agency's DENIED AREA OPERATIONS TRAINING COURSE SYLLABUS, REV 3/10/02)

14.01 The case officer/driver creates a GAP (a distance sufficient enough so that his vehicle is out of direct sight of the surveillance vehicles) between himself and the opposition.

14.02 Once within the GAP, the CIA vehicle slows at a prearranged spot. The case officer/passenger quickly exits the car and seeks concealment. As the CIA vehicle accelerates away, the case officer/driver releases a JIB pop-up dummy.

14.03 If executed properly, hostile surveillance will not detect the JIB maneuver until it is far too late for the hostile team to carry out effective COUNTERMEASURES.

JACK IN
THE BOX

PART I

MOSCOW

CHAPTЭЯ 1

SAM WATERMAN spent the morning of his forty-fifth birthday a hostage to his profession, stuffed rudely onto the rear floorboard of one of the consulate's 1985-vintage four-door Zil sedans, the driveshaft hump wedged uncomfortably against his kidneys, his long legs tucked fetal, his body hidden under a damp blanket. Even though he knew he couldn't be seen through the dark-tinted windows, he still held his breath as the car clunked over the antiterrorist barriers just prior to passing the Russian police checkpoint outside the garage gate. He exhaled slowly when the driveshaft under his side whined as the car merged into the late-morning traffic.

"Keep going, keep going," Sam instructed tersely from under musty cover. "Don't check your mirrors. Just drive. Nice and easy."

"Don't have a cow, man." That was Consular Officer Tom Kennedy, imitating Bart Simpson. Tom, who'd been recruited to do the driving, could impersonate Bart perfectly.

He was still working on his Homer, though, running and re-running the videotapes his sister sent him through the mail pouch, night after night after night. Which kind of told you what Moscow's social life had to offer a reasonably good-looking African-American junior-grade diplomat, even in these post-Soviet days.

Sam grunted and shifted his position slightly, trying to reduce the pressure on his kidneys as the car turned left, heading west.

"We're on Kutuzovsky Prospekt," Homer told him. "*Doh.* Crossroads of the world."

"Tom, put a cork in it." Christ, he'd warned the kid this was serious business, and the youngster still wanted to talk. Not good. Because they weren't safe. Not by a long shot. FSB,[1] the Russian internal security agency, had inherited the KGB's elaborate passive surveillance system. *Vizirs* they were called—long-range, high-power telescopes mounted on sturdy tripods, positioned in buildings along Moscow's major thoroughfares. The watchers would scan for diplomatic plates, and peer inside the cars. If they saw your lips moving, they'd take note. Were you talking to someone hidden in the car? Were you operating a burst transmitter in the open brief-case on the passenger seat? Were you broadcasting? If they thought you were up to no good, they'd dispatch one of the static counterintelligence teams that were all over the city to do a traffic stop—dip plates or no.

And Sam couldn't afford a traffic stop. Not today.

Today he had to meet General Pavel Baranov at precisely five past one, and failure wasn't a viable option. The rendezvous was critical. Baranov had used his emergency call-out signal, an inconspicuous broken chalk line on a weatherworn

---

[1] *Federal'naya Sluzhba Bezopasnosti.*

lamppost sixty yards from the entrance to the Arbatskaya metro stop. Sam had seen the *long-short-short* Morse code signal last night on his regular evening jog—a five-mile run that began outside the embassy's faded mustard-colored walls and took a long, meandering, but unfailingly consistent route that brought him all the way to the western boundary of the Kremlin, and thence back toward the embassy.

The Arbatskaya signal site and the letter *D* were to be used by Baranov only under crisis conditions. Still in his running gear, Sam sent Langley a code-word-secret "criticom," an urgent cable alerting his division chief to Baranov's emergency signal (in the cable Sam referred to Baranov not by his true name, but by his CIA cryptonym, GTLADLE; Sam's CIA in-house pseudonym, which he used to sign the cable, was Cyrus N. PRINGLE).[2] In it, he enumerated all the operational details for the emergency PMP[3] and requested comment. Today he was awake by five, running and rerunning the operation in his mind. By six he was in the office, checking for response from Langley—there was none, which was typical—and removing gear from the duffel he kept in ▓▓▓▓▓▓ walk-in safe.

The next step was to shanghai young Tom Kennedy, one of three greenhorn consular officers Sam had identified as potential decoys. The decoy factor was critical. As CIA's Moscow chief, Sam was "declared" to the Russians. He even held regular meetings with his counterparts at SVR, the Russian foreign intelligence service. And thanks to an American defector, a CIA turncoat named Edward Lee Howard who'd been transferred into FSB, Russia's internal

[2] CIA in-house pseudonyms are invariably three-part names: first name, middle initial, and last name. The last name is always spelled entirely in capital letters.
[3] Personal Meeting Plan.

security and counterintelligence service by Vladimir Putin, the Kremlin's aggressive new director of counterintelligence, FSB pretty much knew who was Agency and who wasn't.

Ed Howard and Sam Waterman had history. In fact, sometimes Sam felt as if the traitor was shadowing him. He and Howard had been members of the same basic Russian-language studies class at Georgetown University. Subsequently, Howard sat next to Sam at the CIA's language institute in Rosslyn during the two-year, advanced Russian course. They'd even shared a room at ██████████████, the Agency's case-officer training facility near Williamsburg also known as the Farm, for the six-week class in advanced tradecraft procedures required of all case officers assigned behind the Iron Curtain.

But that's where the relationship stopped. As he readied himself for his first Warsaw Pact tour, Sam was already an experienced case officer with a successful tour in Germany. He'd run an agent network and worked against a KGB *Rezident*. Howard was a greenhorn trainee who had never handled an agent or worked in the pressure cooker atmosphere of a real-world op.

Despite that lack of experience, Howard had been selected to go to Moscow under deep State Department cover. But then, in the spring of 1983, Ed Howard flunked four separate polygraph tests—and his career was abruptly terminated.

On May 2, 1983, Howard was told to report to the personnel office. Sam had even seen him in the corridor. The distraught young case officer was flanked by two armed CIA security agents. Later, Sam heard that when Howard got to personnel, he was given papers to sign, fired on the spot, and escorted from the building. Although Howard and his wife Mary moved back to their home in New Mexico almost immediately, he was kept on CIA payroll through the end of June. Sam never saw him again.

Then Howard started acting strangely. From New Mexico, a distraught-sounding Howard made open-line telephone calls to the U.S. embassy in Moscow that let KGB eavesdroppers know that he was a disgruntled CIA employee who'd just been fired. After half a dozen similar provocations, including two trips to Vienna, where CIA countersurveillance teams had spotted the former case officer meeting with known KGB officers, the FBI was called in. Howard was interrogated half a dozen times but denied any collusion with the Soviets. The FBI didn't believe him and assigned twenty-four-hour surveillance to the fired CIA operative. His arrest seemed imminent.

But the FBI blew the case. The surveillance crew assigned to Howard were New Mexico locals who never factored into their operations that Howard had been trained to evade KGB surveillance. It didn't take the former CIA trainee long to note their below-average performance. And so, Ed Howard used basic CIA tradecraft to evade the G–men. Late in September 1985, he and his then-wife fabricated a jack-in-the-box device for their car, then went for a drive along a route he had carefully worked out. Once she'd put sufficient distance between their vehicle and the FBI agents to open a GAP, she slowed down. Howard jumped out and hid in some bushes. His wife activated the JIB, sped away, returned home, drove straight into the garage, and dropped the door. It took the FBI almost twenty-four hours to realize Howard had skipped.

In the meanwhile, Howard flew from Albuquerque through Tucson to New York, where he caught a plane for London. At Heathrow, he connected to a flight for Copenhagen, and thence to Helsinki, where he went straight to the Soviet embassy and asked for political asylum. Six days later, using reports from an MI6 source in Helsinki, British counterintelligence cabled Langley's CI[4] gumshoes that Howard had handed the KGB a foot-thick pile of documents. The double-crossing son of a bitch even betrayed (among many other jewels) all the Agency tradecraft he'd learned during the "Denied Area Operations" course required of all case officers assigned to Moscow, Prague, Warsaw, Paris, Bonn, Delhi, and other stations where local counterintelligence capabilities were exceptional and the opposition was active.

Howard presented the DAO course syllabus to his new masters at Moscow Center as evidence of his bona fides. He'd immediately been put to work at the KGB's Second Chief Directorate–counterintelligence, followed by a long tour in the First Chief Directorate, where he trolled much of Western Europe for American agents. And now the rotten son of a bitch spent his days working for Vlad Putin at the FSB, using everything he'd learned at Langley against his former colleagues.

Which meant whenever one of Sam's people drove, surveillance was virtually guaranteed. So Sam went outside the box and used an outsider, a junior consular officer Vlad Putin's FSB understood to be totally uninvolved in intelligence gathering.

At 9:06 A.M., Sam strode unannounced into the expansive office of Sandra Wheeler, the consul general. At 9:12 he returned to his own secure ████████████████. Seven minutes after that, there was a tentative knock on Sam's thick door. *Enter Thomas Jefferson Kennedy, Foreign Service Officer Grade Four, stage left.* Twelve minutes later, a wide-eyed

---

[4] Counterintelligence.

Thomas J. Kennedy headed for the garage, having received his first inculcation into the shadowy Wilderness of Mirrors in which Samuel Elbridge Waterman had lived and worked for almost nineteen years.

1

0:38 A.M. The drivetrain had developed a nasty vibration. Sam could feel it shudder through the floorboard. He was sweating even though the Zil's heater didn't work. He lay silent, eyes closed, counting the seconds off, timing the route he'd painstakingly devised, as Tom drove in blessed silence. They'd be heading northwest now, less than a kilometer from the Ring Road that encircled the city. At the Volokolamskoe on-ramp they'd turn north, toward the M10 and Moscow's Sheremetevo airport.

But they wouldn't go to Sheremetevo. Instead, the youngster would exit south, onto Leningradskoe, and divert to a narrow, deserted strip of parkland where Sam would roll out. Then Tom would drive like hell to the airport, where he'd wait in the no-parking zone—in vain—for a consular official scheduled to arrive from Berlin. And, yes, tickets had been bought. There was even a Russian visa stamped in the nonarrival's diplomatic passport just in case the Russians ever checked. Sam had thought of everything, right down to the smallest detail. "Plausible" and "denial," after all, were the two foremost watchwords of his particular faith.

Sam squinted at the dim luminous dial on his cheap Bulgarian wristwatch. Thirty-nine minutes had elapsed since the car passed through the embassy gates. The Zil banked hard right. In his head, Sam saw the exit and the industrial zone. He felt Tom brake, accelerate, then brake again. *Showtime.* Sam pulled the blanket off, reached up, opened the rear door, and scrambled out next to the pockmarked brick wall of a narrow alley. He rapped the Zil's door. "Go-go-go!"

Alone, he made his way southwest toward a narrow swath

of green parkland. He checked the watch. He was two minutes behind schedule.

10:52 A.M. Sam caught the sparsely passengered ferry with seventy-five seconds to spare, paid for his ticket, and found a hardwood bench in the rear of the smoky passenger cabin for the six-minute voyage to Zaharkovo. Halfway across, he went to the men's toilet. Even unheated, the cramped compartment stank of urine. He stepped across a puddle under the tin trough that served as a pissoir, entered the single stall, shut the door, and quickly shed his long black nylon overcoat. Underneath, he wore a thigh-length brown patchwork leather jacket. He stuffed the coat behind the toilet. He extracted a false mustache from its envelope, exposed the adhesive, and affixed the disguise to his upper lip. He ripped up the envelope and flushed it. Finally, he pulled a short-brimmed, green wool cap from the jacket pocket and jammed it on his head.

He left the men's room just in time to feel the engines reverse as the boat pulled alongside the quay. Without reentering the cabin, he elbowed his way to the rail, nudged up the gangway, walked up the dock and across the street. There he climbed aboard a waiting No. 96 bus, which he rode to the Tušinskaja metro stop. Sixty-nine minutes and three train changes later he emerged from Textilshchiki station, crossed the road, and stepped gingerly over a single, rusting set of railroad tracks into a huge, deserted industrial park where, in the old days, they'd assembled Moskvich automobiles as part of Joe Stalin's workers' paradise.

What Sam had performed since leaving the Zil was an SDR, or Surveillance Detection Route. It was a planned, timed course during which he'd had half a dozen opportunities to spot a hostile tail. Not to shake it, however, simply to identify it. Only in Hollywood did CIA officers *shake* a tail.

In real life, you *spotted* the opposition. Under normal circumstances you did nothing to alert them, because if the other side realized they'd been tagged, they'd change surveillance methods, and the cycle would have to begin all over. Today's SDR was different. If he'd been spotted, he'd have had to go provocative—escape surveillance by using aggressive, evasive tradecraft. That was why Sam had spent six weeks crafting each segment of this particular SDR, even though he'd use it only once.

Six weeks, because he had to provide himself with a number of rabbit holes in case he had to disappear. Six weeks, because he had to make sure that no matter where he might be pinged, he could still go black—vanish in plain sight—without alerting the opposition. Most important, six weeks, because Vlad Putin's counterintelligence people were good. They didn't have the fourth-generation infrared sensors used by American CI gumshoes, or the state-of-the-art, ambient-noise filtering directional microphones built for CIA's countersurveillance teams by National Security Agency audioespionage specialists; instruments that could pick up a whisper across a busy intersection at distances of up to ▮▮▮ meters. But what the Russians lacked in technical means they more than made up for in human resources. The FSB could put a hundred and fifty people on one American case officer. Putin liked to use multiple teams and sophisticated methods, like the Дождь,[5] or rainfall technique, in which scores of watchers were monsooned against a target from all directions. But not today. Today Sam was clean. His finely tuned sonar hadn't picked up even the hint of a ping.

Sam walked until he reached an alley containing a row of

[5] *Dosht'.*

corrugated, sheet-metal gated sheds where Muscovites bribed the watchmen in hard currency so they could keep their autos under roof. The deserted streets leading to these shanties resembled a ghost town. But even if they had been crowded, no one would have paid Sam any mind, because the tall, gray-eyed man looked like any other local.

Careful to avoid getting mud on his scuffed shoes, he stepped around a rusted Latta with a tarp spread under the rear of its chassis. There were two blue-jeaned legs poking out. Sam's knuckles rapped the Latta's hood. "Yuri Gregorovich, is that you under there, or should I call the police?"

Yuri G. Semerov rented the shed next to his. Yuri, Sam knew (the Russian had been checked out by Langley to ensure he wasn't a provocateur), owned a store near the Arbat, where he sold everything from fake czarist antiques to Soviet Army uniforms.

The legs crabbed from under the vehicle, followed by a torso, then a thick arm holding a big crescent wrench, and finally a broad, flat, mustached Tartar face that peered warmly up at Sam. "Hello, Sergei Anatolyvich."

So far as Yuri Gregorovich Semerov knew, Sergei Anatolyvich Kozlov was an up-and-coming businessman with an unhappy marriage in Moscow and a mistress in a dacha near Podol'sk. And if he'd checked—something Sam knew he hadn't—Sam's cover would have been confirmed. "Long time no see. How's it going?"

"Any better I couldn't stand it," Sam answered effortlessly in Moscow-accented Russian. It was a gift. Some people have a natural aptitude for mathematics, or science. Others are innate painters, or musicians. Sam had an ear for languages. He learned them quickly and retained them. He spoke Russian at a five-plus level, in addition to four-plus

French, and workable German, Polish, and Czech. To get any better rating in Russian he'd have had to be born in the Soviet Union. Sam focused on Yuri Semerov and smiled mischievously. "Anytime I escape to Podol'sk for a few hours, life is great."

"I can imagine," Yuri said wistfully. He pulled himself into a sitting position and brandished the wrench. "Hey, have you got a number thirteen socket in there? This piece of shit won't catch on what's left of my tailpipe bracket bolt."

"I'll look." Sam withdrew a bunch of keys attached to a chain clipped to his belt. He squinted until he selected the right three, then unlocked a trio of padlocks the size of paperback books. The locks were carefully placed back on their hasps, then he scraped the battered door across the wet ground and disappeared inside.

There was silence for about forty seconds. What Yuri couldn't see was Sam retrieve a small electronic device from his jacket and quickly check the car for listening devices or locator beacons. The Russian heard only the sounds of an ignition stammering, followed by the hiccuping ca-ca-ca-coughs of an engine starting up, followed by half a dozen puffs of gray-black smoke emanating from the shed. Finally, Yuri watched as a beat-up Zhiguli coupe with local plates backed out onto the uneven dirt, sputtering and backfiring as it jerked clear of the shed.

Sam opened the car door and eased his big frame out from behind the wheel, his hand still playing with the choke. "I'll look for the socket for your Bentley while my Ferrari warms up."

Thirty seconds later he was back. "Nothing," Sam said. "I must have taken them home." He wrestled with the shed door, slapped the hasps closed, and replaced the padlocks. "Sorry, Yuri Gregorovich."

"No problem." Yuri watched as Sam compressed himself into the car. *Lucky bastard,* he thought, *to have a piece of ass on the side.* Then Yuri G. Semerov rolled onto his back and pulled himself under the Latta, cursing the cheap Georgian wrench as he heard the Zhiguli's engine grind off into the distance.

СНАРТЭЯ 2

1:04 P.M. Sam edged north on Prospekt Mira, caught the light, and turned left. Sixty feet past the metro, he pulled over just long enough to pick up a short, muscular man in a cheap fur hat, thick, patchwork leather hunting coat, and construction worker's boots who'd emerged from under the metro canopy, a rolled newspaper tucked under his left arm—that was the good-to-go VRS[6]—as Sam had turned the corner.

Sam extended a gloved hand to the Russian. "Pavel Dmitriyvich."

The Russian dropped the newspaper into the well, then slammed the reluctant door. "Sergei Anatolyvich," he responded, grasping the American's big paw tightly.

Sam gunned the engine, spun the wheel, and the little car accelerated past the botanical garden. "Next meeting on

---

[6] Visual Recognition Signal, which indicates that it is safe to proceed. If the agent believes conditions are unsafe, he/she will display a prearranged Danger Signal to warn off the case officer.

schedule in eight days," he said in English. "I'll leave a call-out signal on the Pushkin Museum mailbox. Letter *G*. We meet at the onetime back-up site—the *stalovaya* off Bolshaya Nitikskaya Street."

"Eight days. Pushkin mailbox. Letter *G*. *Stalovaya* off Bolshaya Nitikskaya. Got it."

"Today is only our second meeting," Sam continued tersely.

"Second meeting. Got it."

Sam turned left onto a small side street. "You have been trying to recruit me so you can pass me along to military intelligence. I have been open to the idea, but you're dubious because you believe me to be a provocateur. Nevertheless you suggested we get out of Moscow to escape CIA countersurveillance and talk things over some more."

"Dubious. Countersurveillance. Got it."

Now Sam made a series of turns, going left, then right, then left along the one-way streets, talking as he drove. "The Arbatskaya lamppost is dead. If you need an emergency meeting from here on, it's an *F* on the first lamppost to the left of the Lenin Library metro stop as you're facing north."

"Lenin Library lamppost, first left as I face north. Letter *F*. Got it."

"You remember what *F* is?"

"*F?*" The Russian harrumphed. "Short-short-long-short, Sam. My Morse is probably better than yours. In fact—"

"I'm changing the backup letterbox," Sam cut him off. This hurried tradecraft was known to case officers as the Mad Minute because it had to be completed within the first sixty seconds of an agent meeting. "Church of the Trinity in Serebryaniki. Third icon on the left. Upper right-hand corner of the frame."

"Serebryaniki. Third icon left side. Upper right-hand corner. Got it."

"Emergency rendezvous changed to fourteen hundred twenty hours. Location remains the same."

"Fourteen twenty. Got it." Baranov paused, waiting. "Is that it?"

"Yes." Sam turned the car north, toward Kaliningrad.

"Got it all. By the way, where are we going today?"

"Zagorsk. I thought we'd take the scenic route."

" 'The scenic route?' Good—no *vizirs,* no static surveillance teams." Pavel Baranov removed the rabbit fur hat, revealing short-cropped blond hair, through which he ran stubby fingers. The scenic route was a series of narrow, largely unused back roads that wound through thick pine forests past dachas and farms for roughly twenty-five kilometers to the fourteenth-century walled town.

Sam scanned the rearview and sideview mirrors and was happy with what he saw. "Okay," he said, "What's your crisis, Pavel?"

"It's not my crisis, Sam," the Russian answered gravely. "It's yours." He unfastened the buttons on his hunting coat, reached inside, and eased a heavy envelope from the game pocket.

Baranov opened the envelope and extracted a single page from between two pieces of cardboard. He looked at Sam. "Are your hands clean?"

Sam shed his thick leather gloves, revealing latex ones beneath. He reached out eagerly. Still, Baranov withheld the sheet. "Gently, Sam."

Gingerly, Sam took the page, laid it atop the steering wheel, and anchored it gently with the edge of his left hand. He glanced down, his eyes skipping between the road ahead and the sheet just below his line of sight. The document bore a Russian Foreign Intelligence Service logo, a top-secret stamp, and the legend "Urgent: Eyes of the President." A paper patch sat at the topmost right-hand corner of the sheet. He focused—

Pavel's voice interrupted. "Sam, Sam, watch out!"

"*Ebat'kopat!* Holy shit!" Sam braked hard, still barely missing the bumper of a slow-moving truck. He lifted the paper off the wheel, used his right hand to steer around the lumbering vehicle, checked the distance between the Zhiguli and the car ahead, then dropped his eyes to devour every syllable.

Devour, because Sam Waterman understood that the neat lines of Cyrillic type signified the end of life as he knew it.

EXECUTIVE SUMMARY

12.10.1998

01 Source OSKAR reports President W. Clinton held a secret meeting on 09.10.1998 with CIA director N. Becker, Deputy Secretary of State S. Talbott, and National Security Council Chief S. Berger regarding terrorist threats to Americans in former Soviet Republics.

02 Clinton was advised by Becker that American business interests in the former republics of Azerbaijan and Kazakhstan have been targeted by al–Qa'ida.

03 Becker suggested that CIA identify, isolate, and neutralize the al-Qa'ida threat through a covert action programme. He was challenged by Talbott, who maintained covert action would violate Azeri and Kazak sovereignty and antagonize the Russian leadership if discovered. Berger argued that if CIA's covert action programme backfired, consequences could include regional instability and jeopardizing lucrative American petroleum partnerships.

04 Clinton agreed with Talbott and Berger.

05 Analysis follows.

Sam felt as if he'd been gut-shot. If the document was *razvedka*—what the old KGB used to call the real thing—the implications were cosmic. There's another traitor in Washington—a high-level one, too. This was a goddamn all-star session, not some low-level policy gang bang with thirty junior staffers drinking lattes.

And if the document was a fabrication, the implications were equally cosmic. Pavel Baranov was a double agent— probably a creation of Vlad Putin and Edward Lee Howard's aggressive counterintelligence operation—and everything the general'd been feeding Sam for the past six months, every rumor, gossipy info-bit; memo, briefing paper, and report: all of it—every syllable—had to be reevaluated. And whether the document was real or a fabrication, Sam was going to develop carpal tunnel syndrome before he finished writing the metric ton of reports this meeting was going to require.

Sam kept his surging emotions under check. "Pavel, where did you get this?"

"I managed to get it. That should be enough."

It wasn't. Not by a mile. "Pavel—"

The Russian retrieved the sheet from under Sam's hand.

"Where's the rest?"

The Russian placed the document atop its envelope. "At Lubyanka. In a safe." He pointed at the sheet with a stubby forefinger. "Where this has to go by tonight if I want to stay alive."

"I need it, Pavel."

"No way."

"Then we go back to Moscow so I can make a copy."

"I can't risk that." Baranov pointed at the thick paper patch. "See that? They hand-numbered these. I don't want you knowing whose copy I was able to get. And who knows what else they did."

Sam understood only too well what Pavel was saying. Highly classified documents were often individually typed, with minor alterations in the punctuation or the writing. Then they were numbered. If the document was leaked, the very wording that appeared in the newspapers—or was intercepted on its way to a hostile intelligence service—could lead counterintelligence to the perpetrator. If this page was genuine, there'd be no way Pavel would allow him to make a copy.

That was on the one hand. On the other hand, if the page was a fabrication, there was equally no way Pavel would allow him to reproduce it. It would be like handing over a signed confession.

Sam took his eyes off the road long enough to give his passenger a piercing glance. "I'll have to handwrite a copy, Pavel."

The general's jaw tightened. He rubbed his wispy mustache with his right forefinger. He bit his lip. He looked into Sam's eyes, trying to read what was going on in the American's brain.

Sam, opaque, gave nothing back. He kept the Zhiguli's speed even; gauged the distance between his car and the truck he was about to overtake. He floored the accelerator and passed the lumbering vehicle, letting silence do his work for him. Silence was a great ally in intelligence. Young case officers often spoke too much—chattered like nervous birds. Better to give your target time to think, ponder, consider. And then, you'd close the deal with a few well-chosen words.

So, Sam waited the Russian out. There was, he thought as he drove, more than a little irony in the fact that it had been a battle royal to recruit Baranov in the first place. Opposition had come from an unlikely direction, too: Langley itself. The problem had begun when CIA sent a delegation headed by a senior case officer named Frank Dillard to Moscow. Dillard was not one of Lubyanka's favorites. He'd been chief liaison to Pakistan's Inter-Services Intelligence Directorate, the remote control organization by which CIA ran the mujahideen fighters who chased the Soviets out of Afghanistan.

Dillard returned in triumph to headquarters, where in 1991 he became chief of CIA's Central Asia Task Force, the successor to the old Soviet/Eastern Europe Division known inside Langley as "The Russia House." Then, early in 1992, he was sent to Moscow to meet with the KGB leadership and discuss common areas of interest. Incredibly, the weeklong sessions resulted in the formation of what Dillard described as "a symbiotic relationship with a fraternal intelligence service."

How Dillard of all people could have called it fraternal was beyond Sam Waterman's comprehension. Especially since it was vodka clear to Sam, who was deputy chief in Paris at the time, that the Russians would never ever stop targeting America. And yet, incredibly, three days after Dillard returned to Washington, he'd sent out a cable over the signature of the deputy director for operations, instructing CIA stations worldwide that every Russian agent was to be dropped, and that all operations against Russian targets were to be closed down. Immediately. Henceforth, potential Russian developmentals would be dealt with by Langley on a case-by-case basis, on an ADDO—assistant deputy director of operations—or higher level. No exceptions.

For Sam, it meant that he could no longer liaise with the French against Russian targets. Worse, the French stopped passing Langley other intelligence they'd previously shared.

When Sam asked Jean-Paul Meric, his French counterpart, why Quai d'Orsay was holding back critical information, Meric shrugged and muttered some diplomatic mumbo jumbo about "entering a transitional period of shifting liaison equities between our services." Meric's subtext was unambiguous: Sam was being told Paris was concerned CIA would leak sensitive information about French sources and methods to its new pals in Moscow and so would henceforth be held at arm's length. He immediately sent an URGENT message to Langley about the development but never received an answer.

Dillard's cable was bad enough. What was worse was that even after the Aldrich Ames and Harold Nicholson debacles (which proved Sam's premonitions correct), neither CIA's leadership, nor the administration, nor the congressional intelligence oversight committees reversed the idiotic no-recruiting-Russians rules.

Which meant, even in post-Ames 1997, Sam had had to fight tooth and nail for Pavel Baranov. He'd done so because it hadn't been EMSI—the tradecraft acronym for the vulnerabilities of *e*go, *m*oney, *s*ex, and *i*deology—that had caused the general to become a traitor. Baranov was different. He saw himself as a soldier whose mission was to rebuild a nation enslaved for more than half a century. He wanted freedom and self-determination, and he was willing to spy for his former enemy to achieve his goals.

And having uncovered this idealistic chink in the Russian's otherwise well-armored personality, Sam Waterman fought for the opportunity to exploit it in America's interests. And he had prevailed over strong resistance from the seventh floor. It had been worth the risk to his career, too—at least until today.

Sam noted Baranov's fretful expression. Their relationship was complex. There was no ethical ambiguity, for example, in the fact that Sam Waterman honestly liked Pavel Baranov, although he often coldly manipulated the Russian. Their association was even fraternal: both were military men. Sam, a Marine, had been awarded the Bronze Star in Vietnam; Baranov, a paratrooper, fought in Afghanistan. The shared experience of combat gave them common ground on which to build rapport.

But when it came to crunch time, Sam knew that despite male bonding and camaraderie, it was he, not Pavel Baranov, who had to exert control. Indeed, control was the key to all successful case officer–agent interaction. He had to run Pavel Baranov. It couldn't be the other way around.

Still, pushing—leaning on an agent—was never pleasant. But Sam understood he didn't always have to *like* what he did—he simply had to get the job done.

And so, he pushed. "I have to make a copy, Pavel. I need a piece of paper in my hand. That's how things work. You know it and I know it."

Silence. He watched as the general blinked thrice, half-nodded, and then said in whispered Russian. "But not the exact language, Sam, please. You *must* paraphrase."

"Agreed," Sam replied, his heart pounding so loudly in his chest he felt Baranov must hear it.

Sam looked at the Russian's worried face. Was it because he really was in danger, or had Pavel sensed Sam's perception that he might be a double.

AS THE LITTLE CAR IDLED on a side street just south of Zagorsk's Sovietskaya Square, the two men worked out the language like a pair of lawyers hammering out a plea bargain. Beyond the square they could see past tourist buses to the walls of the fourteenth-century fortress that held a farmers' market, half a dozen churches, and a classic Russian citadel. When they'd finished, Sam locked the car and they strolled through the old kremlin gates. Pavel bought himself the sorts of fresh vegetables that even generals found hard to come by in Moscow's sparsely stocked stores. Sam bought a decoratively painted balalaika as a thank-you gift for Tom Kennedy. Then he watched as Pavel bargained for a set of *matryoshka* dolls. Sam had never seen anything like them: five fierce-faced KGB goons in red-tabbed green uniforms and brown pistol belts.

Baranov examined the dolls. The largest carried a pistol in

one hand and a pack of cigarettes in the other. "He's about to serve up a Lubyanka breakfast," Baranov said. "You know what that is, Sergei Anatolyvich?"

"A cigarette and a bullet, Pavel Dmitriyvich."

"Correct." The general agreed on a price, handed rubles to the vendor, and stuffed the hollowed-out figures back inside one another. Juggling his groceries, he presented the *matryoshkas* to Sam. "Happy birthday, Sergei Anatolyvich."

Sam was genuinely touched. "Thank you for remembering, Pavel Dmitriyvich."

Baranov flushed, embarrassed. "It is nothing."

He still has a boyish face, Sam thought, even after having been to war. He patted the figurines. "I will treasure them. And to celebrate, let me buy us a late lunch."

The general checked the thick gold Rolex on his wrist. "I think we'd best get going," he said. "I have things to do in town."

"So do I, it would seem."

THEY WERE about halfway to the M8, on a winding stretch of back road bordered on both sides by thick forest, when a Mercedes overtook them. It was a huge car, a 500 series with the opaque windows favored by *Mafiyosi*. The driving lights flashed three times in Sam's rearview mirror, and he steered toward the shoulder to let the black behemoth pass, catching a quick glance of the driver and the front-seat passenger as they drew close, swerved around the Zhiguli, and disappeared around the next curve.

"*Byki,*" Baranov grumbled, using the idiom for *Mafiyosi* muscle.

"*Da*—from the look of the ugly *torpedo* riding shotgun."

Baranov scowled. "Yeltsin surrounds himself with them, you know."

"You've said as much before."

"He encourages them. He even does business with them."

"With who, Pavel?"

"Who?" Baranov flicked his hand dismissively. "It doesn't matter who. They're all scum." The Russian sighed, then stared pensively through the windshield.

A minute or so later a second and a third Mercedes came up quickly behind the Zhiguli. Again, Sam edged shoulderward, but the cars stayed tight on his bumper. Then they dropped back. He glanced ahead, saw a tight curve, and slowed to ease through it. As he came around he saw the first Mercedes, not three hundred yards ahead. It was blocking the road. Behind it crouched men with weapons.

Too late, Sam realized what was happening. They'd been targeted by criminals. Where had all his damn counterinsurgency training gone? "Shit," he shouted. "Pavel—it's a goddamn ambush."

Stay calm, he thought. *You're a professional. Remember what they taught you about running roadblocks.* He gauged the closing distance and measured the amount of space between the Mercedes that sat astride the two-lane road and the narrow shoulder bordered by spruce, birch, and aspen trees. *Just enough,* he prayed, *so I can thread the needle.* He floored the clutch, downshifted into second, and mindless of the Zhiguli's protesting transmission, he stomped the gas pedal and aimed the car at the middle of the narrow gap between the Mercedes's rear quarter panel and the tree line.

Which was when the big sedan behind him came up fast and smacked the left side of his rear bumper—smacked it *hard.*

In the eighth of a second between the time the Zhiguli was hit and Sam lost all control, he realized the maneuver had been so precisely executed that he wasn't up against gangsters, but Vladimir Vladimirovich Putin's FSB professionals. The car spun out. Its front wheel caught the soft shoulder, wavered, teetered, and then rolled, skidding toward the road-block in a shower of sparks.

Sam's face made rude contact with the windshield. The impact ripped him out of his seat belt and he caromed help-lessly around the interior. He smacked into the roof panel and heard himself scream as his shoulder separated. Then his ears filled with the cacophony of shattering metal and splin-tering glass, all color drained away, and he could see nothing but black and white. And then, huge bright spots appeared in front of his eyes. And finally, as if an immense drapery was being pulled from left to right across what was left of his field of vision, he slipped into blackness and disappeared into a terrible crystal funnel of white sound.

It was getting dark when Sam opened his eyes. He groaned, and flopped over onto his back. He was on the shoulder of the road. He licked his split lips and tasted blood. He ran his hand over his face. The false mustache was gone. Christ—it hurt to breathe. He felt as though he'd been worked over by eight guys named Cheech.

Behind him, the Zhiguli rested on its crumpled roof. Veg-etables were strewn about, along with pieces of balalaika and glass shards. Eight feet away, Pavel Baranov's body lay crumpled facedown, legs at an obscene angle, arms akimbo.

"Pavel?" Sam crawled toward the Russian. The going was slow and incredibly painful. He reached Baranov's leg and shook it. There was no response. He pulled himself along-side the Russian and rolled him over onto his back by using his belt.

Which is when Sam saw Baranov's open, dead eyes. And the broken Marlboro stuffed into his mouth. And the bullet holes in the Russian's forehead. He forgot his own pain, raised Pavel's head, and cradled it in his lap, his hands and trousers wet with blood and skull fragments and brain matter. He brushed tobacco strands from between the Russian's lips.

He sat there for some seconds, rocking the lifeless man in his arms. It came to Sam, in the way cruel memories intrude uninvited, that he'd spent a small part of his nineteenth birthday twenty-six or so miles southwest of Da Nang, holding the shredded body of a lance corporal in much the same attitude he was holding Pavel Baranov right now. But then, Sam's training took over from his pain, and he checked the Russian's corpse only to discover what he knew he'd discover: Pavel still wore his gold Rolex, but the envelope with its precious page was gone. He ran his left hand up inside his jacket. The copy was gone, too.

Which, Sam realized even in his present state, didn't prove anything about the document's bona fides—or Pavel Baranov's, either.

But then, in the way men who are about to die understand at the precise moment of their death some precious secret about existence that will, of course, do them absolutely no good at all given their predicament, Sam Waterman realized something else. He remembered Pavel Baranov hadn't known they were going to Zagorsk. No one knew his destination or his route. Until, that is, he'd cabled every single detail about this particular PMP to Langley.

PART II

WASHINGTON, D.C.

CHAPTЭЯ 3

SAM WATERMAN lunched alone on his forty-ninth birthday, a hostage to his former profession. He celebrated straddled atop a wood stool in the crowded Garden Bar of the Cosmos Club, which is located on Massachusetts Avenue two and a half blocks west of Dupont Circle. Retired, at loose ends much of the time, he ate lunch at the Cosmos twice a week, preferring the dark wood paneling and every-man-is-an-island atmosphere of the bar to the politely gregarious hubbub of the club table in the dining room across the corridor.

Sam was a hostage to his former profession because even in retirement he was cursed with the second sight that had come with a quarter century plus of street work. He simply saw things differently. Parks, for example, weren't for lovers' trysts or tourists taking snapshots. They were dead-drop and letterbox locations. Lampposts, mailboxes, and fire hydrants were signal sites. Department stores were multiple entry/exit facilities for a cleaning route—a tradecraft term for spotting surveillance.

He saw people differently, too. FBI gumshoes, plain-clothes police operations, undercover DEA agents—he'd spot them all. Not a week ago, he'd stopped at the Four Seasons for a vodka rocks on his way home and watched, fascinated, as an FBI "honeymooner" counterintelligence team covertly videoed a martini-drinking senior Saudi diplomat who was clandestinely passing what Sam took to be a cash-stuffed envelope to a messy-haired, olive-skinned, bearded man in a black leather jacket who looked like he'd just emerged from Beirut's southern suburbs, while the rest of the customers at the hotel's posh terrace bar drank and bantered and smoked, oblivious to both the transaction and the feds.

It went even deeper. Just like those single-letter characters in *Men in Black,* Sam could identify Aliens, too. There was a whole civilization of them out there, totally undetectable by the population at large.

Sam knew who *they* were. You could even find them at the Cosmos Club. Like Martha, the attractive blonde in her mid-thirties sitting across the bar, nursing an Australian Chardonnay as she chatted up a prospective client. Sure, she looked normal enough. But Martha was an Alien. Oh, Martha's business card said she owned an exclusive gallery in Georgetown specializing in original editorial cartoons and investment-grade photographs. And she did.

But for eight years, Martha had worked for CIA. She'd been a NOC, or Non-Official Cover, case officer. She'd lived under a cover name in a third-floor walk-up two blocks from the main post office in Düsseldorf, Germany. Outgoing, attractive, and demonstrably left-wing in her politics, she'd taken courses at the Universität and worked part-time at a gallery a couple of blocks off the Königsallee, where she sold mediocre, high-priced modern paintings to Gulf Arabs.

And when she wasn't at school, or at work, she was busily cultivating the local cell of the Kurdistan Workers' Party or PKK, an anti-Turkish terrorist group that had bombed half a dozen targets in Germany. Every week, she clandestinely passed her reports to a control officer from CIA's Düsseldorf base, which, before it had been closed because of budgetary cutbacks, had been located in the American ▓▓▓▓▓▓▓▓▓▓▓ on Kennedydamm. And although Martha didn't know it, Sam had created her postresignation legend during his fifteen months in Purgatory (which, incidentally, is an anonymous, glass-fronted office building on Nash Street in Rosslyn, Virginia). Because of Sam's ingenuity, Martha had a credit history, a Social Security record, and all the other detritus necessary to assume life on planet Earth under her real name.

There were thousands of them, Sam thought as he stared into his martini. The Aliens among us: NOCs, defectors, faceless NSA eavesdroppers, anonymous NRO satellite squirrels, and all the case officers who'd left CIA covertly. Ride the Washington metro at rush hour, and it was an absolute certainty you'd brush shoulders with a few. But you'd never know who they were.

Sam, however, had The Knowledge. Once in a great while, an Alien might actually catch him watching. Brahmins—which is how Sam referred to Aliens from the OSS generation—looked right through him. Martha's generation was different. If they remembered his face from Langley, they'd stare back. Or worse, ask what he was doing these days.

Richard Helms was part of the OSS group. Helms had died last night. There'd been a small box on the front page of the *Post,* and of course it made the morning TV news shows. Sam sipped his drink and silently prayed for Richard Helms's soul.

Sam had always thought of Helms simply as The Director.

Helms understood about keeping secrets. He took them to his grave. That kind of dedication was largely unknown these days. During his time in Purgatory Sam had heard about a probie case officer who'd been dumb enough to write dozens of gossipy e-mails to family and friends chronicling her tradecraft training and describing in painstaking detail the foibles and even the sexual habits of her fellow trainees. She'd been fired, of course. Now she was writing a book. It had occurred to Sam that perhaps she should have been executed.

Martha the Alien threw her head back and laughed. It was a professional laugh—and it would be followed directly by an elicitation of some sort. Martha's client didn't realize what was going on. But Sam did. He was impressed. Martha must have been one of the good ones.

Actually, Sam was surprised Martha hadn't gone back to CIA. Between the fallout from 9/11, the buildup to military action in Iraq, and the intelligence vacuum with regard to Iran, Africa, North Korea, China, and the Middle East, the Agency was hiring back every retired or resigned case officer it could make an offer to.

Well, not quite everyone. Sam, and a few others like him, had been deemed untouchables. In fact, Sam had been personally designated as unworthy of reemployment by Nick Becker—Czar Nicholas the Third, as Sam referred to him—the director of central intelligence himself.

It bothered Sam that Czar Nicholas was riding so high these days. Like most of the Vietnam generation in the Directorate of Operations, Sam considered Becker a disaster. To him the evidence was clear. On DCI Becker's watch, CIA had missed gleaning any advance warning about India's 1998 nuclear tests. Because Becker had shut down virtually all of CIA's African stations, Langley hadn't picked up a single ripple in advance of al-Qa'ida's bombings of the American embassies in Kenya and Tanzania. Becker had been unable to provide any prior warning about the suicide attack on the USS *Cole* in Aden harbor because he had neither language-capable case officers assigned to Yemen nor agent networks within al-Qa'ida. He'd lied to Congress about having spy networks in Baghdad when Sam knew for a fact CIA didn't have a single unilateral agent in all of Iraq. He'd thrown so many wrenches into the Robert Hanssen investigation that there were some in what was left of the Agency's CI Division who actually believed Becker, a pudgy, rumpled former think-tanker, to be a Russian agent of influence. And then, of course, there was 9/11.

On a more personal note: in April of 2000, Becker had summoned Sam to his long, narrow seventh-floor office, administered a profanity-laced tongue-lashing, and then gave Sam a choice: a public gibbeting followed by demotion and termination, or fifteen months of total isolation in Purgatory, followed by retirement with full SIS—Senior Intelligence Service—benefits. It still grated on Sam that he'd chosen the latter.

A HAND DROPPED onto Sam's shoulder. "Happy birthday, Cyrus."

Sam swiveled the bar stool. It was Michael O'Neill, dapper as ever. O'Neill was one of the few Agency colleagues Sam ever saw socially—and he hadn't seen O'Neill in two, almost three months.

O'Neill's hand flicked something off Sam's shoulder. "Y'know, Cyrus, I've just been all over town looking for you."

It was a private joke. Michael O'Neill and Sam Waterman sometimes called each other by their CIA pseudonyms. Sam was Cyrus N. PRINGLE. O'Neill's was Edward P. SAMGRASS. For years, Sam had been convinced that Agency pseudonyms were lifted from characters in Dickens novels.

He wasn't far off: in actual fact the odd-sounding names were culled at random from old London telephone directories, and the middle initials were added wherever necessary.

So, Edward P. SAMGRASS had been looking for him. Had he really. "All over town, Eddie?"

O'Neill deflected Sam's query. "Well, all over the part of town that's between my house on Q Street and here, anyway."

Sam laughed and polished off the last of the Boodles. He put his glass down and scrunched his stool over so that O'Neill could sidle up to the bar. Sam Waterman had been Michael O'Neill's mentor in Paris during the early nineties. O'Neill had come to CIA as a thirty-year-old with an MA in history from Cambridge and a law degree from Georgetown. He was a case officer who worked under State Department cover as State's Paris-based French resource management officer—in charge of finding apartments and office space for American diplomatic personnel and missions. Fluent in French and Italian; charming, gregarious, and hopelessly social, O'Neill was a fast learner, a bright kid who had all the God-given talent to hook agents up and drop them in the CIA's creel.

Sam showed the ambitious young case officer the trade-craft subtleties necessary to work successfully against France's first-rate domestic security agency, the DST. He honed O'Neill's natural talent for spotting and assessing developmentals. Most important, he tutored the young case officer about ways of keeping track of Ed Howard's Moscow Center goons without alerting the powers that be. By mid-1992, Langley categorically prohibited recruiting Russian targets and running operations against Moscow Center. But it was obvious to Sam that no one at Lubyanka had ever sent a comparable cable to the Foreign Intelligence Service's *Rezidents,* because Edward Lee Howard's SVR case officers were continually and provocatively trolling American officials in

Paris, Bonn, Vienna, in fact, all over Western Europe. Howard had no compunction about targeting his former colleagues at CIA and State. The question that nagged Sam was whether any of those targets had been snagged.

There were other problems, too. Paris in the early nineties had not been a good post if you were ambitious, and a risk taker. The ambassador, Pamela Harriman, was a millionaire Democratic Party kingmaker. She was egocentric and incompetent in the way only self-important, delusional idiots can be. But she also was personally close to the president.

Harriman, whose late husband, Averell, had once been ambassador to Moscow, had an innate distaste for espionage. In Paris, therefore, CIA's activities were severely limited by ambassadorial decree. Moreover, the ▆▆▆▆ chief had no intention of crossing Harriman, because he knew any attempt to do so would result in a career-ending call to the Oval Office.

Mediocrity and complacency were therefore encouraged, while recruiting—the single most important job of any clandestine service officer when Sam had joined CIA shortly after Vietnam—was actively suppressed. And so, of the thirty-seven case officers working at Paris Station when Sam arrived for a three-year assignment as deputy ▆▆▆▆ chief in 1991, nineteen of them had resigned, frustrated by the Agency's seeming reluctance to gather human intelligence, before he completed his own tour. Among the ships deserting the sinking rat was Michael O'Neill.

Covertly resigned under State Department cover, O'Neill had gone on to pursue life in the real world. He moved back to Washington, crammed for six months, passed the bar, and was snatched up by a multinational law firm, where he made partner in three and a half years. These days, Michael O'Neill owned a nineteenth-century town house in Georgetown and an eighteenth-century cottage just west of Middleburg. He made seven figures representing half a dozen Fortune 500 companies on Capitol Hill and a select number of private clients. Like many former government employees, O'Neill maintained his Top Secret/SCI[7]security clearances—especially useful when he'd been tapped to serve on the presidential commission looking into the 1998 African embassy bombings.

After the change in administrations in 2001, there had even been published rumors that O'Neill might be appointed to the president's Foreign Intelligence Advisory Board, the 9/11 Commission—or even to the deputy's post at CIA. None had happened. But Sam knew O'Neill was highly political. He did favors, like performing classified due diligence work for a handful of politicians, including some on the Senate Select Committee on Intelligence, acronymed SSCI and pronounced "sissy."

Sam looked his protégé up and down. "So, was I hard to find or easy?"

"You, Cyrus? Easy. You leave a wide wake. Besides"—O'Neill hooked a thumb in the bartender's direction—"Miguel here reports to me on a regular basis. He's my principal agent in the keep-track-of-Samuel-Elbridge-Waterman network. He says you're here for lunch two days a week. Like clockwork." The attorney brushed a lock of prematurely gray hair out of his eyes. "Frankly, Sam, as much time as you're spending at the bar, I think Miguel's running some kind of network for you."

"I'm retired."

"And I used to be a diplomat. We diplomats understand that retirement is just another form of cover. C'mon, Sam: What the hell have you really been up to?"

"Up to?" Sam lifted the martini glass six inches off the bar surface, then lowered it back. "I've been working out. Regularly. As you can see, I'm into free weights these days."

[7] Sensitive Compartmented Information.

The attorney ta-tapped Sam on the back half a dozen times like a doctor checking his respiratory system. "Well, you're still alive, so the regimen must be working."

O'Neill extracted a gold pocket watch from the vest of his bespoke tweed suit, checked the dial, returned the watch to its proper place, reached for a blank bar tab and pencil, then pointed at Sam's empty martini glass. "I'll have one of those, please, Miguel—and so will this reprobate." He scribbled the formalities on the chit and slid it back across the bar. "So," he said, his arm clasped around Sam's shoulders, "entering your half-century year today. But I see you haven't had the requisite eye tuck."

"Like *der Raccünvald*?" Just saying the words brought a smile to Sam's face. *Der Raccünvald* had been O'Neill's pet name for the late Jerrold von Brünwald, their station ▓▓▓▓▓ chief in Paris. The day before he'd turned fifty, von Brünwald announced he was taking a week of personal leave. With Jerry's wife in the States, everyone thought he'd be going somewhere romantic with his mistress, a sensational redhead named Chloe. Instead, six days later, he'd reappeared at the embassy, both eyes blackened. From then on, the self-important von Brünwald was known to O'Neill's circle as *der Raccünvald*.

O'Neill waited until Miguel mixed the drinks, filled their glasses, and then left the bar in search of something. He plucked the olives from the glass, ate them, and laid the bare toothpick on a bar napkin. The lawyer lifted his martini and carefully touched the rim of Sam's glass with his own. "To absent friends, Sam Waterman."

"*Pey Dadna*—drink to the bottom, Michael O'Neill. Drink to those who keep the secrets."

Sam watched Michael O'Neill glance across the bar as Martha the NOC and her client made their way toward the dining room. If O'Neill knew she was an Alien, he didn't let on. But then, O'Neill could keep secrets. Or, perhaps he didn't possess The Knowledge.

O'Neill turned back to Sam. "So you miss secrets, do you?"

"I didn't say that," Sam corrected. "But I'll tell you what I do miss, since you asked and I've had a second cocktail." He paused to sip. "I miss the adrenaline rush. I miss the competent chiefs, who taught me what they called 'The Great Game,' and encouraged audacity and risk taking—not the *grands zéros* like Grünwald who were scared of offending the French, or pissing off the ambassador. Believe it or not, I miss writing agent debrief memos and activity reports and even PMP cables." He stared at the back bar. "I miss running agents, Michael."

"The thrill of the chase."

"God, it was so much more than that," Sam said. "It was the Cold War. It was the feeling of commitment. We were the better angels. We did God's work. Life had meaning. And now, what are they doing? Screwing up target information in Belgrade or Baghdad, tapping *drogista* telephones in Bogotá, or chasing transnational terrorists on the Internet. It's all turned so mean, so grimy, so . . . spiritless. It's as desolate as a lunar landscape."

"But valuable nonetheless." Michael O'Neill shrugged. "The end of the Cold War simply meant that we had to refocus our resources on other problems."

"*We?*" Sam wriggled an eyebrow at his friend. "Ah, so maybe the law is just another form of cover, too, eh?" He paused, but got no response. "You're right, of course. But you know what? Let the youngsters deal with asymmetrical warfare, transnational hackers, and trying to decipher the intentions of our unipolar-focused bilateral relationships." Sam tapped the bar. "I'm happy doing nothing."

"Horse puckey."

"The Romanoffs wanted me out," Sam said, using his personal term for the CIA's current leadership. "Nicholas the Third wanted me gone. And he got what he wanted."

"Ah, Czar Nicky—the turd," Michael O'Neill pronounced, cracking a grin. "But was it all Romanoffs, Cyrus? Didn't you bear some responsibility?"

Sam looked at his friend, then turned away, toward the French doors, and stared out into the garden. There were still leaves on some of the cherry trees. Maybe winter would come late this year. Sam loved autumn. He'd especially loved autumn in Moscow—except for his last autumn there. He blinked, and for an instant he was back on the road to Zagorsk, the handwritten document in his pocket. He twisted away from the grim vision to face Michael O'Neill. "You know, afterward, the son of a bitch didn't even give me time to pack," Sam said bitterly.

"Who?" O'Neill said, confused.

"Franklin Dempster Pierce. Our ambassador plenipotentiary and extraordinary in Moscow. Called me into his office before I'd had a chance to change clothes. I was still bleeding. 'The Russians want you out,' he told me. 'They say you were drunk. They say you drove illegally into the diplomatic exclusion zone outside Moscow.' "

O'Neill raised his glass and sipped, giving him time to ponder Sam's words. "What did you say?"

"I said nothing. Because it didn't matter to Franklin Dempster Pierce. 'Don't even bother trying to make excuses. I have it on the highest authority that you screwed up big.' Sure he did: he'd heard it from his pals the Russians. And that was it. I was back in Washington thirty hours after the general was murdered."

Michael O'Neill said nothing.

Sam went silent, too, for some seconds. Then he dropped his voice to just above a whisper. "He was the only one I lost, Michael," he rasped, the hurt still deep enough to keep him from pronouncing Pavel Baranov's name. "Only one. In twenty-six years. That's not so bad, is it?"

"Considering people like Ebenezer J. THREADNEEDLE, they should have given you a friggin' medal."

Sam snorted. In 1996, THREADNEEDLE, a blockheaded Middle East branch chief whose real name is ▆▆▆▆▆▆▆▆▆▆,[8] had managed to lose all forty-three of the CIA's precious assets in Iran in one fell swoop. But ▆▆▆▆▆▆▆▆▆▆ was a Romanoff. And so, as a reward for his agents' torture and executions, Czar Nicholas the Third—who was then CIA's deputy director—promoted ▆▆▆▆▆▆▆▆▆▆ to chief, Near East Division, where he got a lot more CIA assets killed. Currently, ▆▆▆▆▆▆▆▆ is the executive assistant to CIA's assistant deputy director for operations.[9]

O'Neill sipped his martini. "No, Sam, in fact, it's a record to be proud of. But you took your one loss way too hard."

Sam's eyes flashed dangerously. "Who told you that?"

"You did—just now," O'Neill said coolly. "But you're right. I heard things. After all, Romanoffs like to gossip in the corridors."

In the CIA's ingrown culture, corridor gossip was bad juju. Michael O'Neill, whose political barometer was a lot more finely tuned than his mentor's, understood that a DO

---

[8] It is illegal to publish the real names of active clandestine service officers. ▆▆▆▆▆ was recalled to active duty shortly after 9/11.

[9] The debacle occurred after THREADNEEDLE, to save money, ordered that all messages sent to CIA's Iranian agents emanate from the same accommodation address in Germany. He fired twelve Iranian calligraphers, which left only one individual to address all the envelopes—which, incredibly, were written in green ink. Iranian counterintelligence didn't take long to pick up on the fact that forty-three people in Iran were receiving mail from the same address in Germany, and that all the envelopes, which were written in distinctive green ink, had identical handwriting.

officer's formal personnel file, filled (as Sam's was) with awards, two medals, and fulsome, albeit bureaucratic, praise, counted for nothing. What had really mattered was Sam's corridor file—the gossip that reflected how the Romanoffs perceived him.

Sam wagged his head. "I should never have told you about Romanoffs." He saw the hurt look in his friend's eyes and recovered quickly: "You understand, of course, it was the champagne that loosened my tongue."

THE FIRST TIME Sam Waterman ever told Michael O'Neill about Romanoffs they'd been sitting in high-backed, cognac-colored leather wing chairs, isolated from casual eavesdroppers in the Hotel George V bar's denlike alcove. Behind Sam was a fireplace on whose mantel sat a pair of small Remington bronzes. Between the two men stood a small, round wood table covered with a starched white cloth on which sat a magnum of Dom Ruinart in a silver bucket, and a large crystal ashtray holding two well-aged Punch double coronas. They were celebrating Sam's forty-first birthday.

"If you're planning any future at all in the business, you are going to have to learn about Romanoffs," Sam said quasi-solemnly after they'd finished about two thirds of the huge bottle.

"Romanoffs?" O'Neill cocked his head like an Airedale. He'd never heard about Romanoffs. "Who are Romanoffs?"

"The new ruling class on the Potomac." Sam drained his champagne, and while O'Neill refilled his glass he picked up his monologue. Romanoffs, he explained, had almost completely displaced the home office's original dominant caste, Brahmins.

Brahmins were mostly Ivy League. They wore bespoke

suits and Burberry trench coats. They had trust funds, they drank scotch, martinis, and twenty-five-year-old cognac—except between Memorial Day and Labor Day, when they drank gin-and-tonics, martinis, and twenty-five-year-old cognac. Brahmins saw what they did as a noble calling.

Sam paused to draw on his cigar. He blew a perfect smoke ring, paused to appreciate the long gray ash, then carefully replaced the half-smoked Punch on the broad rim of heavy crystal. Romanoffs, he continued, came from schools like Indiana University, Brigham Young, and Kansas State. They wore polyester suits, wash-and-wear shirts, Hush Puppies, and London Fog raincoats. When they drank at all they drank rye-and-ginger or plonk Chablis spritzers. Romanoffs saw what they did as a job.

Brahmins spoke three, four, or five languages fluently and elegantly. Romanoffs had trouble with English. Brahmins, virtually all of whom had served in the military, accepted and tutored the CIA's Sergeants—the generation of ex-military case officers like Sam who had been recruited in the post-Vietnam era—with patriarchal charm and patrician dignity. Romanoffs, most of whom had never served in the military, detested Sergeants and therefore spent much of their time making the lives of Sergeants like Samuel Elbridge Waterman miserable.

In fact, Romanoffs treated everyone below them in the pecking order like serfs. Which is why Sam had started calling them Romanoffs in the first place.

O'Neill's voice brought Sam about halfway back from Paris. "It wasn't the champagne that loosened your tongue that day"—the lawyer winked, "it was the cigars."

Sam grinned at his old friend and savored the memory. "They *were* good."

"They were perfect." O'Neill sighed. "Life was good in Paris, Cyrus—until everything . . ." The lawyer paused.

"Yes?"

"It all just . . . evaporated, Cyrus. Everything good just went away."

CHAPTЭЯ 4

MOVEMENT in the Cosmos corridor diverted Sam's attention. He blinked, refocused on O'Neill, and wrestled the George V bar into the ether. "You're right, Michael. Romanoffs, Brahmins, Paris—even Moscow. It's all water under the bridge. It doesn't matter anymore."

"We both know that's not true," O'Neill said adamantly. "Look, Sam, there's nothing wrong about taking what happened in Moscow as hard as you did. It was murder."

Sam scratched the back of his neck. "The thing that bothered me most," he finally said, "was that I wasn't given any time to pack my stuff."

"Or mourn, perhaps?"

"Mourning wasn't the point," Sam said, much too quickly.

"You sound detached about it now," O'Neill said. "But that wasn't how you were then. When you came back, you were quite zealous—looking for revenge."

How much does O'Neill actually know? Sam wondered. *How much did he ever find out? How much has he been able to piece together?*

"Revenge?" Sam looked poker-faced into his friend's eyes. *You're right about that, pal.* But he said nothing. There was no need to talk about revenge now. Revenge was a dead issue. As dead as Pavel Baranov.

O'Neill, however, wanted to take matters another step. "In point of fact, Sam, after you returned from Moscow, I was told you saw Russian penetration everywhere." The attorney paused. "Well?"

"I never made any secret of that."

"That's a fact," O'Neill snorted. "Christ, Sam, somebody said watching you stampede through Langley looking for Baranov's killer was like watching the bulls running in Pamplona."

"Maybe it was." Sam dropped his forearm onto the marble bar top and turned toward the attorney. "Maybe you're right. But you know what? I was one of six people who came up with the name Robert Philip Hanssen in 1999. And the Romanoff running CI laughed me right out of the room."

O'Neill crooked a finger in Miguel's direction and pointed toward Sam's almost empty glass. "So, they laughed. So what? They still arrested the son of a bitch."

" 'So *what*?' " Sam caught the bartender's quick nod and watched as he began mixing another cocktail. "So *what,* is that they didn't want to know about Hanssen."

"Who's *they,* Sam? The same people who killed Pavel Baranov?"

Baranov again. The caution light went on in Sam's head. He and O'Neill had never really discussed Baranov. And yet, here O'Neill was, trying to draw him out. He'd been doing it ever since he'd walked into the bar, too. O'Neill was *eliciting.* And he was using Boodles to help grease the skids.

Well, let him try, Sam thought, *he should know better.* After all, alcohol was a way of life at the Central Intelligence

Agency. Good case officers used alcohol as a tool, to loosen tongues and lower inhibitions. Sometimes they also used it as a crutch, to deaden emotions, to help them compartmentalize their existence. But the way Sam saw it, those who used booze as a tool generally did well in the field. Those who used booze as a crutch became drunks. O'Neill was wasting his time: Sam had long ago mastered alcohol—and it had never become a crutch.

But O'Neill was indisputably eliciting. And he was using Miguel's martinis to help him do it.

The question, of course, was why. In Sam's world, nothing was ever happenstance. Coincidence was an impossibility. And hadn't O'Neill already admitted he'd been looking for Sam? He'd tried to make a joke of it, but he'd said it right off: *I've just been all over town looking for you.*

What did O'Neill want? Sam decided to release chaff. "Okay, Michael: last question first. Why do Romanoffs laugh? They laugh because they won. Because they forced out a whole generation of people like me, and replaced us with reports officers and analysts who don't give a rat's ass about stealing secrets. They—" Sam broke off suddenly, some primitive protective instinct taking control. He glanced around the room. There was a newcomer at the bar. A professorial stranger in worn, clerical gray worsted with real buttonholes on the cuffs, aged blue button-down, and gravy-soiled Metropolitan Club tie was looking strangely in his direction.

It was an Alien. Again, O'Neill seemed not to have noticed. Sam snuck another look. The old gent reminded Sam of his own Agency mentor, a patrician, courtly, long-dead spy named Donald Kadick. Sam lowered his voice. "So, who are *they*? Y'know, Michael, there's a word in Russian. *Mudak.* It means 'dumb-ass.' Well, *they* are all the *mudaki* who come to the office with blinders on. Who can't see past their noses. Who have no vision. Who take no risks." Sam paused.

"That kind of behavior isn't unique to CIA these days, Sam. There are a couple of corporations I represent who fit that description exactly."

"Yeah—but I'm not paying for their incompetence with my tax dollars. Nobody's running agents. Nobody's recruiting. It's all counterterrorism—and most of that's done through liaison, or PM."[10] Sam made a sour face. "The Agency is completely dysfunctional these days."

Michael O'Neill crossed his arms, his body language betraying the fact that his eliciting wasn't going anywhere.

Sam decided to rub it in. "For chrissakes, Michael—it's my birthday, and I'll bitch if I want to."

"Then bitch away, old chap"—O'Neill sighed patiently—"I'm listening."

Gotcha. Triumphant, Sam picked a filbert out of the small bowl of nuts in front of him and pondered his next move. Today he was on the cusp of his sixth decade. The endgame. *Bishop to queen's pawn 6.*

It had been a decade since the George V bar. Maybe it was time to tell O'Neill something else he didn't know. Or confirm something he did. One of the things Sam had learned over the years was that if you gave a little, you sometimes got a lot. He'd just released chaff. Now he'd drop a small depth charge and see what it brought to the surface.

Sam scrutinized the intricate pattern of the dark marble under his glass. "Lemme tell you a story," he finally said. "I was working in Purgatory."

"At least it was convenient."

"What?"

---

[10] Paramilitary.

"Convenient," O'Neill repeated. "Purgatory. I mean, it was only three blocks from your apartment. Think of all the gas you saved."

Sam rolled his eyes. "Are you listening? This is important. It was on the twenty-first of February 2001—the day after they arrested Bobby Hanssen. I had this . . . epiphany. I realized that all of the successful arrests, prosecutions, and incarcerations were *meaningless*. Hanssen, Ames, Nicholson, Pitts—they hadn't been caught because of counterintelligence. It had all been on purpose. They'd been betrayed."

"Betrayed," Michael O'Neill said. His face was deadpan, but Sam could see the machinery engage and the gears begin to grind behind O'Neill's eyes. Telegraphing was a problem common to young case officers.

"Correct. Betrayed. In order to muddy the waters. Betrayed in order to protect a traitor or traitors operating at the very highest level of America's intelligence apparatus." He paused. "It was an audacious, brilliant op."

Michael O'Neill blurted, "Who ran this incredibly successful operation?"

"Edward Lee Howard."

O'Neill's eyes went saucer-wide. "Ed Howard? The CIA defector?"

"Yup."

Sam saw the attorney's internal engine decelerate. "Sez who?"

"Sez me."

In response, Michael O'Neill extended his right index finger, touched the skin just below his right lower eyelid, and tugged it downward slightly, in the French sign of gross skepticism. "Sam, that is just plain crazy."

"Why?"

"You tell me it was Andropov, and I'd say maybe. Or Klimov—he was *Rezident* in Paris when we were there. He had balls, too—aggressive son of a bitch. Tough opponent. But Howard is a second-rate hack. A drunk. A screwup. Besides, I heard he's out of favor with President Putin and the current leadership at Moscow Center."

Sam said, "Oh?"

"Just last night I heard reliably that Putin distrusts foreign defectors because he thinks they could be doubles."

"I think I read something to that effect in a newspaper, Michael."

O'Neill shook his head. "There was nothing in any newspaper about Putin not trusting defectors."

Sam decided to provoke O'Neill. "Well, you know, Michael, stuff like that, it's all about sources. Depends where you heard it."

"Well," O'Neill said petulantly, "I heard it up on—" And then he thought better of disclosing where he'd been and stopped himself in midsentence.

But it was too late. In the rarefied jargon of Washington officialspeak, "up" always meant Capitol Hill. So, Sam knew that O'Neill heard it somewhere in Congress, which meant someone on one of the intelligence committee staffs was gossiping to O'Neill, which in turn indicated the comment had originated inside the intelligence community. Which confirmed Michael O'Neill was still working on the Dark Side every now and then. *Give a little, get a lot.*

Satisfied, Sam filed O'Neill's gaffe away for later use. "Maybe it's all an act. Remember what Sun-tzu said: 'All war is deception.' Maybe Ed Howard just wants us to think he's a second-rate hack. After all, President Putin is former KGB—maybe he's targeting some kind of *dezinformatsia* program at us."

"That's not the thinking at Langley, Sam."

"It wouldn't be. Czar Nicholas and Vlad Putin are best friends these days."

"Moscow has been extremely helpful since 9/11."

Sam's eyes went cold. "Moscow never acts except in its own self-interest," he said. "Never has, never will."

O'Neill stared across the bar at the clock on the back wall. "Ever the Cold Warrior, eh, Cyrus?"

Sam said, "Some things die hard, Michael." But it wasn't the Cold War he was thinking about.

O'Neill said: "Besides, Ed Howard's never been able to do us any real damage."

Sam said nothing.

"C'mon, Sam."

Sam examined O'Neill's face. The problem was, O'Neill hadn't spent enough time in the street. He'd been a case officer for less than half a decade. He'd been taught most of the moves. But he'd never developed the antennae you get with a quarter century of clandestine warfare. Besides, O'Neill was far too trusting and far too glib. They might be endearing traits. But not on the street. On the street they were vulnerabilities. And vulnerabilities will always be exploited.

O'Neill nudged his friend. "C'mon, Sam."

It was time to give O'Neill an education. "Remember where Ed Howard works these days?"

O'Neill scratched alongside his left ear. "Moscow Center."

"But where in Moscow Center?"

The lawyer shrugged. "Dunno."

"CI," Sam said, tapping the center of O'Neill's vest, an inch above the gold watch chain. "Counterintelligence. The way I see it, about half the agents we lost that were credited to Ames and Hanssen were targeted by Ed Howard and betrayed by his moles in Washington. And I think he's still running people here."

"Impossible."

Sam remembered the broken cigarette jammed in Pavel Baranov's mouth and knew that nothing was impossible.

He looked at Michael O'Neill, his face dark with anger. "Edward Lee Howard has blood on his hands. And Vlad Putin's no friend. End of story."

Michael O'Neill shook his head in disbelief. "But that's only your supposition, Sam. You weren't ever able to prove it, were you?"

"If I'd been able to prove it, I'd still be working at Langley—and Czar Nicholas would be out of a job."

"Wouldn't that be lovely." O'Neill set his glass down. "I'm going to the head," he said. "Back in a minute."

Sam watched the attorney slalom around the tables and chairs, past the tweedy Alien who was staring down at a glass of house red so he wouldn't have to make eye contact. Sam plucked a Brazil nut from the bowl, chewed it, and washed it down with a full glass of water.

Okay, so O'Neill thought his Edward Howard theory was crazy. Hell, this wasn't the first time it had been dismissed out of hand.

O**N FEBRUARY 21,** 2001, Sam drove from Purgatory out the George Washington Parkway, turned off at the entrance to the George Herbert Walker Bush Center for Intelligence, parked in the visitors' lot, badged his way through the turnstile, took the elevator to the sixth floor, marched into the office of the assistant deputy director for counterintelligence, and declared, "Tom, we have to look at Robert Hanssen as a disposable."

The ADDCI looked up at Sam pie-eyed. "You're kidding me, right, Sam?"

"No, I'm dead serious." Sam knew he was probably talking to a wall. Tom Jorgensen was a former reports officer who'd never served overseas or run an agent. He was a Langley apparatchik—yet another archetypal, four-eyed Romanoff, sartorially understated in an ill-fitting Hugo Boss

knockoff, a gray Regis Philbin signature shirt, and nylon burgundy tie knotted in a triple Windsor the size of a child's fist.

But perhaps even Jorgensen could be enlightened. Sam
dragged a chair up to Jorgensen's desk, dropped into it, and
set both elbows on the ADDCI's Grade One walnut veneer.

Jorgensen, who detested such proximity, suppressed the
urge to scream for help. He swallowed hard and said, as
slowly and calmly as he could, "It's your . . . supposition,
your . . . *theory* that it was the *Russians* who allowed us to
uncover Robert Hanssen?"

"Absolutely." Sam slapped his palm on the desk. "Hanssen
is a diversion—just like Ames was—to keep us away from
Moscow's principal agents."

"Ames, too." Jorgensen rolled his chair away from the
desk, putting distance between them. "That's fascinating,
Sam, absolutely fascinating. And the proof?"

"Isn't it obvious?"

Jorgensen eased behind his three-tiered in-box so that Sam
couldn't stare directly at him. His fingertips began to drum
the edge of his desk nervously. "Why don't you tell me."

Sam scraped his chair across the carpet to reestablish eye
contact. "Ed Howard," he said.

"The defector." Jorgensen moved farther behind the in-
box barricade.

Sam played peekaboo. "Putin has put Ed Howard in
charge of a large-scale covert action program."

"Putin. Vladimir Putin."

"Precisely. The Russian president. Putin's making us believe we've plugged all the holes when in fact we're more
porous than we've ever been." Sam paused. "During my tour
in Moscow, the Russians lost Ames and Nicholson, right?"

Jorgensen scratched his chin. "I guess."

"Well, you lose one agent—that's normal. Agents get
caught. But two? With two, you start looking for anomalies."

Sam caught the look on Jorgensen's face and saw he was talking to a wall. But he kept on. "But the Russians never started looking for anomalies." He paused. "Doesn't that tell you something?"

Jorgensen responded by moving farther behind his in-box.

"It told me the Russians weren't worried because they had other, better-placed agents. And Hanssen's arrest proves my case. Now, Moscow let us have Hanssen because he's outlived his usefulness and they've got at least one more highly placed source—most likely here, at the assistant-deputy-director level and maybe even higher. There are others, too. Probably at the White House and State."

The ADDCI's fingers were now moving so fast he looked as if he was playing a fragment from Bach's *Goldberg Variations.* After six and a half very frantic measures, Jorgensen rolled out from behind the in-box and said, as reassuringly as possible, "Disposables? Anomalies? Sam, I think you need to take some vacation time."

Fifteen seconds after Sam had left his office, Jorgensen was on the line to Nick Becker's executive assistant.

SAM WAS PLAYING CHESS with his martini olives as Michael O'Neill made his way back into the bar.

The attorney drained his cocktail, pulled the pocket watch out, and squinted at the dial. "You know, Sam," he said, "Jim Angleton saw conspiracies, too, and talked about them loudly. Remember where it got the late and lamented counterintelligence chief."

"Same place it got me," Sam said.

"Think about that."

Sam had to admit O'Neill was right. He should have kept his damn mouth shut. Indeed, committing truth hadn't done him any good. No good at all.

Which was bizarre. Because for twenty-six years he'd

worked for an organization above whose main entryway, carved in foot-high letters, was the legend: KNOW YE THE TRUTH, AND THE TRUTH SHALL MAKE YOU FREE.

Yeah—right. And if you believe that, Sam thought, *I have some Chechen bearer bonds to sell you, cheap.*

He stared into his glass. Well, at least he'd been right about not committing truth when it had come to Baranov. He'd never divulged what the general had showed him to anyone at CIA. He'd rationalized at the time that if the document had been real, the unknown traitors would manage to cover their tracks and melt away forever. And if it had been a fabrication, the simple act of reporting its existence would have resulted in precisely the kind of confusion the Russians had wanted to generate.

Besides, Sam was punctilious when it came to double-checking agents' claims, and there were just too many questions left unanswered. For example, the page Baranov showed him had been dated October 12—a Monday. But was the date valid, or had it been a fabrication?

After he'd been sent back to Washington, he'd checked online and discovered that on October 15, the Thursday following the meeting described in Baranov's document, the *Washington Times* had run a three-paragraph story by Bill Gertz citing unnamed intelligence sources, and containing approximately the same details as the page of typing he'd been shown on October 23. To Sam, that was reason enough to cause him to doubt Baranov's bona fides. So he'd simply left the document out of his reports.

Not that he'd never told anyone. He had in fact described the Baranov document in March 2000, during an unauthorized trip to Capitol Hill. And in a way, that particular truth *had* set him free—by ending his career. But that was another story for another day.

In fact, Sam wondered if Rand Arthur, the two-faced son

of a bitch who was currently ranking member of the Senate Select Committee on Intelligence, had tasked O'Neill to elicit him on the subject of Pavel Baranov. O'Neill did the occasional odd job for Senate Select.

But if so, why? After all, Rand Arthur already knew all about Pavel Baranov. Sam had told him.

O'Neill was checking his watch again, his face tinged with concern like a conductor whose train is running late. Then he turned toward Sam, his expression suddenly quite grave. "I need your presence, Sam."

"My presence."

"Yes, your presence. It's required."

"Does that mean you want to *hire* me?" Waterman's tone took on a sardonic edge. "Does your firm want someone shadowed? Are you requesting due diligence? That's me: Samuel Elbridge Waterman. Dedicated due diligence done dirt cheap." And then he read O'Neill's face, and realized his former colleague was dead serious.

"No, I'm not talking about hiring you." O'Neill inclined his head so his lips almost brushed Sam's ear. "I'm not here by accident. I really was sent—to find you."

The attorney pushed his empty martini glass across the bar. He stepped back and checked his pocket watch a third time. "Someone needs to see you, Sam—needs to see you *now*."

CHAPTƎЯ 5

SAM DROPPED into the cold leather bucket seat of Michael O'Neill's vintage Mercedes coupe, slammed the door, and snugged the seat belt over his big frame. "Who wants to see me?"

"You'll know when we get there."

"Where are we going"

"You'll know when we get there."

"What's the big mystery?"

"You'll know when—"

"Michael," Waterman interrupted, "are you aware you've started to repeat yourself? It's the first sign of dementia. Pretty soon you'll be hiding your own Easter eggs."

O'Neill grunted in response and nosed the car out of the alley behind the club. He crossed Florida Avenue and turned south. At Massachusetts Avenue he made an illegal right turn, careened three quarters of the way around Sheridan Circle, then went south, back the way he'd come. At Twenty-first and Mass, O'Neill drifted around the corner, sped past the cabs stacked two deep outside the Westin's awning, shot halfway down the block, then abruptly cut into a narrow, one-way alley that ran the length of the block.

"You're going the wrong way." Sam listened to the car's ancient transmission and suspension go through hell. "Michael, what in heaven's name—"

"Tradecraft, Cyrus, tradecraft." O'Neill stared straight ahead. At Twenty-third Street he worked his way across two lanes of gridlocked northbound traffic, turned south, and crossed P just as the light went red. "I'm checking to see if anyone's following us."

"If you keep driving like this, we're guaranteed to pick up surveillance—traffic cops, all waving ticket books."

It began to drizzle. With the single windshield wiper beating syncopation, O'Neill slalomed down Twenty-third Street. Just south of Virginia Avenue, O'Neill flicked his chin toward a gated, fenced compound whose entry sign bore the legend U.S. NAVAL MEDICAL FACILITY.

The sandbagged main gate disappeared from view. O'Neill glanced toward the installation's thick concrete retaining wall, which ran all the way to C Street. "Hey, what good times we had up there, eh, Sam?"

Like many government installations in the National Capital Region, this one was purposefully mislabeled. In point of fact, five structures out of the seven-building U.S. Navy complex, which sat due west of the two-square-block Department of State headquarters building, belonged to the CIA. The Agency's Technical Services Division, known in-house as "Invisible, Inc." was located there. Inside three huge redbrick warehouses shielded by lead, white sound, and electronic countermeasures from any kind of hostile surveillance activity, dozens of creative, dedicated, and resourceful government artists forged documents, concocted disguises, and built a dizzying assortment of high-tech spy gadgets. And the aging three-story, slate-roofed, mustard yellow Big House, built in the late 1930s for the War Department, was used as the staging area for the Agency's denied area operations course, or DAO, a monthlong, eighteen-hour-a-day immersion program in countersurveillance tradecraft required for all case officers assigned to hard-duty stations like Moscow, Delhi, or Paris.

Sam was more interested in finding out what O'Neill was up to. "Michael—"

"Relax, Sam." The light turned green. The sleek black car sped down the hill, cut off an old taxi, and careened onto the Roosevelt Bridge on-ramp.

Sam glanced up the hill at the razor wire. "If the tourists only knew what to look for, right, Michael?"

"You got it." Indeed, the two-square-mile rectangle bordered by the Willard and Watergate Hotels on the east and west, and K Street and Constitution Avenue on the north and south, would be the city's number one visitors' attraction. Because that was the playing field where fledgling special agents from the FBI's Counterintelligence Division and the State Department's Bureau of Diplomatic Security engaged in regular spy games with trainees from CIA and the Defense Intelligence Agency's defense attaché school.

The FBI and DS agents were graded on how many CIA and DIA "hostiles" they could catch taking photographs of the government buildings, filling or emptying dead drops, passing information to "control agents," or receiving it from "sources." The spooks got graded on how many times they could evade the gumshoes and successfully use "sticks-and-bricks" tradecraft to complete their espionage missions. Failure meant that you washed out of whatever program you were a part of, and so the incentives to succeed were high.

Michael O'Neill changed lanes without signaling. "A tourist came to my rescue when I took the DAO," he said.

"Really."

"Yeah. Big black car of gumshoes came after me and my partner—she was a pocket rocket from DIA named Margo something or other. Good-looking babe. She was an Army captain and you just wanted to *salute* all night. They were about to send her to Poland, I think. We'd just cleared a dead drop at the public phone booth in the gas station next to the Watergate, and she had two rolls of film in her handbag when a pair of the ugliest FBI agents I've ever seen tried to wrestle us into their car. They were such Neanderthals—they should have been working for the KGB."

"Maybe Bobby Hanssen was one of them."

O'Neill guffawed. "Anyway, about fifteen feet away there was this tourist family watching our little drama unfold. The daddy had this look on his face, y'know, like he'd made up his mind that Margo and I were the good guys, and the gumshoes were the bad guys."

"Carpe diem, right?"

O'Neill's head nodded in assent. "Exactly. I yelled, 'KGB agents are trying to kidnap my wife because she's a defector,' grabbed the FBI guy closest to me, and wrestled with him. Meanwhile, Margo picked up my cue, and she's struggling with the other FBI agent and screaming bloody murder and help-help-help in a Russkie accent."

"You're making this up."

"I'm serious, birthday boy. Guess what: Daddy came to the rescue. He kicked the FBI agent holding on to Margo right in the balls—got him from behind. And I mean *kicked*. Oh, Sam, Daddy must have been a punter in college, because he lifted the poor schmuck about eight inches off the ground. Makes me cringe to think about it even now, and we're talking seventeen, eighteen years ago. So the guy holding on to me goes, 'Holy shit,' and he shakes me off and goes for his creds and his handcuffs, because Daddy has just assaulted a federal officer. That's when Margo and I got the hell outta Dodge."

"What happened to Daddy?"

"Who knows. Who cares. All that mattered was Margo and I kept the film."

Sam snorted. "The thing about you, Michael, is that you've always had your priorities straight."

In response, O'Neill wriggled his eyebrows.

They were on Route 66 now, heading west. The rain was now coming down in sheets. Sam peered through the windshield. "C'mon, Michael—give it up. Where are we headed?"

O'Neill's knuckles were white as they gripped the leather-covered steering wheel. "Should I repeat myself again, Sam, or just start hiding my Easter eggs?"

SHORTLY AFTER FOUR, Michael O'Neill deposited Sam Waterman outside a rural post office, an ugly, one-story redbrick shoe box of a building, separated from a volunteer fire department by a narrow alley. Across the two-lane blacktop sat a country diner, already closed for the day, and a gas station, still open. "End of the line for me, Sam."

Sam opened the car door. "Now what?"

"Now, you wait here," the lawyer said. "You'll be picked up."

Waterman stretched. He walked around the Mercedes's grille, leaned over the open driver's side window, and put his big hands on the sill. The rain had let up: it was drizzling. It had also turned quite cold, and he wasn't wearing a coat. "Picked up."

"Yup."

"When?"

O'Neill checked his watch and shivered in the chill. "Soon, I hope, for your sake." He looked up at Sam. "Look, friend, this is where I get off. I was asked to find you. I found you. I was instructed to drop you here. Consider yourself dropped. This is obviously a compartmented op, Sam. And just as obviously, I haven't been cleared for the next compartment."

Sam took a single step backward, away from the vehicle. "Okay, Michael—fair enough."

"Happy birthday, Cyrus. Many happy returns." The tinted window ascended, the Mercedes reversed, and headed off in the direction it had come.

Sam looked up at the post office facade. It told him he was in Round Hill, Virginia 20142. He pulled on the post office door and walked into the outer lobby. There were rows of mailboxes along two of the walls. A thick sheaf of wanted posters hung by the door, next to a bulletin board to which were thumbtacked half a dozen notices about lost cats and dogs. Sam thumbed through the wanted posters to see if there was anyone he knew.

He hadn't perused a dozen when bright headlights flashed rapidly three times through the glass door. Sam looked up. Eight feet away was the imposing snout of a big black Range Rover with headlights, driving lights, and fog lamps all turned on. Another triple flash of halogens summoned him impatiently. He pushed on the door with his shoulder and stepped outside.

Senator T. Randall Arthur opened the heavy door, slid off the tan butter leather upholstery, and exited the big SUV. "Thanks for coming on such short notice, Sam."

The senator pulled off pigskin driving gloves, stuffed them in his jacket pocket, and stuck his hand out for Sam to take. "Good to see you, Sam, my boy. It's been a while."

A while, Sam thought. *A while?* It had been two years. Two long years, since Sam made his surreptitious visit to the bug-proof "bubble" used by the Senate Select Committee on Intelligence and committed truth.

He'd told the senator, who had been Sam's company commander in Vietnam, about the murder of Pavel Baranov. After which, his former CO had turned political cutthroat and promptly set in motion the chain of events that ended Sam's career.

Which is why Sam put his spine up against the cold red-brick wall of the post office and kept his hands at his side.

He watched as the senator's extended arm lowered hydraulically slow until it was perpendicular to the ground.

"I can understand your reticence," Rand Arthur said, his deep voice placating in its tone. "That's one reason I called on my personal attorney Michael O'Neill to deliver you. I doubted you'd have come if the request came directly from me."

So Edward P. SAMGRASS was Rand's lawyer. That was something O'Neill had never ever mentioned. Sam crossed his arms. "I was delivered according to your instructions. What's up, Senator?"

"I need your help, my boy."

There was a certain arrogance, Sam had always thought, in the senator's calling him "my boy." They were, after all, only five or perhaps six years apart in age. And yet, Rand Arthur had done it as far back as Vietnam.

Sam gave his old CO a quick once-over. He looked every inch the country squire, the senator did. Double-vented tweed jacket cut in the British style over a soft cashmere turtleneck; thick, dark wool trousers; and stout walking shoes with cleated soles. Yes, Rand Arthur looked exactly like one of your classic, stiff-upper-lipped English shits.

Sam remained where he was, arms crossed. "I don't think you need my help, Senator. You seem to do pretty well on your own these days."

"Sam—please." Rand Arthur came around the hood of the

Land Rover and opened the passenger-side door. "At least let's talk privately."

"Privately? Does that mean you won't call the DCI afterwards and spill your guts?"

"Sam, you gave me no choice. I was compelled to inform the Agency about our meeting. Those are the rules."

"It would have been nice if you'd explained the rules to me beforehand."

Rand Arthur shook the Range Rover's door. "Sam, *please*."

Sam made him wait a full minute. But finally he yielded, noting with some grim satisfaction that the senator held the door for him two-handed, like a hotel doorman.

When he pushed it closed, the seal was so tight Sam's ears popped. The tan leather seat surface was warm. A digital readout in the dashboard told Sam that the interior was sixty-seven degrees Fahrenheit. The senator trotted past the headlights, opened his own door, and climbed in, popping Sam's ears a second time. He settled his well-tailored posterior on the seat, attached his seat belt, gave Sam a professional, reassuring smile, then stepped on the brake and reached for the shift lever.

Sam brushed the senator's arm aside, turned the ignition key to "off," snatched it from its socket, and held it securely in his big hand. "You said, 'Let's talk,' Senator. Okay, talk."

CHAPTƏR 6

EARLY IN 2000, Sam knew he was violating DCI Nick Becker's directive against any officer of the clandestine service contacting members of Congress without authorization when he called his old CO and asked for a confidential meeting in a secure location. But T. Randall Arthur, newly appointed to the Senate Select Committee on Intelligence, seemed happy to oblige. He welcomed Sam to his hideaway office, then guided him through the subterranean U.S. Capitol maze to the committee's bug-proof room in the Hart office building. But not alone. Accompanying the two men was one of SSCI's staff counsels, Virginia Vacario.

Sam protested. But as Rand Arthur explained it, no one went into the bubble room without a witness. "Too many leaks, my boy," he'd said to Sam. "The rules have changed. It's all on-advice-of-counsel legal mumbo jumbo these days."

After they'd secured the thick door, Sam told the senator and his legal shadow about Pavel Baranov, described the events surrounding the general's murder, and laid out Ed

Howard's covert action to destabilize the American intelligence community.

The senator had sat quietly and listened to his former platoon sergeant's one-hour presentation, occasionally asking questions as Lawyer Vacario scribbled notes. When Sam had finished, the senator thanked him for coming and ushered him out. And then, on advice of counsel, he used the room's secure telephone to dial Nick Becker's direct line and convey the high points of Sam's monologue.

Three days later, a story in the *Washington Post* citing "sources close to the intelligence community" described in broad brushstrokes the 1998 assassination of a Russian CIA agent in Moscow, the unnamed CIA station chief's expulsion, and Langley's subsequent embarrassment.

The following morning Sam was summoned to the DCI's office, where Nick Becker, brandishing the *Post* front page, accused Sam of leaking the story to embarrass him. By noon Sam had been banished to Purgatory. The senator never returned Sam's phone calls.

SAM SET HIS SHOULDER against the Range Rover's door and waited, sensing with satisfaction Rand Arthur's unease.

"Sam," the senator finally said, "I am truly, truly sorry. I can see why you—"

Sam cut him off. "Senator," he said, "don't play games. Can the charm and get on with whatever it is you have to say."

Rand Arthur grunted, an uncomfortable half laugh. "Still cut-to-the-chase, aren't you?"

Sam glanced at the senator with hostile derision. "The Directorate of Operations nomenclature for what you're doing is called a cold pitch. They don't work if you dance around. Tell me what you want—and what you've got to offer, then

I'm outta here." Sam hooked his thumb toward the lights in the gas station across the road. "They'll have a phone. I can call a cab."

Rand Arthur looked into Sam's eyes, and saw the determination in his expression. He exhaled a huge sigh that seemed to deflate his whole body. "You're right," he said, his tone contrite. "I knew what Nick did to you—and I did nothing about it. For my inaction, Sam, I am honestly sorry. But sometimes, that is the way things work in the real world. If you ever thought it was tough out there"—the senator's hand waved beyond the Land Rover's windshield—"then you should spend a few days with me. Politics is brutal, Sam. There are casualties. And loyalty? In the United States Senate, loyalty is a dispensable commodity. The Senate is nothing like the Marine Corps, my boy." He paused, his eyes moving quickly across Sam's face.

The senator's voice grew stronger and more resonant. "So, yes—I abandoned you. Two years ago I was just another member of Senate Select. But there's a very good chance I'll become chairman if the elections go well for us. I can facilitate the improvements in policy and budget and oversight that the intelligence community wants—and more important, that it needs. And if your scalp was a small part of the price I had to pay so I could work my way up the ranks in order to achieve a series of greater goals for the committee—and perhaps the country—well, then so be it, Sam. That's the real world. And if you can't deal with what I'm saying, then thanks for coming, walk away, take your cab, and go home. If, however, you want to become a part of something that I believe with all my heart will forever change the course of this nation, then hand me back the keys, fasten your seat belt, and join me for the ride of your life."

What garbage. It was drivel. Political smoke and mirrors. "Stow the speeches," Sam growled. "You're going to have to earn my trust the way my agents used to earn it—by delivering something tangible. Right now, Senator, you're nothing more than a blowhard."

The flash of anger in Rand Arthur's eyes told Sam he'd drawn blood. But Sam didn't let up. "*Die karten auf den Tisch legen,* Senator."

"Sam?"

"Cards on the table, Senator. Tell me what you've got—now."

Rand Arthur's expression changed. "I *could* tell you," he said coolly, "but I'd rather show you."

Sam made him wait. Then he flipped the keys at the senator, who caught them clumsily.

Rand Arthur put the big SUV in gear. They drove for fifteen minutes, the road narrow and hilly. The vehicle's lights played off tall, thick hedgerows rising on either side of the blacktop. The Range Rover came up a short rise, after which it traversed a small wooden bridge. Then the senator braked carefully and steered hard left onto a freshly graveled road that more or less paralleled the creek they'd just crossed.

The going was slower now, punctuated by the undulating crunch of stones under the tires. The hedgerows gave way to a four-batten fence that stretched off as far as Sam could see. The road before them disappeared beyond the range of the vehicle's headlights. A mailbox advertising an equine rescue center came into view on the Range Rover's starboard side. The senator passed it by and went another half mile. There, the road took a gentle turn to the left. Ahead, at the farthest perimeter of the headlights, Sam could make out two imposing pillars. Between the pillars, blocking the road, sat a darkened, four-door vehicle.

Rand Arthur switched his headlights on/off three times, waited two seconds, then flashed the lights once. The rolling roadblock ignited its parking lights, pulled ahead, and the senator drove past.

Sam swiveled in his seat and watched as the big Chevy sedan backed up and barred the road.

"U.S. Capitol police," the senator said by way of explanation.

"They provide security out here?"

"They handle sensitive matters for a lot of senators, including me, if I need them to."

Rand Arthur steered slowly around a long, gentle curve. As the tree line off to his right broke, Sam could see a big stone house, bathed in the kind of dramatic lighting often displayed in *Architectural Digest*. He counted chimneys in the fading light and came up with six. "Impressive place, Senator."

"It was my wife's. She's dead now."

Sam didn't quite know how to respond. "I'm sorry."

"No need to be," Rand Arthur said, quite coldly.

A second car—a dark Crown Vic—with two men in plain clothes sat adjacent to the three-car garage that had been added as an obvious afterthought. Rand Arthur pulled up next to the car, switched on the Range Rover's interior lights, and rolled his window down.

"Reese, this is Mr. Waterman," he said to a black officer with a shaved head who sat behind the wheel of the sedan. "He'll be with us for the foreseeable future. He can come and go as he pleases."

The policeman peered across the senator's torso and took a good look at Sam's face. "Okay, Senator," he said. "Thank you, sir."

"Carry on." Rand Arthur depressed the accelerator and the SUV nudged forward. "I had to tell him something," the senator said, anticipating Sam's response.

" 'Foreseeable future'?"

"I really do think you'll want to stay once you understand the implications," the senator said. "We're roughly the same size, so clothes won't be a problem. Or, I can send an officer to your apartment and get you what you need." He stopped the Range Rover outside the garage, stepped onto the pea gravel, and bid Sam to follow him.

Footfalls scrunching, they marched around the side of the house, past the accent lighting and the neatly trimmed English boxwood, up a shallow set of stone steps. Rand Arthur opened the unlocked castle-size front door without a key and ushered Sam into a huge, two-story foyer. The place had probably been built in the fifties, then gutted and redone very recently. It was impressive. The foyer floor was dark flagstone. Beyond, he could see a slice of the huge living room, whose wide floorboards were covered by antique Oriental rugs.

The senator led him past the living room and along a parquet-floored corridor hung with inscribed photographs from the rich and famous interspersed with testimonial plaques until they came to a thick, antique wood door. On the door at chest level was the same kind of twelve-key cipher lock that secured offices at SSCI, or CIA. Blocking the keys with his body so Sam couldn't watch him enter the combination, the senator punched one-two-three-four-five-six-seven keys in rapid succession. Sam could hear the electronic lock release. Then the senator reached down and turned the door handle.

He looked back. "Please, my boy, go in," he said, holding the door and indicating that Sam should precede him.

The room into which Sam walked was obviously The Library. It had a high, vaulted ceiling from which strategically placed spotlights illuminated half a dozen old masters on the walls. Antique furniture sat atop heart-of-pine flooring and muted Persian carpets. From hidden speakers, a Beethoven trio provided background music. Sam looked around quickly. The big rectangular room was dominated by a stone fireplace with a perfect fire crackling away behind a mesh guard. The fireplace was outlined by an ornate wooden mantel and bordered by a horseshoe-shaped, leather-covered fireplace bumper. A long, kilim-covered sofa accented by a pair of tall black leather wing chairs faced the fireplace. A folded quilt with a bed pillow atop it sat, incongruously, at one end of the sofa. Beyond, in front of the drapery-covered windows, sat a Victorian partner's desk, with two high-backed leather judge's chairs opposite each other.

Sam felt Rand Arthur's hand on the small of his back, and he stepped farther into the room. Behind him, something clicked audibly. Sam turned, to see that the inside of the door had the same sort of cipher lock as the outside. Then he looked across to the partner's desk. Sitting in the big chair facing him was a red-haired woman, half-glasses perched on the tip of her nose, an oversize pen poised three inches above a legal pad. He squinted, and recognized Rand Arthur's SSCI lawyer lady, Virginia Vacario.

She removed her glasses and laid them on the desk. The ice of her tone unconcealed, she said, "Hello, Mr. Waterman."

At the sound of her voice, the second chair, the one facing away from Sam, swiveled.

Edward Lee Howard extracted himself from the dark leather. "Well, at last. Cyrus N. PRINGLE. Thank you, Senator."

CHAPTER 7

YOU—TRAITOR. You son of a bitch." Sam advanced toward Howard. "I'm calling the FBI."

"No—" Rand Arthur inserted himself between Sam and the defector. "This man is under my protection. I gave him my word."

"Your word means nothing, Senator. Get out of my way."

Rand Arthur held his ground. "Let's get one thing straight," he said. "Two years ago, I never promised you anything. You called *me,* Sam. You wanted an appointment. I granted you one. I never pledged confidentiality. If I had, I would have kept my word. And whether you choose to believe it or not, it wasn't I who leaked the story."

Sam remembered things differently. But this wasn't the time or place to say so. "What's your point, Senator?"

"Mr. Howard has asked me for protection. I have granted it to him."

"He's a traitor, Senator. National security trumps politics."

"This *is* about national security, Sam." Rand Arthur paused. "The information Mr. Howard brought with him is paramount to America's national security. Isn't that right, Mr. Howard?"

Edward Lee Howard said nothing.

"You asked Michael O'Neill to get hold of Sam Waterman. He's here." The senator paced slowly across the rug to Howard's chair. He nudged the defector's elbow. "So, tell Sam what you told me."

Howard's round, pasty face turned toward Sam. "The White House knew about al-Qa'ida's plans to fly passenger jets into targets in New York and Washington seven weeks before the attacks occurred. But the president did nothing. The vice president and a cabal of hard-liners in the Pentagon had convinced him that he needed a 'trigger' that would allow the United States to initiate a string of military campaigns under the rubric of counterterrorism; actions that would guarantee American hegemony over the rest of the world. The president concurred with them, and personally suppressed the intelligence that would have thwarted the 9/11 operation. That is why, despite CIA's publicly perceived massive pre-9/11 intelligence failure, Nick Becker and the rest of Langley's top leadership were not fired. I have proof."

"You have proof." Sam was incredulous.

"Yes. I obtained a series of SVR communications intercepts of conversations both CIA and the White House believed to be secure. They are in the form of digital recordings, and can be positively verified by voiceprinting and other technical means available to you. They are Moscow's trump card over this administration. They are in a safe place. I also have information that will allow you to identify a Russian intelligence network operating within the highest levels of the American government. That network is why President Putin can sell nuclear materials to Iran, conventional weapons to Syria, and clandestinely assist the

North Koreans upgrade their long-range missiles with impunity. He can do so because he knows in advance what the U.S.'s reaction will be. His agents have told him. That information is in a safe place, too." Howard looked at Sam with some derision. "Of course I have proof, Sam. If not, why would I risk my life to come back?"

Why indeed. Not two hours before, Michael O'Neill had told Sam that Howard was washed up. A drunk. O'Neill's theory was certainly a possibility. But it was far more likely that the rumors of Howard's unhappy decline had been created by Moscow Center as a way of easing his redefection.

As a case officer, Sam had developed over the years a series of informal rules under which he operated. The first of what had come to be known as Waterman's Rules of Engagement was that, when something seemed too good to be true, it was, in fact, too good to be true. Edward Lee Howard and his protector, Rand Arthur, were living embodiments of Waterman's Rule Number One.

But Sam put not a single word to his thoughts. Instead, he said, "Miss Vacario, may I sit down to take some notes, please?"

The lawyer's eyes shifted toward the senator, then back to Sam. "Of course, Mr. Waterman." She opened a drawer, retrieved a fresh pad and a pen, laid them on the desktop, eased her chair away, and stood up, taking her pad and pen with her. "All yours."

Sam crossed the room and dropped onto the padded seat.

But he didn't say anything. He waited until Howard turned to face him. And then he stared into the defector's face, his own expression as neutral as he could manage.

The silence endured for some half minute. But Sam knew Howard would speak. That was his role. He'd set his hook. Now he was going to play his fish.

And the defector didn't disappoint. "I *worked* for

Moscow," Howard finally said. "No more. I came back because I want to help."

Sam's eyes intently examined every minute detail of Howard's appearance and behavior, conveniently illuminated by a pair of spotlights hidden somewhere up in the rafters. He watched as the defector centered himself in the chair, using his right hand to smooth down the sparse gray hair atop his scalp.

" 'You want to help,' " Sam mimicked Howard's nasal tone.

"Yes, help." Nervously, Howard ran a finger around his shirt collar. "I am truly sorry for what I did and I want to make amends."

Except it was an act, and Sam knew it. He knew it because he hadn't followed Howard's hand as it played with his collar but kept his gaze on Howard's eyes. And he hadn't been disappointed. There'd been a quick, micromomentary flickering in both of the defector's eyes as he spoke. It was a subconscious signal, something Agency psychologists had discovered by watching thousands of hours of film and videotape run frame by frame in extra slo-mo. Sam had been trained to watch for these involuntary micromomentary eye movements in his agents, because they indicated deceit. Ed Howard knew all about micromomentary expressions, too. So, moving his hand had been a diversion—similar to the way a three-card monte dealer uses a flourish to draw the mark's eyes away from the position of the ace.

But Sam had ignored the distraction. His focus never moved from Howard's eyes. And their movements told Sam loud and clear the defector was lying. Which was when Sam confirmed his own longtime beliefs: Ed Howard was no drunk, no has-been, no mediocre hack. Edward Lee Howard was a pro—and a dangerous opponent.

The defector shifted his position again, his face now open and receptive. Which is precisely when Sam struck. "Yeah, right. You just left. Walked away. Snuck out of Moscow unnoticed and came straight to Washington. And what did you say to your pals at Lubyanka as you were walking out the door? '*Do svidániya? Poká?* See you later, alligator. *À bientôt? Sayonara?* You can call me at Senator Arthur's place in Virginia?' *Mudozvon,* Ed. Bullshit. Like all fabricators, you're feeding me garbage."

Howard licked his lips but didn't answer. It was, Sam knew, a delaying tactic. Finally, his thoughts composed, Howard spoke. "I traveled on an Irish passport. The senator has it for safekeeping, It was something I kept in reserve, hidden under the floorboards of my dacha. I slipped out of Moscow. I picked up the passport. Then I took a train to St. Petersburg. From there, I crossed into Finland. It wasn't difficult. I flew from Helsinki to Hamburg. I caught a train to Frankfurt and bought a ticket for Washington, flying through Toronto. Open return."

He's still playing games, Sam thought. *Deflect. Redirect. Sidetrack.* It was an old agent's trick: inundate the case officer with a flurry of meaningless details in order to obfuscate and confuse the issue at hand.

"You've told me nothing. I asked a question and you blew smoke in my face." Sam turned toward Rand Arthur. "Senator, you want my opinion? He's worthless."

Howard swiveled toward the senator. "I risked my life—" he began.

Sam cut him off. "Ed, you may be able to fool these people. But this is me. Sam. I know you. I know how you operate. To me, you're cellophane—I see right through you. So, let me translate for the senator and our learned counsel here what you said—and what you were really doing. You claim you came here out of some long-buried sense of civic duty and remorse. 'The president knew all about 9/11. There are Russian spies in the American government.' That's what you *said,* Ed. But your objective was creating confusion and chaos. You're a double agent, Ed—you work for Moscow Center. And you might have succeeded, except—thank God—the senator got hold of me instead of calling a press conference and putting you on CNN."

He waited for a response, and when he got none, he slapped the desk. "You said you had confirmation. But I don't see any, Ed. You know the game as well as I do: an agent's claims have to be backed up by hard evidence. Paper. That's what we call it, right? You know the rules. No paper, no proof. And without proof, agents' claims are treated as fabrications."

Sam looked at the defector. "So, where's the paper?"

Silence.

"Where's the paper, Ed?"

Silence.

Sam slammed his palm onto the desk. "Show me the paper, goddammit. Show me the *paper.* Show me the *paper.* Show me the *paper.* Show me the *paper.*"

Howard's silence was eloquent. Sam let the senator and his legal counsel absorb its significance. "But you can't show me the paper, can you, Ed? That's because there *is* no paper. No evidence. You're a provocateur, a fabricator. But you still *want* something don't you?"

Sam swiveled toward Virginia Vacario. She'd moved to the sofa, pad on her lap, scribbling away. "If you understood double agents you'd know that people like him always try to get something for nothing, counselor."

Then he looked at Howard. "So, what is it, Ed? Money? Protection? A new identity?"

Sam turned back to Vacario. Her face was a mask. It was like talking to a Romanoff. He continued anyway. "I know what he wants, counselor. He wants *everything.*"

Vacario said nothing. Neither did Ed Howard. So Sam

picked up. "Everything. And what quid pro quo did you bring in return, Ed? You brought *nothing*."

Howard pushed himself out of the chair. He stared past Sam through the wide Palladian window. "I shouldn't have come." He massaged his eyes. Then he dropped his hands to his sides. "You know, Sam, by now Klimov will have discovered I'm gone. And when he learns what I took, he'll be extremely upset. He'll try to find me and retrieve his . . . materials. My life is worth nothing right now. My whole life has been thrown away because you refuse to see what I've just done for you, Sam."

Klimov was Major General Valentin Klimov, the brutal, relentless, ambitious current head of Russia's counterintelligence service. "Don't flatter yourself, Ed. You've been worthless for years." Sam wasn't about to give Howard an inch. "Materials again? Show me the paper."

Howard stuck out his lower lip. " 'The paper,' as you call it, is in a safe place," he said.

"And what's in the paper, Ed?"

Howard's eyes shifted toward the ceiling. He bit his lips. "Nineteen ninety-three," he finally said. "DO wanted to carry out a clandestine site survey of a chemical weapons facility in Ukraine." He looked at Sam. "Remember?"

The operation had been a top priority. Sam nodded but said nothing.

"You were deputy chief in Paris. Long before the end of the first year of your tour you were miserable. You despised the bureaucratic scut work deputy chiefs have to do. You were bored by all the managerial aspects of the job. And so you hit the streets with one of your young officers, a deep cover pseudonymed SAMGRASS, using the excuse that you wanted to mentor him to get you out of the office."

Sam's face betrayed no emotion. But Howard had it right.

Sam had chaffed under the administrative aspects of the deputy's job.

The defector's eyes flashed. "Before long SAMGRASS spots a possible target. An émigré—a defector actually—a former KGB officer from the Second Chief Directorate. His name is—well, you know his name, Sam. His surname begins with *S.* You and SAMGRASS tag-team the émigré, but since it's you who had all the street smarts, it's you who develops him. SAMGRASS is content to watch from the side. It's a fight, but you finally receive POA[11] to recruit Mr. S under alias. The initials you used were RJ, and the Agency cryptonym given to Mr. S was GTREQUIRE." He squinted at Sam. "Am I getting warm, Sam? Am I cutting close to the bone?"

Sam was trying hard not to show anything outwardly. But his heart was pounding. The son of a bitch *knew.*

"So, let's fast-forward. Blah-blah-blah, it's spring of 1993, Langley wants to run the op in Ukraine in the late fall or early winter and needs someone who knows the turf. Your agent, GTREQUIRE, had served a three-year tour in Kiev. And so on April ninth, you slip out of Paris to drop below DST's[12] radar. You drive southeast, to Auxerre. There, you take back roads, heading toward the Côte de Nuits. You go black successfully, and at a clandestine meeting at the Agency safe house in the village of Corgoloin, four miles north of Beaune, you ask REQUIRE to accompany the team." Howard paused. "Correct, Sam?"

Sam wasn't about to confirm or deny anything. But Howard had it all. Every piece.

"REQUIRE agrees," the defector continued. "Langley makes plans all through the summer. Then you receive a re-

---

[11] Provisional Operational Authority.
[12] DST is the acronym for Direction de la Sécurité de la Territoire, France's internal security agency, which conducts counterintelligence operations against foreign espionage activities.

quest from Langley to flutter GTREQUIRE. You comply—
actually, you don't box him yourself, because you're in
Washington, setting up the Ukraine op. You get back to Paris.
Everything's ready to go. But at the last minute the mission is
scrubbed. You assumed the bosses back at Langley were
averse to taking risks—at least that's what you complained
loudly to your colleagues. But in fact, the plan was scuttled
by SCARAB, one of our longtime American agents at the
National Security Council. And immediately after it fell
apart, Langley orders you—despite your strong protests—to
cut REQUIRE loose and write off all the information he gave
you as tainted. You're furious, right, Sam?"

Sam said nothing.

"Furious." Howard cocked his head. "You'll be angrier
when you hear the real story. SCARAB slipped the word to
Aldrich Ames to make sure GTREQUIRE was tagged as a
double."

"Slipped Ames the word. How?"

"SCARAB operates a safe house. Had it for years under
true name. SCARAB will only meet with his control under
certain conditions." Howard paused. "He's leery about dead
drops and mailboxes. Said the FBI had them covered. I always thought he was slightly paranoid."

"He?"

"I'm not sure whether it's a he or a she," Howard said
quickly.

Yes, he was. But Sam wasn't about to pursue the matter
right now. "So SCARAB met with Ames in the safe house."

The defector nodded in the affirmative. "Frankly, it made
me nervous. If Ames was being followed, it would have compromised SCARAB."

"Ames wasn't followed?"

"Apparently not." Howard shifted his legs. "We took a big
chance, Sam, using Ames so late in the game. But we had to.

REQUIRE had stories to tell. He worked in counterintelligence. He'd heard all the rumors floating around Moscow Center about the KGB's American moles—and we knew that sooner or later he'd tell you about them." Howard's tongue flicked across his lips.

"Now, there were some who wanted REQUIRE silenced permanently. I argued against that, Sam." The defector's tongue repeated the reptilian gesture. "But if he'd been killed, then his information would have been taken seriously. No—I wanted Mr. S to be a discredited source, not a dead martyr. Besides, I convinced Primakov in March of 1993 that Langley's CI capabilities were so pitiful we'd get away with it, even though Ames was under suspicion and was being monitored." Howard's tongue flicked over his lips once again. "Monitored. Just like the FBI monitored me in September 1985." His lips drew back in a nasty smile. "And we know what happened then, don't we, Sam?"

When Sam didn't respond, the defector continued, his tone growing more confident. "Y'know what, Sam? Primakov called when he got back from Washington in July to tell me I'd been right on the money. He even met with SCARAB."

"Actually met with him?"

"In plain sight. During a diplomatic reception on the eighth floor at State. Shook his hand. Shared a glass of champagne." Howard saw the skeptical look on Sam's face and made a fist. "You don't believe me? Well, Primakov told me he watched SCARAB's control brush-pass a tasking right under the secretary of state's nose"[13]

---

[13] Yevgeniy Primakov, an academician, was nominated by Boris Yeltsin to be head of Russia's foreign intelligence service, the SVR, on December 26, 1991. In July 1993, while his organization was running Aldrich Ames and more than a dozen other American moles, Primakov visited Washington, where he held a series of highly publicized meetings with incoming CIA director James Woolsey and other American intelligence community, congressional, and State Department officials.

Sam gave the turncoat a dirty look. "You just told me SCARAB would only deal with his control officer at the safe house, Ed."

"Then I misspoke."

"You're lying, Ed."

"No, Sam." The defector's head wagged. "I simply misspoke. I confused SCARAB with another agent." Howard's tongue slicked across his lips. "We *do* have more than one agent, Sam. After all, we've totally penetrated you. But CIA's porosity isn't the point I was making. The point I was making is that we convinced Langley GTREQUIRE was a double."

He paused to see how Sam would react. When Sam didn't react—outwardly, at least—Howard said, "Of course REQUIRE *wasn't* a double, Sam. He was twenty-four-karat gold. And the information he gave you was genuine. But you knew that all along, didn't you, Sam? You always had good instincts in those matters. Better than Langley's." He paused to scratch a red blotch on his pale cheek. "Much better, actually. What you don't know is SCARAB's identity. I do."

Howard pursed his lips. "Let's proceed to 1997. Moscow Center was informed about another DO op, this one on the Tajik-Chinese border, by another of our agents—I knew him—I'm assuming he's a man—only by his cryptonym SCEPTRE. The corridor gossip at Moscow Center was that SCEPTRE had access to the highest circles of the American government. Because of his information we were able to roll up your network before the operation ever got off the ground—we even made it look as if the whole thing had been done by the Chinese."

"And you know who SCEPTRE is."

Howard frowned. "I can point you in the right direction. I—"

"Wait a minute," Rand Arthur broke in. "You never told me anything about any SCARAB or SCEPTRE. You said you had information about the president—and a Russian spy network."

"SCARAB and SCEPTRE were for Sam's ears, Senator. That's why I asked you to send for him. He understands the significance of what I have to say."

Rand Arthur bristled. "I receive the very highest-level briefings, Mr. Howard, and I have never heard word one about any SCEPTRE or SCARAB."

"Senator, please." Sam interrupted. "I have a lot of ground to cover." He watched as Rand crossed his arms. Then he focused on Howard. "*We?* Who is we, Ed? And where's the paper to back up your claims?"

"Uh-huh. Not so fast, Sam." The defector's right index finger waved, windshield wiper–like in Sam's direction. Then he put his finger upright against his lips. "Shhhh—quiet." The defector smiled in Rand Arthur's direction. His voice took on new authority. "I'm no fool. I'm not about to hand anything over until we come to a formal understanding."

Sam focused on the defector. "A formal understanding."

"An agreement. You are correct, Sam: I want everything. A new identity. Enough money to be able to start a new life. A safe place to live. And then, I want to be left alone."

"You and Greta Garbo." Sam glanced toward Rand Arthur. "He doesn't want much, does he?"

"Look, Sam." Howard's voice took on an assertive tone. "I didn't have to turn myself in. You said the senator could have called a press conference. Well, I could have just as easily gone to the *New York Times,* or the *Washington Post.* Hell, I could have met with the *Times* of London in Switzerland and sold my story for half a million pounds—maybe more. But I wasn't interested in making headlines or piles of money. I'm interested in making amends. I want to come home. I want to set things straight. I made mistakes, I admit it. I can't erase what's already happened. But I can attempt to help fix the problem. Because CI has a problem, Sam, a huge problem—and you know it as well as I do. America has no counterintelligence capability right now. Everything's counterterrorism these days. Putin's our friend, right? So: thousands of FBI CI personnel shifted. The Oracles?[14] They're all retired. Headhunters at Langley? Decimated. All reassigned to CTC.[15] The doors are wide open, Sam. The United States is porous. Porous. I can point you in the right direction."

"Okay." Sam centered the defector in his sights. "Tell me what you have."

"There's so much," Howard began. "Hundreds of pages—"

"Hundreds."

"Yes, hundreds."

"Where are they? Did you bring one page with you, Ed? Just one."

Howard's silence was all the answer Sam needed. "He's fabricating, Senator."

"I'm telling the truth, Sam."

Sam's expression darkened. "Don't insult me any more than you already have, Ed. Give me one straightforward answer—just one: Where did you put all these alleged documents?"

"They are in a safe place."

"Don't play games. No more chaff, Ed."

Howard's dark eyes locked on Sam's. "All right, Sam. Let's talk about an important case."

"Why?"

"You want me to demonstrate good faith." Howard smiled—somewhat malevolently, Sam thought. "All right," the defector continued, "that's fair. After all, you were kind

---

[14] The Oracles were a group of women who initially worked for James Jesus Angleton's counterintelligence operation, and stayed on in CI until they were finally forced out by Nick Becker when he was CIA's deputy director.
[15] CIA's Counterterrorism Center.

enough to come at a moment's notice to meet with me. So, let's talk about a case with real significance. A case that is relevant to the counterintelligence problems America is facing right now. Let's talk about Pavel Baranov."

CHAPTЭR 8

SAM TRIED to maintain his composure. But the earlier conversation with O'Neill had brought all the nasty memories flooding back. He fought the surge of emotion. "Pavel Baranov," he said.

"Yes, Baranov." Howard's eyes flashed. "You remember Pavel Baranov, don't you, Sam? Brigadier general? Close friend of General Lebed's? One of your developmentals. He was killed during a rendezvous with you."

"I remember Baranov very well, Ed."

"Your fists are clenched," Howard said. "Bad tradecraft, Sam. Tacit reaction. Projection. Body language and all that. Very basic mistake, Sam." The defector displayed visible satisfaction as he watched Sam's face redden. "I doubled Baranov against you. It was a hugely successful operation."

Sam finally reined his emotions in. "How did you spot him?"

"By accident, actually." Howard caught Sam's expression of momentary confusion and he half smiled. "President Yeltsin wanted Lebed watched," he explained. "He was afraid of a coup from the Army—with reason, too, if you remember. And so, within a week after Putin took over FSB in August 1998, he ordered surveillance on all of Lebed's old staff from Kabul. Pavel Baranov may have only been a junior officer in Kabul, but he was a drinking buddy of Lebed's. So we tailed him." He shrugged. "And then ten days later we saw you. You were at the opera. So was Baranov. So there it was: you and Baranov were in the same venue. We both know there's no such thing as coincidence in our profession, Sam. And then: confirmation. You brush-passed him a message in the foyer after the performance. Great tradecraft, Sam. The foyer was jammed and it was a very smooth bren[16] indeed. But we knew what to look for and we saw it." Howard smiled. "Bingo, Sam. Jackpot."

Sam said nothing.

"That was enough for Putin. He ordered me to put Baranov under active surveillance. I knew at once you'd received POA." Howard turned toward Rand Arthur. "That stands for provisional operational approval, Senator—and you'd re-cruited Baranov. So I took one of my best teams and assigned them to him, twenty-four-seven. Eighty people per shift, Sam. Just think of the man-hours. I discovered all your signal sites and letterboxes. Your rendezvous sites, too. Arbatskaya lamppost—that was a Morse code signal site, as I recall. Your Prospekt Mira metro pickup spot. The mailbox at the Church of the Trinity in Serebryaniki. Even the hollowed-out tree just north of the police station in Red Army Park."

Sam's eyes never wavered. But he drew a small measure of grim satisfaction in the fact that Ed's four score gumshoes had screwed up—if just a little. Red Army Park had never been one of Pavel Baranov's dead drops. The park was right next to a cluster of army staff offices. The chance of being compromised by Russian counterintelligence was too great.

---

[16] CIA jargon for brief encounter.

And even if Russian CI hadn't been active in the area, Sam would not have used that portion of the park as a dead-drop location because it was close to a *vizir* site and police station.

Maybe Red Army Park had been one of *Howard*'s dead-drop sites. Sam took appropriate note.

Howard appeared not to notice his gaffe. "I even knew about your car at the Moskvich factory," he continued eagerly. "You never discovered the microphone, did you?" Howard cracked a smile at the flicker in Sam's eyes. "So, we called the general in for a little tête-à-tête and I gave him a choice. I told him, 'Work for us, Pavel Dmitriyvich, and perhaps you'll escape the gulag. If not—'" Howard looked at Sam, his moist eyes absolutely cold. "Well, Sam, you know the alternatives as well as he did."

Sam knew the alternatives all too well. "You murdered him."

"No," Howard objected. "No way. I didn't have him killed. Why would I? I was never told they were planning anything like that. Matter of fact, Sam, I was devastated when they executed Baranov, because I was about to use him to cause you—and Langley—a great deal of discomfort."

"You said 'they.' Who had Baranov killed, Ed? Was it an American?"

The defector smiled. "Ah, yes. You started looking for Russian moles the minute you got back from Moscow, didn't you, Sam? It was quite devastating to your career, one hears."

"To hell with my career. Who had Baranov killed?"

"Your career did indeed go to hell, Sam." Howard shrugged Sam off with a spiteful smile and shifted his gaze. "Miss Vacario, I'd like to settle a few particular arrangements about my future before I get any more specific with your interrogator here."

That was when Sam realized he'd lost control. He wasn't doing any better than a frigging Romanoff reports officer. It was Howard who'd just determined the entire tempo of the exchange. Dammit, he had to shake things up. *Provoke. Goad. Incite.* Sam gazed across the room at the defector's smug face.

Then he slapped his big palm on the leather-inlaid surface of the desk like an explosion. "You're crazy—Senator, Miss Vacario. Both of you." When they looked at him, wide-eyed, he continued. "What the hell is going on here?" He focused on Virginia Vacario. "You—you're an attorney—an officer of the court. Hell, you're the SSCI minority counsel. So you know exactly what you have to do." Sam swiveled toward the senator and explained himself. "She gets on the phone and she calls the FBI. And then the two of you turn this . . . *thing* over to them. Let him make his crazy accusations—and let the FBI deal with it. Whatever happens, happens. But the bottom line is, he's a traitor, a defector. He works for Moscow Center. Brave people died because of his treachery—including one of my agents. He deserves whatever he gets."

Howard said, quite coolly, "The senator knows what you suggest is impossible. It wasn't part of the agreement."

Jeezus H. Kee-rist. Had Rand had already cut a deal with the defector? Sam's voice took on an edge. "Senator?"

Now it was Rand Arthur's turn to release chaff. The senator ignored Sam's question. Instead, he crossed his arms defensively and blurted, "He showed up unannounced."

"Unannounced."

Rand Arthur continued. "Two days ago. Just after midnight. He rang the front doorbell. I came down and answered it. He stood there and said, 'Senator, I'm Edward Lee Howard and I want to come home.'"

"Just like that. And you agreed not to turn him in."

"I agreed to listen to what he had to say," Rand Arthur protested. "I told him that if he was honest with me, I'd do my best to help him."

"So, has he been honest, Senator?"

"Motive be damned, he has a lot to offer, Sam." The senator gave Sam a guarded look. "Besides," he continued, "there are a lot of questions he can answer; a lot of old cases he can solve for us. But he has conditions . . ."

Motive be damned? Sam was shaken. But the senator continued undeterred. "One of them was seeing you. This morning, out of the blue, he demanded to see you." The senator looked over at Howard. "Right, Ed? You told me you wouldn't say another word until you'd had a chance to meet with Sam Waterman. Only Sam would do."

Sam looked over toward the defector. Edward Lee Howard's opaque expression never changed. He remained silent.

Rand Arthur picked up the slack. "I had no idea where you were these days. Luckily, Michael O'Neill was here. He knew where to look." The senator paused. "I guess Ed thought you'd be the best person to take his information and help us put it to good use."

That's when the warning light went on in Sam's brain. "Good use."

"About the president. About Russia's network of agents. Their penetration plans. The other materials he brought."

"He hasn't produced a shred of evidence so far, Senator."

"But he will," Rand Arthur insisted. "Now that you're here. You'll see, Sam."

"He says he is willing to hand everything over to us," Virginia Vacario explained.

The senator cleared his throat. "Not to us, Ginny." The senator tapped his chest. "To *me*. He said once he'd met with Sam he'd be willing to hand everything over to *me*."

That was when Sam realized how bad the situation actually was. Edward Lee Howard had snagged them both. He'd tagged their vulnerabilities and exploited their egos and was playing them like game fish. The damn senator and his chief counsel, and they were both *his*. Couldn't they see what the hell was going on here? They were bloody well being *recruited*.

"Senator, I'd like to talk to you outside."

Rand Arthur blinked. "Why?"

"Because I'd like to talk to you—*alone*."

Rand Arthur's eyes flicked in Virginia Vacario's direction. Sam couldn't see her reaction without making a clumsy move.

He didn't have to. The senator filled the blank in for him. "If you'd like to tell me anything, Sam, I think it preferable that you do so in front of my counsel."

Been there, done that. "Whatever you say, Senator." He pushed out from behind the desk, crossed the big room, and stood by the heavy wooden door. Virginia Vacario followed him, her pen clutched like a dagger, the legal pad shielding her bosom.

The senator dropped his hand onto Ed Howard's shoulder. "This foolishness won't take more than a few minutes," he said. "Can I bring you a drink?"

"Thank you, no, Senator." Howard shook his head. "I'll be just fine."

Rand Arthur joined Sam and the attorney at the door. He stood so as to block Sam's view as he punched the combination into the cipher lock. When he heard the soft click, he opened the door and stood aside so that Vacario could lead the way. Then Sam walked through the doorway and watched as the senator pulled the door shut, double-checking to make sure it couldn't be opened. Then both men followed the staccato castanets of the lawyer's heels on the intricately patterned wood floor.

THE CHIEF COUNSEL led them down the hall and then turned left into a narrow passageway, past a small wet bar and into a pantry, which in turn led to a huge kitchen, floored in rustic Spanish tile. She dropped her legal pad on a granite-covered island, unsheathed the pen, and turned toward Sam. "What was so important?" she asked impatiently.

"He's playing with you. Can't you see it?"

"Of course I see it," she said, irritation evident in her tone. "But so what? What's so bad about letting him think he's running things?"

"Because that puts him in control," Sam said. "It means he decides what happens—not you." He paused. "Senator, I really do advise strongly that you bring the FBI into this."

"I'm surprised that you of all people would suggest that course of action," Rand Arthur said.

"His allegations—" Sam began.

Rand Arthur cut him off. "Things are a lot more complicated than they may appear at first glance, Sam."

Virginia Vacario said: "The FBI's still recovering from Hanssen. The so-called counterintelligence czar is a figurehead. They've moved ninety percent of the agents working CI into counterterrorism."

"Besides," Rand Arthur said, "the FBI is just too porous these days." The senator turned toward his chief counsel. "The committee has had major problems with leaks coming from the Bureau, hasn't it, Ginny? And the Department of Justice is just as bad." Rand Arthur gave Sam a worried look. "Any hint of this in the news media before we can substantiate Howard's assertions would be ruinous."

Sam was equally adamant. "He's a traitor, Senator. Turn him over to the proper authorities and let nature take its course."

Rand Arthur took on a resolute tone. "You're making an open-and-shut case out of this, Sam. You know that in intelligence, most things are shades of gray."

Sam said nothing. *Wait them out. Make them explain themselves.*

"There's a lot at stake," the senator finally blurted.

Sam decided that Ed Howard had obviously hooked these two up, and they were going to do whatever they were going to do no matter what he said. But all of his instinct and experience told him everything about the situation was wrong. *Something was terribly hinky here.*

Like Howard, Rand Arthur was holding something back. He was omitting some essential element of information, and he was trying to draw Sam's attention away from noticing it. *What does Rand Arthur really want? What's the goal here?*

And then, as if on cue, the senator answered it for him. "Time," Rand Arthur said definitively. "Time is the single most critical factor we have to face, Sam."

"Why, Senator?"

"Because you can't look at Ed's redefection in a vacuum, Sam. There are huge consequences to what's taking place here in this house tonight. Huge political consequences. Huge national consequences. Huge global consequences."

And that was when Sam understood exactly what Rand Arthur wanted from him—and what he wanted from Ed Howard, too. Rand Arthur wanted what a lot of politicians want: he wanted to be president.

But Rand Arthur possessed something no other politician had. He controlled Edward Howard's information. And to achieve his political objective, he was about to use Howard's allegations to launch a covert action the likes of which had never before been attempted anywhere.

Not an hour earlier, Rand Arthur had admitted he'd sacrificed Sam's scalp in order to play a political chess game merely to improve his position on the Senate Select Committee on Intelligence. Now Sam understood that Rand Arthur wanted very, very much to become president of the United States. How many scalps was he willing to sacrifice to get there?

Because Ed Howard's revelations—especially if they were true but even if they weren't—were political dynamite of a potency heretofore unknown in American politics. There were huge potential pitfalls ahead for the administration. The inevitable war in Iraq could go badly—or worse, turn into a guerrilla war and drag on for years. Al-Qa'ida could reconstitute itself and strike the U.S. Iran's nuclear program could become operational. So could North Korea's. The Middle East could erupt into a new regional war.

It wasn't only the Democrats waiting for George W. Bush to slip up either. A Republican challenger was a long shot now, with the president's polls running 70 percent positive. But late in 2003, with the economy still dragging, unemployment hovering around 6 percent, and the world stage in turmoil, anything might be possible. Rand Arthur was neither the brightest of men nor was he particularly blessed with what the first President Bush had called "the vision thing." But he was charismatic, charming, and, above all, media-wise. He gave great quote—and he gave a lot of it. His presence was ubiquitous both in print and on the Sunday-morning talk shows. And with reason: Rand had spent twelve years in the House and fourteen in the Senate assiduously cultivating Washington's media movers and shakers. And so, if the force of Rand Arthur's political explosion was properly controlled, accurately tamped, and above all, perfectly timed, the kinetic force generated by its energy might just propel Rand into the White House in slightly over two years—or position him nicely for 2008.

CHAPTΣR 9

THINGS WERE MOVING way too fast. And fast was dangerous. It wasn't that intelligence gathering didn't demand initiative, ingenuity, and resourcefulness. Nor did a spy's tradecraft exclude quick, decisive, decision making. And certainly, the case officer's holy trinity of *spot, assess,* and *recruit* required both intuitive and spontaneous behavior. But Sam also understood from experience that risk taking, which was the essence of what recruiting and running agents was all about, wasn't the same as being either impetuous, or reckless.

Rand Arthur was propelling him straight toward both. Indeed, one of the first questions Sam asked himself, as he stood in the kitchen under Rand Arthur's intense gaze, was whether the chairman's behavior simply reflected characteristic, senatorial impatience, or was there a deeper, and potentially more sinister political purpose at play here, with Sam recast as the sacrificial lamb.

Now, a Romanoff profiler might conclude from a quick analysis of this inner turmoil that Sam was one of those cynical conspiratorialists who look at "two plus two" and know in their hearts that "four" is simply a cover-up to keep the hoi polloi from discovering the presence of the second gunman on the grassy knoll. But they'd be wrong. His motivation was pretty straightforward: Sam Waterman had been taught from the very start of his career never to accept anything as it appeared to be. The term "face value" appeared nowhere in his operational lexicon.

Which is why Sam stood in the senator's huge kitchen wobbling precariously on an operational high wire. He understood that Rand Arthur's political ambition was pushing him toward imprudence—and disaster. And Virginia Vacario was doing nothing to rein the senator in. *Hell,* Sam thought, *he's probably promised to make her the first female director of central intelligence.*

He had to make them perform by his book, not theirs. The point was, Edward Lee Howard was a Moscow walk-in—and Moscow walk-ins more often than not were provocateurs. Moreover, Sam's quarter-century-plus of street smarts had given him a certain advantage in spots like this. It wasn't the first time he'd been squeezed by impatient superiors, or agents who wanted him to rush to judgment so they could get paid—or extracted. And *taking control,* as unlikely as it might appear on the surface, wasn't going to be all that difficult.

Sam, after all, understood what made Rand Arthur tick. He was aware of the senator's intentions—even if all his motives were still unclear. And he had a pretty good idea about Rand Arthur's vulnerabilities, too. Like most politicians (and Sam had recruited his fair share), Rand Arthur would be receptive to flattery and praise. He'd be susceptible to the sort of subtle ego stroking that demonstrated just how important, influential, and all-powerful he was. And Rand Arthur's worst fear? It would be public humiliation. The thing all politicians fear most is loss of face, followed by loss of votes.

So, he had to reel Rand Arthur in. Sam cast his fly into the water by placing both his hands on the dark polished granite as if resting them on a lectern. "Senator," he said in his most deferential tone, "you were right and I was wrong. We have to act—and act decisively." He watched as Rand Arthur's face brightened.

The senator said, "I'm gratified, my boy."

Sam worked the fly along the surface by rapping his knuckles on the cool stone. "Okay, then. Let's look at the situation tactically." He inclined his head in Virginia Vacario's direction. "Let's assume he is genuine. The Russians are definitely going to come after Howard. They're going to try to cover their tracks; destroy anything that might hurt them— and that includes the guy down the hall. You're both right. Time *is* of the essence."

Rand Arthur said, "My sentiments precisely."

"So, we must take the initiative. Remember what they taught us before we left for Vietnam, Senator? If you're ambushed, you initiate a counterambush with such ferocity and violence of action that the ambushers are forced to retreat."

"That's right," Rand Arthur said.

Sam continued. "I say we initiate from the get-go, Senator—we take the offensive."

Rand Arthur's satisfied expression told Sam that the fly had been taken. Now it was time to set the hook. Sam paused, then said: "Senator, so far as I'm concerned, there's only one aspect of this situation that might leave you politically vulnerable."

Rand Arthur's sunny expression clouded over. "Politically vulnerable," he repeated.

"Oh, yes," Sam said as neutrally as he could. "But it's only a small thing, and I believe we can deal with it on the run." He looked straight into Rand Arthur's eyes and said, "So, Senator, how do you suggest we proceed?"

"I don't like problems, Sam," Rand Arthur growled. "And I certainly don't like surprises."

"No one does, Senator."

Rand Arthur's tone chilled another ten degrees. "I'm not in the mood for games, Sam. What's the problem?"

"He's a walk-in," Sam said.

"So?"

"Obviously you brought me into this because of my experience. Here's the most basic fact about walk-ins: unless they've brought documents to establish their bona fides, you don't know anything about their motivation."

Rand Arthur looked back at him but said nothing.

"That's why we're taught to treat walk-ins differently. We look very carefully at their motives, and we always demand something concrete that will establish their bona fides."

"Well—" the senator began.

Sam cut him off. "Think about it, Senator. What do you really know about Ed Howard's motives? And more to the point, what did he bring you?"

Rand Arthur stroked his chin. He started to open his mouth, but Sam cut him off again. "Senator, every single American who betrayed our country in recent years was a walk-in. Ames, Walker, Nicholson, Hanssen—all contacted the KGB, not the other way around. And each one of them gave the Russians classified materials to establish their bona fides. Ed Howard followed the same pattern. When Howard defected he took three hundred pages of CIA documents to Lubyanka, including one of our crown jewels: the denied area operations course syllabus. We had to invent a whole new way to work in Moscow because of him."

The senator's expression reflected his impatience. "So?"

"Senator, what did Howard bring when he showed up on *your* doorstep?"

"He told me—"

Now it was Sam's tone that grew cold. "What a walk-in *says* doesn't matter, Senator. I'm no politician," Sam said. "But let's look at this situation as if it was a headline in the *Washington Post*. 'Senator Claims President Knew About 9/11 on Say-So of Defector Who Murdered American Intelligence Assets.'"

Rand Arthur's head bobbed up and down twice. "I see your point," he said, his tone grave. "Well, my boy," he said, ready for the creel, "how do you think we should handle this—given the time limitations, of course."

It was at that point, just as Sam was congratulating himself, that he happened to catch Virginia Vacario in his peripheral vision. Her expression, absolutely kaleidoscopic, refracted awareness, comprehension, bemusement, skepticism, and incredulity, all in the space of about half a second. And then her lawyerly instincts overrode whatever else she might have been thinking and her face turned impassive, unreadable, deadpan.

Sam picked up Rand Arthur's train of thought. "I think I should handle him the way I normally handle walk-ins, Senator."

Rand Arthur looked intently at Sam. "Which is?"

"Interrogate him for hours. Polygraph him. Make him repeat his story over and over to pick up any inconsistencies."

"But—"

"I know we don't have the time to do all that. So we're going to have to cut to the chase. You have to make Howard turn over his documentation, or threaten him with the FBI."

Rand Arthur turned toward his general counsel. "What do you think, Ginny?"

"I think Mr. Waterman is right, Senator."

Rand Arthur pursed his lips. Finally, he said, "Agreed."

He pulled at the cuffs of his jacket and started toward the pantry door.

With the senator leading the way, the trio retraced their path. Rand Arthur punched the combination into the cipher lock and opened the door, stepping aside so that Sam and Virginia Vacario could precede him.

Sam crossed the threshold. There was a draft in the room.

That was because the thick drapes behind the desk were parted. Behind them, the Palladian window was open—and Ed Howard had vanished.

It didn't take Sam more than a few seconds to realize what Howard had done—because he'd left the evidence behind for them to find. The defector had used the senator's sterling-silver letter opener and a large, straightened paper clip to pick the cheap, keyed hardware-store lock on the window. It was par for the course when it came to such matters, Sam thought somewhat ruefully. He'd seen it before, during his overseas tours: penny-wise Soviet ambassadors who installed two-thousand-ruble KGB-approved cipher locks on the doors because Moscow paid for them, and one-ruble, seventy-nine-kopek tin Romanian locks on the windows, because window locks came out of the embassy budget.

That sort of approach to security had made his life a lot easier when he'd been working the streets. But it complicated the hell out of the current situation.

At least, Sam thought, no one panicked—outwardly. The senator called for a quick search of the grounds and the woods, but to no avail. Well, that was to be expected: the cops were city boys who'd sat cold and uncomfortable inside their Crown Vic cocoons. They were dressed in suits and tasseled loafers, but even if they'd been wearing BDUs and boondockers they'd still have no idea how to comb the thirty acres of bramble-and-thorn-covered hillside behind the house, or the two hundred acres of dense woods to the south and east.

Moreover, given the circumstances, there was no way the senator could even put out a proper APB. Why? Because Rand Arthur couldn't tell anyone, including his precious U.S. Capitol police and, more significantly, the FBI or any other state or federal law enforcement agency, precisely for whom he was looking, and why.

Which was when Sam realized how carefully Ed Howard had planned his arrival—and factored in an abrupt departure. The defector had obviously surveilled Rand Arthur's estate, located a caching spot for a car, and identified an escape route—all before he'd made his presence known.

THEY WERE SITTING in the library, Rand Arthur scowling frostily in Sam's direction. The senator hadn't said anything, but Sam understood he was being blamed for Howard's disappearance. It was Sam, after all, who'd caused Howard to be left alone.

Sam stared the senator down until Rand finally shifted his gaze. It wasn't his fault—Howard's move had been part of an elaborate scenario. Of course the senator didn't see things that way. That was to be expected: Rand Arthur was the center of his own universe. Everything was about *him*.

Well, it was time to open his eyes to the real world. "Senator," Sam said, "you told me Howard 'just showed up'—your words, Senator—at your front door two days ago."

"Correct," Rand Arthur said. "He rang the doorbell. I came downstairs and answered it." The senator was nursing a large crystal tumbler of single malt in which floated one lonely ice cube. "I recognized him at once, of course, from surveillance photos I'd seen during closed hearings. Sam, you could have knocked me over with a feather."

Sam had refused whiskey. He wanted his mind uncluttered. "How'd he get here?"

The senator pondered the question for some seconds, and then said, his head wagging, "I don't know—I never even thought about it." He sipped his drink. "And now that you ask, I don't remember seeing a car. Frankly, I was so excited to see him, it never occurred to me to look."

That was when Sam knew precisely how it had *gone down,* as they said on all those TV cop shows he'd been watching on cable lately. Sam knew, because it was exactly what he would have done if he'd been in Ed Howard's shoes. Howard was a professional. Just like Sam, he'd understand exactly what sort of emotional response his appearance would trigger in a politician like Rand Arthur. There would be shock, surprise, astonishment, and disbelief to name a few of the immediate reactions, all accompanied by a tsunami-size adrenaline surge. Which would, in turn, knock out Rand Arthur's ability to act rationally—like, for example, to peer out into the driveway for a car and take down the license plate.

Ed Howard's performance reinforced Sam's belief that the redefection had been part of a carefully scripted CA—covert action—operation. But who had written the script? And what was the ultimate goal? Those were the million-dollar questions. Because the outcome of covert action was never obvious. Like the plot of that old movie, *The Sting,* the goal of a successful covert action was to nick the target without that target—or anyone else—knowing they'd been had. Like the way CIA had supported the Polish trade union Solidarity in the 1970s and 1980s. One of Sam's jobs in Warsaw had been the clandestine dispensing of millions of Solidarity buttons, posters, broadsides, and leaflets through a series of Polish agent networks who were convinced the support was coming from European trade unions. It wasn't: the materials had been printed by CIA to assist Lech Walesa's struggling organization when it was broke and under attack from Poland's Communist government. CIA's CA program kept Solidarity alive—and neither the Communists nor Walesa had ever known.

Right then, all Sam knew for certain was that Rand Arthur had been the target of a covert action. Or had he? Certainly, had the defector's charges been allowed to go forward, the entire government, from the White House on down, would have been thrown into chaos. So, Howard might have been running an op designed by Moscow Center to cause what was left of the United States's counterintelligence apparatus further turmoil. Or, he might have been initiating a sleight-of-hand strategy to deflect attention from an audacious, large-scale Russian destabilization program. It could be anything.

The senator finally looked away from his scotch. "I don't suppose there's any way we can assess his information now, Sam." He peered at Sam, who saw, ever so fleetingly, the wide-eyed, feckless, optimistic features of a six-year-old staring at a shattered toy, hoping daddy can somehow make it all right. Then the image passed; the professional politician's face reappeared. "Are you listening, Sam? There's got to be some way I can still use what he told us."

"Senator, it's over. He's pulled a Yurchenko." Vitali Yurchenko was a KGB security officer who'd defected almost twenty years before, in August 1985. He'd walked into AMEMBASSY Rome, identified himself as a KGB colonel, and demanded to speak to Alan Wolfe, who was Rome's ▮▮▮▮▮ chief at the time. Flown to Washington under tight security, he'd pointed his CIA debriefers at NSA analyst Ronald Pelton, and a fired CIA case officer trainee named Edward Lee Howard who lived in New Mexico but had made two trips to Vienna in the past eight months. Yurchenko claimed that Howard had met with KGB case officers.

The Romanoffs were euphoric. A high-level defection like Yurchenko's would cement their ascendancy—perhaps even cause Bill Casey's downfall. So they kept Yurchenko isolated from Langley's Counterintelligence Division, which was still under the control of Brahmins. And when the Brahmins complained, the Romanoffs leaked the story that CI was trying to wage a turf war so it could augment its already bloated budget.

Undeterred by Ed Howard's September 1985 defection, the Romanoffs flaunted their defector's revelations within the community and leaked hints of what he said to their favorite reporters. In fact, they flaunted "their guy" Yurchenko and the "crown jewels" he'd brought with him all over town, right up to the chilly November night, three and a half months later, when, during a dinner at a Georgetown bistro, Vitali Yurchenko excused himself to go to the men's room, escaped from his Romanoff handlers by slipping out the kitchen door, walked up Wisconsin Avenue and straight through the gates of the Soviet embassy. At a press conference the next day he claimed he'd been kidnapped by CIA.

Rand Arthur's chest deflated. "A Yurchenko," he sighed. "But still, Sam . . ."

It was time to put a stop to this nonsense. "Senator," Sam said, "you've been had."

Rand Arthur bit his lips and set down his drink. "Of course, if you hadn't been here, Howard wouldn't have gotten spooked," the senator said bitterly.

Then he caught the dangerous look in Sam's eyes and instinctively threw up his hands. "No, no—that's wrong. That's wrong—I apologize. I do. Ed Howard demanded to see you. It was his idea. I'm glad I sent for you. Glad, Sam, glad. If I hadn't, and it turned out he was peddling a story . . ." The senator retrieved his glass and took a long, regretful pull on his single malt. "Still . . ." Rand Arthur's voice trailed off. "Just think of the possibilities."

Possibilities were exactly what Sam was thinking about—although they were homicidal in nature. Finally, he calmed himself down and stared at Rand Arthur in the same detached way he used to deal with his developmentals. "Didn't he say he gave you his passport?"

The senator set his drink down. "Yes—it's in my safe."

"May I see it?"

"Certainly, my boy." The senator rose, and crossed the room, to where an arrangement of three small nineteenth-century hunting-dog oils clustered around a large pastoral scene framed in ornate gilt wood. He swung the large painting to his left—the frame was obviously on hinges—revealing beneath it a small green safe door with an electronic lock. He punched the combination, turned the handle, opened the foot-square door, reached inside, and extracted a dog-eared, burgundy-covered booklet, which he handed to Sam.

Sam ran his thumb over the faded gold leaf harp embossed on the cover then opened the document. "Seamus Haitch Maloney of Ballyragget," he pronounced in a cartoonish Irish accent. "Born twenty-five February 1955. The 'haitch,' incidentally, is for Harold." He thumbed through the well-worn pages until he came to a Lufthansa seat stub, Frankfurt–Dulles, dated October 10, for seat 23D, stuffed between two pages near the back of the passport.

Sam blinked. He riffled through the pages again. There was a passport control stamp from Frankfurt/Main, dated 10.10.02. But no INS stamp. Which told Sam Howard hadn't used the Maloney document to enter the country. This was 2002, after all. The nation was at war. And even the hugely inept INS managed to stamp the passports of foreign nationals when they arrived at a major U.S. airport in these days of heightened security.

He peered down at the seat stub without disturbing it. October 10. Seat 23D. Twenty-three. That was today. Sam's birthday—and the date of his final meeting with Pavel Baranov. Seat D. *Long-short-short* in Morse code. That was the call-out sign Pavel Baranov had used to signal Sam. October 10. The same date that was on the document Pavel Baranov showed him in Moscow. It was a message. It had to be. *There are no coincidences.*

Sam closed the passport, then opened it again and flipped through the pages, looking a second time for an INS stamp. There was none. Still, he kept the pages moving so as not to call attention to himself—or the significance of what he'd discovered. Even so, his pulse beat so loud in his ears they had to hear it.

"Can I see?" Virginia Vacario extended her hand over the arm of the wing chair.

"Sure." Sam closed the passport and passed the document over to her.

She retrieved the half-glasses that sat on a delicate gold chain around her neck, placed them on the bridge of her nose, and flipped through the pages. "He's done a lot of traveling in the past few years, has our Mr. Maloney."

His mind spinning, Sam shook his head; tried to focus so he wouldn't be overwhelmed. "Don't be so sure of it."

"Oh?"

"Visas and entry stamps can be forged," Sam said, knowing that one of them wasn't. Knowing that one of them was a key that would sooner or later open a series of doors for him.

"I see." She nodded, blind. She handed the passport back to him without further comment.

He took the Rosetta stone between his fingers and slipped it into the pocket of his jacket. Seat 23D. October 10. *There are no coincidences. There is no happenstance.* Edward Lee Howard was trying to tell him something. *Him*—Sam. Not Rand Arthur. Not Virginia Vacario. That's why Howard insisted Rand Arthur contact him.

All Sam had to do was figure out where Howard was pointing.

The date did bring Sam to one quick deduction: Ed Howard had been around for almost two weeks. That was plenty of time to set up whatever he'd been setting up. Sam had always been good at intelligence pathology—the art of deconstructing the opposition's moves. So, perhaps there *was* a way to salvage this mess—or at least expose a big part of it. He tapped his jacket pocket. "Mind if I keep this for a couple of days?"

Rand Arthur shrugged. "It's not going to do me much good."

Maybe not you, Rand, Sam thought, both his heart and his mind now accelerating at warp speed. *Maybe not you.*

And then he realized what was happening to him, and he let the huge emotional wave pick him up and carry him forward. Oh, God, how good it felt to be inundated by all the old feelings, all those familiar back-in-harness sensations: shallowness of breath, tightening of sphincter, accelerated heartbeat, and palpable adrenaline surge. Oh, yes, he was back. Sorting out the possibilities, working the angles, creating the compartments, operating under Moscow Rules.

Moscow Rules. It had been years since he'd thought about Moscow Rules. *Moscow Rules* meant one of him against hundreds of them. *Moscow Rules* were about never surrendering, never giving up, never ever considering the possibility of failure. *Moscow Rules* was about winning at all costs.

He brought himself under control, hoping he hadn't given himself away. A quick glance told him he was all right.

Good. His next move was simple. He had to distract them—focus them on something—so that he could get out of here and make his own plans. Set up his own three-card monte game. Create his own covert action plan.

"Senator," Sam said, "and Ms. Chief Counsel, too, I need a favor from the both of you." He waited until they'd turned toward him, then continued. "I'd like you to write down everything you and Ed Howard talked about before I arrived—every detail, no matter how unimportant it might seem."

Sam looked at Virginia Vacario. "Put down every single thing you can remember. Everything, no matter how trivial."

The lawyer nodded, her expression grave. "I've been doing that all along, Mr. Waterman."

"Oh?" Sam was dubious and his tone reflected it. "Complete notes?"

"Verbatim, Mr. Waterman. Every single word."

"Can you show me?"

The lawyer riffled through the legal pad. Finally, she stopped, perched her glasses on the tip of her nose, and began to read. "Timestamp, five-eighteen. Waterman: 'You've told me nothing. I asked a question and you blew smoke in my face. Senator, you want my opinion? He's worthless.'

"Howard: 'I risked my life.'

"Waterman: 'Ed, you may be able to fool these people. But this is me. Sam. I know you. I know how you operate. To me, you're cellophane—I see right through you. So, let me translate for the senator and our learned counsel here what you said—and what you were really doing. You claim you came here out of some long-buried sense of civic duty and remorse. "The president knew all about 9/11. There are Russian spies in the American government." That's what you *said,* Ed. But your objective was creating confusion and chaos. You're a double agent, Ed—you work for Moscow Center.

And you might have succeeded, except—thank God—the senator got hold of me instead of calling a press conference and putting you on CNN.' "

Vacario flipped her eyeglasses onto her forehead and looked up at Sam. "Is that about right, or was something missing?"

Sam was impressed. "Where on earth did you learn to do that, counselor?"

"I was a young single mother, Mr. Waterman. I had to work my way through law school. I did so as a legal secretary. Thus, I take shorthand. It's come in handy, especially at the committee."

"I'll bet it has," he said earnestly. He gave the senator an encouraging smile. "Senator," Sam said, noting Rand Arthur's reticent body language, "I really need your support here."

Rand Arthur drained his scotch. "If you really think it's necessary, Sam, I'll be happy to comply." The senator pulled himself to his feet, walked to the big partner's desk, extracted a laptop from one of the big file drawers, switched the closest of the two banker's lamps on, dropped into the chair facing the window where Howard had made his escape, then unlatched and booted the computer.

Sam looked on approvingly. "Thank you. This is going to be a big help, Senator." He watched as Virginia Vacario settled behind her side of the partner's desk, lips pursed in thought, Montblanc poised above the legal pad.

"Now," Sam said, "I need something else."

Rand Arthur looked up. "What is it, my boy?"

"I'd like to borrow a car."

"Oh?"

Sam's tone was decisive. "I have some thinking to do. I want to do it in the city. We can meet early next week and decide how to proceed."

Rand Arthur's eyes widened. "Proceed? But you said this was a dead issue, Sam."

Sam set the hook. "I need time to reassess the situation, Senator."

"And?" The senator raised an eyebrow in Sam's direction.

"There may be a good chance I can salvage things."

CHAPTЭЯ 10

SAM WATERMAN pressed the intercom button outside the locked unmarked door of Rand Arthur's hideaway office in the U.S. Capitol. "It's Sam Waterman."

The senator's abrupt "Come" was followed by dissonant buzzing, The electronic door lock released. Sam turned the ornate brass knob, pushed the thick door inward, and stepped onto luxurious royal blue carpet patterned with ivory fleurs-de-lis. Michael O'Neill followed in his wake. The lawyer leaned on the heavy paneled wood until it snapped shut.

"Make sure the door's secured, Sam." Rand Arthur was sitting behind the desk, his back to the door, looking at a flat, widescreen television screen atop the credenza. It was tuned to one of the all-news channels. A blond woman anchor was talking but the senator drowned her out. "They killed another American today. A diplomat from USAID. In Jordan—Amman," he said, shaking his head. "Where the hell was CIA? According to Nick Becker, we *own* Jordan—lock, stock, and camels. We pay the damn Jordanians millions in foreign aid. And for decades—*decades!*—CIA station chiefs carried suitcases of cash to King Hussein. Like clockwork. And this is what we get? For chrissakes, Sam, it's a travesty what's going on around here."

Then Rand Arthur swiveled around, saw O'Neill, and frowned. "You said you wanted to see me alone, Sam. What's he doing here?"

"In a minute, Senator." Sam waved a single sheet of paper under the senator's nose. "I pulled this off the AP site fifteen minutes ago."

Rand Arthur shrugged. "So?"

"Let me read it to you. It's slugged Urgent. Quote: Dateline, Moscow. Edward Lee Howard, fifty, the only CIA officer ever to defect to the KGB, died at his home outside Moscow this afternoon, according to Russian government sources. Howard is said to have broken his neck in a fall down the steps of his dacha outside the Russian capital, according to a friend who asked not to be identified. A spokesman at the Central Intelligence Agency had no immediate comment about Howard's death but said the Agency was following developments in Moscow with interest. End of quote."

The color drained out of Rand Arthur's face. "My God," he said, slumping in his big leather chair. He fumbled for the TV remote, hit the mute button. "My God." He looked at Sam. "But *why*? Why, Sam?"

Sam shrugged. "I have no idea, Senator."

"But . . . but—" Rand Arthur rubbed a hand across his face. He looked up at the ornate design of the narrow room's high ceiling. "Why?" he asked again.

Michael O'Neill walked to the window, fingered the curtain aside, and peered out. "Spectacular view, Senator," he said. "Inspiring. You can see the entire Mall." O'Neill allowed the curtain to fall back into place. He turned toward Rand Arthur. "A slightly different version of 'why' is precisely what Sam and I have been trying to puzzle out for the past three days. Our line of inquiry centered around the possible location and motives of your former houseguest. The uncertainty surrounding our first focus—if not the second—has now been answered definitively."

Rand Arthur's eyes narrowed. "Whatever happened to the lawyer-client relationship, Michael? You are my personal attorney—as well as a special counsel to SSCI. Your involvement in every aspect of this matter was to be absolutely confidential."

"I understand, sir." O'Neill brushed his unruly forelock out of his eyes. "But in this particular case, our lawyer-client relationship gets trumped by the deputy chief–case officer relationship I have with Sam Waterman. Lawyers and clients—even you and I—don't have the kind of secret handshake Sam and I do."

"*You* were a case officer?" The senator was dumbfounded. "A spy?"

O'Neill nodded. "I was."

"You never told me that. All the time I thought you'd worked at State. And now you're telling me you and Sam have your own secret handshake."

"I take secret handshakes seriously. It's one of those situations where I could show you, Senator, but then I'd have to kill you."

O'Neill paused just long enough to realize his attempt at humor wasn't being well received. "Senator," he continued, "Sam came to me straight from your house. He was furious."

Rand Arthur shot Sam an angry glance. "Furious?"

Sam's peripheral vision caught pictures of a car on the TV screen. There were bullet holes in the door and bloodstains on the upholstery. For an instant he was back on the road from Zagorsk. Then he forced the memory aside and focused on Rand Arthur. "You blindsided me, Senator. It was unnecessary. No—worse: it was a recipe for disaster." He jerked his thumb in O'Neill's direction. "He should have known better. I should have been told what I was getting into."

"That was impossible. I swore Michael to secrecy—that's why he lied to you—and I'd made an agreement with you-know-who."

"A lot of good that agreement did you."

"I'm not in the mood to be lectured, Sam."

Sam slapped the AP story on the senator's desk. "We're in a nonsecure room, Senator, so I won't be specific—and I'd suggest that you follow my lead. But let's just say that had I been given some advance notice, I might have been able to wring something useful out of your . . . houseguest."

Rand Arthur started to say something but Sam cut him off. "I was coming in to see you today to lay out a plan that would perhaps allow us to pick up some of the pieces. But that's moot now. According to AP, Edward Lee Howard is dead. Maybe he died from a fall down the stairs, just like it says in the news story. But maybe he was pushed. Anything's possible. Your houseguest said just as much at one point in the conversation." He looked at Rand Arthur. "Remember, Senator?"

The senator's head bobbed up and down. "I do," he said. "He said the . . . opposition would know what he'd taken, and they'd come after him." He scratched the side of his nose. "Maybe that's what happened."

"It's a distinct possibility."

Rand Arthur tapped the single page on his desktop. "You mean *his* death could be confirmation of the things my houseguest told us."

"Yes. Or, it could be accidental—just as written." Sam

paused. "It could also be a provocation. I want to take Michael to Moscow and see what we can find out."

The senator's eyes widened. "Michael? Moscow?"

"Your houseguest provided a few clues I may be able to follow up," Sam said.

"Oh?"

"Nothing certain, but I think it's worth a try."

Rand Arthur nodded. "Hmm."

"But it's not a one-man job," Sam continued. "I'd feel a lot more secure if Michael came along. And we'll need cover."

"Cover?"

"Given my background, there's no way I can go to Moscow as a tourist," Sam said. "But if you, as a senior member of Senate Select, were doing—as you are—some digging into the events surrounding 9/11, and Michael and I had credentials as your investigators, then we'd have cover for status."

"What's cover for status?"

"It's a Langley term meaning we'd have a legitimate reason for being in Moscow."

Rand Arthur's eyes widened. He pushed back in his chair and focused on the ceiling. "I don't like the idea. I don't want to make this matter into committee business."

"It wouldn't be. We'd be working for you."

"It becomes committee business if I get credentials for you. Once you represent me, you represent SSCI, and you fall under Senate rules."

Sam said, "So what?"

Rand Arthur's fingertips came together, forming a steeple. "If something were to go wrong," he said, "it would reflect badly on me."

"We will be models of discretion," Sam said. "I'm not talking about breaking into Lubyanka, Senator. I just want to do some nosing around."

"Some very quiet nosing around," Michael O'Neill said.

Rand Arthur said, "Hmm." And then, after a quarter minute of contemplation, he flung himself forward, reached for the telephone, and punched five keys. "Ginny? It's me. Meet me in the bubble in ten minutes."

SAM KNEW she was opposed to the whole idea, even though she hadn't said a word. He could tell it from her body language: arms crossed tightly across her bosom, legs locked together at the ankles, lips pursed, listening as Sam laid out his case. Her legal pad and the big Montblanc sat unused on the bubble room's bare wood table—another bad sign.

When Sam stopped talking she said nothing for fully half a minute. And then she looked at Rand Arthur, and said, "Senator, I agree with Mr. Waterman. This operation should come under the sponsorship of Senate Select. A formal SSCI visit—a STAFFDEL. Official passports, country clearance—the whole nine yards."

Sam started to say something but she cut him off. "With one proviso."

"And that is?"

"I will lead," she said matter-of-factly.

Sam didn't like that idea at all, and told her so.

"You misunderstand me, Mr. Waterman," she said.

"I don't think so." Sam knew exactly where she was coming from. She was another in a long line of ambitious bureaucrats engaged in a never-ending campaign of influence building. She was probably related to the Romanoffs. Hell, she probably wanted to become czarina. The first woman DCI.

"You think I'm trying to horn in on your operation because it will benefit me in some way."

That was pretty close to the truth. Sam said nothing.

"Just the opposite, Mr. Waterman."

"Oh?"

"If you and Mr. O'Neill went to Moscow by yourselves, even with SSCI credentials, the FSB would be all over you from the moment you arrived."

Sam had to admit what she said was true. Moscow Center had thick files on him. And they'd probably spotted O'Neill in Paris. He'd had deep embassy cover, but he'd also worked the émigré community. The SVR kept tabs on all American diplomats who met with émigrés. Sam had to admit that traveling incognito was impossible.

Vacario tapped her legal pad with the end of the big pen. "But if we make it clear from the get-go that you are working for me, we may be able to find a way for you to disappear long enough to actually get something done."

Sam hated to admit it, but she was making sense.

Vacario saw the change in his expression and pressed on. "We'll have to dazzle them with footwork, Mr. Waterman. Mr. O'Neill and I can distract them with 9/11—demand endless briefings about the Chechen connection to al-Qa'ida, ask to visit the theater where Chechen terrorists took hostages—while you take a cleaning route, slip surveillance, and do the cloak-and-dagger stuff."

She paused. Sam looked at Vacario, impressed with her knowledge of tradecraft terms.

The lawyer's fingers brushed her legal pad. "I have been reliably told, Mr. Waterman, that you were remarkably good at making yourself disappear."

"Not according to the senator's houseguest."

"As you said the other evening, Mr. Waterman, there is a good chance that the senator's houseguest was a fabricator."

"You didn't seem to think so at the time."

"Distance gives perspective, Mr. Waterman." She tapped the table with a fingernail. "So, do you accept my proviso?"

Sam had never been one to turn a good suggestion down, and this was a good suggestion. "I like it," he said simply.

She smiled at him warmly. "Good."

Sam grinned back at her. She wasn't so formidable when she smiled. And she had green eyes. "What's your estimate for wheels-up?"

Vacario ran a hand through short-cut red hair. "Next week sometime. You and Mr. O'Neill will need official passports. That's two days, if I can wring the paperwork out of State. Russian visas—another twenty-four hours minimum. Country clearance, appointments in Moscow, hotel reservations—three, four days, maybe more. Of course, that's if everything falls into place." She looked at Rand Arthur. "Senator, you're going to have to call Nick Becker and notify him."

Sam broke in. "I don't think that's advisable."

"Protocol," Rand Arthur said. "Has to be done, my boy." He paused. "I won't be telling him our real intentions, of course."

"There's something else," Sam said.

Vacario looked up from her notepad.

"We need to elicit some information. I want to know where Ed Howard lived. Address, phone number, that kind of stuff. I may need directions to his dacha." He paused and saw the quizzical look on Vacario's face. "Sometimes dachas don't have regular street addresses—you know—'it's the second cabin past the clump of pine trees two kilometers outside Popelkovo.'" He paused. "And Ed Howard's file. I'd like to see the latest material Langley's got."

Virginia Vacario said, "A lot of red flags will go up if I start pressing those buttons, Mr. Waterman."

"*Sam,* Ms. Vacario," Sam said. "Please—just Sam. It's an old Agency tradition to be on a first-name basis when you go operational."

She offered her hand. "Sam it is, then. And I'm Ginny."

Sam took her hand. And held it.

Michael O'Neill watched the two of them as their eyes locked. "Perhaps you two should post the bans," he said, laughing as Vacario reacted. "Still, if you're Ginny and you're Sam, that officially makes me Michael." He struck a heroic pose. "So here we are. MIG-1."

Vacario raised an eyebrow. "MIG? Like the plane?"

"Moscow Insertion Group." O'Neill tapped his vest with a thumb. "I'm See No Evilovich." He pointed at Vacario. "You're Speak No Evilovska." He tapped Sam on the shoulder. "And he's Hear No Evilovich."

"What about me?" Rand Arthur said.

"You, Senator? You're just Evil."

There was another awkward pause. O'Neill cleared his throat. "About the Howard stuff . . ."

Sam said, "Yes?"

"Let me handle Langley, Sam. I've still got a few friends in low places out there."

Sam said, "I never thought of you as a penetration agent, Michael."

"Obviously, Sam, you never kept track of me when I was single."

PART III

MOSCOW

СНАРТЭЯ 11

NOVEMBER 6, 2002

SAM SQUINTED through the windshield of the embassy sedan. It had started to snow as they'd pulled onto the M10 shortly after passing Sheremetevo's perimeter fence. Not quite a blizzard, but enough to make the drab city picture-postcard attractive. Out of habit, he glanced left as the Volvo flew down the divided highway that was still called Leningradski Prospekt, just able to make out the hulking outline of Sportkompleks Dinamo through the blowing snow. During his Moscow tour, Sam had become a fervent Dinamo fan and had gone to many of the soccer team's home games.

Of course he had. He genuinely enjoyed watching the team play. But he had a professional interest in soccer as well. During the Soviet era, Dinamo had been sponsored by the KGB, and its stadium still contained the offices of several former high-ranking KGB officials. Moreover, the huge stadium had dozens of entrances and exits, multiple ramps, tiers of staircases, and long tunnels. There were two nearby metro stations and numerous bus stops close by, as well. The

Sportkompleks made it possible for him to slip away during the tumult of a game in case he had a meeting to which he didn't want to be followed.

Sam snuck a quick look at the driver's stoic profile, wondering if he was FSB. It was madness, he'd always thought, to hire foreign nationals[17] as embassy drivers and maintenance workers. After a while, you simply forgot they weren't cleared, and you spoke openly in front of them.

Quickly, the snow-covered parkland surrounding the soccer stadium gave way to a residential neighborhood of towering apartment blocks. Some had been built in the 1930s by Stalin as rewards for the Communist Party's top cadre. In a matter of minutes they'd be coming to the Garden Ring— roughly two kilometers from the Kremlin—and a block or so farther on, their hotel. Thankfully, there was nothing on the schedule for tonight. There'd be a meeting at ten tomorrow morning at the embassy, followed by a session at the Russian Foreign Ministry, followed by a lunch with the deputy ▓▓▓▓chief—the COS was on home leave through the end of the year.

Sam had been riding in silence since they'd left the airport. It wasn't a matter of security so much as that he was caught up in a maelstrom of conflicting emotions and memories. Now, as they neared their destination, he felt compelled to say something. So he swung around and caught Michael O'Neill and Ginny Vacario peering openmouthed at the sights.

"Impressed?"

Vacario's eyes were wide. "The buildings are so huge. The scale is quite incredible."

---

[17] Foreign Service Nationals (FSNs in State Department terminology), often outnumber U.S. citizens at American embassies two to one. Some FSNs invariably report to the local intelligence service.

"Stalin believed the bigger the building, the grander the political movement."

"Really?"

"So the story goes. Still, it takes getting used to. It seemed a lot bigger before there were so many cars."

"That's hard to imagine."

O'Neill asked, "How far are we staying from the Kremlin?"

"About a mile and a half."

"I hope we have time to see Red Square."

"We'll make time," Sam said. "And visit the Arbat so you can buy *matryoshkas* and icons."

"I'd settle for one of those big Russkie hats—the fur ones," O'Neill said. "God, it's cold."

Sam laughed. "It's only late autumn, Michael. Just getting chilly."

O'Neill extracted a handkerchief from his trouser pocket and blew his nose. "'Scuse me." He wedged the big white square back into his pocket. I don't think I'd like to spend the winter here."

Sam grunted in response. He rubbed at his face, which was bristly. He wanted a shower and a shave and a couple of shots of good vodka in the bar just off the Marriott's big atrium.

They'd been traveling for almost twenty-four hours now, and he was getting tired. Because they were flying on government tickets and at least one leg had to be on an American carrier, they'd flown a joint Delta/Air France flight to Paris. They'd arrived in the middle of a cold downpour, climbed aboard a crowded tram, and chugged from Terminal F through the rain to Terminal B. There, while O'Neill and Sam snagged a quick breakfast of *petits pains* and cafés au lait at the cleaner of two crowded, greasy-spoon coffee bars, Virginia Vacario tested her new GSM cell phone by checking in with her deputy back in Washington. It was way past midnight in the nation's capital, but she guessed he'd be up watching election returns—and if he wasn't, he should have been.

She returned to the table elated. The Republicans were going to take back the Senate. The current ranking member of SSCI was going to become chairman of the Senate Foreign Relations Committee, which meant Rand Arthur was moving up two notches. When the session started, he'd become SSCI's new chairman. His ascension meant Vacario would become the committee's chief counsel as soon as the new Congress convened.

To celebrate, Vacario and O'Neill hit the duty free. He bought a box of Cuban Punch double coronas and a liter of twenty-one-year-old Irish whiskey. She snagged a half ounce of Chanel No. 5 and an Hermès scarf. Sam didn't feel much like a party animal. The thought of Rand Arthur in charge of SSCI made him uneasy. Still, he bought a bottle of Jack Daniel's and two cartons of Marlboros out of habit. He'd put them to use in Moscow.

They'd hustled through security and then, when they'd arrived at the departure lounge—and were unable to go back through security into the terminal proper—they'd discovered the Air France flight to Moscow would be delayed two and a half hours.

So, instead of arriving in Moscow just after 3 P.M., they'd touched down at five-thirty. The tarmac was clustered with knots of security troops, dressed in bulletproof vests and carrying automatic weapons. Armored personnel carriers sat adjacent to the terminals. The customs and baggage areas were heavily patrolled. Bomb-sniffing dogs checked every incoming suitcase.

The embassy driver, whose name, appropriately enough, was Boris, had been waiting impatiently just outside the customs area. They knew he was from the embassy because he was holding a foot-square sheet of cardboard on which had been written US CONGRES DEL. "Nothing like great OPSEC," O'Neill commented drily.

BORIS SWUNG LEFT down a side street, then veered right, accelerated past a squat yellow taxicab, slid to the curb adjacent to the Marriott's marquee entrance, and popped the trunk lid. He jumped out and opened the rear door for Vacario with a flourish. "*Pazhalsta,* Mrs." he said, beckoning.

Vacario slid out into the cold night and peered through the snow at the brilliantly lit facade, atop which sat a huge sign that despite being in Cyrillic, obviously said MARRIOTT in four-foot-high, red neon letters. O'Neill followed, shivering and sneezing. Boris unpacked their suitcases and set them on the sidewalk, where they were picked up by a pair of uni-formed bellmen.

The driver turned to Sam, his hand brazenly outstretched. Until now, Sam hadn't used his Russian. Now he turned on the FSN. "*Shto?* What? You're looking for something extra? The embassy doesn't pay you enough already?" He knew how much embassy drivers made, which was more than Russian generals. Embassy drivers even got paid in dollars. It was just another scam. Boris was greedy.

Boris shrugged. "I waited so long," he said. "The plane was late."

Sam was having none of it. "Then put in for overtime." He raised his hand in a dismissive gesture. "*Atyebis',* Boris. get lost." Then he turned and followed the others into the hotel.

The embassy had booked rooms for them on the eighth floor. The bellman led them through the huge atrium to one of the elevators, then showed them how to insert their room key cards into a reader next to the floor-selector buttons. Sam machine-gunned some Russian at the young man, who smiled and launched into a fifteen-second monologue.

Vacario gave Sam a quizzical look.

"He was explaining the security procedures," Sam explained. "You can't ride these elevators unless you have a room key card. There are readers, which compare your key card with your room number. You can't use the elevator to go to any floor except the one your room's on. He says they put them in after 9/11."

At eight, the bellman pushed the luggage gurney into the hallway and turned left. The three Americans followed. They were lodged in adjoining rooms. Sam watched from the corridor as his bag went onto the bed, then tipped the bellman as he came out. "I'm going to grab a quick shower. What say we meet for a drink in an hour and then go out and have some dinner?"

"I'll take a pass on drinks and dinner if you don't mind, Sam." O'Neill sneezed messily. "I think I caught a bug in Paris, or on the damn flight. I'm gonna take a pill and try to sleep it off."

"Counselor?"

"Count me in." She turned and followed the bellman down the brightly lit hallway.

"An hour, then—in the bar," he called after her. "It's in the lobby—opposite where we registered."

SAM WAS WAITING at a table in the rear, his back to the back wall, as she came through the door, her fur coat folded across her arm. She'd changed into a knit skirt over which she'd layered a thick, patterned turtleneck sweater. And she wore calf-high boots. He rose and held a chair for her. "Ginny."

"Thanks." She seemed to hesitate just slightly before sitting down, then smiled brightly as she scrunched her chair closer to the table. "How's Michael?"

"I knocked on his door just before I came down. He sounds dreadful."

"I hope he'll be better in the morning. We have a hellish day. I had a message from the embassy moving our first appointment back to nine." She let Sam order—which he did in Russian. She shifted slightly in her seat, craning her neck to look around the bar.

"Nice hotel. We could be in New York or Chicago."

"The hotel is new. It was finished just before I left."

She gestured around the room. "Who comes here?"

"To this bar? Guests—businessmen mostly, and of course tourists. Plus locals: the new Russian entrepreneurs who do *beeziness*. And, you know . . . others."

"Others?"

He grinned. "*Mafiya*. Hookers. Take a quick peek to your left—about ten o'clock . . ." Sam waited as she twisted around, then turned back to face him. "Those two bald guys with the bottle of Dom Pérignon are *Vory*—*mafiyosi*."

"How do you know?"

"Look at the three tables surrounding them."

She did. "You mean the seven bodyguards drinking Chivas by the bottle who look like they're all named Cheech?"

He smiled. "Exactly. They call them *byki* here. It means bulls." He paused as a waiter in a Cossack-style tunic placed a hundred gram tin of caviar set into shaved ice, a platter holding a stack of warm blini, and a pile of buttered black bread in front of them. Next, he set a half-liter bottle of vodka, which had been frozen into the center of a milk-carton-size block of ice then wrapped in a starched napkin, in the center of the table.

The waiter unwrapped the napkin so Sam could see the label through the crystal-clear ice. When Sam nodded, he unscrewed the cap and poured the syrupy liquid into two delicate crystal shot glasses.

Sam said, *"Spaciba."*

"Pazhalsta." The waiter withdrew with a flourish.

"The traditional welcome to Moscow, Virginia Vacario: caviar, vodka, *vory,* and *byki.*" Sam lifted his glass and inclined it toward Vacario. *"Za vashe zdarov'e,* Ginny."

She returned the toast, touching the rim of his glass with her own. "Your health, too, Sam."

Sam took the vodka down in one gulp. He caught the waiter's smile as the man watched Vacario sip tentatively from across the room. *"Dadna,* Ginny. Drink it to the bottom, or you'll embarrass me."

"I wouldn't want to do that." She drank it all down and slapped her glass onto the tablecloth. *"Da svidanya!"*

"Good-bye?" Sam was confused. "You're leaving already?"

Vacario laughed. "It's the only expression I remember from the guidebook I read on the plane." She leaned forward, scooped beluga from its tin, spread it on a pair of blini, and placed them on the small plate in front of Sam. "They don't serve chopped eggs or onions here the way they do in the States."

"The good caviar is so fresh you don't need anything except a squeeze of lemon—if that." Sam waited until she'd served herself, then ate with relish. He hadn't had any caviar since returning from Moscow, and this stuff was just as good as he remembered it could be. He wiped his mouth with the starched napkin and poured them another round of vodka.

They finished the second round, and Sam was just pouring a third when he felt the ping. The signal was so strong in Sam's head as to be almost audible. He stopped short, the bottle held immobile in midair.

Vacario sensed his unease. "What's wrong?"

"Nothing." He tilted the bottle, filled her glass to the rim, set the bottle down, and then lifted his glass. "To absent friends." He drank, his eyes panning slowly across the room, unable to identify who might be watching.

"Something's wrong." Ginny said. "Sam—"

He smiled at her, then opened his mouth wide and laughed. He put his glass down and took both of her hands in his. He inclined his head toward her, still smiling. "Let it alone, Ginny," he said, his voice low and serious.

She blinked. But she didn't pull away. And then she realized what he was saying. She stroked the back of his hand tenderly, looked into his eyes soulfully, leaned across the table, smiled, and mouthed, "We're being surveilled, aren't we?"

He squeezed her hand and winked. "This is an official visit."

She let go of him, sat back, spooned beluga onto a blini, leaned across the table, and fed it to him. "This bar is so Western I almost forgot."

"You can't forget," he said, wiping at his mouth. "Ever. And believe me when I tell you old habits die hard."

She nodded. "Understood." She spread the last of the caviar on a piece of buttered black bread, took a delicate bite, chased it with vodka, and sat back in her seat. A satisfied, alcohol-amplified smile spread across her face. "I could get used to this—if I didn't have to work ever again."

"But work we must." Sam finished his vodka and signaled the waiter to bring the check. "So, what would you like for dinner? Shashlik? Herring? Borscht?"

She watched as he pulled four twenty-dollar bills out of his wallet, folded them around the check, and handed everything to the waiter. "To be honest, Sam, after all this rich food, I'd like something plain. A steak and a salad would be fine with me. We could probably eat here in the hotel."

"Nah." He stroked his chin. "I know a place. It's about a ten-minute walk. If you're up for it, that is."

"Lead on, Macduffski." She folded the big napkin, stowed it on the table, and raised the fur coat high enough off her lap for him to see it. "I came prepared."

"Well, I didn't," he said. "Let me run upstairs and grab my coat."

CHAPTЭR 12

THEY LEFT THE HOTEL and turned northwest along Tverskaya Street, their chins buried in upraised collars against the wind. It had stopped snowing, but the wind was fierce, and there were still flakes blowing. Ginny tucked her arm through Sam's and stayed close, the cold far more bitter and penetrating than she'd expected. Even in her fur she was chilled clear through by the time they'd walked a hundred yards past shuttered stores that made her think of Howard Avenue's Gold Coast. Off to her left she saw the lights of what was obviously a metro station. Just beyond it, a huge ornate arch was bathed in floodlights. "What's that?"

"On the bottom, Mayakovskaya metro stop," Sam said, pointing. "Built in the late thirties by Stalin. Named in honor of the great poet Mayakovsky."

"I never heard of him. Was he a contemporary of Pushkin? Chekhov?"

"He was a commie," Sam said. "He once wrote a poem celebrating the Soviet passport. 'Read it and envy me! I am a citizen of the Soviet Union!' "

"My kind of guy."

"Stalin's, too. Actually, the metro station is remarkable. The main platform is about the size of Union Station back in Washington. There are probably fifty or sixty arches. The ceiling is made up of a series of domes, with Art Deco lighting. Uncle Joe used the station to hold meetings during the war because it was so deep he felt safe from German artillery."

"God, it is really cold." She hugged his arm tighter. "What's the ornate pillared palace right above the metro stop?"

"It's a concert hall."

Vacario pointed at her one o'clock. "And over there?"

"That's the Triumfalnaya Arch. Can you make out the statue of the charioteer on top?"

She squinted, putting a hand to her eyes to shield them from the wind. "Of course—it's huge."

"The joke used to be that he was the only sober coachman in Moscow."

"More humor from Stalin's time, right? And the big street we're coming to right now?"

"Garden Ring. We saw it from the other direction as we were driving to the hotel." He gestured to his right. "We cross here." He ushered her quickly across the busy, wide street, sprinting the last ten yards as one of the fast-moving vehicles almost ran them down. He stopped and turned to look.

Vacario tugged at his arm. "What's up?"

"That was an ARV."

"Arv?"

"Armed response vehicle. Ministry of Interior special-tactics police—counterterrorist units. They're known as OMON."

"What are they doing?"

"They're floaters—on call in case of an emergency. I guess they've increased the number of ARVs since the theater takeover."

Sam turned and trotted Vacario across a small narrow strip of parkland. They dashed across another wide avenue, a wide plaza with its massive arch to their left. Sam turned east, then left into a narrow one-lane street that shielded them from the gusting wind. He guided her a hundred yards, turned right again, walked another fifty yards, and turned left.

Vacario said, "My God. Sam, gridlock." More than two dozen snow-covered cars were jam-packed on the sidewalk and wedged atop the high curb of the narrow street, blocking the sidewalk and apartment-house doorways.

Sam laughed. "Valet parking Moscow-style." He gave the parked vehicles a quick once-over. The vehicles all appeared to have been there awhile. Sam saw no sign of recent windshield-wiper action or window defrosters, except for one steamy-windowed sedan that sat up close to the restaurant's entrance. Sam was careful to take a peek as they sidled past. Two men, smoking cigarettes. Probably bodyguards. Besides, the car had been there for a while. It was wedged in by half a dozen others with snow on them.

At least whoever was pinging on him wasn't leapfrogging. Sam pointed at the neon sign in red, white, and blue blinking in the plate-glass window of the obviously bustling restaurant. "You wanted a steak and a salad. This is the American Bar and Grill. Best steak in town. They even have Budweiser on draft."

"I'd rather have a California Zinfandel. A bottle of Ridge would be nice right now."

"You don't ask for much, do you? What about a nice Georgian *Mukuzani*?"

"What if I told you Zinfandel or nothing, Sam. In case you haven't noticed, I'm used to the very best: beluga caviar and Golden Ring vodka."

"Oh, I noticed." He grinned. "Caviar by the pound. And vodka by the bottle."

She let go his arm and pushed through the door. "And Chanel No. 5—by the gallon."

IT WAS PAST TEN when they emerged. The wind had died down, but snow had begun to fall again and the streets were white. Footfalls muffled, they returned the way they'd come, walking quickly and in silence. Sam hadn't sensed a ping since the hotel bar.

Sam let her precede him into the hotel lobby. He crossed the atrium to the desk and checked for messages. There were none.

They met at the elevator. He inserted his key card into the reader, waited for the green light, and pressed the eighth-floor button.

They rode in silence. At eight, Vacario stepped off and turned left. Sam followed her down the hall, past his own room. There was a room-service tray on the carpet next to O'Neill's door. He'd ordered soup, tea, and toast—and hadn't consumed much of anything from the look of it.

Vacario stopped in front of her doorway. She turned. "Sam, thank you."

He shrugged. "It wasn't much—drinks and dinner. The weather wasn't being very accommodating, so I couldn't take you to the Kremlin and Red Square."

"Is that your usual itinerary?"

"Everybody wants to see Red Square the first night."

"And you always play tour guide."

"That was a big part of the job when I worked at the embassy."

She turned, reached up, pulled him to her, and kissed him softly on the cheek. "Well, even without the tour, thanks for a lovely evening."

"You're welcome."

She didn't step back. "I had a wonderful time." She kissed him again. This time on the lips.

Then she took a step back, inserted the key card into the reader, and opened the door. "Nightcap?"

Sam started to say no. But he didn't. Even though he knew better.

He knew he should have said no because he was hugely attracted to her. He should have said no because there was palpable chemistry between them, something they'd both tacitly acknowledged over dinner. He should have said no because there were such obvious and potentially nasty complications to any involvement.

Sam realized he'd been hooked shortly after he'd started a professional elicitation of her background and found himself both charmed and impressed with what she told him. She was from Detroit. She'd married at nineteen and divorced at twenty-two with a two-year-old daughter, born the very day Richard Nixon had resigned the presidency. She'd put herself through law school and after passing the bar had gone to work as a prosecutor in the office of the U.S. attorney for eastern Michigan. Two years later, when her boss had been selected as a deputy assistant attorney general and moved to Washington, he'd brought her with him as a special assistant.

She'd obviously thrived. Her boss's purview included intelligence, violent crime, and public integrity. At the age of twenty-nine, Vacario was promoted to chief of the Terrorism and Violent Crime Section of the Justice Department. Thirteen years later, she'd been sought out by Rand Arthur, then a freshman senator, to become his legislative assistant for justice and intelligence matters. She'd been ready for a change, she told Sam, and so she'd accepted the offer once Rand had promised to match her Justice Department pay. She'd worked for Rand ever since—shifting to Senate Select when he'd been appointed to SSCI in his second term.

She'd spent enough time dealing with Nick Becker to dislike him, although she was smart enough not to disparage the DCI in a busy Moscow restaurant. She was also smart enough not to ask Sam to tell his own story in public. Not that he would have. Sam seldom talked about himself.

But Ginny had been absolutely voluble. She was bright, politically astute, charming, attractive, and sensual. Sam spent much of their dinner asking himself why he hadn't seen those qualities sooner.

Which was why, instead of protesting, or heading for his own room in a levelheaded tactical retreat, Sam stood in the hotel corridor experiencing simultaneous pangs of anxiety and arousal.

Vacario took him by the hand and led him inside. "I know," she said as she closed the door behind him.

"What do you know?"

"There are complications."

"Uh-huh." Sam watched as she shed her fur on the bed. He draped his overcoat across the plaid-upholstered sofa. Instinctively, he glanced around the room for any sign of surveillance equipment. Of course, there'd be nothing. Although the facade of the Marriott looked vaguely nineteenth century, the hotel had been built shortly after the collapse of the Soviet Union. Which meant that FSB had been able to conceal whatever sorts of electronic bugs they'd wanted to during the construction phase. There were going to be no KGB-style two-way mirrors or walnut-size microphones in the lampshades of this room.

He walked to the television, picked up the remote, and turned the set on. It was pretuned to CNN International. He adjusted the volume until the sound was loud enough to mask normal conversation, and then beckoned Vacario over to the TV set.

Sam put his hands up to her face, took it between his fingers, gently brought her close, and kissed her. She responded. He held her close and kissed her once more. He said, "This is madness, you know," and then he kissed her again, with more intensity.

She bit his lower lip gently. "Oh, I know, I know." She broke away from him, but didn't let go of his jacket sleeve. "This isn't like me at all, y'know."

"What isn't?"

"This—us. I'm not an impulsive person, Sam. I don't do this. I'm very disciplined."

"Me, too." He stared at her, sensing her fragility. She was as translucent as Limoges. "Except, I'm very attracted to you."

"Oh, damn."

"Why damn?"

"Because I feel the same way. And here we are, in a hotel room. Worse, in Moscow of all places. And everything's been telescoped and compressed, and I'm feeling all sorts of things I shouldn't be feeling, especially here, and especially now."

"Like?"

"Panic. Terror. Temptation."

"Welcome to the club." He shook his head. "You know, we were trained to resist this sort of thing."

"And did you?"

"Until now." He took her back into his arms and kissed her passionately. They stood, their bodies pressed against each other. Sam nuzzled her neck. God, she smelled good. His hands moved up and down her back, slipped under the bulky sweater. Rubbed her skin. He kissed her again, his tongue touching her teeth. He bit her lower lip and she moaned softly.

Now he put both hands under her sweater and massaged her back, and her rib cage. She moved against his body. He brought his right hand around in front, his thumb moving under her breasts.

She responded by slipping her hands under his jacket and rubbing his back, her fingers probing and pulling him closer.

He brought his hand out from under her sweater and held her head, running his fingers through her hair. "Ginny . . ."

They were moving in syncopation now, like dancers, closer and closer to the king-size bed. Finally, they toppled onto it, landing atop the spread without letting go of each other.

He rolled on top of her, his hands moving on her body. She wrapped her legs around him; held him tight against her. "Oh, Sam, Sam, it's been a long time since I felt like this."

Their clothes came off quickly after that, scattered recklessly onto the floor. Their lovemaking was quick and passionate.

Afterward, they lay entwined atop the covers. Sam rolled over just enough to grab an edge of the spread and cover her with it. "You must be chilled clear through."

"No. I'm quite warm." Vacario ran a hand through his hair, then stroked his shoulder, her fingernail tracing the faint crescent-shaped scar that ran down his arm. "What's this?"

"From Vietnam. Shrapnel."

She raised her head and kissed his shoulder. "Does it ever twinge?"

"It used to."

Idly, he stroked the curve of her back, running his hand along her bottom. "My God, you have a lovely body."

"It's all that caviar and champagne."

He nuzzled her neck. Her skin smelled of roses and cloves. "Not to mention the gallons of Chanel No. 5."

She laughed out loud, rolled over on top of him, and kissed his nose. "I like you, Sam Waterman."

He hugged her close. "I like you, too, Ginny Vacario."

They kissed again passionately. He cupped a breast in his hand, bent over, and kissed the nipple. She put her hand between his legs and rubbed softly, gratified to sense his arousal. He rolled atop her and they made love again, this time more slowly and deliberately but no less passionately.

When they were lying side by side, his left hand clasping her right hand, his right hand tracing her body, she looked at him earnestly. "So."

He rolled onto his side but didn't let go of her hand. "So?"

"So how do we deal with this, Sam?"

He grinned. "First, we ask FSB for the videotapes."

She smacked his hip. "Be serious."

"First, we ask FSB—."

"Sam . . ."

"I think," he said, choosing his words carefully, "that we have to be very . . . circumspect in public for the foreseeable future."

"No posting the something-or-others. What was it O'Neill said back in Washington?"

Sam thought about it. "Posting the bans. No—definitely no posting the bans." He caught her flash of concern. "Well, not yet anyway."

She rolled onto her back and took his chin in her hand, her index finger on his cheek. "But in private, Sam?"

He licked between her breasts, then kissed them. "In private, we can let FSB have their cheap thrills."

IT WAS SHORTLY past midnight when Sam slipped the key card into the slot and pushed the thick door open. He tossed his overcoat onto the back of the closest chair and pulled off the clothes he'd only minutes before climbed into, noting with a satisfied smile that his Jockey shorts and his socks were both inside out.

He hung his suit in the closet, balled the rest of his clothes up, and dropped them into a plastic bag. They'd go to the valet in the morning. He was on his way to brush his teeth when he noticed an envelope sitting on his pillow, where the mint should have been. His name was written in block letters.

Carefully, Sam took the envelope by its edges, went to the desk, turned on the lamp, and held it up to the bulb so he could make out what was inside. There was a single sheet of paper—nothing more.

He laid the envelope on the glass top of the blond wood desk, went to his shaving kit, and dug through it until he fished out a small Swiss Army knife and a pair of latex gloves. He pulled the gloves on. Then he used the sharp blade to slit the envelope. Carefully, he slid a single page of white copy paper out of the envelope and unfolded it.

He held the sheet up to the desk lamp. The watermark told him the stock was American manufactured. Centered just below the top of the page was an image of Edward Lee Howard's Lufthansa boarding-pass stub from Frankfurt to Washington on October 10. The same stub for seat 23D Howard had left for Sam to discover in the Irish passport. In the middle of the page was the letter *G*, and the number 0800.

Sam refolded the sheet and put it back in the envelope. He'd have both checked for prints when he got back to the States. But he was reasonably certain he'd find neither prints nor DNA. Then he went to his document case and checked to see whether the surreptitious entry seals he'd placed on his luggage and clothes had been disturbed. They hadn't. Sam removed them, unlocked the big leather satchel, unpacked the maps he'd brought, unfolded them, and spread them out on the bed. He checked his watch. Six and three quarter hours to go. Not enough time to prepare for Moscow Rules. But it was all the time he had.

CHAPTЭЯ 13

SAM WAS UP just before five. He'd planned to run in the mornings and packed cold-weather gear for that purpose. It wasn't the only specialized clothing he'd brought. He'd traveled looking like an archetypal American, carrying a lined Burberry raincoat, and sporting lace-up black wingtips. Indeed, the baggy cut of the suit he'd worn to dinner with Ginny identified him immediately as a Yankee. But he'd brought other accoutrements, too. There were two specialized jackets, a pair of thick-soled Russian boots, and other things—tradecraft equipment he'd accumulated before he'd retired.

It looked like everyday clothing. But it wasn't.

By six-fifteen he was dressed. He slipped his official passport into the compartment hidden in his left trouser leg, stuffed a wad of local currency in his pocket, pulled a rough, thick sweater over his Marks and Spencer thermal T-shirt, then shrugged into a tan, military-style insulated car coat that could have been bought at TsUM or one of the other old-line Moscow department stores. An eight-section, short-brimmed tweed cap gave him the retro look of a 1930s *Pravda* vendor. He checked to make sure he was carrying everything he'd need, placed intrusion-alert devices on his satchel, suitcase, and carry-on, then cracked the room door and peeked outside.

Michael O'Neill's room-service tray had been picked up. Sam bent down and retrieved the *International Herald Tribune* that sat on his doorsill and tossed it onto the bed. Then he eased the door shut, double-checked to make sure it locked securely behind him, and headed for the elevator.

Holding one fluorescent green-and-black-striped ski glove in his left hand, he called Ginny Vacario from the lobby phone.

She picked up after a single ring. "Vacario."

"It's me."

Her voice softened. "Morning."

"Morning. You're going to have to give my regrets at the embassy. I have some shopping to do."

Her tone changed. "I see. Will you make lunch?"

He didn't like standing in the lobby. There were too few people to give him the level of cover he needed. "I'll do my best. But don't count on me until later in the day."

"Will you be on your cell?"

"No." He paused, noting the pair of security men watching him from the check-in counter. One put a cell phone to his ear and began speaking. "Gotta go." He replaced the receiver, turned, and pushed through the big glass doors.

6:28. It was still dark, but rush hour was definitely under way. There was traffic. Pedestrians, bundled up against the numbing cold, moved briskly on the pavement. Sam waved off the five taxi drivers stomping to keep warm, turned left, and strode south on Tverskaya, the thick soles of his brown suede boots scrunching on snow.

Because he'd measured the distance, Sam knew it was just

under five hundred meters from the hotel to the Tverskaya metro stop. The canopied entrance sat at the opposite side of the street, roughly two hundred meters of some of the most heavily traveled sections of the four-lane Boulevard Ring. Sam crossed Tverskaya Street opposite the Stanislavski Theater, walked quickly into the northernmost section of the big Pushkin Plaza, slipped into the entrance, dashed down the stairs, turned onto the topmost gallery, and walked east, then north, then pushed onto one of the crowded escalators and descended toward the platform.

Tverskaya was one of Sam's favorite metro stations when he was running a cleaning, or countersurveillance route. It was a three-line interchange with intersecting passages that ran hundreds of meters under the streets between the No. 2, or Green Line, the No. 8, or Gray Line, and the No. 6, or Violet Line. Tverskaya was a No. 2 Line station. A passage running vaguely north took you to the No. 6 Line's Pushkinskaya station, and from there another two-hundred-meter underground tunnel led to Chekhovskaya and Line No. 8.

As Sam stood on the escalator, he kept his hands below the rail and shed his brightly colored gloves. Then he used his bare right hand to pull the big tweed cap from his head. As he did so, his left hand worked a release cord hidden in his coat pocket. By the time he'd reached the bottom of the escalator and stepped off. He was no longer wearing a car coat, but what looked like a knee-length, zipper-front lined raincoat. No one noticed. The tweed cap he'd been wearing, turned inside out as he held it out of sight, had metamorphosed into a round, brimless Russian fur hat. He waited until he'd stepped off the escalator and turned into a new passageway to replace the headgear. From his pocket, he pulled a second pair of gloves—thin brown leather.

Two of the benchmarks for any successful surveillance include paying careful attention to the opposition's color and silhouette. In the space of half a minute, Sam had changed both—in plain sight, and without attracting attention. He walked up to the ticket booth, laid a fifty-ruble bill on the counter, and in flawless Russian bought a one-month *transportnaya karta,* ignoring the rude stare of the clerk who was visibly inconvenienced to have to make so much change.

Quickly now, Sam headed for the Green Line platform. He slipped the *karta* into the turnstile slot, watched as the red light turned green, retrieved the ticket from the upper slot, and pushed through. A rush of air told Sam a train was coming into the station. He loped to the escalator and charged ahead. He reached the platform and, moving as nimbly as a running back working the tires during spring training, picked his way through the crowd and made it onto a northbound train just as the doors smacked themselves closed.

Sam elbowed his way into the crowded car. He'd always been fond of the Moscow subway. The cars themselves were often carpeted, and the seats covered in plush, patterned fabrics. He pulled his coat off—between the crush of bodies jammed cheek by jowl and the heaters going full blast, it was warm—and hung it over his left arm. His sonar swept the subway car. Nothing. Then Sam relaxed, looking like just another Russian worker in the former workers' paradise. He hung on to the tubular handrail above his head, peered down, and snuck a glance at the back page of the newspaper being read by a chubby little man in a pair of greasy overalls and short black leather jacket who moved his lips, silently mouthing every syllable of copy.

Sam rode the Green Line two stops, got off, and waited on the platform until the train had pulled out. Then he made his way through the passageway to the No. 4—or Brown Line— which he rode for one stop. Abruptly he left the car, bounded up the escalator, and changed trains for an incoming southbound Gray Line train.

He left the Gray Line train at Chekhovskaya and walked north through the passageway to the Violet (No. 6) Line station, where he pulled on his overcoat and rode the escalator up to the street. But it wasn't the same coat he'd worn when he entered Tverskaya station.

During his odyssey, Sam had nonchalantly flipped the tan raincoat inside out as it lay over his arm, refolding it in stages. So, what Sam wore as he exited Pushkinskaya was a blue, calf-length wool overcoat with a half belt in back and sloping, raglan shoulders—another change of shape. The fur hat had grown a short leather brim, altering his silhouette. And during his transit from the Brown to the Gray Line, he'd stopped in the crowded passageway just long enough to retie his boot laces—and simultaneously peel off the brown suede "skin" that covered them. Now Sam sported a pair of what looked to be shiny black leather boots that could have been bought in London, Paris, or the Dr. Martens store one block south of the Marriott on Tverskaya Street.

7:22. Sam emerged into gray light and the subzero cold of Pushkin Square, roughly two hundred meters from where he'd originally entered the metro. The Boulevard Ring was clogged in both directions, the sidewalks bustling with pedestrians. Quickly, he crossed Tverskaya Street, passed through one of the arched facades of the imposing Soviet-era building facing the metro, and scampered up a narrow side street.

His sonar was working overtime. But Sam hadn't picked up a single ping so far. He turned south and walked past a small police station. Two half-frozen OMON Special Unit soldiers from the Interior Ministry stood outside, plainly miserable, AK74 submachine guns in their mittened hands, cigarettes dangling from painfully chapped lips. Washington wasn't the only city with a heightened threat level. It hadn't been two weeks since Chechen terrorists had taken hundreds of hostages at a theater in northwest Moscow. Ministry of Interior SWAT teams had used knockout gas during the rescue—and killed more than a hundred of the hostages in the process.

On the corner, Sam stepped into a small store. Under the watchful eye of a babushka wearing an Order of Lenin medal on her stained sweater, he plucked a *Moskovsky Komsomolets* from the display rack, pointed at a tin of Cuban cigarritos on the shelf, and lifted a box of wooden matches out of a jar on the counter. *"Pazhalsta?"* He laid two ten-ruble notes on the scratched glass.

She picked the bills up and held them to the light, rubbed the surface with her thumb, finally dropped a handful of change into his outstretched palm, and only muttered *"spaciba"* as he was going out the door.

Sam dropped the tin of small cigars and the matchbox into his pocket. He rolled the newspaper so only its masthead was visible and tucked it like a football under his left arm, scrunched his neck into his collar, and walked south until he reached the boulevard. There, he turned east, crossed back over Tverskaya Street, and descended into the maze of underground passages that splayed out beneath the grass-covered expanse of Pushkin Square.

7:56. There were no hostiles blips on Sam's sonar screen as he passed the crimson and gold-crested, colonnaded facade of the five-story, eighteenth-century building that housed the mayor's office. Beyond him to the south, the wide expanse of Tverskaya Street ran downhill all the way to the Duma—the Russian legislature—and just beyond it, to the Kremlin walls. But he wasn't going there. One block below the mayor's office Sam turned west, walking through a huge granite arch, into a wide lane on both sides of which sat blocks of identical houses. Four decades ago they'd been handed out to high-ranking Communist Party officials. Today, they were co–ops and condos, bought for suitcases of hundred-dollar bills by oligarchs, entrepreneurs, and *Mafiyosi.*

The lane angled north, then took a shallow dogleg southwest. Sam ambled past a small, seventeenth-century orange-and-white church with a gold onion dome. Just past it was a small, deserted square. Sam turned north into the square. As he did, he applied an appearance-changing prosthetic by

.[18]

7:58. Sam walked purposefully past a school, cut through a narrow alley, then backtracked south again, crossed the lane, turned west, then south, into Bolshaya Nitikskaya Street. He walked fifty feet, then immediately turned left in a narrow, unmarked alley. Twenty yards in, the alley took a ninety-degree turn to the right. Ten yards beyond, on the right side, Sam saw the steam-streaked window of the sort of neighborhood joint Muscovites call a *stalovaya,* or canteen. He pushed through the door, grunted a greeting to the sweating, bald man in a grease-stained white chef's jacket behind the counter, and looked around.

There were six tables in the narrow room. The three closest to the door were occupied. As Sam turned to the counterman he took the rolled newspaper from under his right arm and stuck it under his left. "White coffee and *syrniki,* please." He made his way to the rearmost table, shed his coat, and took a seat against the back wall. Then he reached into his trouser pocket, pulled out the tin box of Punch cigarritos, slit the seal with his thumbnail, took one out, and lit it, leaving both cigars and matches on the scarred marble tabletop.

The counterman smacked a cup of coffee with milk in front

---

[18] This particular technique is still being used by case officers operating in denied areas.

of him. When he'd left, Sam unrolled his newspaper, flattened it with his hand, and spread it out. That was the "okay to make contact" signal. If he'd left the newspaper rolled, or taken it off the table unread, it would have meant "abort."

He slid the coffee to the side and concentrated on the front page, which told him that right-wing fascists had regained power in the United States, endangering the good relationship between President V. V. Putin and President Bush Jr.

"That smells good. Would you mind to give me one?"

Sam looked up. It was Irina—Edward Lee Howard's Russian wife. She was six years older than the surveillance photographs Michael O'Neill had managed to snag from Langley, but she hadn't changed much. She was thin but attractive. Dark hair. Her accent wasn't Moscow, but somewhere east and south. Ukraine? Georgia? Sam hadn't heard enough to decide. Obviously, Howard had provided her with the language to use—the same phrases Sam had employed with Pavel Baranov for this onetime handoff site, known as G.

Irina wore a purple nylon down-filled overcoat that came almost to her ankles. She was nervous. Sam could hear it in her voice. He hoped her tradecraft had been adequate. If she'd been followed, this whole morning would turn out to be nothing more than a charade—and a dangerous one for her.

"They're Cuban, so they're very strong," Sam said, reciting the opening sequence.

"I wouldn't bother you, but I taught Russian in Spiriti Sanctus Province fifteen years ago and developed a taste for them."

"Then it is my pleasure." Sam flipped the tin open. "Please."

"Would you mind? My hands are cold."

The password sequence complete, Sam took a small cigar and offered it. "Would you care to sit down?"

She smiled and complied. "Thank you."

The counterman brought Sam's *syrniki*. He asked for sugar. Sam looked across the table. "Coffee?"

"No, thank you—the cigarrito is enough." She reached for the matches. "Do you mind?"

Sam lifted a forkful of the sweet cheese fritter. "Be my guest."

She smiled, took the matches, fumbled for one, struck it against the box, and lit the small cigar. Her head went back as she drew the smoke in.

Sam watched as she struggled not to cough. Her face went red. But she maintained control. She exhaled. "Good. Stronger than I remembered."

"But rich. Tasty in the mornings—especially with coffee."

"Yes," she said. "Very rich and tasty." She pushed the box of matches back across the table, picked up her coat, and stood. "Do you think I could have another one—to smoke later?"

"Of course."

"You are very generous. Thank you."

"Are you sure you don't want a coffee? Some breakfast?"

Her hands made a dismissive gesture. "I'm already late." She brandished the cigarrito between thumb and forefinger. "This was enough. You've been awfully kind."

"Then you're welcome." He resumed reading his newspaper, his eyes following her as she left. She disappeared into the cold without looking back and Sam's full attention returned to the headlines. He polished off his breakfast and his coffee, had a second cigarrito, dropped a handful of coins on the table, then stood up and pulled his coat on.

To anyone observing him, it would have appeared that Sam took the matchbox almost as an afterthought. He started to leave, remembered the matches, swept them off the table-top, and pocketed them.

СНАРТЭЯ 14

8:56. Sam plunked himself down on a granite bench in a small park a few blocks off the Arbat and reached into his coat pocket for the cigarritos and matches. He lit one of the small cigars and, hiding his actions, unfolded the slip of paper that the woman in the canteen had slipped into the box, concealed it in his palm, and glanced down.

In small, precise Cyrillic handwriting was the message

I. Alexandrova, 31, 2.pr. Mar'inoj Rošči, 1130.
III-И Code 826.

It wasn't an address Sam was familiar with. But there was no way he was going to check his map while sitting in plain view. Sam rolled the message into a ball between the fingers of his left hand and, as he took the small cigar from between his lips, rolled the paper into his mouth and swallowed it.

He checked the street. There was a bar about a hundred meters away. He finished his cigar, then rose, and made his way there. The door was painted wood. It was a neighborhood joint that smelled of old beer and stale cigarette smoke, similar to the Irish bars on Second and Third Avenue when Sam was growing up in New York. Sam pulled the door open and stepped inside the smoky gloom.

It was just like walking into a Blarney Stone. Four regulars hunched over the stained wood bar, their right feet raised on the bar rail. All were drinking vodka in the tall, narrow shot glasses that held a tenth of a liter. Three of the four chased the vodka with beer—Baltika—drunk straight out of half-liter bottles.

In 1950s New York it would have been Three Feathers or Four Roses, chased with draft Knickerbocker or Ballantine.

Sam ambled up to the bar and slapped three coins on the sticky surface. *"Baltika tri."*

The bartender swept the change off the bar and threw it in an antique cash box sitting on the back bar. Then he reached down, unlatched the door of an old wooden cooler, extracted a half-liter bottle of lager, flipped the top off, and slapped the beer in front of Sam. *"Pazhalsta."*

"Spacibo." Sam wiped the mouth of the bottle with his hand, picked it up, and gulped. It was good, even at this hour. "Ahh."

He pulled out his cigars and lit one. The rich tobacco balanced the cool beer nicely. Sam glanced around. He probably had a little time to kill, although he wanted to check the map in order to see where the hell Mar'inoj Rošči was located. For all he knew, it could be in one of the suburbs. No—it couldn't. If it had been, Irina would have added the information.

He sipped the beer, then rapped on the bar. "Where's the toilet?"

The bartender looked up from his newspaper and indicated with his chin.

"I'll be back." Sam walked to the rear and found the toilet. It was empty. There was the usual pissoir, and a single stall.

Sam was happy to see it had a working door. He took it, closed the thin metal behind him and latched it, then turned to discover there was no commode—only what he knew as a Turkish toilet: two size-sixteen concrete footprints flanking a hole in the floor. There was a half-filled ancient bucket with no handle, and a dripping spigot.

God help those whom nature calls. Sam pulled the street map out of his pocket. Quickly he checked the street index, found what he was looking for, and unfolded the map. He located 2 Mar'inoj Rošči. The street was in the northern part of the city—at least a mile from the closest metro stop. But it was close to a couple of trolley-bus lines. From Arbat, Sam guesstimated it was a thirty-minute trip.

He had just refolded the map when the toilet door opened with a thump and there was a rude pounding on the thin sheet-metal door of the stall. "Get out, goddammit, I have to take a huge dump."

Sam smiled in spite of himself. Direct, these Muscovites. "Keep it in your pants another ten seconds, comrade." He tossed the bucket of water down the hole, adjusted his clothes, opened the door, and stepped out. "Bucket's empty."

A large, red-faced man in a black sheepskin coat lurched by him, his shoulder bumping Sam's. "I'll piss it clean, asshole."

9:37. Sam climbed aboard a boxy, red-and-cream-colored No. 13 trolley bus heading north. The old-fashioned vehicle reminded him of the buses he'd ridden in New York as a kid. The seats were covered in the same rough, hardy velour as metro cars. In Washington, which was a graffiti-rich environment, there was nothing used on public transportation that couldn't be power-washed or steam-cleaned.

He'd walked from the Gray Line's Zwetnoi Bulewar metro stop, using tradecraft to make sure he wasn't being surveilled. His appearance had changed once again, too. Now

Sam sported a thick brush of a mustache on his upper lip, and the fur hat had metamorphosed back into a tweed cap.

Sam checked his watch, an anonymous stainless steel Rolex with an adjustable bezel. The trolley bus would take eight or nine minutes at the most. He knew he'd be early at Mar'inoj Rošči by almost two hours. But he wanted the time to do countersurveillance just in case Irina had been careless.

The trolley bus lurched up Olimpiskij Prospekt, then took a hard left that bounced Sam against the door guardrail. He peered through the dirty window only to be rudely bumped again, when the trolley bus swerved right and slammed to a stop.

The doors swung open. The street sign caught Sam's eye. It read ULITSA DUROVA. That was the street Howard mentioned in connection with a dead drop. Impulsively, Sam swung through the rear doors just before they smacked shut with a pneumatic hiss.

He found himself on the wide sidewalk in front of the old Red Army staff headquarters. To his right stood a 1930s, Art Deco police station. Behind and to his left, in the middle of a small plaza, was a statue of Field Marshal Suvorov, the greatest of the imperial Russian generals and one of the most successful tacticians who'd ever lived. It was Suvorov who had invented the dictum "Train hard, fight easy."

On the roof of the building just beyond Suvorov's statue was the old *vizir* site. Involuntarily, Sam glanced up to see if it was still active. He was too far away to be certain.

He sensed no untoward activity. The radar screen in his head clear, Sam turned right and walked east, slaloming his way past half a dozen blue-and-white police cars parked provocatively up on the sidewalk, impeding pedestrian traffic. A pair of cops, their chins tucked into the high collars of thick bulletproof vests, stomped booted feet as they patrolled a fifty-foot beat between the police cars and the sandbagged doors of the station, submachine guns hung around their necks.

The increased police presence in the streets made Sam nervous. Sure, the cops were deployed to guard against more terrorist attacks. But their very presence made his own work a lot more difficult. Sam turned the corner, heading against the traffic flow on Samarskij Lane. Abruptly, he cut behind the station and turned into the park.

Ed Howard had described the site as a hollowed-out tree just north of the police station. Sam scanned the vista. There was a ragged line of leafless poplars. Beyond them, across the snow-covered parkland, lay a bottle-shaped pond.

Idly, Sam took the path that paralleled the tree line, his eyes probing for Howard's dead drop. He made his first pass without result. He turned, pulled a cigarrito from the tin, stopped to light it—which gave him half a minute to take a closer look at the poplars—then ambled back the way he'd come.

Nothing. He made his way back to Samarskij Lane, turned north, walked as far as the edge of the pond, where the lane merged with Olimpiskij Prospekt, then stopped. Frankly, he was getting nervous. There was almost no one else in the park. A lone man, poking at trees, was bound to attract attention.

Sam turned north again and strolled along the prospekt, trying to put himself inside Howard's head. If this was his dead drop, where would he locate it?

He paused and looked back to the south. Certainly, nowhere near the police station. Too much chance of being discovered in flagrante delicto. That ruled out the poplar trees. He panned his gaze west. The pond was bordered by a wide pathway, flanked by a smattering of birches and some evergreens. Nah: too much open space. You wanted someplace you could pass quickly, insert your package, and move on.

Sam's eyes kept moving. In the northwest corner of the

park stood the Red Army Museum. Directly north of where he stood was an unmarked, L-shaped street—more of a lane, actually. A row of removable cast-iron stanchions blocked each end of the *L,* where the twenty-meter-wide band of asphalt merged with the prospekt. No doubt it had been built as an athlete staging area during the Olympics.

Between the apex of the lane and the museum's back entrance, a path meandered in a wavy sine curve. Just below the path, roughly half the distance to the museum, stood a square, green-painted steel shed perhaps twenty-five feet on each side. It was a utilitarian structure—probably used to house and maintain tractor-drawn lawn mowers and other park equipment. A small grove of mature birch trees stood between the front of the shed and the pathway.

Sam turned. From where he stood, it appeared that the shed was almost directly north of the back side of the police station. He walked between the stanchions, his boots making deep prints in virgin snow. At the top of the lane he veered onto the path leading to the museum.

As he walked, Sam said aloud, "Good tradecraft, Ed." It *was* good tradecraft, too. Now Sam had what the instructors at the Farm call cover for status—he had a reason to be on the path. He was going to visit the museum.

He slowed down as he came up on the maintenance shed. It was shielded from the path by one-two-three-four-five-six-seven trees. He passed the first, then the second. He stopped at the middle tree. It had been pruned. Sam squinted. The cuts were recent, too. Certainly, the work had been done within a month or so. Quickly, he scanned all seven birches. The middle tree—number four—was the only one that had been touched.

Sam examined the pruning. The work was all on one side of the tree. Two of the lower branches had been cut back extensively. The stubs were very short—less than an inch. Just above them, a third cut had been made. But the pruner hadn't been so careful. The stub stuck out almost three inches from the tree trunk.

Sam stepped back and looked at the trees again. Seven trees. The middle tree had been pruned.

The middle tree. It was tree number four no matter which direction he counted from. Number four. Number four. His mind raced. Four—*a-b-c-d.*

D was the fourth letter of the alphabet. *D.* And the letter *D,* in Morse code, was *long-short-short.* Letter *D—long-short-short.* Letter *D* was the emergency call out signal for Sam's fateful meeting with Pavel Baranov. Was it reaching? Maybe. But as Howard had said during the short face-to-face at Rand Arthur's house, in the spy's trade there are no coincidences.

From the way the pruning had been done, it was obvious Howard had completed this dead drop before he'd left for the United States. The defector's trip had been as well planned out as was his subsequent escape from Washington. But what was Howard's true purpose? The only thing Sam knew for certain was that Howard's clues were for Sam and Sam alone. Of their ultimate intention, Sam had not a clue.

There are no coincidences. His heart pounding, Sam left the pathway and walked up to the tree. On the far side, inconspicuous but unmistakable, the bark had been peeled back, the area beneath it hollowed out, and the bark strip resecured with dark, unnoticeable tacks.

Don't rush. Work smoothly. His pulse racing, Sam pulled the flap, reached inside, and discovered something small and cold. He removed the object and dropped it into a pocket. He replaced the bark strip, then walked away toward the museum.

Sam's fingers examined the packet. It was small. It was wrapped in some kind of thick plastic. There was tape.

He very much wanted to pull the package out of his pocket

and take a look. But that was impossible right now. Right now he had to depart the area safely; extract unnoticed.

Sam made his way along the pathway to the broad rear courtyard of the Army Museum. There was an exit doorway to his left. Cutting through buildings with multiple entrances was basic denied area tradecraft. He stepped over a mound of plowed snow, edged between the parked cars, and made his way to the door. A sign taped to the gunmetal gray entrance instructed him to use the front unless he was a staff member. So much for that idea.

He turned right, walking along the windowless rough-hewn stone rear wall of the museum. As he turned the corner, a Zil coupe passed him. Sam let it go by. Had the driver seemed unduly interested in him? Sam wasn't sure. But he wasn't going to take any chances either. Not now. He double-checked to make sure he was alone and unobserved. So far, so good. Suddenly Sam's head snapped backward, as if in anticipation of a huge sneeze. Sam's right hand flew into his trouser pocket. It emerged with a balled-up handkerchief. Sam shook the white linen like a flag, put it to his face, and sneezed hard. He brought his left hand up, blew his nose, and then returned the handkerchief—which now contained the false mustache—to his pocket.

Newly clean-shaven, he turned the corner onto Sovietsky Armii Street and stood for a few seconds, monitoring the traffic.

Sam checked his watch. It was almost a quarter of eleven. There was going to be precious little time for countersurveillance on Mar'inoj Rošči Lane. He saw a No. 13 trolley bus making its way up the one-way avenue and jogged north so he could intercept it and climb aboard at the next stop.

CHAPTƏЯ 15

SAM APPROACHED 2 Mar'inoj Rošči Lane from the north. There were, in fact, more than half a dozen separate streets and lanes in this neighborhood, all with that very same name. Only the prefix numbers—1 Mar'inoj Rošči, 2 Mar'inoj Rošči, and so on—differed. The same sort of repetitive pattern appeared in every section of the city. It was one of Moscow's more maddening topographical traits.

Sam left the trolley bus at 10:58 six blocks north of his target. His mental sonar, radar, and FLIR[19] were all fully operational. He made his way past the Satirikon Theater, walked three streets east, then turned south, his boots crunching on frozen slush as he followed the chain-link perimeter of a deserted vegetable canning factory on whose puke-colored wall was spray-painted a six-foot-high hammer and sickle under which, in crude Cyrillic, was scrawled FUCKING JEWS OUT OF THE MOTHERLAND.

He paused, checking for pings, and, sensing none, peered

---

[19] Forward-Looking Infra-Red.

east. Half a kilometer beyond the deserted factory, Sam could make out the railroad tracks of one of the commuter lines that brought workers into Moscow from the northern suburbs, and a few hundred meters beyond that, where a broad, six-lane highway traversed the railway, sat the Sputnik memorial and the Rizhskaya metro stop.

He resumed his route. The streets were largely deserted. Even the normally busy ones adjacent to the Satirikon had been strangely empty. Sam walked south on 4 Mar'inoj Rošči Street, turned west onto 3 Mar'inoj Rošči Lane, then veered south again on 2 Mar'inoj Rošči Street. Obviously, nobody was paying off the city workers in this neighborhood, because the streets had not been plowed. The sidewalks were slippery and the cars unlucky to have been trapped curbside were encrusted in sooty ice shells.

From the time he'd departed the trolley bus, the weather had taken a sudden and definite turn for the worse. The skies were overcast. Oppressive pewter gray clouds had moved in from the east, roiling so low they formed a drab drop ceiling above the apartment blocks and rusting factory roofs. In the space of half an hour, the city had been plunged into an unnatural midday dusk that gave it a grim, forbidding, Stalinesque aura.

The cold, always pervasive, was now tinged with a bitter, frozen dampness that made Sam remember how much he detested Moscow winters. No wonder Russians drank the way they did.

11:27. Sam hunched his shoulders against the cold, shoved his gloved hands as deep into his pockets as he could, and turned onto 2 Mar'inoj Rošči Lane.

The building Sam wanted—number 31—was on the left side of the street, about sixty-five yards south of where he was. Eyes moving, he noted that every vehicle on the street was either snow-covered or ice-coated. Sam brushed the plastic-wrapped object in his pocket with the tips of his gloved fingers. Yes, it would have been nice to get out here before ten so he could find a safe spot and surveil the location for a full two hours to make sure he wasn't going into a trap. But the trade-off had been worth it.

Maybe. He'd only know for certain when he opened the packet.

Sam crossed the street and scanned the windows of the five-story building opposite number 31. Only clear glass— he could see inside virtually every apartment. No gauzy curtains or black netting to hide surveillance cameras. He turned his attention to the target building itself. It was light-colored brick and stood five stories high, just like every other building on the block. The boxy design probably dated from the late 1950s or early '60s. More than two dozen satellite television dishes faced the sky, bolted beneath old-fashioned louvered windows. They gave the place a contradictory, techno-ancient appearance.

What struck Sam most was how unremarkable it all was. This was an anonymous building in an anonymous neighborhood. It was most certainly working class.

This fact in particular gnawed on Sam. Ed Howard was most definitely not the working-class type. The reports Sam had read thanks to Michael O'Neill's ingenuity indicated Howard had a large, well-appointed dacha northwest of the city, and an in-town pied-à-terre only a short walk from his office at Lubyanka.

So what was this place? And what had Howard used it for? The possibilities were infinite, and almost all of them unpleasant.

The rendezvous could be a setup. The FSB wasn't above that sort of thing, and the compromising of a former CIA chief could prove valuable in the current and often prickly liaison negotiations between the two intelligence services.

* * *

SHORTLY after Sam had returned from Moscow, a Soviet intelligence officer named Stanislav Borisovich Gusev had been caught monitoring a sophisticated electronic eavesdropping device that the Russians had somehow managed to secrete in a seventh-floor conference room at the State Department. It was a huge scandal. First of all, the Russians had hidden the bug inside the chair-rail molding on the wall. Which meant they'd been in the conference room enough times to obtain photos of the molding, and paint samples so they could turn out a piece of molding with the bug, cut out a section of molding, and insert their section—all without being discovered.

Second, the bug had been in place for more than a year. The only reason Gusev got caught was that he got careless. Because he enjoyed diplomatic immunity and therefore had State Department–issued plates on his car, Gusev habitually parked in one of the numerous no-parking zones within a block or two of State Department headquarters, where it was inevitably ticketed by DC traffic officers. His activity pattern escaped the FBI gumshoes at Buzzard Point.[20] But it was caught by a sharp special agent in the Counterintelligence Division of the State Department's Bureau of Diplomatic Security, who took the time to chart the position of Gusev's car when it received each of its sixty-two parking tickets. All, she discovered, had been written within two blocks of Main State. Sixty-two appointments in thirteen months was some kind of record, especially because the diplomatic list identified Gusev as a junior-grade cultural attaché. Then the DSS agent checked the diplomatic visitors' log, only to find that Gusev had never actually entered the building.

---

[20] The FBI's Washington field office, out of which the CI (Counterintelligence) Division, operates.

It was at that point that the FBI finally realized something untoward might be going on and started surveilling Gusev. Two weeks later, they caught him sitting on a park bench across from Main State, holding a small radio monitor that was broadcasting the proceedings of a meeting in the seventh-floor conference room two hundred or so yards away. Despite his vehement protests, Gusev's monitor was confiscated.

Immediately thereafter, following a lot of undiplomatic publicity (not to mention blanket television coverage), Gusev was booted out of the country. Ever since, Moscow had been looking for an "equalizer," and Sam, having been declared persona non grata by Moscow once before, was an ideal candidate for public ignominy.

Or, it could be a honey trap. The Russians had a history of trying to compromise their adversaries by setting them up with women. Sam's CIA mentor, Donald Kadick, who had served in Germany, Poland, Bulgaria, and the Soviet Union during the early days of the Cold War, had once told Sam about the time the ploy had been tried on him.

Kadick had been on his way to a white-tie-and-decorations embassy reception in Warsaw. Dressed like a dandy, he'd walked onto the elevator in his apartment building. The doors shut. One floor below, an elegant woman swathed in a thick sable fur coat and the high-heeled, up-to-the-knee boots fashionable in the mid-1960s joined him. She nodded in his direction. Kadick amiably nodded back.

Just as the doors opened on the ground floor, the woman jettisoned her fur coat. She was wearing nothing beneath it. She threw herself on Kadick and kissed him passionately just in time for her performance to be captured by the six Polish government cameramen who were waiting in the lobby.

Before Sam left for Moscow, a terminally ill Don Kadick had taken him to the Metropolitan Club for what turned out to be their farewell dinner. Cancer was eating away at the old Brahmin's body. Kadick's decades-old bespoke suit hung from the retired case officer's shrunken frame. Frail and watery-eyed, he walked with the aid of a knobby stick that he brandished as he spoke. But the man's will was as indomitable as ever. And he hadn't lost his sense of humor—or irony. Over perfect martinis Kadick related the Warsaw story. "The moral is simple, Samuel," he'd said with mock severity. "Never, ever, get on an elevator with a naked Polish woman."

11:29. The keypad was on the left side of the battered security door. Sam noted screwdriver scars around the metal casing. He punched the numbers 8-2-6 and waited for the electric buzz that would signal the lock had been unlatched.

Silence.

He punched the sequence a second time. Again, there was no reaction.

Sam had visited places like this before. He took hold of the doorknob, twisted, and pushed the steel door open. It was yet another reality of Moscow life. People got tired of punching buttons with their arms full of groceries. So they disabled the security locks on the front doors of their apartment houses—and then they complained bloody murder when the burglary rate went sky-high.

Apartment III-И would be on the fourth level. At least Irina's place had a number. Most of the apartments in Moscow didn't. Ask where someone lived, and it was more than likely you'd be told, "We're the second door on the right, on the first-floor landing off the third stairwell, far left-hand side of the inner courtyard."

Sam walked into the dingy, narrow foyer. To his right a cluster of cheap metal mailboxes were bolted to the wall. About half of the covers had been pried open. This was definitely not the kind of place Ed Howard would have sought out to live.

But it would have been a perfect safe house.

Now, *that* made sense. An anonymous apartment on an anonymous block of working-class apartment houses. An out-of-the-way place to stash things for safekeeping. To be honest, Sam had done something similar. During his tour in Paris he'd rented a safe-deposit box using one of his Agency aliases—a German businessman named Koch. He stored documents that he felt uneasy about keeping in his flat (DST had the habit of breaking into diplomatic residences), as well as a handgun, a sterile[21] Belgian Browning Hi-Power complete with a suppressor.

Sam hadn't even wanted the damn thing. The weapon had been a gag gift from an old Marine colleague of his from Vietnam who worked in the Agency's Paramilitary Division, performing what was euphemistically known as "special action." The pistol had initially been bought in Europe for use at one of the CIA's high-risk stations. Once it was appropriated by the Paramilitary Division, it had been modified with a threaded barrel and a suppressor and all of the weapon's identifying marks had been erased.

Sam had always been nervous about having the Browning at his apartment—possession of suppressed weapons was illegal, even for diplomats—and so he'd stored the gun, the holster, the silencer, and the unmarked brown cardboard box containing fifty rounds of subsonic hollow-point ammunition he'd been given with the weapon in a safe-deposit box. Later, the Hi-Power and its accoutrements resided in the same small, fireproof safe lag-bolted to the floor of his condominium in Rosslyn in which Sam kept German, Irish, and Belgian passports and half a dozen other forms of alias iden-

[21] Untraceable.

tification. But Sam had always been uneasy about having a gun in the apartment. And so the pistol and all its accoutrements currently resided in the library wall safe of "Rose House," Michael O'Neill's 1730 stone cottage on the outskirts of the fashionable horse-country town of Upperville, Virginia, seventy-five miles from Washington.

Right now, though, Sam wished he had the old Hi-Power cocked, locked, and tucked into the waistband of his trousers.

SAM PUSHED the *minuterie,* a single dim bulb came on, and he proceeded down a shabby, narrow hallway. The first apartment on his left belonged to the concierge. No one was home. Sam knew that because the door, which had a plaque bearing the word "concierge" stenciled on it, was locked with a padlock and hasp. The light went out. *Minuterie,* hell. This was a damn *thirty-secondrie.* He fumbled along the wall until he found the button. When the light came on again he made his way to a narrow stairwell.

Sam glanced down. There was water on the tiled floor—from the shoes of people coming in from the snow-covered street. Directly ahead was another *minuterie* button. Sam pushed it and a light somewhere above him came on. He put his gloved hand on the utilitarian wrought-iron handrail and started to climb, stepping gingerly on the concave marble treads. Wet marble was more slippery than Teflon-coated ice.

Carefully, he mounted the stairs. On the first-floor landing he peered into the hallway, sniffing like a dog catching scent. Someone was cooking cabbage in vinegar. He saw lights under two doors. He moved across the landing, pushed the light button, and continued his climb. There was no sign of life on the second floor. He pressed the *minuterie* button to sustain the light, and continued his climb.

On the third-floor landing he paused to get his bearings.

The hallway plunged into darkness. Sam cursed silently, found the *minuterie* button by running his hands along the wall. He hit it with his thumb. Nothing happened.

He sighed, descended to the second floor, and hit the button with his gloved fist. When the light came on he scampered tiptoe up the stairs and started down the hallway to his left, searching out doors for Irina's flat number. He was halfway down the hall when his world was plunged into darkness. He ran his hand along the cold, rough stucco until he felt a button, which he squished. A single bulb at the end of the hall came on. But it was enough to see by, and Sam pressed on, only to discover he was in the wrong wing. Then the lights went out again.

This alleged encounter was turning into a frigging comedy of errors. Sam made his way back to the stairwell in the dark, then felt his way down the opposite hallway, running his hands along the wall until his fingers located a *minuterie* button. And having found the damn thing without killing himself, he depressed it with his index finger.

Yet another ten-watt bulb came on, illuminating the dingy hallway. Sam turned and quickly scanned the doors. He was in the right place. Apartment III-И should be on the right side of the hallway as he faced the rear, three doors down. Sam searched for another wall button just in case the lights went out. There was none. He tapped the one in front of him again, then moved quickly toward his target. Just as he reached the door, the hallway went black.

A fissure of light spread along the length of the frame. The door to apartment III-И was slightly ajar.

CHAPTЭR 16

SAM STOOD in the hallway for some seconds considering possible scenarios. As a case officer, he had been trained never to make a move without having at least one alternative plan up his sleeve. Right now he felt sleeveless.

The simple answer was that Irina had left the door open for him. More probable was that she'd been trailed and there were half a dozen FSB goons in the closets just waiting to pounce.

But if that were the case, Sam's radar would have picked up a blip. And there had been no blips today. Not a single one.

Sam slowed his breathing until he felt the tom-tom beat of his own pulse in wrists and neck. Then he stood, silent and immobile. Every environment, he knew, has its own natural rhythm. As a young turkey hunter, Sam had learned how to wait out his prey. The turkey is a cunning bird, with sharp eyes, and a keen sense of its natural habitat. Sam was taught by experience in the field that anything he did to disturb the turkey's surroundings spooked the birds and spoiled the hunt.

And so he became both practiced and patient. He'd find a

position up against a tree and camouflage himself and his shotgun to make it hard for the gobblers to spot him. He would mask his human smell by using scent blockers. And most important, he would establish his hunting site early enough so that the forest would return to its normal and natural rhythms long before the turkeys moved into Sam's area. By the time Sam was ready, the songbirds would be chirping, the insects buzzing, and the other critters doing whatever they did naturally.

Now, in the darkened hallway, Sam opened his mouth ever so slightly, and then . . . just . . . listened.

After some seconds, he heard the gurgle of water running through pipes somewhere above his head. He heard muffled voices. He heard the sound of faint music. The apartment-house habitat was in its natural state. He cocked his head. There was no hint of ominous creaking of floor; no giveaway squeak of stealthy soft rubber boot soles; no adrenaline-heightened shallow breathing close by.

Then Sam inclined his head slightly and put his ear close to the door of the apartment. There was nothing coming from inside. No breathing. No water. No muffled voices. Only silence.

Sam eased the door open, mouthing a silent prayer to the god of spies to keep it from creaking. His prayer was answered. He stepped over the threshold into a small, low-ceilinged living room and closed the door behind him, careful to turn the handle so as not to make any noise when the latch caught.

The door firmly shut, he looked around. The furniture—what there was of it—was sparse and utilitarian. A daybed sat against the far wall. In front of it, on an imitation Azeri rug, were a pseudo-Scandinavian coffee table and a teak-colored armchair with a concave, burnt orange upholstered seat. Two narrow windows looked out on a brick air shaft just wide enough so that a hint of daylight came through the filthy glass.

To Sam's immediate left was the kitchen: a stove that used bottled gas and a four-foot-high fridge were the only appliances. There was a dinette with two chairs. A single cup and saucer, and an aluminum ashtray holding a number of cigarette butts, sat on the scuffed metal table.

To his right, he could just see into what he guessed was the bedroom. There was a light on. Quickly, Sam scanned for closets and other places to hide. There were none in the living room.

He checked the kitchen. There was a no coffee in the cup, but a lot in the saucer, and some puddled on the tabletop. He picked up the ashtray in his gloved right hand and checked the bottom with the back of his bare left hand. It was warm. There were eight butts in it. One was dark brown—the Punch cigarrito Irina had taken earlier. The others were filters; all identical. They were smoked only halfway down. Then they'd been carefully stubbed out.

He examined one. It was American—a Marlboro. They were all Marlboros. He opened the fridge, which held a single bottle of beer. There were six glasses, three plates, and two cups and saucers in the single metal cabinet above the tiny, cold-water-only sink that stood opposite the stove and fridge. Sam ran his fingers under the empty drawers on either side of the sink. Nothing had been secreted there.

Sam pulled his glove on, left the kitchen, and made his way toward the light. In the short passage between the living room and the bedroom stood a tall, dark, Art Deco armoire. He opened one of the burled wood doors. It was empty except for a dozen or so wire hangars that jangled when the armoire's base moved on the uneven floorboards.

He peeked into the bedroom. A single window, shade lowered, provided light. Obviously, it looked out on the inner courtyard. The room was devoid of furniture except for a bare double bed. Not quite a bed, just an ancient, stained, ragged-around-the-edges box spring, sitting on a cheap wheeled metal frame. He backed away. The whole place absolutely reeked of safe house. With the exception of the cigarrito, there was not a single sign of Irina, or anything that linked the place to Ed Howard.

Sam paused. Something was terribly wrong here. The pieces didn't fit the puzzle.

To his right was the bathroom door with its frosted glass panel. No light shone through. He tested the handle. The door was unlocked. He tried to open it but the door wouldn't budge. He leaned his shoulder against the frame and pushed, gently at first, then with increasing pressure. But the damn thing was wedged shut.

He pushed hard. Whatever it was that had held the door shut slipped. Sam saw bright light through the frosted glass panel.

He shoved, forced the door open, and saw Irina in the bathtub.

That was when it all began to make sense.

The bathroom had no windows or vents. They'd used the mattress to muffle the sound of her screams. She lay in the empty porcelain tub, eyes open, lips rolled back from her teeth, frozen in a pitiful smile that Sam knew wasn't a smile at all. Animals, crushed on the highway, often display similar, upturned lips. But roadkill didn't smile in death. And neither did Irina.

He stepped across the mattress very carefully so as not to disturb anything. There was blood on the tile floor and the sides of the tub.

They'd bound her arms and legs with some kind of wide, dark tape. He wrestled the mattress on end and examined both sides. There was blood on it, as well as urine—wet splotches in three separate areas. At one point they'd laid her atop it and worked her over. He examined the black-and-white tile of the bathroom floor and saw the drag marks. Then they'd moved her to the tub, where they'd finished their . . . work.

He wasn't ready for this level of butchery. The urge to get the hell out was overwhelming.

And yet . . . and yet, Sam forced himself to stay, understood that he had to stay, because this, just like Pavel Baranov's murder, was a message—a form of communication. It was a hideous message. And it had to be deciphered.

And so, he went on autopilot, relegating every response and reaction that might be detrimental to forward progress to a mental shredder. There was no time for compassion now. Nor empathy, nor sensitivity.

There are no coincidences. Sam had to read the signs here—they'd provide the road map. That was his job. Nothing else.

And so, he slammed the emotional door shut and started to reconstruct what the hell had gone on—and more important, why.

Sam backed out of the bathroom, careful to ensure that he wasn't leaving any bloody boot prints, and went to the front door. From his trouser pocket he took a fresh handkerchief inside of which was folded a pair of latex gloves. He stuffed the ski gloves in his jacket and pulled the rubber ones on. He went to the front door, listened to make sure no one was outside, turned the handle, and opened it. Quickly, in the dim light, he examined the lock. It was a simple cylinder lock. He reached into his pocket for the box of matches, struck one, and held it up to the plug. There were scratches around the keyhole. The match burned down and he blew it out before it burned his gloved fingers, then struck another and squinted at the lock again. There were three fresh scratches around the keyhole.

He turned the handle from the inside, revealing a simple and unlockable spring-loaded latch. The lock itself was a keep-it-simple two-turn dead bolt. There was a T-shaped knob just below the inner door handle that secured the dead bolt manually.

Sam snorted. These things could be opened in a matter of seconds—even by someone as rusty as he. There were no tumblers or pins—the key was an old-fashioned one, which turned the dead bolt directly.

He closed the door, made sure the two matches were fully extinguished, and dropped them into his jacket pocket. So they'd broken in and surprised her. That explained the coffee in the saucer and on the table.

Quick in the door—and grab her. He moved to the kitchen, turned the light on, and dropped onto hands and knees, examining the floor. There were faint but unmistakable fresh scrape marks on the scuffed linoleum.

Sam stepped back and examined the kitchen with a critical eye. The front legs of the small refrigerator had been moved recently. He knew that because half an inch to the left was the indentation. Sam eased the fridge from the wall and checked behind it. Nothing had been concealed. He slid it forward and tilted the four-foot-high box backward. Nothing underneath but wads of accumulated dust.

The living room appeared to be undisturbed. But Sam's practiced eye saw that every piece of furniture in the room had been moved and then replaced. The armoire, too, had been searched. He pulled a chair from the kitchen and stood atop it. The dust on its top had been touched. It was unmistakable: someone had dragged a finger along the back edge, feeling for a cache, or an envelope, or something.

He probed the walls and tested the floors for places where Howard might have hidden materials—and came up dry.

After a quarter of an hour, there was nothing left to examine. The place had obviously been gone over by professionals—and from the look of it, they hadn't found anything. Why professionals? Because Sam knew that normally, the premises looked like a disaster zone after having been searched. Tossed, Sam remembered, was the police term for the procedure.

But Edward Howard's safe house hadn't been tossed. Nothing was out of place. Which suggested to Sam that whoever had done this knew Howard wouldn't keep anything sensitive at the safe house.

Which bothered Sam. Because there had to be a reason why Irina had summoned him to this place. Had to be something tangible for her to give him.

Sam returned to the bathroom. He went over the mattress inch by inch, looking for slits, tears, or resewn seams. There was nothing.

He put the hard part off until last. Finally, he stared down at Irina. Her throat had been slashed. Blood ran down her chest, coating her breasts. She'd lost two fingernails on her right hand. They'd been discarded, bloody, next to the tub.

They—whoever *they* were—used the cigarettes on her body. The Mafiya used cigarettes—especially Chechens and Georgians. There were burns on her nipples. On her stomach. Her cheeks. Her shoulders. Sam was nauseated. But he kept looking.

That was when he saw they'd left him a message.

It had been burned onto her forehead with a cigarette. It was unmistakable. Two long raw red dashes and an ash-crusted dot where they'd stubbed the cigarette out. He looked carefully. They'd branded her with the letter *G*.

The same call-out sign that had been left on his pillow last night to establish the bona fides of the message he'd received. The same call-out sign he'd arranged with Pavel Baranov to use a onetime site: the same *stalovaya* where Irina had showed up three and a half hours ago.

The cigarette was there, too—a Marlboro. The filter had been shoved between her lips. The rest of the cigarette had broken off, leaving strands of tobacco between her blood-soaked breasts. That was when he remembered the Marlboro crushed between Pavel Baranov's dead lips.

Sam gagged. He almost lost it. But he fought the nausea, sustained by a white-hot hatred of those who'd done this unspeakable damage—first to Pavel Baranov and now to Irina Howard. So he swallowed hard, sucked the stale air that smelled of blood, and continued examining the broken corpse of what had been Ed Howard's wife.

He was sweating buckets now. Sam realized that if he stayed much longer he might pass out. And he'd seen everything he had to.

Quickly, he wrestled the mattress up against the door the way he'd found it. He squeezed past it out of the bathroom and eased the door shut. The mattress fell into place and blocked most of the light. Gasping, Sam checked the bottoms of his boots for blood once more. The soles were blessedly dry.

Bile rising in his throat, Sam opened the front door, slipped into the darkened hallway, and silently closed the door behind him.

Get a grip, Sam. He leaned up against the wall and forced himself to concentrate. *Why had they tortured Irina?*

The obvious answer: to see if she knew where Howard stowed his paper. The hundred-dollar question was what Howard had told his wife.

There was, perhaps, a way to get some sort of rough idea. Sam made his way down the hallway to the landing. His outstretched hand found the banister in the dark, and using it as a guide, he headed toward the street. By the time he'd reached the second level and the cabbage fumes hit him again, he felt as if he was suffocating. In the building's foyer, he paused long enough to change his appearance once more. The tweed cap morphed into the fur hat; the long blue overcoat became the military-style tan padded jacket; he pulled the latex gloves off, and shoved his wet hands into the black-and-green ski gloves.

Finally, he lurched onto the snowy street. Checked for watchers. Sensed none. He stood there for some seconds, hyperventilating. He rubbed his hand across his chest. He'd sweat completely through his thermals and thick sweater.

The weather, he noted, had gone from bad to worse. It struck Sam right then that the deterioration was visible bad karma—a meteorological reflection of his current psychological condition. He walked in a trance through the sleet north one block, turned west, and made his way to the trolley bus stop on Šeremet'evskaya Street. Seven minutes later he climbed aboard a southbound No. 15, displayed his *transportnaya karta,* and found a seat on the left-hand side.

Six and a half minutes after he'd dropped onto the unrelenting bench seat, Sam got his answer as the trolley bus came to a jerky stop a hundred yards north of the Army Museum. Verdict: Irina hadn't known about the hollowed-out tree. If she had, the location would have been staked out by now, and there would be signs of whoever had killed her— FSB agents, Ministry of Interior counterintelligence goons, or the Mafiya *byki* and *torpedos* they hired to do their dirty work. But Sam saw no evidence of surveillance. Not a single indicator.

He craned his neck to see if he could spot hostiles on the museum's roof. *Nada.* It was deserted. With a hiss, the trolley bus driver released the vehicle's brakes and moved on. Sam closed his eyes. He opened them when he saw Irina's body. Then he drove the image from his mind, his right hand resting on the packet in his trouser pocket.

1**:24.** Sam was still feeling queasy when he checked for messages at the Marriott's desk and was handed two envelopes. Hands trembling, he ripped the first one open. It was from Ginny, and it read: "Embassy canceled all our meetings today—they are nervous. Afraid of a diplomatic flap. Tea in the bar at 4 P.M. with DCM. Be there. Impt. you are at this meeting." It was signed "V."

Sam recognized the writing on the second envelope. It was Michael O'Neill's distinctive hand. The note was uncharacteristically brief for the usually loquacious lawyer: "Criticom—must talk." He jammed both messages into his pocket and headed for the elevator, feeling sick to his stomach.

1:29. Sam pulled himself off his knees and wiped the vomit from his mouth with a hand towel. It was the wanton brutality that got to him. It was all just so goddamn needless. Tears welled in his eyes. He fought hysteria with the rage that boiled in his gut. He tossed the wet towel into the shower stall, went to the sink, turned the cold water on full, rinsed his hands, and then splashed water on his face, the wetness running down his neck onto his thermals. He reached for a fresh towel, wiped his face and neck, flushed the toilet, then lurched into the bedroom, dropped exhausted onto the floral coverlet, and fell immediately into a deep sleep.

3:14. Sam examined his face in the bathroom mirror and decided that he'd aged noticeably in the past few hours. Then he forced the image of Irina into an emotional lockbox and got to work. He turned the shower up full and switched the bathroom radio on. He pulled on a pair of latex gloves. Using the small knife in his shaving kit, Sam carefully slit the tape, unpeeled the plastic wrapping, examined it for any messages, and, finding none, washed it to remove any fingerprints he might have left, wiped it dry, then laid it on the counter next to the sink. Under the plastic skin was a layer of bubble wrap, which Sam cut away. Inside the bubble wrap was another layer of greenish black plastic that looked as if it had been snipped from a contractor-grade garbage bag. He sliced the taped seam and unrolled the wrapper, revealing a red, white, and blue plastic key-chain fob, decorated in a cartoonish American flag motif. A ring was attached to one end.

The fob had two sections. He pulled them apart. Just as he'd thought, the fob was a USB pen drive—a portable computer data storage device.

Sam didn't have a laptop. And he wasn't about to borrow Virginia Vacario's Dell, or the lightweight Sony that Michael O'Neill had packed. Whatever was on the pen drive would have to wait until he was back in Washington. Sam bundled up the wrapping materials and shoved them into the pocket of the trousers he'd be wearing so he could dispose of them surreptitiously. Then he went to the closet and burrowed in his satchel until he found his house keys. They were on a souvenir key chain—a miniature Eiffel Tower he'd bought a decade earlier at Charles de Gaulle airport.

He returned to the bathroom, took his keys off the old key chain and slid them onto the pen drive's ring, and placed the old key chain in the same pocket as the plastic wrap. Then he dropped the pen drive and keys into the big leather book bag. When you need to hide something important, Sam understood, it's often best to do it in plain sight.

Sam shed his wrinkled, soiled clothes, shrugged into the thick terry bathrobe that lay across the bed, took his cell phone, and punched Michael O'Neill's number into it. The phone rang twice, then a voice growled, "O'Neill."

Sam said, "Criticom? What's the crisis, Michael?"

The was a momentary pause. "Oh, *hi* there," O'Neill answered. "Can we do this some other time, sweetheart? I'm not in a position to talk right now."

"Do you have all your clothes on, Michael?"

"As a matter of fact I do. But let's chat later, shall we? Ta."

The phone went dead in Sam's ear. O'Neill was obviously in one of his eccentric moods. Sam hung the robe on a hook and stepped into the shower.

CHAPTƎЯ 17

YOU CAN'T IMAGINE how touchy things are right now. I have to be perfectly candid and tell you this is absolutely the worst time for you people to be poking around."

"We're sorry to inconvenience you, Mort." Of all the places Sam didn't want to be right now, this topped the list. But work was work. He stared across starched linen at the slightly built man who was running his hand nervously through thinning, butterscotch-colored hair. "But Senator Arthur wants answers—and he's sent us to dig them out."

The deputy chief of mission nudged the cup and saucer of untouched Earl Grey out of his way. "The Russians are hugely sensitive about matters of national security. You of all people should know that, Sam."

Sam let the veiled affront pass. "This isn't about Russian national security, Mort—it's about ours."

"Even so, we're at a critical stage of bilateral discussions right now in the counterterrorism arena, and I'm hesitant to do anything that might cause offense."

" 'Cause offense'?" Virginia Vacario broke in. "Mr. Hazleton, how can a discussion relating to 9/11 do that?"

"Because, Ms. Vacario, it would. The Russians have just been subjected to unreasonable second-guessing by the international media over the hostage rescue at the Palace of Culture Theater."

Sam cocked his head. "Unreasonable, Mort? Putin killed a hundred and twenty-four hostages trying to rescue them. If that had taken place in the U.S., there'd be calls for the president's impeachment."

Hazleton sighed. "All I'm saying is that just raising the subject could offend my Russian counterparts—and then, where would we be?"

Sam eased his leather tub chair back on its rollers and polished off his espresso. "Where? Precisely where we are now, Mort: without any of the information we've been tasked to obtain." Sam set the cup back in its saucer and glanced to his left where Ginny Vacario sat, lips pursed, her right leg pumping impatiently.

"My requests are quite straightforward, Mr. Hazleton," she said. "You can tell your Russian counterpart no offense is meant. But I want a background briefing from one of the embassy's political officers about Russian-U.S. counterterrorism cooperation in the days before 9/11. I want a meeting with someone from the Ministry of Defense who will update us about the transfer of Russian weapons to al-Qa'ida. I want to learn about Russian concerns regarding their missing weapons of mass destruction. And I want a meeting with the Foreign Intelligence Service to learn about links between al-Qa'ida, the Chechens, and Saddam Hussein."

"That is a very tall order." Hazleton worked the tip of his sparse mustache. "I'm not sure how much we'll be able to accomplish for you."

"A briefing at the embassy shouldn't be much trouble."

"We are extremely busy these days," Hazleton said. He lifted a water goblet and took a swallow. "My staff is overworked, and as you know, it takes a lot of preparation for a proper brief."

"I'm sure you'll find a way to squeeze us into your schedule. The chairman—Senator Arthur is now the incoming chairman of Senate Select, Mr. Hazleton—takes a very personal interest in the subject, and I don't think you'd want to disappoint him."

Hazleton blinked rapidly half a dozen times. "Of course, we'll see what we can do to accommodate you, Ms. Vacario."

"I'm sure you will. Now, as to the weapons of mass destruction—"

"As you know, Ms. Vacario," Hazleton interrupted, "the Russians insist they do not have any missing WMD."

"I'd like to hear that directly from a Russian official, not an American diplomat." Vacario looked at Hazleton pointedly. "What about weapons transfers?"

"The Russian position is that none of their weapons have been sold by official sources to any terrorist group."

Vacario smiled. "I understand the precision of their language only too well, Mr. Hazleton. That is why I have brought a list of serial numbers, as well as photographs of the arsenal markings on one hundred separate weapons, including rocket-propelled grenade launchers, AK-47 assault rifles, and 7.62 RPD light machine guns, all of which were retrieved from al-Qa'ida terrorists in Afghanistan, Sudan, and Yemen."

"I can tell you that the Ministry of Defense will refuse to receive your list."

Vacario poured herself two fingers of bottled water and sipped delicately. "How can you say that, Mr. Hazleton, when we haven't submitted the list yet?"

The diplomat looked at Vacario and smiled ingratiatingly. "That's how I earn my salary, Ms. Vacario."

No, Mort, Sam thought, *you earn your salary by making sure we don't upset anybody's applecart—especially yours.*

As deputy chief of mission or DCM, R. Morton Hazleton was the embassy's second-ranking diplomat. The question in Sam's mind was whether Hazleton actually worked to promote the U.S. government's interests, Moscow's—or his own.

This sort of modus operandi was endemic at State. Discipline was so lax at State that career foreign service officers who disagreed with an administration's policies often simply ignored instructions from Washington and freelanced, advocating their own agendas. Leaks to the press were so widespread the department was known as an information sieve. Equally appalling, the foreign service culture had little appetite for security, and so classified information was treated carelessly. Laptops with code-word information on them were routinely left turned on in unlocked conference rooms; red-tabbed materials[22] sat on desktops in empty offices.

Sam had long ago decided that as an instrument of meaningful diplomacy, the State Department was essentially worthless. Some of the problem had to do with the technical advances of the twenty-first century. State still functioned for the most part as if CNN, Fox News, Al Jazeera, MSNBC, or Sky News did not exist. The foreign service bureaucracy routinely operated as if diplomacy could be accomplished only between the hours of 8:00 A.M. and 5:30 P.M., Washington time.

The majority of cables written by today's FSOs were little more than rehashes of what had already appeared in the press. Genuine political intelligence and insightful analysis

---

[22] A red tab indicates material classified as "Secret."

were virtually nonexistent. From what Sam could discern, neither the secretary of state nor the president was being given any information about what was really going on inside the Kremlin these critical days. And how the hell would they be able to formulate a coherent policy that would keep Moscow on America's side during the inevitable war with Iraq if they were essentially blind?

But the problem went much deeper than that. An epidemic of risk aversion had infected the upper echelons of the department. Ambassadors often seemed more interested in avoiding what they referred to as "flaps" than in doing the president's bidding. In the early days of the war against terrorism, several career ambassadors assigned to Middle East and Gulf states had actually forbidden the FBI to mount full-court-press investigations against the perpetrators of bombings. Ginny Vacario had shown Sam one ambassador's confidential cable following a bombing that had taken seventeen American lives. "Our host nation," it said, "will become seriously offended when the FBI's investigation proves that local terrorist elements with tacit governmental support have in fact been involved in causing the deaths of American uniform service personnel. Offending our host nation could do grave harm to the political interests of the United States."

So far as Sam was concerned, R. Morton Hazleton was the living embodiment of State's abysmal condition. Mort—the French-language pun was not lost on Sam—had all the right pedigrees: degrees from Georgetown, the Sorbonne, and Johns Hopkins. His first overseas assignment had been Cairo, where he'd been staff assistant to the ambassador. From there, he'd been assigned to the U.S. consul general's office in Jerusalem. After three years he'd returned to Washington as a senior staff officer at State's operations center. During the previous administration, Hazleton had put in three and a half years of seven-day weeks as the nose-to-thegrindstone executive assistant to the deputy secretary of state. His reward had been a three-year assignment to the NSC and the title of special assistant for national security affairs to the president. Two years ago he'd been handed another plum assignment: this Moscow posting. Mort understood that if he kept the embassy running on an even keel, his next assignment would be as ambassador to a major post: Warsaw, perhaps, or even Prague.

Which is why Hazleton ordered the embassy staff to cancel all meetings with the SSCI delegation so he could meet with them privately and lay out the operational parameters under which they'd be constrained for the duration of their visit. Until they'd agreed to his rules of engagement, Mort didn't even want them in the building.

THERE WAS a thirty-second period of what radio talk-show hosts call "dead air" while Vacario glared angrily at the DCM.

Sam looked around impatiently. Where the hell was O'Neill? He was good at this kind of stuff. The lawyer was nonconfrontational, diplomatic, tactful—all the things Sam wasn't.

Right on cue, O'Neill appeared in the double doors of the restaurant. He scanned the low-ceilinged room, then immediately made his way to the table, skirting the three DynCorp contractor bodyguards who'd taken up seats in a protective arc around the DCM's chair. "Sorry, all." He cocked his head in Sam's direction. "You're looking a bit glum, old chap. Pale, too. Coming down with something?"

He didn't wait for Sam to answer, quickly extending a hand in the DCM's direction. "Michael O'Neill, Your Excellency," he said. "We were at Georgetown at the same time. You were a year behind me. We took the foreign service exam six months apart."

Hazleton's face lit up. "Morton Hazleton. Call me Mort. Nice to meet you, Michael."

"Mutual." O'Neill tossed his overcoat over the back of an adjacent chair while the others resumed their seats. He rolled a chair between Sam and the DCM and plunked himself down. "You edited the literary magazine, didn't you, Mort? First one ever to do so as a junior."

"I did," the diplomat said. "How ever did you remember?"

"Googled you before we left Washington, of course." O'Neill paused. "But in point of fact, when I saw the reference, I remembered how good the magazine was. You wrote one of the short stories. Didn't it win an award?"

OVER THE NEXT HALF HOUR Sam watched the coldness fade from Hazleton's face, read the shift in the diplomat's body language, and gave silent thanks for O'Neill's arrival.

The DCM drained his second cup of tea and set the delicate china precisely in its saucer. "Michael," Hazleton said, "if there is anything you need, all you have to do is ask. I'll do everything I can to be of assistance."

"You're an old-school gentleman," O'Neill said. "Thanks, Mort. I can tell you that the senator is going to be very impressed with the level of cooperation exemplified by you and your people." He raised his arm and signaled for a waiter. "I need another cuppa and so do you," he said, nodding in the DCM's direction. "Earl Grey and lemon, right? I can't get past the afternoon without it, either." He smiled amiably in the DCM's direction. "You probably know this joint, Mort. You got enough pull to get me crumpets and jam?"

6:15 P.M. Sam and O'Neill exited the Marriott's atrium, went through the double front doors, and began to stroll slowly around the perimeter of the Marriott.

Sam was happy simply to get outside. He'd started to feel claustrophobic in the low-ceilinged bar. His system needed the shock of Moscow's subzero temperature; he craved icy wind slapping him in the face. He'd been feeling queasy for most of the last half hour. Still, O'Neill's special brand of diplomacy had brought positive results. Ginny and Mort Hazleton had departed for the embassy on civil terms, and it appeared as if she was going to get her briefing after all. Sam put his arm on O'Neill's shoulder. "Nice work, Michael."

"Just doing my job." They turned the corner and moved off Tverskaya Street. "You okay?"

"I'll live." Instinctively, Sam had guided his friend against the traffic flow.

"I hope you're not coming down with the same bug as me." O'Neill adjusted the big fur hat he wore.

"I don't think so." That was the absolute truth. Sam's sickness wasn't the twenty-four-hour variety. He bit the inside of his cheek until he tasted blood. Irina's face disappeared. "Looks like we'll get a little cooperation from Mort, thanks to you."

"Well, I'd hate to be PNG'd[23] by one of our own diplomats, wouldn't you?" He saw the look on Sam's face. "Oops."

Sam's gloved hand went up, fingers spread wide. "No offense taken." They walked ten yards in silence. O'Neill hunched his shoulders and pulled the collar of his overcoat up against the wind.

Sam said, "So what was the criticom?"

"It has to do with Bonn."

"Bonn."

"Bonn. During the time you and I were in Paris, Ms. Virginia Vacario worked in Bonn."

[23] Declared persona non grata.

"What?" Sam was flabbergasted. "I didn't know that."

"It was a special position created by Justice. She did a fourteen-month tour as the assistant LEGATT[24]—concentration on counterterrorism and public integrity."

"Public integrity?"

"You know—bribes, visa fraud." O'Neill paused. "Traitors."

"She was working CI?"

"You got it, bud."

"Michael—where the hell did you hear this?"

"Remember, I still have friends in low places, Sam. And some of them even work in Moscow these days."

"When did you hear this?"

"Today. At lunch. My source served in Bonn the same time she was there."

"You certainly made a fast recovery, Michael. Last night I thought you were going to croak on me."

"There's nothing like strong tea, dry toast, a shot of Georgian cognac, and a double Imodium on the rocks to ease the pain," O'Neill said. "It was a twenty-four-hour bug, only I managed to compress it into twelve." He looked at Sam. "The LEGATT thing is only the half of it, Cyrus."

Sam wasn't in the mood to be playful. "Drop the other shoe, Michael."

"The CI operation was an Agency program. She was ultra-deep-cover. Recruited by and working for Langley."

"Bullshit."

"My source wouldn't BS me, Sam. My source owes me."

"Impossible." After all, Sam had The Knowledge. He'd never missed an Alien. Never.

But it wasn't impossible—and Sam knew it. The Agency was constantly running ultra-deep-cover programs. Two of

---

[24] An embassy's LEGal ATTaché. Most often an FBI special agent.

Sam's Marine Corps buddies had been recruited right out of the military. One had gone to the air marshal program and from there to the U.S. Customs Service, where he still worked delicate undercover assignments in the Middle East, playing the role of an arms dealer. The other was a twenty-year veteran of the State Department's Diplomatic Security Service, currently serving as the lead RSO, or regional security officer, in Tel Aviv.

But both former Marines served two masters. They performed their official jobs. They also reported to Langley, working under a special U.S. citizen's contract agreement, and reporting through a series of cutouts. There were scores—perhaps hundreds—of Langley operatives similarly embedded at other government agencies.

O'Neill paused. "So the question has to be asked, don't it, Cyrus?"

Sam halted as well. "The question."

"The question is, just who does the delectable Ms. Vacario really work for?"

"Delectable?"

"C'mon, this is me—SAMGRASS. I read you like a book. I was sick last night. You and Ms. Vacario had the evening all to yourselves."

"Come off it."

"Deny what you will, Cyrus," O'Neill said. "Body language don't lie." He took Sam by the arm and drew him close. "But here's where the prob gets thorny, old friend. Our late and unlamented pal Ed Howard was prowling and growling at about the same time you and I were in Paris and carry-you-back-to-old-Virginny was in Bonn. And we both know how . . . anxious Ed was to prove himself to his masters at Moscow Center."

Sam said nothing. But his emotions were churning.

"Who's to say he didn't do a little trolling, Cyrus?"

"It doesn't make sense."

"Oh, it makes perfect sense. A false flag recruitment—maybe through one of Moscow's BND[25] penetrations, or a Langley mole."

"You've always been skeptical about my mole theory, Michael."

"Skeptical don't mean I can't run some scenarios, old friend."

Sam bit his lower lip. It was perfect operational logic for the opposition. The Justice Department was one of Moscow Center's prime targets. And a false flag recruitment would be the obvious way to get inside. Sam had to admit to himself that O'Neill might be right. But he didn't say so. In fact, he said nothing.

It was O'Neill who picked up the slack. "Hence, my criticom," O'Neill said. "By the way, where were you all day?"

"I had a couple of meetings, too," Sam said obliquely.

"Get anything?"

"Nah." Sam shook his head. "Blind alley."

"Hmm," O'Neill grunted in response. "Well, if I can be of any help, Cyrus . . ."

Sam nodded. "You've already been a great help, Michael." But he said nothing further, and the two men walked in silence for the next few hundred yards.

It wasn't that Sam Waterman didn't trust O'Neill. He had—and he did. Now more than ever. But Sam considered his day's work as a compartmented op. And O'Neill didn't need access. Not yet, anyway.

Besides, unlike many of his former colleagues, Sam had never gossiped about his operations or his agents. Others

---

[25] Germany's intelligence service, formally known as the Bundesnacrichtendienst.

considered him paranoid. He simply thought of himself as prudent.

More pertinent was the fact that Sam hadn't established Ed Howard's true motives yet. And wouldn't do so until he'd had a look at what was on the pen drive—which wouldn't happen until he was securely back in Washington, if then. Indeed, while Sam had been shaken to the core by Irina's brutal murder, he wasn't about to be goaded into doing anything rash or impetuous.

From his very first days as a case officer, Sam had been schooled in prudence. The inculcation began during his initial overseas tour in the West German capital. In Bonn, Sam had been taken under the wing of the ▆▆▆▆ chief, a disheveled, pipe-smoking, fifty-eight-year-old veteran named Donald Kadick. Kadick was a soft-spoken, genteel Brahmin whom Sam at first dismissed as yet another of CIA's professorial eccentrics.

But he soon learned that Don Kadick was no muddle-minded academic. In fact, he was a legend in the Clandestine Service. He'd been one of Bill Donovan's ostiaries at OSS. A slightly built, bespectacled twenty-five-year-old Princeton grad, Kadick survived three nighttime jumps into occupied France, where he'd coordinated networks of anti-Nazi resistance fighters in the eight months prior to the Normandy invasion. By the age of thirty-six he was a tough-minded professional intelligence officer, fluent in Russian, Polish, German, and French. He'd recruited not one but two Soviet officers (one of whom Kadick convinced to purloin the complete technical manuals for the Red Army's T-54 battle tank), during his first overseas tour in postwar Berlin. In 1961, at the age of forty-two, Kadick had been selected by Director of Central Intelligence Allan Dulles to be one of two CIA case officers to meet, debrief, and then help run a GRU colonel working for MI6[26] named Oleg Penkovsky.

Sam first worked for Kadick in 1978. He'd been assigned to West Germany under consular cover, and his days were spent standing behind a teller's window in the consulate, stamping visas, answering inane queries, and examining reams of documents. It was tedious, boring, mind-numbing work. But at least, Sam rationalized every time he pored over yet another execrably written visa application, all his compulsory interaction with the locals allowed him to improve his German.

Kadick was a demanding boss, but generous with his time. He loved tradecraft, and often took time to show Sam one or another of the tricks he'd developed over the years. The reversible hat, the two-color boots, and the jacket that turned into an overcoat that Sam had worn to meet Irina had all originated with Don Kadick.

IN BONN, Sam was given three developmentals to run—handovers from his predecessor. The most promising seemed to be a Turkish émigré named Yavuz Ozkan, cryptonym DSBRONCO, who worked as a part-time janitor at the Polish embassy.

Sam, restless, ambitious, and energetic, was anxious to recruit the Turk after his fourth rendezvous. Don Kadick took a more cautious approach.

"He was a walk-in," the veteran explained.

"So what? Let's take yes for an answer and snap him up."

The ███████ chief scrunched closer to his desk, dropped his elbows onto the leather-bordered blotter pad, and peered

---

[26] MI6 is Britain's secret intelligence service, also known as SIS, whose operatives often work under FCO—Foreign and Commonwealth Office—cover.

at Sam through round-lensed, gold-framed glasses. "How long has he been a developmental, Sam?"

Sam thought about it. "Three months."

"How long have you been meeting with him?"

"Three weeks."

Kadick's watery gray eyes focused on Sam's face. "What's BRONCO's motivation, Sam?"

Sam blinked. It occurred to him at that instant that he hadn't the foggiest idea why Yavuz Ozkan had walked into the embassy, asked to speak to a security officer, and volunteered to spy for the United States. He lowered his gaze, embarrassed. "I don't know, Don."

The ████████ chief nodded. "Lesson one," he said. "Slow down. Before you take that final step, you have to learn everything about your developmentals. You have to discover what makes them tick. Sure, you have to probe their vulnerabilities, just the way you were taught at the Farm. But you also have to establish their motivation. You have to learn their quirks, their foibles, their idiosyncrasies." Kadick paused, allowing his words to sink in. "How much time did you spend reading Harry's reports before he turned BRONCO over to you?"

"I read 'em."

"Carefully?"

Sam's face reddened. Between eight hours a day in the teller's cage, a vigorous social schedule encouraged both by his State Department superiors and his bosses at the Agency, and the time required to learn the layout of the West German capital so he could perform surveillance detection routes, locate dead drops, and pinpoint agent meeting sites, Sam had put off studying his agents' files. But he was a Marine. He didn't make excuses. He simply sat there, embarrassed, humiliated, and silent.

The chief's tone softened. "I know how tough the schedule

is, Sam. But you have to do the homework. If you're going to do this job the way it should be done, you have to get inside people's heads. You have to be able to pick up inconsistencies—and that happens only if you're carrying the whole bloody case file in your head—which is why we spend all that time writing such detailed postmeeting reports—and reading them over and over and over before we go for a meet. Because if you're running six agents, it's nigh on impossible to keep all the details about each one of them in your head." The ███████ chief studied Sam's face to see what effect his words were having. Satisfied, he continued. "I don't believe in paperwork for paperwork's sake, Sam. But writing a good report is one of the keys to great agent handling. Because the more detail you are able to provide, the better armed you'll be to deal with these sons of bitches."

The ███████ chief looked at Sam's surprised expression. "Yes—no matter how much we coddle them, or play to their vulnerabilities, or encourage them, they're still sons of bitches to me. Don't forget: they're traitors. Spies. They're the ones betraying their side to us. And so, we have to know for sure whether they're on the up-and-up, or they're agents provocateurs." He looked across the desk at his protégé. "Slow down, Sam. Learn how to read this guy like a book. Take your time. Establish BRONCO's bona fides. And always, always remember that he was a walk-in."

Sam was confused. "What does being a walk-in have to do with it, Don?"

The ███████ chief lifted the antique Rosenthal cup at his elbow, sipped cold coffee, and gently replaced it on its scalloped saucer before he spoke. "Look," he said, "walk-ins can be extremely valuable. They're motivated by something external. Maybe they're being treated badly by the other side. Maybe they want revenge. Maybe they just want to get paid—or get laid. The key here, Sam, is that we weren't introduced to this guy at a cocktail party and then decided to target him. We didn't spot him at the Foreign Ministry and decide he could do us some good. We haven't singled him out because he guards the door of the defense minister's office and can tell us who comes and goes. We spot those sorts of targets, then we evaluate what they can do for us, and then we assess the possibilities while we develop them, and then, finally, after we've done our homework, we either recruit them or we drop them."

"I know—" Sam broke in.

"But walk-ins," the chief said before Sam could shoehorn another word in, "walk-ins, Sam—they're different. They target us, not the other way around. I'm not saying you should be paranoid. Paranoid is counterproductive. But you have to be careful. Take nothing at face value. Probe. Examine. Scrutinize. We don't want to get burned. If you're dealing with a walk-in, I say it's worth the trouble to go extra slow. Uncover his motivation. Double-check his stories, then check them again for inconsistencies. And finally, after you're sure he's proven himself, after we have established to our satisfaction—yours and mine—that he won't double on us, only then do we recruit him and run him."

I T WAS almost seven by the time Sam and O'Neill turned back onto Tverskaya Street and marched lockstep toward the bright lights of the Marriott's entrance. When they got there, O'Neill turned left and allowed the doorman to open the heavy glass door. But Sam took him by the arm and held him back. "Let's get a little more air, Michael." He waved the doorman off and guided the younger man around the corner.

Sam had planned to spend the next morning checking out the second site Ed Howard had mentioned—Pavel Baranov's mailbox in the Church of the Trinity in Serebryaniki. But Sam was so shaky emotionally he knew he'd have a hard time going "black." Operations demanded total focus and concentration. Sam's head was nowhere close to the black-ops zone. But there was a solution. O'Neill still had his Top Secret/SCI clearance. He'd send O'Neill to the Ukrainian quarter, have him scope the church out, and if everything was okay, check the mailbox for a second message from Howard.

Sam guided his old friend around the corner before he began speaking. Yes. It was time to open a compartment door for O'Neill.

And shut one for Virginia Vacario.

CHAPTER 18

THE WEATHER cleared overnight. The morning was stunningly bright and fiercely cold. Sam spent a second night with Ginny, returning to his own room a little after four.

But their lovemaking was far from successful. Sam found her withdrawn, even remote. The previous night she'd been delightfully open and candid—and her eyes reflected her state. Now she was guarded and cautious, her eyes probing, her questions attempting—although subtly—to breach the defenses around his state of mind.

After what he'd been through that day, Sam didn't waste any time at all. He dropped the portcullis, raised the draw-bridge, and retreated behind his emotional bulwarks.

So for her, too, there was a sensation of distance; a sudden aloofness in Sam she hadn't sensed before.

It was, she said to his back as he pulled his clothes on, "as if a wall of glass has come between us."

Sam knew she was right, of course. But he wasn't about to agree. So he reacted in exactly the way the instructors had taught him to deal with hostile situations at the Farm: *deny everything, admit nothing, file countercharges.* Glass-shmass. Everything was just fine. Didn't she understand this wasn't the time or the place to put their relationship under a microscope? Hadn't she herself told him the previous night that she hadn't been with anyone in a long time? "You said, 'I'm not used to this level of intimacy,'" he'd chided. "Well I'm not, either, Ginny—especially under the circumstances."

There, he was telling the truth. As a young case officer, Sam Waterman had had virtually no personal life. Indeed, shortly after he first arrived at Langley, the old-timers told him that recruiting a girlfriend would be tougher than recruiting a KGB *Rezident.* He didn't understand what they meant until he was posted to Bonn. Sam spent a fair amount of his time trolling for assets in the bars lining the streets of Bad-Godesburg, the picturesque suburb across the Rhine and near the embassy. At O'Halloran's, one of three Irish pubs where diplomats and German government workers hung out to drink draft Guinness and snack on *weisswurst,* he met a statuesque redhead bartender named Deirdre Shaughnessy and was smitten.

But there was a problem. Deirdre Shaughnessy was Irish. And so far as the Agency was concerned, her Irish nationality was a security problem. The unwritten rule was that case officers could date Americans, but that all foreigners with the exception of Brits, Canadians, and Australians—all of whom could be vetted through CIA's close liaison with their respective intelligence services—were off-limits.

Sam decided to disregard the rule. Three months later, he found himself the subject of a security investigation, when someone—Sam never learned who—turned him in on an LW-JAR report.

IT IS a little-known fact that the Security Division at Langley sends forms known as LW-JARs, twice a year to all

CIA facilities. Replies are mandatory. In the LW-JAR, case officers are required to disclose whether or not they are cohabiting with a foreign national in what the form describes as "a close and continuing relationship." Sam was therefore obligated to reply in full detail, describing the relationship with his cohabitee Deirdre, and providing information about said cohabitee's background.

Given the fact that Deirdre Shaughnessy had an Irish temper and every other week or so would toss his belongings out the third-story window of her tiny apartment, Sam rationalized that "close and continuing" did not accurately describe their relationship. Moreover, he guessed that any cohabitee with an Irish surname might fall under suspicion of being an agent for the Irish Republican Army—even though he knew that in Deirdre's case, the assumption was absurd. And so he submitted his LW-JAR form without disclosing the "close and continuing" nature of their relationship.

Someone else, however, snitched. The IRA was, after all, active in Germany. And since the organization was known by CIA to use Irish pubs to launder money and smuggle weapons and explosives, Langley was concerned enough to send a gumshoe to Bonn to interview Sam, who realized far too late that he could be reprimanded, sent home, or even fired if the Security Division deemed his relationship with the delectable Deirdre detrimental to the nation's interests.

The investigation was halted only after Don Kadick intervened. The ███████ chief told the investigator he'd done a clandestine background check on Deirdre Shaughnessy and it had come up negative. He insisted he had complete confidence in Sam. Then, in the presence of the security officer, he gave Sam a severe tongue-lashing.

At dinner that night, Kadick lectured the contrite young case officer on the need to keep the folks at Langley happy, ordered him to break things off with Deirdre, and advised him to date only Americans—preferably Americans with Top Secret security clearances—for the foreseeable future. Two weeks later the COS wrote a strong recommendation for Sam's early promotion to his old friend the assistant deputy director for operations.

Sam did exactly as he was told. He married an Agency reports officer six months before he was scheduled to leave Bonn. Her name was Janet Prescott, and Don Kadick, who was Sam's best man, referred to the pair in his wedding toast as Sam and Janet Evening. They put off the honeymoon until Sam's tour ended, then took three weeks to bicycle through France before returning to the States.

It was, however, a marriage of convenience. Passionate indeed, but closer in its frenetic rhythm to the short-lived romances of cruise ships or ski resorts. The relationship didn't last past Sam's second overseas tour. The break was amicable. There were no children, and his ex-wife soon remarried. The groom was a Romanoff who currently was assistant deputy director for collection.

After the divorce, Sam had had half a dozen long-term liaisons, always with American women, most of whom did in fact have Top Secret clearances. His most recent had been a two-year affair with the Moscow embassy's chief admin officer.

So Ginny had been right, Sam had to admit to himself as he stood in the shower. A wall of glass had indeed descended between them. Of course it had. O'Neill's revelation had rocked him—and had changed the way he thought about her.

He was tremendously attracted to her. He wanted a long-term relationship and all the trappings that went with one: intimacy, sharing, and trust, to name just three. But Vacario's motives were now suspect. Sam couldn't put out of his head the possibility that she was playing a long-term political game, and she was using him as a fulcrum to achieve her goals. And then there was the fact that she'd been working for CIA covertly in Bonn at the same time Edward Howard had been trolling for American assets in the German capital, and had not told him about it. *There are no coincidences.*

The implications of that truism were hugely unsettling. Unsettling because Sam believed with every molecule of his body that moles did indeed exist burrowed deep inside the American intelligence community. Unsettling because Sam was convinced he'd always been correct in his contention that Rick Ames, Harold Nicholson, and even Bobby Hanssen were disposables, set up to draw attention away from Moscow's most valuable human assets. Which meant secrets were still being stolen, and the Russians had high-ranking agents still in place. And where better to find secrets than to work for Senate Select, where many of CIA's jewels were displayed on a regular basis.

But if that scenario was true, what were Vacario's motivations? Sam understood that all recruitments, whether ours or theirs, could be defined under four broad categories of vulnerability, those being money, ego, sex, and ideology. Once you spotted a target you thought might be suitable, you assessed their vulnerabilities. Did they need money? Could you cajole them through flattery, or with sex? Could you prey on their ideology?

In France, Sam had recruited a left-wing member of the French parliament by using a Palestinian access agent to tweak the target's blatant anti-Semitism. The Palestinian convinced the lawmaker he would help defeat Israel by handing over reports detailing DST surveillance of Mossad operations tracking Fatah operatives in France so that the Palestinian groups could take countermeasures that would increase their security. In fact, CIA was passing the reports to Mossad so that the Israelis knew what the French were up to.

In return, Israeli intelligence passed CIA information about French-supplied components for Iraqi weapons of mass destruction, as well as updates on Moscow Center's activities in France.

Sam knew Howard had used false flag operations in the past. Could Vacario have been recruited through one? He had to admit that the possibility existed. She might have been approached by a German official and asked to exchange information—something innocent. Then the ratcheting up would start. It wasn't so far-fetched. Once Vacario had passed even a single sensitive document, she would be compromised—especially if there were photographs. Hell, if he were in Edward Lee Howard's shoes, Ginny Vacario would be a prime target.

Why the hell hadn't she told him? What was she hiding? Sam tilted his face under the showerhead and let the water cascade over him. Nothing was simple. Nothing.

SAM CALLED Michael O'Neill at seven-fifteen. "Drop by for breakfast, will you?"

"I'm already on my way."

Sam turned the television set on and adjusted the volume. Sixty seconds later there was a "shave and a haircut—two bits" tapping at Sam's door. He saw O'Neill adjusting his tie through the peephole and unlatched the security lock.

"C'mon in." Sam pointed at the tray holding a pot of coffee, two cups, a platter of coarse black bread, and a ramekin of butter. "Serve yourself."

"*Bal'shoye spaciba,* Sam." O'Neill poured himself a coffee, added milk, stirred, and sipped.

"*Nichevo,* Michael." Sam pointed toward the television. "I see you've been studying the Russian phrasebook. You ready?"

"Locked and loaded."

"Good. Then have a look at this."

O'Neill followed Sam to the set. Atop it, Sam had placed a map of central Moscow. He unfolded the map and put his finger atop the site of the Marriott. "This is us." He traced the cleaning route he wanted O'Neill to take. "Make sense?"

The lawyer's head bobbed up and down. "Just as we discussed."

Sam pulled the wallet from his jacket, extracted his *transportnaya karta,* and handed it to O'Neill. "You'll need this for the metro."

O'Neill pulled an identical ticket out of his shirt pocket. "Keep it. I already bought my own." He ran his finger along the route Sam had shown him. "Okay: I walk the first two legs—sixteen minutes each. Then I take Green to Belorusskaya, grab Circle Line to Taganskaya, then Line Six to Kitay-Gorod. I walk the last three legs. Ten minutes, sixteen minutes, twenty minutes."

"Right. The whole route should take you about one and three quarter hours."

"And if there's surveillance, I'll—"

"If there is any sign of surveillance whatsoever, Michael, you break off. You abort—full stop. We don't want a flap. Remember what the senator said."

"Amen to that." O'Neill nodded, his face grim. "But if it's clear for a go, I'll be prepared."

"You have gloves?"

O'Neill patted himself down. "Oh, for chrissakes, Cyrus . . ."

"Not to worry." Sam went to his shaving kit, unfastened the secret compartment, extracted a set of latex gloves, and handed them to O'Neill. "Here you go, Edward."

"Thanks." O'Neill stuffed the gloves into his the breast pocket of his jacket so the fingers poked out like a handkerchief. "Will that do?"

"Get serious."

"I am serious." O'Neill stuffed the gloves into his pocket. "Sam, what if the letterbox is empty?"

"Then it's empty," Sam said.

"And if there's mail?"

"If there's mail, do nothing. Come back, let me know, and I'll find a way to get at it. I don't want you running around Moscow with anything that could get you in trouble. You need to be discreet."

"I take great offense at that remark." O'Neill slurped his coffee noisily. "I am the sine qua non of discretion."

"Just be careful," Sam said. "With Howard dead, we have to assume that we are being tracked. Every move."

O'Neill's expression grew serious. "Understood." He pulled the pocket watch out of his vest. "I'll split in fifteen minutes—height of rush hour." He looked at Sam. "What's on your schedule today?"

Sam had plans but he wasn't about to divulge them. "I'm meeting Ginny for coffee at ten. She has an appointment at the Foreign Ministry at one, and wants to go over some questions."

"How's the relationship coming?"

"There is no relationship."

In response, O'Neill's index fingertip tugged at the skin just below his right eye. "C'mon, Cyrus . . ."

Sam wasn't about to say anything more. "You're not cleared high enough to know."

AT TEN-TEN Sam was standing in the lobby waiting impatiently for Ginny to show up when his cell phone rang. He pulled it out of his pocket. "Waterman."

"Sam, it's me."

"Michael?"

"I'm, ah, in a police station," O'Neill said. "I was wondering whether you could come on down and help me straighten things out. There has been a humongous misunderstanding."

"Where are you?"

There was a pause. "It's a police station on the edge of the Ukrainian quarter. The chap who speaks English says you walk east on Ulitsa Maroseyka from the Kitay-Gorod metro stop, past the Belarus embassy. The station is opposite—" There was a pause. Then O'Neill, sounding hugely stressed, said, "It's across from Petrovsomething alley. Sam—they put a machine gun to my head. A machine gun! Get me the hell out of this mess."

CHAPTƎЯ 19

10:45 A.M. They'd locked O'Neill in a cage. He was sitting manacled to the arm of a steel chair that was bolted to the floor in the center of a four-foot-deep, four-foot-wide, eight-foot-high, steel-framed cube made of chain link and roofed over with razor wire. He looked as pitiful as a pound dog.

When he saw Sam he strained against the cuffs. "Sam—I'm getting claustrophobic. Get me out. Get me out."

"I'll do my best." Sam gave O'Neill a hopeful smile and a thumbs-up. Then he flashed his official passport at the desk sergeant and asked to speak to whoever was in charge of the man in the cage. The officer picked up a phone and made a call while Sam stood there. Five minutes later, he was escorted through a steel door, ushered down an L-shaped, puke green corridor, marched around the corner past a lavatory, parked on a sturdy wood bench with graffiti carved on its arms and seat outside a pockmarked metal door with a pane of frosted glass so old it had turned yellow, and instructed to wait until summoned.

After forty-five minutes the door opened and he was beckoned into a messy office by an overweight, bushy-haired man who carried a Tokarev pistol jammed in the waistband of a pair of brown tweed trousers shiny on the seat. A set of American-style handcuffs hung loose over the rear of his belt. Without a word the Russian closed the heavy door behind them and walked to the desk, standing with his back to the American, concentrating on some documents. Finally, he flipped the papers over so they couldn't be read, then turned. "You wanted to see me?" he said in English.

Sam spoke in Russian. "Good morning, Detective. My name is Samuel Waterman. I'm a member of a United States congressional staff delegation visiting Moscow on behalf of a committee of the United States Senate, and I understand you have arrested one of our members over a misunderstanding of some sort."

"Ah. So we have here a misunderstanding," the policeman said in Moscow-accented Russian. He walked around the desk and pulled a pack of Marlboros out of the suit jacket he'd tossed over the chair back. He took one then flipped the pack atop the desk, tamped the filter end of the cigarette on the crystal of a thick chronograph, lit it with what looked to Sam to be a vintage Zippo lighter, inhaled deeply, and then turned to focus on his visitor. "You have extremely good Russian, Comrade Congressional Staff Delegation Member Waterman."

Sam said, "Thank you, Detective."

"It is not common for an American visitor to speak with a Moscow accent."

"I used to live here."

"Did you, now." The Russian nudged a pile of documents with his buttock, then sat on the edge of the desk. "My name is Danilov." He looked evenly at Sam. "Chief Inspector Danilov."

Danilov extended his hand. Sam took it and shook it, noting that it was cold. So that was why he'd been kept waiting. Danilov had been called in. Police? Perhaps. But more likely FSB. Sam looked past the desk and saw a second doorway, partially concealed by a coatrack.

The Russian looked evenly at Sam. "May I see your credentials, please?"

Sam took out his pocket secretary and extracted the black official passport and laminated U.S. Senate photo ID, and handed them over.

"Thank you." Danilov examined the passport. He looked first at Sam's Russian visa, holding it up to the light. He ran his thumb over the ID card and squinted at the photo page of the passport. "Recently issued. Congratulations on your new job, Congressional Staff Delegation Member Waterman." He paused, then said, "Excuse me, please," and left the room.

Three minutes later he was back, holding a photocopy of the passport and ID. He handed the originals to Sam, who stowed them.

Danilov waited for Sam to say something else. When he didn't, the Russian said, " 'Arrest' is a very strong word, Congressional Staff Delegation Member Waterman." He took a deep drag on the cigarette and expelled smoke simultaneously from both his nostrils and his mouth. "As of this moment, we have simply detained your colleague." He brandished the cigarette at Sam. "Good. American. Would you like one?"

"No, thank you . . ." Sam watched as the hint of a smirk crossed the Russian's thick-browed face. "*Comrade* Danilov."

The Russian grinned. "Ah, the good old days. No, today I am simply Citizen Danilov." He paused. "That sounds like something out of *Les Mis,* doesn't it?"

Sam said, "You're no policeman, Citizen Danilov."

"Oh, I am," Danilov said. "But I handle . . . sensitive matters."

Sam cut to the chase. "On what charges is my friend being held?"

"He was tampering with an icon in the Church of the Trinity in Serebryaniki," Danilov said matter-of-factly. "One of the priests thought he was a Chechen terrorist planting a bomb and called the police. A special operations team responded. They detained your colleague."

"He says they put a machine gun to his head."

"I wouldn't be surprised. That is generally the practice when a special operations team is summoned."

"But my colleague—"

"A priest thought your colleague was planting a bomb. We have only recently experienced a terrorist incident in which more than a hundred people died. Chechen bombers could be anywhere. Our churches are obvious targets for these Islamist scum. Frankly, Congressional Staff Delegation Member Waterman, your colleague is lucky he wasn't shot dead. We are very touchy about bombs these days." Danilov paused. "In any case, the OMON team brought him here, where it was discovered he was an American working for the government and carrying an official passport. The second-in-command of this station called me in, as I have experience in diplomatic matters."

"Where do things stand?"

"At the moment," Danilov said, "no formal charges have been made. As yet, no paperwork has been filed."

Sam nodded. "That is good news."

"Yes, but there are complications."

Sam cocked an eyebrow. "Complications?"

"Your colleague says he picked up the icon because he found it fascinating." Danilov switched to English. " 'Unique and exceptional' were the precise words he used. But . . ."

Sam wasn't surprised at the Russian's fluency. "But?"

"He was wearing latex gloves, Congressional Staff Delegation Member Waterman. This is not something tourists generally do."

"Maybe he has allergies," Sam said. "Perhaps he is extremely sensitive to dust."

"Allergies." Danilov cocked his head. "Then he should stay out of old churches."

"If life were only that simple, Citizen Danilov."

"If only it were, Congressional Staff Delegation Member Waterman."

"But nothing was damaged," Sam said. "And nothing was taken, correct?" That was important. If the mailbox had been empty, then O'Neill had nothing incriminating on him—except the gloves. Which meant there was little the Russians could do, except try to scare the hell out of the poor guy, something they were obviously doing.

"Correct." Danilov interrupted Sam's train of thought. "Nothing was disturbed or taken."

"Then I am hoping this episode can be solved without making unnecessary waves." Indeed, Sam had the means to smooth things over right in his pocket, too: a thick wad of hundred-dollar bills. "A sizable contribution to the church might go a long way in making the incident disappear, don't you think? And perhaps a contribution to the OMON widows and orphans fund as well."

"It might be possible," the Russian said. "If we could reach a suitable agreement. Of course—" The phone on the desk bringg-bringged. Danilov stopped in midsentence and picked it up. "Danilov." He listened in silence, then replaced the receiver without saying good-bye. "It would seem, Congressional Staff Delegation Member Waterman," he said grimly, "that your enlightened suggestion has just become moot." He looked at Sam. "Your friend outside has just done a very stupid thing."

"What happened? Is he all right?"

"Physically? Yes. Mentally, I'm not so sure."

"What the hell did he do?"

Danilov slipped into Russian "Your friend had a cell phone in his pocket. For some reason—and believe me I intend to find out why—it wasn't taken away from him after he called you. Somehow, he has just managed to place a call to the American embassy. He was yelling about being tortured before they got the phone away from him."

"Oh, Christ." How could O'Neill have done something so stupid?

"Your embassy is responding. So matters are no longer in my hands," the Russian said. "I am truly sorry." He looked at Sam's face, his expression somber. "You are known to us, of course. You served your country as best you could, just as I serve mine. But your colleague out there—" Danilov hooked his thumb toward the front of the building. "Worse than an amateur."

"How do you mean?"

"This cell-phone business is stupid. And from what I understand he entered the church, walked up to the icon, and took it without even a cursory check to see if anyone else was in the sanctuary. Between the latex gloves and the manner in which he acted, the priest thought he was a Chechen planting a bomb. What was he *thinking*?"

Sam shrugged. But the Russian's description rocked him. O'Neill's tradecraft had always been acceptable, if not gifted. Of course, O'Neill hadn't practiced tradecraft in almost nine years. "My colleague is a former diplomat," Sam said, tossing a handful of chaff in Danilov's direction. "He's a lawyer."

"He must not have been very good as a diplomat," Danilov snorted derisively. "He's *zalupa*—a dickhead."

12:20 P.M. By the time the embassy contingent arrived, Sam had already negotiated O'Neill's release from the cage. Danilov had seen to it straightaway. Then Sam browbeat the contrite O'Neill. The last thing they'd needed, he said, was to cause a flap. Phoning the embassy had been incredibly stupid and imprudent. Adverse publicity, he told O'Neill, would cause Rand Arthur, who'd been nervous about sending them to Moscow in the first place, to go ballistic. "It was bad enough for you to get yourself picked up doing something dumb like handling an icon without permission." Sam spoke loud enough for Danilov to hear. "But once you were detained, it was imperative to keep this whole mess quiet." Sam shook his head. "I was on the verge of straightening everything out, Michael. What on earth were you thinking?"

O'Neill appeared to be on the verge of tears. "You disappeared for like an *hour,* Sam. I didn't know what was happening. I was claustrophobic. I couldn't breathe. Sam, they rushed me. They were all dressed in black. Wearing masks and carrying guns. They put a *gun* to my head. A machine gun. The *muzzle,* Sam, the muzzle was pressed against my head." He touched his left temple with a finger. "See? They cut me with the front sight thingy."

Sam examined O'Neill's forehead. "Michael—it's just a scratch."

"It didn't feel that way." O'Neill's eyes widened. "And they dragged me, Sam. Handcuffed my arms behind my back and dragged me by my hair."

"They thought you were a Chechen terrorist, Michael." Sam exhaled. "And no matter what happened, you saw me arrive. You knew I'd get you out."

O'Neill hung his head. "I admit it. I panicked. I hadn't heard a word from you in an hour and I just bloody panicked."

"That's an understatement." Sam eased his tone. He looked down at his friend and tried to sound reassuring. "Let's hope for the best."

But Sam understood *merde* had really hit *ventilateur* when the embassy motorcade pulled up in front of the police station. He peeked outside. Mort Hazleton, Ginny Vacario, the vice consul, two junior political officers, and an FSN interpreter were riding in the DCM's armored Caddie Brougham, the U.S. flag displayed on the right front fender. The limo was tailed by a Diplomatic Security war wagon flashing red-and-blue bar lights, complete with two junior consular officers armed with clipboards and pens, plus three ARSOs[27] dressed in ninja black and toting submachine guns and sidearms.

The DCM swept into the police station followed by the rest of the entourage from the limo.

Sam didn't like it. Danilov liked it even less.

The Americans were immediately met by a line of Moscow policemen who blocked their way. When the DCM tried to push his way through the human wall, Danilov barked an order. The police drew their batons and raised them horizontally, creating a barrier. Then the line of cops moved forward, forcing the Americans back toward the doors.

Sam caught Danilov's eye. "Please . . ."

The Russian's arm went up. The police line stopped moving.

Sam edged between the line of officers just as Mort Hazleton pushed his way forward, the interpreter at his shoulder.

---

[27] Assistant Regional Security Officers are Diplomatic Security Service special agents assigned to embassies.

The DCM cocked his head in Danilov's direction. "Ask if he is in charge."

Danilov didn't bother waiting until the FSN finished. He answered in English, "Yes, Mr. Deputy Chief of Mission, I am Chief Inspector Danilov and I am in charge."

Hazleton waved his right index finger petulantly under Danilov's nose. "How dare you chain a United States official in a cage like some animal. How dare you beat him. I am planning to send a démarche to the Foreign Ministry over the mistreatment of this important U.S. government official."

Danilov shrugged helplessly at Sam, turned toward Mort Hazleton, and switched into Russian. "Then there is nothing more to be discussed, sir. You and your invaders will leave this police station immediately or you will all be detained," he said. He waited for the translator to finish. "Moreover, you should understand that your so-called official was caught using espionage equipment. If you choose to make an official protest, we will be forced to publicly identify him as a spy and demand his immediate expulsion from sovereign Russian territory."

Before the interpreter had finished, Sam stepped between the two men. He looked at Danilov. "*Pazhalsta*—please, Chief Inspector," he said in rapid Russian, "let me try to work out something mutually agreeable?"

Danilov cocked a thick eyebrow in Hazleton's direction and answered Sam in Russian. "If that asshole can be made to see reason," he said, watching as the translator suppressed a bemused look. "But I doubt it."

"At least let me try." Sam beckoned Virginia Vacario over. Then he put his hand on the DCM's shoulder. "Mort, let's the three of us talk in the corner for a second, okay?"

Hazleton opened his mouth to protest, but when he saw the look on Sam's face and read Vacario's concerned expression, he snapped his jaw shut. The diplomat scowled at Danilov, but also moved in the direction Sam was indicating.

Sam herded the DCM and Vacario around the cage and across the stone floor to the far corner of the drab station. He made sure that the DCM had a clear view of Michael O'Neill, who was sitting on a bench behind the cage, sandwiched between two uniformed officers. "Take a look, Mort: Michael's just fine. He panicked." Then Sam pointed at the Russians and Americans, who were standing nose to nose. "Mort, this is overkill."

The DCM crossed his arms. "You should have heard his voice," he said. "He reached me on my cell phone. He was screaming that he was chained in a cage and the police were beating him."

Vacario said, "Obviously, Mort, that's not the case."

When the DCM nodded in agreement, Sam said, "Nobody wanted this situation." He moved his head in Danilov's direction. "Look—Michael was sightseeing. He picked up an icon. A priest thought he was a Chechen terrorist and called the cops. An OMON SWAT team responded, and they roughed O'Neill up a little bit. Then they brought him back here and the cops discovered who he was. Michael called me, I rushed over and met with Danilov. He realized the gravity of the mistake, and was willing to make the whole thing go away."

"He is?"

"He *was*—until you showed up with machine guns and started making threats."

Hazleton blinked. "Michael said—"

"I don't give a damn what Michael said," Sam interrupted. "Michael was obviously having the mother of all anxiety attacks."

Hazleton said, "What was that crack Danilov made about spying?"

"O'Neill was wearing rubber gloves inside the church," Sam said quickly. "It's nothing."

"Rubber gloves?"

"It's an allergy thing—dust."

The DCM looked perplexed. "But—"

Vacario caught the look on Sam's face and broke in. "This is a complete disaster, y'know." She shot the DCM a nasty glance. "It's all your fault, Mort."

"All *my* fault?" Hazleton crossed his arms. "I'm not the one they took for a bomb-throwing Chechen. You insisted you wanted a strong response. You said—your exact words, Ms. Vacario—'I want a strong response, or the chairman will hear about this.'"

"That was before we got here and discovered Sam had the situation under control."

"Nobody knew." Hazleton looked accusingly at Sam. "You should have called and explained what was going on."

"Mort," Sam said, "the whole idea was to solve this problem without involving the embassy."

"Well, the embassy has become involved." The DCM removed his eyeglasses, fogged them with his breath, and rubbed them clean with a pocket handkerchief. "So what do you suggest?"

"Honestly? A tactical retreat," Sam said. "Declare victory. Congratulate Danilov for taking O'Neill out of the cage as soon as he realized what was happening. Assure him there will be no démarche. Then take everybody back to the embassy and make sure nobody—*nobody*—writes anything down. You save face, and you allow Danilov to save face."

The DCM said, "Hmm."

"As soon as you're gone, I'll work things out. Then I'll bring Michael straight back to the hotel so we can pack." Sam gave Vacario a quick glance. "We're going to have to cut our visit short."

She looked at him quizzically.

"There's no way we can get the information the chairman's looking for now," Sam said. He turned to face Mort Hazleton. "Look, Mort: let me try to fix this my way. Once I get O'Neill released, I promise we'll be out of your hair as soon as we can get seats."

The DCM looked hugely relieved. "I'll do everything I can to help you leave quietly."

I'll bet you will, Sam thought. But he stuck his hand out. "Thanks, Mort."

"My pleasure," Hazleton nodded. "But no reports filed—by either side, right?" He stared at Sam. "That's critical."

Sam understood only too well. If Danilov filed a report and Hazleton didn't, the American would be put at a disadvantage in the bureaucratic paper wars.

"I can't guarantee anything," Sam said. "But obviously, keeping this whole matter quiet is in everyone's interest— theirs as well as ours." He glanced over his shoulder. "So, shall I talk to Danilov?"

The DCM straightened his glasses, and adjusted his French cuffs to better display his blue, white, and gold enamel White House cuff links. "Do it," he sighed.

EVEN WITH THE EMBASSY pulling strings, the earliest flight on which the three of them could get business-class seats was the next day's Air France to Paris. That meant spending the night at Charles de Gaulle and taking a connecting Delta flight to Dulles the following morning. So they spent what was left of the afternoon sightseeing, driven about in an embassy station wagon and accompanied by an unhappy FSO Grade Four minder from the consul general's office, who ushered them through Red Square, the Patriarchs' Palace, the Cathedrals of the Assumption and the Annunciation, the tombs of the czars, the huge czar's cannon, and the Kremlin Armory.

The FSO kept up a constant mantra reminding O'Neill not to touch anything. Mort Hazleton was obviously taking no chances.

The three of them had dinner in the Marriott's rooftop restaurant, shadowed by an American minder and two Russian gumshoes. O'Neill was uncharacteristically glum, and his mood affected the other two. Sam understood the lawyer was feeling pretty guilty about his screwup.

Well, he should. Sam had planned to slip outside Moscow and search Edward Howard's dacha. That hunting trip was now out of the question.

Ginny excused herself early. Her demeanor and body language told Sam loud and clear not to visit. So Sam and O'Neill drank Georgian brandy and smoked Cuban cigars, but hardly spoke. Just past ten-thirty, they left their Churchills half-finished and took the elevator, rode in silence to the eighth floor, and walked awkwardly in side-by-side lockstep to their rooms.

Sam inserted his key card halfway into the reader and turned toward O'Neill's back. "G'night, Michael."

The lawyer waved offhandedly and disappeared through his door without a word.

Sam looked past O'Neill's room toward Ginny's door. Then the electronic latch opened, he turned the handle and went inside to spend the night alone.

SAM SPENT the following morning walking the Arbat alone, too—alone, that is, except for the FSB surveillance team that picked him up as he came through the Marriott's atrium. They were so obvious that he understood the Russians wanted him to know he was being followed. So he made things easy for them. He walked at a leisurely pace to the Pushkinskaya metro stop, then followed the underground passage to the No. 8 Line, rode one stop to Borovitskaya, took the escalator to the street, then strode along Znamenka Street until he came to the pedestrian underpass at the huge square leading to Ulitsa Arbat.

He emerged near two armored personnel carriers with counterterrorist troops lounging in the morning sunlight, then elbowed his way along the crowded Arbat, past the fast-food joints and the old Peace Wall with its Cold War, anti-Reagan Star Wars tiles. He riffled through stacks of old prints, examined antique maps, and pawed over trays of Soviet-era military medals. He found one exquisite—and authentic—Order of Lenin decoration and bought it for Ginny. Fifty yards down the street he purchased a reproduction of an OMON SWAT-team patch for Michael O'Neill.

At a *matryoshka* vendor just off Kalosin Lane, opposite the old Vakhtangov Theater, he bought two set of dolls. The first one chronicled the love life of William Jefferson Clinton; the second displayed the Bush-family political dynasty—with a camouflage-and-kaffiyah-clad Usama bin Laden as the final minidoll. He looked for, but could not find, a set of KGB *matryoshkas* like the ones Pavel Baranov had bought for him in Zagorsk.

When Sam got back to the hotel just after one-thirty, he found a message from Mort Hazleton advising that an embassy car would pick them up at four, and that he, Ginny, and O'Neill would be given diplomatic courtesy at the airport. He also discovered that the subtle intrusion-alert devices he'd placed on his baggage and his briefcase had been tampered with. He conducted a thorough examination of his belongings, making piles of his stuff as if he was laying everything out prior to packing—which of course he was.

The search had been professional. Every sheet of paper and news clip in his files had been replaced in exactly the order Sam had put them—although they'd probably been photographed. His shaving kit, a common venue for concealed items, had been gone through. Sam knew that because he'd set the jar and tube tops in a certain way and he could see they'd been opened and rescrewed. His tradecraft clothes had been examined. He wouldn't be able to use them in Moscow again—not that he'd ever visit.

He picked up his keys and examined the flag-themed plastic egg he'd removed from Ed Howard's dead drop. The pen drive had been opened—the light film of dust he'd sprayed on a portion of its surface at 6 A.M. was gone. But the USB tab hadn't been inserted in a USB slot. Sam knew that because the eyelash hair he'd positioned just inside the slot opening with his tweezers was still in position. He snapped the egg closed, dropped the keys back into his book bag, and resumed packing.

3:20. Sam finished and gave the room a once-over. He pulled his coat and scarf out of the closet, running his hand along the high shelf to make sure he hadn't left anything behind. He locked his suitcase, shoved the scarf through one of the overcoat's arms, draped the coat over his one-suiter carry-on bag, then propped himself on the bed, hands clasped behind his head, staring at the blank TV screen across the room.

Seventy-two hours ago, he'd come to Moscow all pumped up, excited to be back in the game. As they'd driven into the city from Sheremetevo, Sam had experienced a surge of self-validation he hadn't experienced in some years. He'd been elated, energized, euphoric. Now he was leaving unfulfilled, depressed, and miserable, unsure of what he'd accomplished—if, that is, he'd accomplished anything at all.

Irina Howard was dead—certainly in part because of him. He'd become involved with Ginny Vacario against his better judgment. O'Neill had volunteered to check Pavel Baranov's mailbox in the Serebryaniki church in the Ukrainian quarter, and even that simplest of ops had gone terribly wrong. Sam ran his hand into his trouser pocket and jingled his house keys, fingering the pen drive. If *that* turned out to be worthless, then this whole trip had been for nothing, and a woman was dead.

But the signs had all been clear—unmistakable. Messages that left no room for interpretation. And each one had been carefully constructed by Edward Lee Howard, as if he knew he would be murdered, and wanted to leave a trail that could be followed. *There are no coincidences.*

No coincidences indeed. And then, in an epiphany, Sam realized what had happened. He'd lost control. He was being moved to and fro like some damn chess piece on a board. Manipulated. Pushed. Directed.

Don Kadick would have known how to deal with the problem. Sam wished he could call his old mentor for advice. But Kadick was long gone. Eaten alive by cancer. Sam cracked his knuckles.

So, how would Don Kadick have dealt with this? He would, Sam quickly surmised, have found some way to go on the offensive.

Russians are like submariners, he'd once told Sam. When Sam looked puzzled, Kadick had elaborated. "Russians make lists and operate off those lists. Look at their military doctrine: it's inflexible; unyielding. They're fighting in Afghanistan the same way they did in World War Two. What does that tell you, Sam? It tells you loud and clear that the Russian game plan is rigid. The KGB's no different than the Red Army. It's a huge, centralized bureaucracy. And Moscow Center doesn't give its case officers the same operational flexibility we give you, because Moscow Center doesn't trust its people to think for themselves. So, if you provoke, goad, incite—anything to disrupt Lubyanka's game plan, you will prevail."

The phone rang, jolting him out of his reverie. It was the desk. The embassy car had arrived. He swung off the bed. It was time to move. Oh, yes it was.

PART IV

PARIS

CHAPTЭЯ 20

SATURDAY, NOVEMBER 9, 2002

IT WAS RAINING when they arrived at de Gaulle; a steady, drenching downpour that could be felt even inside the concrete-and-glass terminal. Sam shifted his carry-on bag from his left to his right shoulder as they trudged along a damp carpet down the long, chilly passageway leading to the passport control barrier between the F and D Terminals.

If they'd been traveling as everyday tourists, passport control would have been unnecessary. They could have simply shown their passports to the guard at the exit barrier, then left the terminal and caught the tram to the de Gaulle Sofitel. But they had French visas in their official passports, and so the documents would have to be stamped.

They were about halfway to passport control when Sam made his move. Abruptly, he veered toward one of the stairways that led down to the street-level exits. "See you guys back in Washington."

O'Neill came to a sudden halt. "Where the hell are you going?" he shouted at Sam's back.

Sam stopped and turned. "Into the city," he said. "There's something I have to do."

O'Neill dropped his bag onto the carpet in obvious exasperation "But we have to get our passports stamped."

Sam reached into his jacket pocket and withdrew a blue-covered passport. "I brought the regular one, too. They'll wave me though at the control kiosk downstairs."

Virginia Vacario set her carry-on down. "Sam, what in heaven's name is going on?"

"I told you. There's something I want to check out."

Vacario shot a worried look at Michael O'Neill. "We didn't bring regular passports. Wait for us to get our passports stamped, and we'll all go together."

He looked back at her. "Sorry, Ginny—no can do." He hefted his carry-on higher onto his shoulder and adjusted his grip on the leather document case. "I'll call you later." Then he bolted. At the bottom of the stairs he stopped long enough to check his six and was relieved to see they hadn't tried to follow him.

Sam pushed through the revolving doors and headed for the cab stand. He jogged to the *station de taxis* and, checking to make sure O'Neill and Vacario were still nowhere in sight, jumped into the cab at the head of the line. *"Paris—8 Place St. Augustin, s'il vous plaît."*

11:20 P.M. The Cercle National des Armées, Paris's largest military club, takes up much of the northern side of the Place St. Augustin, which lies at the intersection of the Boulevard Malesherbes and Boulevard Haussmann in the city's fashionable eighth arrondissement. Sam had become a member during his tour as deputy ████ chief, sponsored by a colonel in the French Army's Centre d'Exploitation du Renseignement,[28] and he stayed at the Cercle whenever he visited Paris. It was like an old pair of boots: comfortable and well broken in.

He barged through the automatic doors, shook himself off like a wet dog, walked to the desk, showed his membership card, and asked for a room facing the square. Most of the rooms on the club's north and west sides looked out on the drab rear end of an Army barracks, and Sam preferred the view of the square, with its shops and cafés and the Eiffel Tower in the distance, or a northwest view that looked out on the hulking Cathedral St. Augustin.

The receptionist checked the computer, punched in Sam's membership code, then gave him a key card. He handed his bags and a two-euro coin to the bellman, who took them upstairs. Then he bought a ten-euro phone card at the cashier, borrowed one of the club's big black umbrellas from the concierge, and headed out into the rain to find something to eat.

1:45 P.M. Sam furled the umbrella, and stomped inside Café Rome, one of half a dozen anonymous bars and cafés sitting cheek by jowl on the rue de Rome, directly across the perpetually under construction Place Péri from the Gare St. Lazare railroad station. Most of the bistros were closed. But the Rome, a favorite of taxi drivers, was open every day but Sunday until 2 A.M. and served food until half past midnight.

Sam found a table in the rear with a good view of the square and sat with his back against the wall. He'd used this place before. The location was ideal. There were seven

---

[28] The Center for Intelligence Exploitation is a subsection of the army's Second Division, known as Division du Renseignement, or Intelligence Division, which reports to the national defense staff.

streets that emptied into the bustling square, all of them one-way. The restaurant—depending on where one sat, the hour, and the volume of the traffic—afforded a view of up to five, which allowed for effective countersurveillance.

When the laconic waiter finally deigned to visit his table, Sam ordered a half-liter *pichet* of Fleurie, a hangar steak *à point,* and *une chlorophylle,* café shorthand for a greens-only salad. He waited for the wine to arrive, poured a half glass, and sipped. It was fresh, fruity, and cellar-cool. The steak and salad followed. Sam ate quickly, hungry after the long day of travel. He finished the food and polished off the last of his wine, called for the bill, and laid cash on the small tray. Then he pushed away from the table and headed to the pay phone affixed to the wall between the end of the bar and the short corridor leading to the lavatories and the manager's office. He punched the phone-card numbers into the keypad, waited for a dial tone, and then entered a telephone number.

The line rang with the distinctive French double ring. After six repetitions, Sam heard a familiar voice. "Hello?"

"Alexei, hello. It's Richard Jordan—I'm visiting from overseas." Sam used the alias under which he had dealt with the man. Sam's French, which was fluent, was spoken with a Canadian accent, something he'd worked very hard to achieve.

There was a slight pause. And then: *"Salut, Richard. Comment tu vas?"*

"Fine," Sam answered in French. "Busy. I'd like to see you, if that's possible. There's something I'd like to talk about."

He was answered with silence.

"It's important, Alexei."

There was another momentary pause. Then Semonov's distinctive voice growled, "But of course, dear Richard. I'm booked all day tomorrow—Mona's leaving to visit her family for two weeks—and the next two days are so busy it will be impossible to see you. But on Wednesday come and have breakfast with me in the morning. First thing—ten o'clock. I'm still living in the same place."

This was not good news. Sam didn't want to spend that much time in Paris. But there was no choice. "I'd rather meet somewhere more . . . out-of-the-way." Sam took for granted that DST—and perhaps other intelligence services as well—tapped Alexei Semonov's telephone, and he wanted the Russian to understand that he should take precautions before they met.

Alexei Alexandrovich Semonov was former KGB. He'd defected to France in January 1992, and had been debriefed extensively by DGSE, the intelligence agency formally known as the General Directorate of External Security but commonly referred to as "La Piscine," because its old headquarters, in a former Army base on the city's east side, had stood adjacent to a public swimming pool.

Semonov's defection, like many others in those days, had more to do with idealism than ideology. "The last straw," he'd once told Sam, "was November of ninety-one. That was when the Duma voted to privatize the apartments that had been set aside for legislators by the old Soviet government. Two thirds of Russians were living in poverty, and here were these vocally pro-democracy, pro-free-economy, pro-equality legislators voting themselves the right to purchase millions of dollars' worth of real estate at less than one cent on the dollar. Worst of all, they did it in secret. It made me sick."

Sam had targeted Semonov as a developmental during the spring of 1992. By July Fourth he'd received POA and recruited the former KGB major. It was a nice catch. Semonov had worked counterintelligence in Moscow Center, and was privy to details about the émigré networks the Russians were still running in Paris in the nineties. Before Moscow, he'd served four years in the KGB's huge Kiev Station, and he'd provided Sam with details not only about the Ukraine, but also the condition of the old USSR chemical and nuclear weapons facilities there.

Then, in the summer of 1993, Sam had been abruptly ordered to drop all contact with the tall, aristocratic defector. The bosses at Langley were convinced Semonov was a double agent. Semonov had done badly on the polygraph, Sam was told. Cut him loose.

Sam did as he was ordered. Semonov hadn't been happy with Langley's decision. Still, he seemed to take the bad news like the professional he was. After all, he didn't lack for money. After being granted French residency he'd quickly become a successful businessman, a consultant (*"un combinard"*[29] he self-deprecatingly called himself), whose wide range of contacts in the old Soviet Union were helpful to the many French companies that wanted to establish themselves in Russia.

By 1994, he'd married Mona Abboud, a beautiful, successful French-Lebanese clothes designer half his age and moved from cramped quarters in the seventeenth arrondissement into an expansive, opulently decorated apartment that looked out on rue Clément Marot, just off the Champs-Élysées. He entertained at the Plaza Athénée just around the corner from his apartment house, or the George V, a four-block walk, and frequented a series of trendy, expensive one- and two-star restaurants.

Sam heard rumors, in the months after he'd severed contact with the Russian, that Semonov had formed a relationship with DST, as well as continuing his association with La Piscine. The move made sense. It gave Semonov political protection as well as demonstrating to his French hosts that he was willing to help defend France's internal national security goals in deed as well as word.

"Somewhere out of the way? We can go anywhere you

[29] French for "fixer."

like. How about lunch at the George V? Shall I pick you up?
Where are you staying?"

Sam didn't like that either. He wanted to talk about Ed
Howard, and do it where they wouldn't be noticed. "I'd like
this to be private, Alexei. Can we meet at the spot we used to
rendezvous, and under the same conditions?"

There was a pause. Then the Russian-accented French
came back at him. "Ah, yes. Of course. What time?"

"Ten past ten."

"Done and done. Until Wednesday morning, Richard."

"Until then, Alexei." He rang off abruptly. If DST was listening, they'd be zeroing in on the location of the pay phone
already. French intelligence had the technical ability to identify any telephone in Paris within seconds, which is why Sam
had kept the call as short as possible.

Sam took up his umbrella, shrugged into his coat, and
walked quickly into the night. The downpour had diminished
to a cold drizzle, but the wind had picked up. He hunched his
shoulders under the umbrella and walked south on the rue de
Rome. There were no vehicles coming in his direction. That
was good news.

Twenty feet from the corner of rue de l'Isly, Sam jay-
walked, turning west and heading down the rue de l'Ar-
cade. Ten yards down the deserted, unlit street, he quickly
reversed his overcoat so the tan side faced inward and the
dark blue wool lining faced out. Then he pulled off the
thick mustache he'd applied to his upper lip as he'd made
his way to the café. If DST checked, he'd be described as a
tall man with a mustache wearing a wrinkled suit and a tan
raincoat.

At Boulevard Haussmann, Sam turned right and walked
up the wide street, ignoring the shuttered stores. Semonov
had worked in Moscow Center just before he defected. He'd
been there when Ed Howard was running his games in Paris

and in Bonn. Maybe he'd heard stories. It was certainly worth a stopover in Paris to find out.

Sam had never questioned the Russian about Howard. There'd been no reason to do so. But now Sam had to identify as many pieces of this particular puzzle as he could, lay them on the table, and see if they belonged anywhere, or if they were extras.

That was both the problem—and the challenge. Sam had come to understand that the intelligence-collection process is indeed something akin to assembling a vast jigsaw puzzle. The trouble is that you never have just one puzzle. There are always a dozen or more to be solved simultaneously. And each one has millions of tiny pieces to be collected. And once they've been collected, all of the pieces of all the puzzles are dumped onto the same table.

So, intelligence collection is a lot more complicated than simply fitting the pieces together. The real craft is having the ability to recognize which piece belongs to which puzzle. And the problem becomes much more difficult when you realize—after a fair amount of time on the job—that all of the pictures on all of the puzzles are copies of Jackson Pollock paintings.

Politicians and civilians had no idea how complicated a process it was. On television, intelligence operations lasted about an hour—less commercials—and they were all neatly solved by the time the credits rolled. That simplistic, idiotic perception was one of the reasons Congress and the press had jumped all over the IC[30] after 9/11, asking how come the community couldn't put all the pieces of the puzzle together when the signals were so clear.

Clear? Even from the outside, Sam had understood how complex and thorny the situation had been. Sure, more

[30] Intelligence Community.

should have been done. But as much as Sam detested Nick Becker, he also understood that Czar Nicholas and the Romanoffs couldn't be held entirely responsible for the failure represented by 9/11. It was a lot more complicated than realizing in some sort of epiphany that Tab A fits neatly into Slot B, and so you go out and scoop up all nineteen bad guys and their support network.

Nick's problem was that he refused to see 9/11 as a failure in the first place. *That* was the real reason the son of a bitch's head deserved to be on a pike.

SAM LOOKED UP to see the bright lights of the Place St. Augustin half a block ahead. He passed the boarded-up metro stop, crossed the street, threaded his way between the portable police barriers that ringed the Cercle, shook the water from his umbrella, closed it, nodded *"Bonsoir,"* and displayed his room-key card to the submachine-gun toting gendarme standing uncomfortably outside the canopied entry, pressed the doorbell, then waited for the welcoming hiss of the automatic doors.

He was starting toward the elevator when the desk clerk caught his eye. "Monsieur Waterman?"

Sam turned. "Yes?"

She held two small rectangles of white paper between outstretched fingers. "There are messages for you."

Sam unbuttoned his coat, stowed his umbrella in an urn, and took the slips. The first read, "WTF? MO." The second, "Imperative you contact me at once. The chmn is very upset. So am I. VV." "He's not the goddamn chairman yet," Sam growled. He crumpled the papers into a ball, dropped them in the fireplug-high ashtray that stood adjacent to the elevator, then pressed the up button.

CHAPTER 21

SAM SLEPT IN, pulling himself out of the hard, narrow bed only at seven. He threw back the heavy drapes. The front had finally blown through on Tuesday and now the streets were dry and the skies beautifully clear. He opened the window and took a deep breath of the crisp, diesel-tinged morning air. The temperature was in the low forties, but after Moscow it felt like summer. He had a double café au lait brought to his room. Then he showered, shaved, and dressed in a suit he'd bought more than half a decade before at Galeries Lafayette. He called the club valet, who picked up the clothes Sam had been wearing the previous day. They'd all be returned by late afternoon. He pulled his key chain out of the document case and dropped the keys and pen drive into his pocket. The Russians had missed it. The French wouldn't. And when DST searched his room, which he was certain they would do, they'd be carrying the technology to copy the damn thing.

At eight-thirty he went downstairs, crossed the boulevard's light traffic, bought three newspapers at a kiosk, and carried them back to a small café on rue de la Pépinière. There, he found a table that afforded him a view down rue La Boétie, ordered a café au lait and a *petit pain au beurre,* and sat, reading, for three quarters of an hour.

He had the whole morning in front of him. He and Semonov were meeting under their old rules. He'd told the Russian ten-ten on the phone. It was a code. A straight-up hour meant the stated time plus three hours. Every five minutes past an hour really meant forty-five minutes past the stated time. So when he'd said ten-ten, Semonov knew to add ninety minutes. The rendezvous would actually take place at eleven-forty. And Sam would arrange for their subsequent conversation to take place in a venue so crowded that overhearing them would be difficult if not impossible.

Precautions were necessary. The DST's Parisian teams, Sam knew from bitter experience, had probably the best surveillance and countersurveillance capabilities on the face of the earth. They were smarter than the Russians, better equipped than the Brits, and more cunning and less principled than the Americans. Teams of more than a hundred watchers were not uncommon, if the quarry was important enough. The French had pioneered techniques such as la Cascade (the Waterfall), in which hundreds of watchers were surged against the target head-on. DST's radios worked inside the deepest tunnels of the metro system because repeaters had been strategically located. DST had a fleet of vehicles that ran the gamut from speedy Citroëns, Renaults, and BMW motorcycles, to unobtrusive vans, panel trucks, taxis, even big lorries. Their watcher teams included Arabs, Africans, fake Japanese tourists, pseudo ugly Americans, bums, postmen, cops, students, housewives, and pensioners, all of whom could change clothes, hairstyles, and (most important) footgear on the run. Sam had been taught that one way to spot surveillance was to check people's shoes. If you saw the same pair twice, you knew you were being pinged. That technique didn't always work in Paris.

Another reason for DST's success was because nettlesome legal impediments like right-to-privacy laws didn't exist in the land of *Liberté, Égalité, Fraternité*—at least where issues of national security were concerned. Indeed, much of the U.S.'s current war on terrorism was being challenged by domestic civil rights organizations who objected to the new and, they claimed, intrusive methods being used by American law enforcement. The Justice Department was being sued. Worse, the folks at ACLU and other organizations often found left-wing judges to agree with them. No such obstacles existed in France.

Tradecraft was mandatory because even though Sam was retired, he remained on DST's permanent watch list. CIA has liaison relationships with only two intelligence services that do not include covert American targeting and recruitment of the very foreign operatives with whom they are working. The two forbidden services are ▆▆▆▆ and ▆▆▆▆. All the others are considered legitimate targets of opportunity. In fact, CIA policy has historically been to obtain unilateral human assets as a normal by-product of liaison relationships. Of all America's historic allies, the French resent CIA's liaison recruitment doctrine the most.

Even so, the often-prickly Paris-Washington relationship had produced many first-rate intelligence successes. François Mitterrand, France's late Socialist president, bonded closely with Ronald Reagan in July of 1981 by giving the American president access to material from France's top Soviet agent, a high-level KGB Line X[31] officer code-

---

[31] Line X was KGB's science and technology collection branch.

named ADIEU. Until he was caught by KGB counterintelligence and executed in 1984, ADIEU, whose real name was Vladimir Vetrov, was instrumental in making it possible for the U.S. to put a halt to a ten-year Soviet espionage program that siphoned off much of America's cutting-edge defense technology.[32]

The French had been helpful in keeping track of Islamist extremists and other Middle East and European-based Muslim terror organizations through productive networks of agents in the Algerian, Moroccan, and Palestinian émigré communities. DST also provided support to U.S. intelligence during the FBI's botched investigation of American diplomat Felix Bloch.

Corporate spying, however, was another matter. The Americans resented DST's habit of breaking into the rooms of American businessmen to steal corporate secrets in order to allow French companies to underbid lucrative contracts. During Sam's Paris tour, French agents broke into a suite at the Ritz, copied a proposal sitting in the briefcase of the vice president for international sales of a huge U.S. petroleum services corporation, and passed the document to a French conglomerate. The Americans lost a two-billion-dollar contract with the Saudis.

But the U.S. company had given half a million dollars in soft money to the Democrats during the 1992 election cycle, and so a call was made to the White House. Three months

---

[32] Among the most valuable secrets stolen by Moscow were the computer programs that governed the grinding of submarine propellers. The props of America's nuclear submarines leave almost no signature in the water, a result of a seven-axis grinding and polishing process that helps mask the sub's blade tonals and cavitation as the propeller changes speed. Vetrov let the Americans know that their grinding technology had been compromised, and that in the future, Soviet nuclear submarines would be able to operate as quietly—or even more quietly—than their U.S. counterparts.

later, sixteen of CIA's Non-Official Case officers, nine of them female, were sent to Paris to initiate an aggressive program targeting French businesses. The operation was a bust. The NOCs, woefully undertrained and lacking in sophisticated French-language skills, were quickly identified and caught by DST, much to Langley's embarrassment.

The unlucky Americans escaped jail sentences only through the direct intervention of the ambassador's close personal friend, the president of the United States. At Pamela Harriman's urging, Bill Clinton called his French counterpart François Mitterrand, begged for mercy, and promised never again to target spies against French business interests.

Clinton kept his word, too. Instead of human beings, he ordered NSA's sophisticated eavesdropping capabilities to focus on French corporations. It didn't take La Piscine long to figure out what was going on, either. So, in return, the French subjected CIA's Paris Station to the kind of aggressive blanket surveillance and intrusive eavesdropping that is usually reserved for adversaries. The prickly relationship had continued into the present, even though France and the U.S. were working closely in the current war against global terror.

Sam had arrived in Paris and registered at the Cercle under his true name. Within hours—perhaps even minutes—of his arrival, DST's 24/7 computer scan of Paris's hotel registries would ping on his name and alert the bureau's counterintelligence branch, which is located in the basement of an anonymous Ministry of Interior office building tucked away on rue de Penthièvre. DST wouldn't mount a full-court press. Sam wasn't a significant enough target. But there would probably be some sort of response. Perhaps they'd do a sneak-and-peek at the Cercle. Still, Sam had decided that a cleaning route might be in order.

9:25 A.M. Sam ambled east on Boulevard Haussmann. At rue Tronchet, he darted across the heavy traffic against the light, descended into the Havre Caumartin metro stop, where he shouldered his way through the crowded station to the caisse and bought a *carnet* of ten tickets. Then he climbed the stairs and quickly loped into one of the twenty entrances to Au Printemps. He jogged up the escalator to the second floor, walked quickly through aisles of trendy women's clothes, found a staircase, scampered down to the first floor, crossed several aisles, and then made his way quickly across a glass-and-steel skyway thirty feet above a narrow alley to the men's store.

He walked past racks of suits and blazers to the end of the aisle, where the fall coats were displayed. He examined several, his radar searching the area for any untoward signals as he moved between the racks. Except for several bored-looking salespeople, the floor was largely deserted. Sam spent a quarter of an hour trying on a series of overcoats and then replacing them on the racks. When he was certain he wasn't being observed, he sauntered off, took the escalator down to street level, made his way to the rear of the store, and slipped out a side door. He walked quickly against the traffic flow, crossed the boulevard, went past the American Express office, down rue Scribe, and across Place de la Madeleine.

From there he walked down rue Royal to the Place de la Concorde, and entered the Hotel Crillon. Inside, next to the lavatory, was a pay phone. He ran his phone card through the reader, dialed a number from memory, and made a lunch reservation under the name Miller. He hung up, walked back outside into the chilly sunlight, and crossed the broad street, pausing to look past the obelisk across the bridge to the National Assembly. Then he galumphed down the metro stairs, ran his ticket through the turnstile, caught the next eastbound train, and rode four stops to Châtelet. There, he waited six minutes, caught the second Porte d'Orléans train, and rode three stops to Odéon. At Odéon, he trudged up the well-worn stairs into the diesel fumes and bustle of Boulevard St. Germain.

10:38 A.M. Sam came out from under the metro marquee and paused on the narrow concrete island. Behind him lay the dark stone walls of the Sorbonne. Across the boulevard lay a string of bars, cafés, and small restaurants interspersed with boutiques, *tabacs,* and bookstores. He waited for the light to change, then crossed while taxi drivers gunned their engines as if they were waiting for the starter's flag at Le Mans. He walked west, window-shopping. Just off the corner of the rue Grégoire de Tours he pushed through the glass-enclosed terrace of a small, sparsely populated café, sat down at a table with a view of the sidewalk, ordered a double espresso, opened his newspaper, and perused the headlines.

Six minutes later, a tall, attractive redhead dressed in the sort of urbanely chic style that Parisian women affect pushed through the door, plunked herself and her Vuitton shopping bag three tables down from Sam, pulled out a newspaper, and started to read. The ping was so loud Sam almost reacted physically. He took a second look. Her hair was too perfect. It was a wig. A very good wig, but a wig nonetheless.

She ordered a bottled water and paid for it in advance. That was final confirmation for Sam. You don't pay in advance unless you might have to leave quickly and you don't want to draw attention to yourself by having an angry waiter pursue you into the sidewalk.

The question was why. He hadn't sensed anything untoward all morning. He certainly wasn't in Paris to work against French targets. All he wanted was a quiet conversation with an old source who might give him some insight about Edward Howard's motives. And now here were the French, putting on a full-court press.

It didn't make any sense. Unless, of course, Alexei had given les Frogs a heads-up. That was possible. He lived here.

He had to do business. Maybe he was just protecting his interests—providing advance notice about a meeting with an old colleague.

She sat on his blind side. Good tradecraft. He wondered how many others of them there were. And then he realized that it didn't matter how many there were, or why they'd decided to target him, or whether Alexei had told DST or not. Sam shook his head, sipped his coffee, and turned his attention back to the newspaper. This had nothing to do with the French. So let them follow. Let them work overtime for all he cared.

A **T ELEVEN-THIRTY** he tossed a handful of euro small change into the saucer in front of him, tore the bill in half, folded his newspaper, and, tucking it like a football under his right arm, walked out of the café. He turned left, walked around the corner into a bustling neighborhood market street crammed with vegetable stands, butcher shops, fishmongers, and bakeries. He shouldered his way through the morning shoppers, turned left, walked another block, then turned right, onto the quiet rue de Seine.

It had been almost a decade since Sam had walked this route, but nothing, it seemed, had changed. The narrow cobblestone street was one of Paris's oldest. The houses, mostly eighteenth and nineteenth century, were narrow three- and four-story stone-and-brick structures. The ground floors of most had been converted into art galleries and artisans shops. Sam took the time to look around. Except for the steel and glass, this was Hemingway's Paris, or Toulouse-Lautrec's.

He made his way slowly, pausing to peer through the plate glass at the displays inside, until he reached his destination, a small gallery that featured nineteenth-century posters. Alexei Semonov, dressed in a thick black turtleneck and an expensive, muted gray herringbone suit, was standing outside, his hands jammed in his trouser pockets, peering at the Cheret posters in the window. He had a folded newspaper tucked under his left arm. It was his VSS—the visual safety signal. If the paper had been rolled and tucked under his right arm, it would have meant Semonov had detected conditions unsafe for a meeting.

But all was clear. Sam said, "Morning, Alexei."

The gaunt Russian's eyes flicked in Sam's direction. But he didn't shift his body. "Richard," he said, pronouncing the word *ree*-charr. *"Bienvenue."*

Sam responded in French. "Nice to see you again." He stared at the posters in the gallery window. "You look very well, Alexei. How's your wife?"

"Mona? Fine, thank you. She's just off to Lebanon, visiting her parents. They're close, these Lebanese, y'know." He laughed. "I discovered that you don't marry the woman, Richard—you marry the entire damn clan." The Russian paused long enough to give Sam a cursory head-to-toe glance. "You look good. Fit." Semonov gestured with his head, pointing down the street. "Shall we walk?"

"Of course." Sam looked around. The street was largely empty. He saw no sign of the woman from the café. "I thought we could have an early lunch. I've booked a table at Ma Bourgogne at noon." Ma Bourgogne was a bustling wine bar in the eighth arrondissement. Using the name Miller, Sam had reserved a specific table in the rear, a location he knew from experience would be impossible to eavesdrop without being obvious.

"If you wouldn't mind," Semonov said, running a hand through thick, graying hair combed straight back, "I'd rather eat in this neighborhood." He glanced down at a thin gold Piaget on a crocodile band. "I have an appointment afterward."

"I don't want to inconvenience you."

Semonov stopped long enough to peer into a shop window. "I booked a table. The restaurant is close by."

"Anything you say, Alexei."

"Thank you." They came to an intersection. Semonov gestured right. "We go this way."

They turned into a cobblestone street no more than eight feet wide, rimmed by narrow sidewalks. At the far end, a red, white, and blue tricolor fluttered from the gated, padlocked rear entrance to a government building. The street was deserted except for a dozen parked cars. Semonov walked slowly, hands clasped behind his back. "So, Richard," he said after half a dozen leisurely strides, "what is it you wanted to talk about?"

"The old days," Sam said. "I wanted to gossip about Moscow Center."

"Just like that." Semonov's pace never changed. "No, 'Sorry Alexei.' No, 'Here's what happened.' You want to pick up where you left off nine years ago."

"Alexei, I—"

"How typically American of you. No wonder the Europeans see you Yankees the way they do. Blunt. Obtuse. Clumsy. No finesse." He stopped walking just long enough to stare down at Sam's feet.

"What are you looking at?"

"I thought you might be wearing cowboy boots and spurs." He glanced up. "Watch out—" The Russian nudged Sam out of the way as a low-slung BMW convertible careened around the corner toward them. The two men sprang to opposite sidewalks to let the vehicle pass.

"*Éperons.*" Sam cracked a bemused smile. "That's funny, Alexei." He stepped back onto the cobblestones. "I'm sorry to be so direct, but there's no other way."

The Russian sighed. "Then get on with it." He paused. "Are you still working? Is this official?"

"I'm retired," Sam said. "This is personal."

"Retired? You're still a young man, Richard. You never seemed much the type to retire."

"It wasn't my choice."

"Ah. They cut you loose." The Russian's head bobbed up and down. "Just like you cut me loose."

"Something like that."

"I'm sorry." Semonov walked on. Finally, he said, "I wish we'd gone to Kiev."

Sam looked at his former agent's face. "So do I, Alexei," he said honestly.

Semonov said: "What happened?"

"I don't know," Sam said. "The op was scrubbed."

"It was scrubbed because of me."

"Why do you say that?"

"We went to the safe house. Your technician put me on the polygraph. Less than a week later you and I meet. You tell me the op is canceled, and that our relationship is over. Au revoir. *Bonne chance. Fin.* Poof—all gone."

Sam tried to sound sincere. "It wasn't you, Alexei. It was us."

The Russian pulled at the skin under his right eye with an index finger.

Sam shrugged. "Believe what you will." He looked up as another car bore down on them and he pulled the heedless Russian out of its path. They'd no sooner stepped back into the street than they had to give way once more for a loud Ducati whose leather-clad driver cut a little close for comfort. "Careful, Alexei—"

When the motorcycle noise subsided, Sam said, "Alexei, did you ever hear anything in Moscow about American agents?"

"American agents?"

"Soviet moles buried in Washington."

Semonov pulled at his ear. "I was only a junior officer, Richard. I had no direct knowledge of such things. Besides, it wasn't my area. I was Second Chief Directorate—and way down the totem pole, as you Americans say. You know as well as I do that agents were run by the First Chief Directorate out of Yasenevo."[33]

"But there must have been stories."

"There are always stories. Gossip."

"And?"

"And? Of course there were rumors." They'd reached the corner. Sam could hear the rumble of trucks, buses, and cars on the busy quai. Beyond the three lanes of fast-moving traffic, die-hard art dealers were opening their kiosks for the tourists. Semonov turned right, heading upstream against the traffic flow. "We go this way." He took Sam's elbow to guide him. "There are always rumors, Richard. You can't have an intelligence service without rumors, can you?"

Sam allowed himself to be led. "No, I don't suppose you can."

"But to be honest, I heard more rumors that the Americans had a mole inside Moscow Center than I heard rumors about KGB moles in Washington."

"I wish we'd actually had one." Sam paused. "You heard nothing at all, Alexei?"

"Like I said, only the usual gossip."

It didn't make sense. Howard claimed the Russians had considered a wet operation to silence Semonov. That's what he'd told Sam at Rand Arthur's house. It was the info-shard that had brought Sam to Paris. And now Howard's lead turned out to be just another dry hole. And yet, Sam couldn't get the defector's voice out of his head. *There are no coincidences.*

---

[33] The headquarters of the KGB's foreign intelligence operations, located on Moscow's outermost Ring Road.

The two men walked in silence for a few hundred feet. Sam could hear police sirens coming from the *préfecture de police* on the Île de la Cité. He glanced toward the Seine. The quai's art dealers had given way to *bouquinistes*—used-book dealers—whose dog-eared wares sat inside huge, green-painted boxes that were bolted to the quai's walls and parapets. Ahead of them was the Boul'Miche—Boulevard St. Michel—and beyond it Notre Dame. On the corner of a busy one-way street Semonov turned right, then opened a heavy glass door for Sam. "Please."

CHAPTƎЯ 22

THE RESTAURANT was called Les Bouquinistes. The place was modern—trendy earth tones, with plank wood floors accented by woven rattan rugs and dark bamboo shades. They were met by a maître d' in a somber three-piece suit who greeted Semonov warmly (and by name) and ushered them past empty tables to a large corner banquette set for two where both men could sit with their backs to a wall and still command a view of the entrance. The table settings were formal. The crisp, pale, lemon yellow tablecloth was counterpointed by a flower arrangement in a simple but exquisite blue-and-charcoal-patterned vase. Three stemmed crystal glasses—a *tulipe* for white wine, and *ballons* for Bordeaux and Burgundy, fanned out from each austere service plate. The silver—it was real silver or good plate—was oversize and heavy. Semonov winked at Sam as they settled onto firm black leather. "They know me here."

No sooner had they unfurled the starched napkins than a trio of waiters appeared. One presented a woven African bowl holding slices of rustic pain Poilane sourdough and a crock of pale Normandy butter. A second presented a square white plate on which were four small triangles of toast, each holding a perfect round of foie gras on top of which sat a dollop of port wine sauce accented with crème fraîche. The third waiter brought a bottle of Pommery Apanage, two long-stemmed flutes, and a champagne bucket on a stand to the table. He set the stand at the Russian's elbow then displayed the label to Semonov. The Russian nodded approvingly and watched as the bottle was uncorked and the champagne poured.

"If you don't mind, Richard, I have taken the liberty of ordering in advance." Semonov lifted his glass. *"Za vashe zdarov'e."*

Sam swallowed. It was very good champagne. "To dead comrades, Alexei." He watched as the Russian plucked a toast triangle off the plate and put it in his mouth. The restaurant had started to fill up. Sam's internal radar flicked on, but picked up no bogeys.

Semonov washed down the foie gras with champagne. "Y'know," he said, "I don't understand how I can eat like this every day and not put on weight. I don't even exercise, Richard. If I ate like this back in Moscow, I'd look like a sumo wrestler."

"It must be the water."

"Water?" Semonov cocked an eyebrow. "Never touch the stuff."

"Then it's all the walking."

Semonov's eyes twinkled. "Perhaps." He paused. "Whatever it is, I don't care. I love this city, Richard. It has become more of a home to me than Moscow ever was."

"I'm happy for you, Alexei." Sam's peripheral vision caught her as she came through the door: a young Chinese woman so beautiful it was frightening. She was fragile as Ming porcelain; dressed simply in monochromatic Chanel and accented by multicolored Hermès. The maître d' treated her with great deference, seating her at a prime window table and immediately producing a half-liter carafe of red wine.

Semonov's French broke into Sam's consciousness. "I find myself smiling as I walk the streets. I am thinking, 'This is *my* city.' You know how it is—you visit le Furet-Tanrade for *des confitures,* and they know you. You stop in at Androuet for some cheese—and you are welcomed like a relative. Ah, Richard, Paris is like a small village to me. I know my neighbors, and I am known. It's an incredible sensation."

Sam looked back across the room. The Chinese woman had shed her jacket. Underneath, she wore a sleeveless brown turtleneck that revealed beautiful arms bedecked with simple gold bracelets. Sam had to force himself to concentrate on the Russian. "I believe you, Alexei," he said wistfully. It was the sort of emotional involvement with a city that he himself had never felt.

Semonov filled their glasses. "I didn't mean to sound bitter earlier."

"No offense taken."

"Good. Because in a way I'm happy things worked out as they did. I have a certain . . . arrangement . . . with the French. It is a good thing for me—and occasionally a good thing for them, too, if you understand."

Sam nodded but said nothing.

"Especially with the current unpleasantness."

"Ah, that."

"If I were a Middle East specialist I would be a rich man," Semonov said. "Keeping track of all the Saudis and their money-laundering schemes. And the others, too. Of course, I can help the French with some aspects of the problem. The Chechen angle, for example." He looked at Sam and whispered conspiratorially, "Did you know that fully twenty-five percent of al-Qa'ida's fighters are Chechens?"

"I think I read something about that in the papers."

Semonov's expression fell. "It is a fact." The Russian scanned the room then nudged the plate in Sam's direction. "You must try the foie gras," he said insistently.

Sam took a piece and tasted. It was perfect, and he said so.

Semonov gave Sam a self-satisfied smile. "This bistro—it was a find of mine almost ten years ago. It has become quite popular lately. Hard to book a table."

"I bet it is." Sam paused.

"But for me . . ."

Sam gave the Russian a reassuring glance. "Alexei—"

Semonov's head tilted in Sam's direction.

"The rumors . . ."

The tired look in Semonov's eyes told Sam the man didn't want to talk about old business. But the Russian uttered a soft sigh, and said, "Yes?"

"Of course there were rumors," Semonov said, switching into Russian. "The KGB lost a large number of agents in the 1980s. The whole Walker ring. Others. You lose one, it is expected. Two, maybe. But three, four, half a dozen in a year and a half? That is called an anomaly, and it requires counterintelligence to do a thorough search."

"And?"

"What was done precisely I don't know. I was very junior and the bureaucracy at Lubyanka was not very trusting. But there were rumors that the First Directorate tasked its American agents to try to pinpoint the leak." He paused. "That's really all I know."

Sam, too, now spoke in Russian. "Northing more specific?"

"Nothing." Semonov took the last of the foie gras, wiped crumbs from his lips with the starched napkin, returned it to his lap, then drained the champagne. A waiter padded up to the table, removed the plate, and efficiently poured the two men more wine. Semonov waited until he'd left before resuming. "I can only repeat what I told you earlier," he said, his lips barely moving. "There was a lot more gossip about a CIA mole in Moscow than there was about KGB moles in Washington." The Russian sipped champagne. "In fact, more than one time I heard the name of Edward Lee Howard."

Sam blinked. "The CIA defector?"

"Justement." Semonov inclined his head toward Sam, and put a hand up to mask his mouth from being seen and continued in Russian. "General Krassilnikov and even more, Krassilnikov's deputy—Colonel Klimov—never liked Howard. That I know for sure—because the general was my boss and he told me so more than once."

Major General Rem Krassilnikov had been Moscow Center's relentless and uncompromising chief of counterintelligence. In the 1980s, using information supplied by the American traitors Ames, Hanssen, Nicholson, and others, he'd mounted a series of spectacular CI operations against both CIA and the Soviet spies working for the United States. By the end of the decade, America's assets in the USSR had been decimated. Sam had met Krassilnikov once during his tour. The general had struck him as a dangerous man; a direct operational descendant of Dzerzhinsky, Beria, Andropov, and Chebrikov. A jowly, gray-haired True Believer with the piercing, steely-eyed gaze of a grand inquisitor.

In his shadow was Valentin Klimov—a tall, ascetic-looking wraith with a leonine head of thick dark hair and the sharp white teeth of a predator. Klimov had been *Rezident* in Paris in the 1990s. He'd run double agents against Langley with some success. But these days Rem was retired and Klimov had come in out of the cold to take over FSB's CI operations. He was, so rumors in Purgatory had circulated, the perfect CI chief: more intense than Angleton and crueler than Krassilnikov. It was even said that Klimov was tearing SVR apart from the inside, searching for the traitor who'd betrayed his priceless spies Ames, Nicholson, and Hanssen.

Sam had never believed a word of it. His instincts told him the stories were disinformation. Active measures from Moscow Center. But by then he'd been banished to Purgatory. He was an Untouchable. No one at Langley listened to him anymore.

The Russian polished off his wine, refilled his own glass, then drank it halfway down. "Urinal gossip was that Krassilnikov believed Howard was a deep-cover double—a mole. I'm told Klimov still does."

Ed Howard? A mole? It was inconceivable—it would have been an incredible operation to mount and sustain. Sam sipped his wine, then watched as Semonov topped both glasses off. "Why, Alexei?"

The Russian drank again, emptying his glass. "It was a running gag: Rem Krassilnikov had spent so much time in the Second Department[34] he took John Le Carré's novels seriously."

"You're not serious."

"I am, Richard. It was rumored—half seriously—that Krassilnikov started to perceive Edward Howard as an American Alec Leamas. Whether that story was actually true or not I don't know. I was pretty close to the bottom of the food chain in Moscow. But Krassilnikov and I were in the hallway once, and Howard passed us going the other way. Krassilnikov stopped, turned, pointed at Howard's back, and whispered to me, 'Alexei Alexandrovich, I believe it was Felix Dzerzhinsky who told the initial selection of Cheka officers, "The only trustworthy defector is a dead defector."' And it is undeniable fact that Krassilnikov had Howard trans-

---

[34] The Second Department of the KGB's Second Chief Directorate was responsible for monitoring British intelligence activity in the Soviet Union. The Second Chief Directorate's First Department targeted America's USSR intelligence operations.

ferred out of the Second Chief Directorate. 'Banished' was the word I heard. Reassigned into the First Chief Directorate, where he was ordered to make trouble for the Americans as a way of demonstrating fealty to our great Soviet motherland. Howard was trolling in Paris at about the time you and I first met, y'know."

"Was he." Sam's tone remained neutral.

"I met with him once. He was looking to put a network of émigrés together."

"You never told me that, Alexei."

The Russian's face grew sad. "I know. I should have. I think, Richard, that meeting with Howard was what made me flunk the polygraph."

Sam was stunned. "They asked you about Howard?"

"The polygrapher spent most of the session asking me about my relationship with Ed Howard, about Howard's relationship with Krassilnikov and Klimov, and about rumors of a KGB mole in Washington. I wasn't much help on any of them, Richard."

Sam blinked. No one at Langley had ever filled him in on that little fillip. All he'd been told was that Semonov had flunked lunch and he was to be cut loose. Who the hell had tasked the polygrapher?

"Besides," the Russian continued, "Howard wasn't even working for Second Chief Directorate at the time. Afterward, I told that to the case officer who oversaw the polygraph—I forget his name, but he was the one who was with you when we met."

O'Neill? O'Neill had run the flutter session? That was a surprise to Sam, because O'Neill had never mentioned it—not then, and certainly not since.

"Whatever, it was irrelevant." Semonov took a big swallow of the wine. "Howard wasn't working counterintelligence in the early 1990s—he was out at Yasenevo.[35] Putin brought him back to Lubyanka after he became head of FSB—over Klimov's strenuous objections, I might add. But that was long after I left."

"That's ridiculous. I—"

"Yes?" Sam started to say he'd only recently heard exactly the opposite: that it was Putin who mistrusted defectors. But he'd forgotten where he'd heard it and he held his tongue. Besides, he was here to elicit, not to inform. And so, he elicited. "I tell you, Alexei, it sounds implausible to me."

"Perhaps. But it's what I heard. And the gossip going around these days . . ."

"Yes?"

"The gossip is that Klimov's more paranoid than Rem ever was. There were whispers after Putin's support of Washington post-9/11 that Klimov told a few of his closest pals that Putin himself had been flipped by the Americans." The Russian sighed deeply. "Try to make sense of that one, by God."

"Well, there were people in my shop who believe Clinton was a Chinese asset."

"But wasn't he?" Semonov grinned. "I heard—"

"Klimov, Alexei." Sam brought the conversation back on track. "Klimov. Klimov didn't like Edward Lee Howard, right?"

They'd finished the champagne. A waiter brought a carafe of red wine. Semonov poured it himself, swirled the wine around the bowl, slurped noisily, then swallowed. "Klimov? Howard? I *told* you, Richard. Klimov didn't like him at all. Hated him." He filled Sam's glass. "You're going to like this. It's a classified Bordeaux."

[35] The headquarters for KGB's First Chief Directorate, which handled Soviet-era foreign intelligence.

The Russian smiled at his little joke. When Sam didn't appear to get it, Semonov gave him an earnest look and shifted into English and French. "A *classified* growth, Richard. A pun. *Un jeu de mots. Un vin classé secret.*" When Sam finally smiled, Semonov went back to Russian. "It's a Graves to be precise, and a Y2K to boot—great vintage, Y2K. But Guy—that's the owner—has it brought in as *vin aux tonneaux.*"

Sam let the chaff about the wine go by him. *So Klimov hated Edward Lee Howard.* If that were true, it made Klimov a prime suspect in the mysterious deaths of Ed Howard—and Irina, too. Klimov had motive, means, and the opportunity to get them both out of the way. Sam caught Alexei's anxious expression and realized he was meant to taste the wine. He sipped—and wasn't disappointed. He couldn't tell a Graves from a Pauillac or a St. Emilion, but he knew good wine when he drank it, and this was spectacular stuff. "Absolutely lovely, Alexei."

"Thank you." The Russian broke off a piece of the brown Poilane bread, dipped it in the red wine, popped it in his mouth, chewed, then washed the bread down with a glug of red. "So that's the Edward Lee Howard story as I heard it—except . . ."

"Except?"

The Russian's face had become slightly flushed. He dabbed at his lips with the napkin. "I remember two other things. I had a dinner with an old friend. A colleague from the trade. Maybe five, six years ago. I don't exactly recall. And the guy mentioned—he laughed about this—that when Putin brought Edward Howard back to Lubyanka, my friend said people in the Second Directorate told him you could hear Valentin Klimov screaming bloody murder about it from his office—even if you were sitting in the bottle."[36]

---

[36] "Bottle" was the KGB term for a Sensitive Compartmented Information Facility (SCIF), or bug-proof room.

A female waiter—one of the few Sam had ever seen in a Paris restaurant—set a plate of salad in front of him. The baby lettuce leaves had been individually arranged so they resembled an open artichoke. The salad had been dressed in a walnut-oil dressing so pungent he'd smelled it before she'd even approached the table.

Sam waited until she'd left. "And the second?"

"Recent. I was told Howard was desperate."

"Desperate?"

"After Putin became president he had other things to think about. Chechnya. Al-Qa'ida. Eleven September. The oligarchs. Oil and gas. Centimeter by centimeter, Klimov took over FSB. Once he'd concentrated his power, he marginalized Howard. It was death by a thousand cuts. Klimov took away his responsibilities one by one." Semonov took a forkful of greens. "Klimov assigned Howard to an office so small a desk wouldn't fit in it. No telephone either. Howard had a chair and a lamp." He looked at Sam and grinned.

"How recently was this?"

"Six months ago I heard the story from someone still active, Richard, someone who still thinks of the United States as the 'Main Adversary.' Someone who still believes that Washington has a mole buried deep inside the Kremlin. This person told me Howard had become a bitter, bitter man. He was drinking a lot. And always looking for some way to get even with Klimov—ruin Klimov's career."

"What did Howard have access to that might do that?"

"Dunno." Semonov punched the salad with his fork, shoved the greens in his mouth, and munched. "But I was reliably told Klimov cut him off from any sensitive material by the end of Y2K. By eleven September, he'd even revoked Howard's clearances, my friend said."

"Why didn't they just fire him?"

Semonov chewed another forkful of salad, then smiled

ruefully. "Your people fired Howard and look what it got them. I don't think Klimov wanted a mirror image."

Sam stayed quiet.

Finally, Semonov spoke. "It's funny you should bring Edward Howard's name up. I hadn't thought about him for years. I read about his death—you have to admit he died under very strange circumstances, Richard—and I thought, well, Klimov caught the son of a bitch with his control officer and dealt with him once and for all."

Deflect. Redirect. Sidetrack. Sam disturbed the nicely arranged leaves with the tines of his fork. "Rem's long retired, Alexei. Left the job in 1991. Meets with CIA veterans. Writes books. I don't think he'd chase Howard down these days."

"Not Rem, Richard. Comrade Klimov. Besides, you know what they say at Moscow Center. They say retirement is just another form of cover. You *say* you're retired. And yet here you are in Paris, wondering aloud whether Edward Lee Howard was a double."

Except that Sam hadn't wondered aloud whether Ed Howard was a double. He hadn't even brought Howard's name up. He'd wanted to. But he'd asked instead about Russian moles. It was Alexei Alexandrovich Semonov who'd brought up Edward Lee Howard. And mentioned the American in the provocative context Sam hadn't ever considered. And totally contradicted what Sam had reliably heard from . . . from . . . *O'Neill.* It had been O'Neill. On Sam's birthday. At the Cosmos bar. And O'Neill had heard it from a source on Capitol Hill.

Given the provenance, Semonov's version appeared on the surface even more far-fetched. Still, Howard had defected on Bill Casey's watch. Casey was a big-picture guy who loved ambitious operations. Could the Old Man have tried to pull a *Spy Who Came in from the Cold* on Moscow?

Knowing Casey's OSS-born affinity for covert ops, anything was possible. Casey loved the black side. He'd even run a few covert ops himself—keeping everyone else out of the loop. But then Casey had died, abruptly. Sam knew how secretive Casey had been. What if the DCI had croaked without handing Ed Howard off to another control officer? Holy mother of God—that would have left Howard all alone. No one to run to. Nowhere to go. No one to trust.

But it was all so unlikely. Howard's defection had thrown CIA into real turmoil. He'd betrayed at least half a dozen of America's top agents in Moscow. He'd handed the Soviets the denied area operations manual. And then, after more than a decade and a half of working for Moscow, the sudden redefection—going to Rand Arthur, no less. If Semonov was to be believed, Howard was a drunk. A bitter, marginalized drunk. That, at least, made sense out of Howard's redefection. If that's what it had in fact been.

That was all on the one hand.

And on the other hand? *There are no coincidences.* That's what Howard had told him. Not a coincidence that he'd showed up at Rand Arthur's. Not a coincidence that he'd demanded to see Sam. Not a coincidence that he'd fled back to Moscow—where he was murdered.

Sam couldn't put his finger on it, but there was something . . . missing. Something hinky. He had the same bone-deep uneasiness he'd felt in Rand Arthur's library listening to Ed Howard's spiel. *Dammit, Sam, you're getting old. What the hell have you missed? They're running a GAP on you—whoever* they *are—and so you can't see what they're up to. They've set a jack-in-the-box and they're about to spring it.*

Sam had to close the goddamn GAP. But how? The one thing he'd do when he got back to Washington was to call Charlotte Wells. She'd know how to decipher this mess. Charlotte and Sam had worked together in Purgatory. She was one of the originals. As a prim, eighteen-year-old Royal Air Corps secretary, Charlotte Harvey had been seconded to OSS during the buildup prior to the D-Day invasion. She worked for General Wild Bill Donovan himself, as well as a pair of Donovan's young acolytes named Bill Casey and Richard Helms. After the war, she'd been swept off her feet by a young Jedburgh, a handsome mustachioed captain named Carl Wells. Donovan himself had been best man at their wedding. He'd also seen to it that Charlotte became an American citizen within eighteen months after she and Carl moved to Washington.

She'd joined CIA in 1951 as a secretary, three years after Carl was recruited by the fledgling Central Intelligence Agency as one of its first case officers. It had been Allen Dulles who'd initially assigned her to work for James Jesus Angleton's counterintelligence operation. That was in the late 1950s, six months or so after she lost Carl at the age of forty-seven to a heart attack. Alone and childless, Charlotte threw herself into the work with white-hot intensity. In less than nine months she'd become Angleton's most trusted subordinate.

In later years, she and her colleagues, all of them women of a certain age, background, and eccentricity, became known as the CIA's Oracles. The Oracles wore tennis shoes in the office. They dressed . . . bizarrely. Some—Charlotte was one—read and spoke Russian. The Oracles didn't trust computers. Instead, they kept their records on file cards jammed into shoe boxes, which were secured in a series of huge, double-locked, fireproof safes, in the fireproof-safe room on the third floor of Langley where they spent their days. The place came to be known as Delphi—and many was the case officer who made a pilgrimage to Delphi to check out a developmental, query about a possible double, or ask an opinion about a recruitment gone bad. Even in a day of

PowerPoint presentations, intuitive rational databases, and sophisticated analysis software, Oracles still hand-lettered their association and activities matrices, and used rulers, compasses, and colored pencils to draw link diagrams and time-event charts.

Oracles were old school, and therefore protected by Brahmins, so the Romanoffs had to hate them and their quirks from afar. But immediately after the Romanoffs elbowed their way to power in the months after Bill Casey died, they began the purge. The counterintelligence files were too important, they said, to be left to a bunch of little old ladies wearing tennis shoes. Within two years, Delphi was razed and turned into a computer center. The Oracles were disbanded—reassigned as secretaries or filing clerks.

Most of the women chose to retire. But some, including Charlotte, did not. When the general counsel's office informed Czar Nicholas he couldn't fire the refusenik Oracles, he banished them from Langley, revoking their building passes and scattering them across Northern Virginia by assigning them to anonymous CIA satellite offices in Herndon, Reston, Chantilly, and Tyson's.

Charlotte was sent to Purgatory. The last five years of her half-century-plus career were spent in Rosslyn, answering phones and making coffee while Untouchables like Sam Waterman created retirement legends for NOCs.

The day he'd arrived in Purgatory she'd stared and stared at Sam. When he'd asked why, she told him he reminded her of her Carl. He did some quiet checking and came away impressed. For the next ninety days, they spent much of their free time in conversation. It wasn't just that she had a prodigious memory for facts, figures, names, and events. It was the pure intellectual passion she radiated when she spoke about the subject. To Charlotte Wells, counterintelligence had become an obsession; one that had endured longer than any other. It enveloped her like an intense perfume.

Sam was miserable the day she walked out of Purgatory for good. She'd listened to his stories about disposables, doubles, and Pavel Baranov. And she'd agreed with his assessment. Like Sam, Charlotte Wells was convinced beyond a shadow of a doubt that at least one high-level Russian mole still worked at Langley. That belief, she whispered more than once, was the real reason they'd both been sent to Purgatory.

And then after three months she was gone, leaving Sam miserable and alone in Purgatory. She moved to the West Coast of Florida. "God's waiting room" was how she'd described it to him in a handwritten note six months ago. If anyone could make sense of this Edward Lee Howard conundrum it would be Charlotte.

SAM GLANCED at Semonov, who was obviously enjoying himself. The wine had made the Russian voluble and garrulous. It was often like that with agents. Some drank to make themselves feel better about themselves. Others—Semonov was one of them—drank to loosen their own reticent tongues. And others drank simply because they liked to drink, and a meeting with a case officer gave them the opportunity to do it when someone else was picking up the tab.

Sam was perplexed. Ed Howard had flagged Semonov. Put up a flare right in Rand Arthur's library. And yet, Semonov had done more to confuse the situation than unravel it.

It was all absolutely crazy. He focused on the oblivious Russian. *The son of a bitch has managed to throw a wrench into the machinery and he doesn't even know it. Or does he? What the hell is he doing?*

And then Sam realized what Semonov was up to. Now that he thought about it, he realized Alexei hadn't asked him a single question about what he was doing in Paris. Except for perfunctory remarks about Sam's being retired, he hadn't inquired about what Sam was doing at all. Not a word. No, "How are you keeping busy? What are you doing making personal inquiries to former agents?" None of that.

The reason Semonov hadn't asked was because he already knew what Sam was doing. Probably knew he'd arrived from Moscow. Probably knew Sam was nosing around about Edward Lee Howard. Maybe even knew he was working for Rand Arthur and SSCI.

Alexei had no doubt called his control officer the minute he'd hung up on Sam, and DST had run a check for him. Sam's name and transit status to and from Moscow were on his French visa application. La Piscine—and therefore DST—had to know. Or maybe Semonov had called one of his old KGB pals. There were dozens of them in Paris these days. Either way, it meant that Sam was currently being fed—both literally, and figuratively. The question was, fed what?

THEY ATE SADDLE of rabbit perfumed with fresh sage, served with turnips and Italian broad beans. The Graves was finished before they were halfway through the entrée, and Semonov signaled for more.

When they'd polished that off—accompanied by a small selection of farmhouse cheeses—and cleansed their palates with grapefruit sorbet, Semonov whispered to the maître d', who produced a bottle of twenty-five-year old cognac, two generous snifters, and a heavy, rectangular ashtray. The Russian pulled a slim, brown crocodile cigar case from the inside breast pocket of his suit coat and uncapped it, revealing two gold-banded Romeo and Julieta Churchills.

He offered one to Sam, who took it, then used the Russian's gold cigar cutter to guillotine the cap.

Sam struck a wood match, waited for the sulfur to burn off,

then lit the cigar. "Thanks, Alexei." He looked past the Russian. The Chinese woman had vanished. Her table had been reset.

Semonov held his Churchill over the ashtray, cut the tip, lit up, and puffed contentedly. "Ahh." He sucked on the big cigar, exhaled, set it down on the ashtray, swirled the cognac, in its snifter, then put his nose into the narrow rim of the glass, inhaled, then sipped. "What a combination, eh?" he said, slipping back into French. "The day after God created great cognac He realized He'd done only half the job and so He created great cigars. Then, He knew it was better than good." Semonov laughed. "And it was the evening and the morning of the eighth day."

IT WAS PAST TWO when Semonov called for the bill. Sam snatched it from the waiter's hands before the Russian could react. "It's mine," he said. "My pleasure, Alexei Alexandrovich."

"If you insist, Richard." The Russian pouted. "But this was to have been my treat."

"Next time," Sam said. "I'll be back soon."

"Oh?" The Russian's eyebrows went up. "When, Richard?"

"Soon," Sam said. "There's unfinished business here."

Semonov looked at him quizzically. Then the expression faded. The Russian watched as Sam dropped a pile of euro notes into the folder. "You're being very generous."

"It was a very good meal."

"Agreed." Semonov pushed the table away so the two of them could stand up. "The French really know how to live," he said. "Except for one thing."

"What's that?"

"No siestas. They could learn from the Spanish or the Portuguese."

"Guess what, Alexei: the European Union has asked the Spanish and the Portuguese to drop the siesta so they stay in sync with the rest of the Europeans."

The Russian's eyes went wide as saucers. "The fools," he said. "Richard, this European Union stupidity will be the death of us all. It is socialism pure and simple. And I, for one, have had enough socialism to last me a lifetime."

Sam followed the Russian toward the doorway, watching as Semonov reached into his pocket and slipped a folded euro note into the maître d's palm as he shook the man's hand. It was as smooth a brush pass as Sam had ever seen. Obviously, Alexei hadn't lost his tradecraft.

Sam held the door and they walked out into bright sunlight and traffic noise. Across the quai, a bookseller in a waxed cotton coat was displaying a matted, antique map. The client was the same woman Sam had seen in the café earlier. The Vuitton shopping bag was slung over a shoulder. In her left hand she clutched the newspaper she'd been reading. She had, Sam noticed, uncomfortably high stiletto heels on her over-the-calf boots. Her ankles were probably killing her. Well, too bad. That was DST's problem, not his.

From far across the Seine, Sam heard the hee-haw of a police vehicle moving east. He turned to face the Russian. "So, Alexei, where are you off to?"

Now another hee-haw rose above the cacophony of traffic. The Russian shrugged almost apologetically. "I have a three-fifteen at the Foreign Ministry."

"Friends from La Piscine?"

"Please." Semonov placed an index finger in front of his lips. "The walls have ears." Then he dipped his head and threw both his hands up in the classic Gallic expression of frustration. "What am I supposed to do, Richard? I live here."

"It's no skin off my nose, Alexei. I'm retired." Sam swiveled, catching a glimpse of the shadow across the quai.

She'd turned and was watching them, the newspaper tucked under her arm. The lyrics for "You'll Never Walk Alone" came into Sam's head, and it made him happy to know that, given his route, her damn ankles were going to swell like melons before the day was over.

He turned, facing west, and gestured for Semonov to start moving. "I'll take you as far as the Solférino footbridge. No need for the two of us to make an appearance on camera." The Foreign Ministry backed up to the French National Assembly, and the entire two-square block area was surrounded by barricades and saturated with surveillance devices—a recent development in homage to al-Qa'ida.

Sam glanced back across the quai. He'd lost sight of his high-fashion tail. Maybe her feet hurt so much she'd handed him to another watcher. It didn't matter. He'd walk back to the Cercle, stopping on the way at Caves Auge, a formidable wine store on Haussmann, to buy a bottle of the fifty-year-old Bas-Armagnac they kept in stock—a belated birthday present to himself. Maybe, if he was lucky, he'd get to share it with Ginny.

They were coming to the rue du Bac. Sam checked the cross traffic to his left. The street was clear. They were halfway across when something made Sam stop dead in his tracks and turn around. Behind them by just over half a block, he saw the redheaded woman, Vuitton bag over her shoulder. She was still on the opposite side of the quai, standing on tiptoe and using her newspaper to hail a cab—waving the damn thing so frantically she looked as if she was trying to burst-transmit in semaphore. She'd just missed one, too—it was careening down the quai, the driver hunched behind the wheel, oblivious to her entreaties.

Too bad, lady. Sam shook his head and turned back to follow Semonov, who'd ambled another three yards across the wide street.

He hadn't gone six paces when he heard the squeal of rubber on pavement. He whirled around and saw the taxi driver's face behind the windshield as he steered dead on toward them. "Alexei—watch out!" Sam shoved the Russian hard—toward the opposite curb.

Semonov stumbled, then regained his footing and headed toward safety.

The cab bore down on Sam. He feinted right. The cab changed direction but didn't slow. He feinted left, then right again. The cab jerked, missed him by a hairbreadth, then swung wide, smacking Sam with the rear quarter panel and flinging him like rag doll into the air.

Everything went into slo-mo. The pace picked up again when he smacked down hard onto the hood of a parked Citroën in painful real time.

Sam rolled off the hood and landed with a thump on his hands and knees. Then time stood still again. Sam watched, as distant as if he were looking at a movie, as the driver reversed, the taxi's tires smoking as he floored the accelerator. Sam smelled burned rubber and rolled out of the way just in time to escape being run over.

He crawled onto the sidewalk behind a parked car—a big BMW. The taxi tried to crush him using the BMW but the Beemer was too heavy.

The taxi shot forward. Sam pulled himself up. He looked in horror across the BMW's trunk. Semonov had stopped dead in his tracks in the middle of the street, a deer caught in headlights. He was looking back toward Sam. "Alexei, Alexei—*move!*"

The taxi shot thirty yards across the pavement. That was when Sam realized through his pain that the goddamned vehicle didn't have any license plate.

The driver hit the brakes, sending the vehicle into a four-wheel drift. The cab caught Semonov broadside and flyswatted the Russian into a parked car. There was a sickening crunch of metal and a single, horrifying scream.

Sam lost his balance and collapsed. Semonov disappeared from view. Sam struggled like a turtle on its back, finally flopped over, and, using the BMW for support, pulled himself onto his feet. He tried to move toward the Russian.

But his knee was gone and no sooner had he let go of the car than he crumpled onto the pavement in agony. He watched as the taxi slalomed into the fast-moving traffic stream and disappeared down the quai. To his right, cars screeched to a stop. People were coming to his aid—and Semonov's. He heard the approaching hee-haw of sirens, shrugged off two men who wanted to help him stand up, and pulled himself across the pavement to where Semonov lay crumpled against the rear wheel of a smashed Citroën.

Someone was already trying to help. Sam elbowed his way through the growing crowd of onlookers. The Russian's head lolled back, eyes open, a narrow streak of blood washing down his upper lip. Sam reached for Semonov's neck and felt for a pulse.

There was none. He rolled onto his back, covered his eyes with his hands, and lay on the pavement, dry-heaving as the sirens hee-hawed closer and closer.

PART V

WASHINGTON, D.C.

CHAPTƎᴙ 23

SAM SENSED he might be in trouble after he called the SSCI offices Thursday morning to give Ginny Vacario a heads up and didn't hear back. Semonov's death made the papers, of course. CIA SPYMASTER WORKING FOR U.S. CONGRESS INVOLVED IN MURDER OF EX-KGB OFFICIAL was how *France Soir* headlined the story. Not to be outdone, the Russians leaked the story of O'Neill's detention to AFP's[37] Moscow correspondent. Unnamed U.S. embassy officials in Moscow linked Sam to that incident as well, suggesting he might have precipitated it.

Sam spent thirty-six hours holed up at the Cercle National popping aspirin and being interviewed by successive teams of gendarmes and DST investigators. He gave the same answers to each. He had no idea why he and Semonov had been targeted. Or by whom. And he didn't. But obviously, it had something to do with Ed Howard. *There are no coincidences.*

---

[37] Agence France Presse, France's leading wire service.

On Saturday the French gave him permission to leave. A police Citroën drove him through the rain to de Gaulle. There, he was met by an armed DST agent in a shiny brown suit and a short black raincoat who escorted him through a maze of corridors to the departure lounge, took him through security, walked him past the duty-free, and held his elbow as he hobbled down the gangway to the Air France flight to Washington.

Michael O'Neill was waiting for him in the Dulles customs area, a plastic visitor's ID clipped to the lapel of his overcoat. Standing at his shoulder was a statuesque customs special agent in blue fatigues cinched by a cumbersome pistol belt. O'Neill took Sam's hands in his. "Gawd almighty, Cyrus, you look terrible."

"Nice to see you, too, SAMGRASS."

O'Neill watched as Sam pulled himself out of the wheelchair and tipped the baggage handler who'd been pushing. "You sure you want to do that?"

"The chair wasn't my idea." Sam nudged the luggage cart. "But you could wheel this."

"Done and done." O'Neill turned to face the customs agent. "Sam, please meet Special Agent Montgomery, U.S. Customs."

Sam nodded. "Good to meet you, Special Agent."

"Nice to meet you, too, Mr. Waterman."

O'Neill pointed toward the exit. "Lead on, Special Agent Montgomery. Escort us through the Bat Cave."

Sam cocked his head in O'Neill's direction. "What's up?"

O'Neill hooked his thumb toward the automatic doors that led to the international arrivals area. "You're a celebrity, Cyrus. There are camera crews out there. And reporters. They'd like to spend a little time with you discussing your most intimate secrets—as well as your professional relationship with a certain senator."

"Oh, Christ."

O'Neill put both hands on Sam's luggage cart and wheeled it away from the exit, toward a door that said OFFI-CIAL USE ONLY. "Y'know," he said, turning back to watch Sam hobble in his wake, "if I were you I'd get a better picture to hand out."

"Picture?" Sam didn't have any photographs of himself, except for the ones on his driver's license, passport, and Senate ID.

"From the Agency. The day you were awarded the Career Intelligence Medal. Somebody gave it to the AP."

Sam remembered the photo. It had been taken the day before he'd retired. He looked awful—tired, drawn, haggard. Nick Becker, who'd just come from his regular Tuesday-morning assignation with ████████████████, a stunning female the DCI had had transferred onto his security detail, was absolutely beaming. Sam never asked for a copy of the photo and Langley had never sent one.

They made their way through the steel door and down a long corridor at the end of which was another steel door. Agent Montgomery was wearing a deck of magnetic key cards suspended round her neck. She selected one of them and slid the card through an electronic reader. The latch buzzed. She swung the heavy door open and stood aside until the two men and the luggage cart had passed through, then closed the door and double-checked to make sure the lock had engaged.

They were in a small, rectangular foyer facing an elevator door. O'Neill pressed the up button. Nothing happened.

"Excuse me." The customs agent slid a second card into a reader, and from somewhere above, Sam could hear the sound of the motor engaging. Half a minute later the elevator door opened and they crowded inside.

They emerged on Dulles's main departure level, were escorted through two more locked doors, each manned by an armed security guard. With the special agent on point, they made their way through the terminal and out the front doors, turned right, and walked to the very end of the sidewalk. There, guarded by a pair of Virginia State Police officers, was O'Neill's vintage Mercedes. The lawyer turned and bowed. "Special Agent Montgomery, I am in your debt." He gave the tall officer his business card. "If there is anything you ever need—a favor, a dinner, a bottle of world-class champagne, or a week with yours truly lolling on the pink sand in Barbados—you just let me know and I am your obedient servant."

Agent Montgomery's cheeks flushed bright red. "Why, thank you, Mr. O'Neill."

"Oh, no—thank *you*." O'Neill pressed a remote, released the latch, hefted Sam's carry-on into the carpeted trunk, and pressed the lid closed. "You'll be happy to know I picked up your suitcase after you abandoned us. It's at my place."

"I'm grateful."

"You should be."

O'Neill slammed the trunk lid shut then opened the passenger door and watched as Sam gingerly shoehorned himself inside. "You won't like where we're going."

"Where's that?"

O'Neill eased the door shut. "Round Hill. The senator wants to see you."

Sam straight-armed the door before it latched. "No way."

O'Neill wagged his index finger at Sam and mimicked the senator's accent. "Don't be stubborn, my boy."

Sam peered up at his old friend. "Michael—you drive me straight to my place—right now—or I'll pull myself out of this heap and take my chances with the press back there—and believe me, I won't have anything good to say about Rand Arthur and his meeting with Ed Howard."

"Your place, old cock, is staked out, too. C'mon, Sam, the

senator just wants to debrief you before anybody gets to you."

So he can dictate the party line, Sam thought. "Bull. He wants to make sure I spin the story in his favor." He watched as O'Neill came round the nose of the car and climbed inside. "Before we go anywhere," Sam growled, "I have a question."

O'Neill slammed the door. "Shoot."

"You never told me you fluttered REQUIRE."

O'Neill put the key in the ignition. "You never asked."

"He told me you pressed him hard about Ed Howard."

"I did. Those were my marching orders."

Sam put his hand on O'Neill's shoulder. "From whom?"

O'Neill's scratched his chin. *"Der Raccünvald,"* he said.

"Jerry von Brünwald?"

"Himself. Our beloved ▓▓▓▓▓ chief. He said he'd had instruction from on high."

"Christ." Von Brünwald was dead—a heart attack not two years ago. Another missing witness.

"What's the point, Cyrus?"

"You gave REQUIRE a failing grade, Michael."

"That I did. Because he showed deception."

"Semonov told me the polygrapher spent most of the interrogation asking about Ed Howard, Valentin Klimov, and Russian moles in Washington."

"When you bolted at de Gaulle I knew it was Semonov you stopped in Paris to see."

"Michael—"

O'Neill's expression was contrite. "Sorry, Cyrus. Look—I was on my way out the door. All my effects had been shipped home. I was living at that little hotel on rue Boissy d'Anglas down from the embassy—they changed the name after I left. Jerry asked if I'd handle something sensitive for him on the q.t. Sure, I told him. My pleasure. 'Polygraph GTRE-QUIRE,' he sez. Cyrus, you could have knocked me over with a feather. I told him REQUIRE was your recruitment and I didn't want to meddle. He told me not to mention anything to you. He emphasized the assignment was all code-word stuff. Hup-too, hup-too, get on with it and do it in the black."

"Which you did."

"Which I did. By the numbers. And the script I was given was full of questions about Klimov and Krassilnikov and Russian CI." O'Neill put the car in gear. "But as I recall— and this is years ago—there was nothing about moles in Washington, Cyrus old chap. What I do remember is my instructions were to probe about American agents in Moscow."

Sam nodded. O'Neill had just unwittingly buttressed Semonov's recollection.

"And the deception? Where did Semonov screw up?"

"He insisted he hadn't met with Howard. But Langley had evidence he had done. We had pictures—I saw them. From the Bureau—taken by the LEGATT, I was given to understand."

"And the script?"

"I had to read the briefing file in *Der Raccünvald*'s office. I wasn't allowed to take notes. The folder was blue-striped, Cyrus. Had to have come from on high."

They were approaching the airport exit. O'Neill looked over at Sam. "Where to, Cyrus? I recommend we head to Round Hill."

Sam growled, "You drive where I tell you, SAMGRASS."

O'Neill saw the determined look in Sam's eyes. "You're a big boy, Cyrus."

SAM STOOD outside the entrance to the Wolf Trap Motel and watched O'Neill edge into the traffic onto Route 123 and head north, into Vienna. The lawyer'd clapped his mo-bile phone to his ear before he'd even turned out of the driveway. Sam shook his head. *More bad tradecraft, Michael.*

He pushed the plate-glass door open and limped to the reception desk. As crows flew, the motel lay seven and a half miles southwest of CIA headquarters. It was a convenient and, just as important, out-of-the-way location to stash case officers visiting from overseas for a few days or a couple of weeks.

Which is why Sam had no intention of staying at the Wolf Trap. He dropped his bags next to the reception desk and used one of the two dedicated phone lines to summon a taxi. He asked loudly for a ride to Dulles airport. Only after he'd climb into the cab would he tell the driver to take him to the Vienna metro stop, a mile and a half away, instead. Desk clerks have memories and cabdrivers keep records. There'd be no way to track him on metro.

3:40 P.M. The escalator at the Dupont Circle metro stop was working, thank God. Sam rode to the top and flagged a passing cab. Four minutes later, he was standing in the deserted foyer of the Cosmos Club. He gave his carry-on and document case to the porter, limped to the concierge's desk, and booked himself a room. He'd hide in plain sight. The club would be largely deserted until Monday morning. Until then he'd use the side entrance to slip in and out. There were plenty of restaurants and coffee shops within a two-block walk. And more important, there was a computer store over on P Street. More than anything right now, Sam needed a brand-new laptop.

5:15 P.M. Sam plugged the pen drive into the USB port on the laptop. A small icon appeared on the lower right side of the screen. Sam sent the cursor to his Windows Explorer program, and clicked on the removable disk. There were four items, three of them jpg files, and one Adobe Acrobat document.

He clicked on the pdf document. When the damn thing finally opened, Sam saw the cover page of an SVR transcript, marked top secret. He scrolled down. This was the "evidence" that Ed Howard had cited about the president and 9/11. Sam snorted in derision. The document was an obvious fabrication. Howard had to know there'd be no way to authenticate the damn thing from a computer-generated printout. If Rand Arthur had produced this crap as evidence of the president's complicity in a conspiracy, he'd have been laughed out of the Senate.

Sam closed the pdf file and opened the first of the jpg files, bringing up a panoramic view of Red Square and the Kremlin. The second was another panorama, this one of the sixteen ornate golden domes of the Novodevichy Convent, a huge sixteenth-century compound west of the Kremlin surrounded by thick fortified walls and crenellated towers. And the third was a beautiful photograph of dawn breaking over Army Park with the museum in the background.

It didn't make sense. Was Howard playing some kind of joke? Sam opened each of the files once more and scanned the pictures carefully, zooming in as much as he could, to see whether a message had been embedded in the pixels using microdot technology.[38] But he found nothing.

He removed the USB drive. Then he opened the word processing program and, using the cryptic notes he'd made for himself in Moscow and Paris, began work on a series of memos detailing what he'd seen, what he knew, and what he

---

[38] Microdot technology is the art of clandestine communication by reducing information—photographs of documents, or weapons, or diagrams—to microscopic proportions in order to conceal the information by placing it in an otherwise innocent message as a period, or the dot of an *i*.

suspected. His arms were still sore, but it was important to get the words down quickly, because the longer he waited, the more details he'd forget.

At eight he shut the computer off and walked over to Twenty-first and P Street, where he wandered into BeDuCi, a Mediterranean-style French restaurant, sat in the rear of the dimly lit dining room, and wolfed down a braised lamb shank with orzo and a half bottle of Morgon. By nine-fifteen he was back in the small room that looked down onto Florida Avenue, working on his memos. It was past three in the morning when he finally fell asleep atop the narrow single bed.

HE WAITED until nine-thirty Sunday morning to make the call, dialing from a pay phone outside a drugstore on Dupont Circle.

The line rang once, twice, thrice. Finally the familiar voice answered. "Rensin."

"Dave, it's Sam Waterman. Got a minute?"

"Hold on, Sam." There was a momentary pause and a hand was clapped over the receiver. Sam heard Rensin's muffled voice saying, "Go play in the kitchen with mommy because daddy's got to talk on the telephone, honey." There was an instant of silence, then: "Sorry, Sam. How the hell are you?" Rensin laughed heartily and answered his own question. " 'How the hell are you?' Heck, you're deep in the doo-doo again. At least that's what I read in the papers."

Dave Rensin had retired in 1999 as head of CIA's Directorate of Science and Technology. He was recalled immediately after 9/11, and subsequently had been instrumental in developing software that had reduced the "kill chain"—the ability to find, track, verify, target, and destroy—from hours to mere minutes. In the late 1990s, Rensin had designed the initial software that allowed the arming of Predator UAV drones with Hellfire missiles linked to gyroscopically stable

video cameras and GPS satellites. CIA had flown the Preda-
tors as early as 1998. But using Hellfires against targets had
been forbidden until after 9/11. Once he was back in harness,
Rensin fine-tuned his kill-chain programs. The results in
Afghanistan had so far been spectacular.

Rensin finally stopped laughing at his joke. "So, what's up
at this hour on a Sunday morning that you had to call?"

Sam said, "I have a technology problem and I need your
help."

"Hi . . . Sam," Rensin answered in a robotic monotone. "I
am Computer Dave in tech support. To unfreeze your
screen, please press one. To download drivers, please press
two. To—"

"Dave, I'm serious."

"So am I. You want to talk on the phone? Call Microsoft.
You want my help? You know where I live. You're Katie's
godfather, for chrissakes. So, you come to my home, you
make a fuss over my kids, you play with the dog, and you
drink my coffee. *Then* I'll help." He paused. "The coffee's always fresh at Rensin's House o' Bytes, Sammy boy."

"It's very sensitive. I wouldn't want to get you in trouble."

"Trouble? Fuggetaboutit. I know you're hot. BFD. What are
they gonna do, can me? I'm already drawing an SIS pension
plus a day rate. Heck, I make more than the president these
days. And I bet I have a higher clearance than he does, too."

Sam had spent enough time in the field to know when to
take yes for an answer. "Thanks, Dave. I'll see you in an hour
or so."

11:00 A.M. Rensin pulled a two-foot USB connector from a
file cabinet, stepped over a battery-powered Harry Potter
Nimbus-2000 broomstick, plugged Sam's pen drive into the
cable, ran a virus check, then downloaded the images onto a
second portable hard drive. "Let's take a look-see."

He typed in a series of letters from the command line. Almost immediately, the four files on Sam's pen drive—which showed on Rensin's computer as an H drive—were listed on the screen.

"What did you do?"

"I ran something called StegDetect."

"Steg?"

"For steganography. *Steganos* is Greek for 'secret.' I'm going to take it for granted you know what *graphos* means." Rensin sipped vanilla-scented coffee from a Disney World souvenir mug. "It's kind of like digital microdots. With steganography you can hide files in plain sight—either in digital images, like jpgs, or in wav files, which hold music."

"Is it hard to do?"

"Depends who's doing the work. Pull up a seat."

Sam settled gingerly onto the only one available, a kindergarten-size Hogwarts School chair, and scrunched it closer to the screen, his knees at chin level. He felt as if he should be holding a Crayola.

Rensin continued, oblivious to Sam's discomfort. "There are programs and there are programs. We have some at Langley that are pretty sophisticated. But what I have here—" He squinted at a line on the screen. "—everything is totally unclassified, I'd like to emphasize that just in case Big Brother is listening—is pretty basic stuff. Even so, I can pick up an amazing amount of material."

"Like?"

"I can perform due diligence using OSINT and public records. I can get into some credit reporting—and all sorts of public records."

"Show me."

"Let's check up on . . . Sam Waterman." Rensin typed Sam's name into one of his search engines. "I wrote this program about six months ago when I couldn't sleep one night."

Sam watched as the screen filled up with links. Rensin clicked on one. It was the electric bills for Sam's condo in Rosslyn. "Amazing."

Rensin exited the program. "All this and I can decrypt stego, too—if it's not real complex."

He saw the look of concern on Sam's face and tapped the pen drive. "Hey, don't worry. Whoever put this together used one of the easily available stego programs. Maybe J-Steg, or Invisible Secrets."

It made sense. Ed Howard wasn't the techno type. Sam scratched his chin. "What about the pdf file? Could it be hiding material, too?"

Rensin's head bobbed in the affirmative. "You could use something like Camouflage, which secretes data in normal-looking files. Appends your material to a Word file, or Excel—anything, really. Bring up the file, and it looks normal, except that it's read-only. But if then you use the decamouflage program to decrypt the file,—*viola*, there's your secret material. All you need to know is the password."

"Isn't that the hard part?"

Rensin smiled. "For you it's the hard part. That's why I made you come all the way to Bethesda."

Sam stood up, reached over Rensin, and took his mug of coffee, which he'd stashed on the top of the five-drawer government-surplus file cabinet that sat next to the computer table. The mug was emblazoned with the black-and-gold tip-of-the-spear U.S. Special Operations Command seal. "Amazing. Has this stuff been around for long?"

"Believe it or not, al-Qa'ida has been using steganography since the early 1990s. It's a favored form of comms for terrorists. They send jpg images back and forth using AOL, or Wannadoo, or some other commercial Web-hosting sites. That's why you see all those porn pictures on captured terrorist laptops—" He cast a glance at Sam's computer.

"C'mon, Dave—"

"Just wondering." Rensin grinned. "I know how all you sticks-and-bricks guys like to get into the minds of your targets." He turned back to his keyboard. "Problem is, most stego is easy to decode, because the keys are short. But if the key goes half a gig or more, then it starts to get a little problematic, especially if you're working on deadline." He tapped the screen. "But this? I bet we crack this in less than an hour."

4:20 P.M. The message light was blinking on the phone. Sam punched keys and retrieved the message. O'Neill's voice told him Rand Arthur was mightily pissed. "He says sending you to Moscow was a huge mistake, Cyrus. And he believes that meeting with a known double agent during an unauthorized stopover in Paris might hurt relations with the French. And the French, if you haven't been reading the papers, are critical to our current war against terror, and they're leaning toward opposing the upcoming fight in Iraq. I'm trying to sway him, but I'm not having much luck. You know how headstrong he is. I just wish you'd consulted with me before skipping off the reservation on your own."

Sam replaced the receiver, unpacked the sandwiches Lia Rensin had packed for him, unwrapped one, stuffed the other two in the minibar refrigerator, then turned his computer on. The three jpg images on Ed Howard's pen drive held more than a hundred pages of documents. The defector had encrypted the material using an old shareware program called Encrypt-It. Rensin's descrambling software had broken the early-1990s sixty-four-bit keys in a matter of minutes. The documents camouflaged inside the pdf file had taken him a bit longer—but he'd finally broken those ciphers, too, and pulled down half a dozen photographs and another fifty pages of documents.

While Sam played with his goddaughter, Rensin installed

a Blowfish algorithm-based encryption program on Sam's laptop, along with the latest version of the Camouflage program Ed Howard had used, allowing Sam to reencrypt the defector's documents and hide them in plain sight on the same pen drive Howard had left behind in Army Park. It also gave Sam a way to secure the thirty single-spaced pages of memos he'd written.

4:30 P.M. A turkey sandwich at his elbow, Sam decrypted the first batch of Ed Howard's documents. He began scrolling through the pages and examining the photographs. When he finished, he went online, tapped into the *Washington Post* site, registered with the newspaper's archive, transmitted a credit-card number, and pulled down three dozen stories about Yevgeniy Primakov's 1993 visit to Washington.

It was past midnight when he stopped making notes. The sandwich still sat, untouched.

CHAPTЭЯ 24

SAM WAS WAITING in the reception area of Hart 211, Senate Select's office suite, at a quarter to eight, his document case tucked between his knees. Twenty minutes later Virginia Vacario came through the thick steel door with an armload of files, looking downright haggard. And her expression didn't improve when she saw him.

"My office, Sam."

He stayed where he was. " 'Nice to see you, Sam. How are you, Sam? Pleasant trip? Eat well in Paris? Hear you had both lunch and a floor show.' "

"I'm not in the mood for playful this morning." She lowered most of the files onto her secretary's desk and looked at him mournfully. "We really do have to talk."

He rose and hefted the document case. "That's why I'm here."

She walked to her office door and attempted to block Sam's view with her back while she keyed in her cipher combination. But Sam was too fast and he caught the last four of the five-number sequence. Using the nub of pencil and half index card that he invariably carried in his right-hand trouser pocket, Sam wrote down the numbers 0-8-7-4. Vacario waited for the electronic lock to unlatch, then opened the door wide and stood back. "After you."

He followed her inside and watched as she turned the lights on. He heard the door click closed behind him. Sam gave the place a once-over. The office was unusual in that it was entirely characterless; neutral; impersonal. There were no photographs or souvenirs, and only a trio of mementos. On the credenza behind Vacario's desk a Plexiglas case held an English bobby's helmet, a truncheon, and old-fashioned manacles. A presentation-quality nightstick from New York City Police Emergency Services Division sat displayed like a samurai sword. Next to the nightstick, a two-foot, ornately decorated machete from the Mexican National Police extended, Excalibur-like, from a rough chunk of black granite.

The windows were covered by thick, sound-absorbing drapes. Flanking Vacario's credenza stood a three-foot-high, industrial-strength shredder, a wastebasket holding a burn bag, and an American flag on a stanchion. On the wall was the Great Seal of the United States, flanked by seals of the Central Intelligence Agency, the National Reconnaissance Office, No Such Agency, and the Defense Intelligence Agency. And thus, Sam thought, endeth all ornamentation.

A utilitarian wooden table held piles of manila file folders. Next to the table sat three four-drawer fireproof file cabinets with combination locks. On the opposite wall was a six-foot-tall, four-foot-wide bank-size safe, with a third-generation electronic lock. A brown leather sofa with an afghan tossed over the arm was pushed up against the safe. It was obviously the place where Ginny grabbed a combat nap when she worked a twenty-hour day, because there was no coffee table or overstuffed chairs to invite discussion or suggest hospitality.

The starkness of the place was reinforced by the four old-fashioned, rail-back oak-wood armchairs that fanned out in front of Vacario's desk. It actually occurred to Sam to check and see whether they came equipped with arm straps, leg restraints, and power cords.

Vacario set the file folders on the desktop. She unlocked one of the drawers and dropped her handbag into the lower right-hand drawer, locked it again, settled into the austere fabric chair behind the desk, and indicated for Sam to take a seat.

When he did, she rolled the chair forward, put her elbows on the desk, and cupped her chin in her hands. She looked like a little girl just then. "Oh, Sam," she sighed mournfully, "what the hell am I going to do with you?"

He shrugged. "There's always vodka and caviar."

"It was vodka and caviar that got me in trouble."

He examined her face. It was, despite the tiredness and obvious tension, a lovely face. He wished he could trust it.

"Sam, what makes me hurt so much is the fact that I'm so damnably attracted to you. I do like you. I like you a lot."

"Feeling's mutual," he said. "But you should have told me the truth."

"The truth?"

"Bonn," he said. "You didn't tell me about Bonn."

"I couldn't. I can't. You know how these things work, Sam." She fumbled in her desk drawer. "You signed the same papers I did. Besides, that's not the point."

"What is the point?"

"Oh, dammit, Sam, give me your credential. Please."

He pulled the laminated ID from his shirt pocket, lifted the chain from his neck, and slid the card across the desk. She took it, unfastened the chain, then dropped the ID into the shredder. "Chairman's orders."

"So I've been declared a nonperson." He snorted derisively. "How Stalinesque. Well, I guess that shows *me*." His expression softened. "What about us, Ginny?"

"Oh, Sam." Vacario bit her lower lip. "This isn't me talking right now. It's Rand Arthur."

"If you say so."

"Your services are no longer required by Senate Select."

"Just like that."

"You haven't made things easy. You met with a French agent in Paris, Sam—after entering the country as a tourist, and without notifying the French government, you planned to contact one of their assets, even though Paris was aware you were working for this committee. Then the man is killed on your watch. The Quai d'Orsay[39] was furious. The foreign minister sent a démarche to State. Some wet-behind-the-ears DAS at EUR[40] contacted the senator and demanded—*demanded*, Sam—an explanation. Which, of course, the senator couldn't provide, since you were operating completely off the reservation."

"I had my reasons."

"Perhaps. I'd like to give you the benefit of the doubt. But then, you refused to see the senator when you returned from Paris. State leaked the whole story to the press. The senator's been badgered all weekend by questions—and he's had to duck them. You know Rand Arthur, Sam. He doesn't like to duck reporters."

"What about O'Neill?"

"Michael's been a big help—he smoothed things over with

[39] The French Foreign Ministry is located on the Quai d'Orsay, directly opposite the Invalides metro station.
[40] In bureaucratic jumble-speak shorthand: a DAS is a Deputy Assistant Secretary; and EUR is the Department of State's Bureau of European and Eurasian Affairs.

State, and he handled the press beautifully. But you, not he, were the focus of all the attention. We needed you—working in support of the senator. Rand Arthur asked for your help and you refused. He sees it as dereliction of duty."

How like Rand—everything was about him. "It's not that simple, Ginny."

"It is to him." She paused. "So, what's the story about this Russian, Semonov?"

Sam wasn't about to go into detail under the circumstances. "He's a Russian I used to know. We were having lunch. He got killed. End of story."

She looked dubious. "No connection to Edward Lee Howard?"

"None."

"O'Neill told the senator Semonov was a double agent who had been terminated by Langley because he worked for Ed Howard."

Admit nothing. "O'Neill's wrong."

"How do you know?

Deny everything. "Because I was deputy chief in Paris with access to every single compartment and O'Neill was a wet-behind-the-ears greenhorn with access to perhaps one or two."

"Then why was Semonov murdered?"

File countercharges. "How the hell should I know. Maybe Semonov was involved with the Russian Mafiya. Maybe he got on the wrong side of his Lebanese in-laws. Maybe the French got tired of paying him."

"You're being defensive. Does that mean you're hiding something?"

For a minute, Sam had forgotten she was a Player—a pro, just like he was. She'd gone to tradecraft, too. *Provoke. Goad. Incite.*

He used the countermoves. *Deflect. Redirect. Sidetrack.*

"It means I'm pissed off at Rand Arthur, Ginny." He gave her the wistful smile and the crinkling eyes. "Okay, the senator says I'm gone, then I'm gone." Pause. "What about Senate Select's chief counsel?"

Vacario bit her lower lip again. "Sam, please. Don't make this any harder than it already is." She pulled a document from a folder, gave it a quick glance, then laid it on the desk. "Sign this please."

He leaned forward, pulled the single sheet of paper to him, and looked at it. It was a boilerplate agreement stipulating that everything Sam had learned while working for SSCI was confidential and proprietary to SSCI, and that all materials of any sort and in any form that were in his possession during the period he'd been working for the committee were the property of the committee and must be handed over. He scrawled his name at the bottom and slid it back toward Vacario. She stared at him. "Are you carrying any documents?"

"I brought your transcripts. I knew you'd want them back."

"Do you possess any other materials?"

"No."

"Nothing from Moscow—or Paris?"

"Nothing from Moscow or Paris."

She struggled to her feet, holding the transcripts to her chest, and walked across to the big safe. She punched at the dial and turned the handle but the safe remained locked. She waited ten seconds and repeated the sequence. This time Sam caught it. He flipped the index card and wrote the numbers down.

Vacario opened the heavy black enameled steel door, knelt, and lay the Howard transcripts on the bottom shelf. The top shelf contained an accordion file that was labeled SEN. ARTHUR—PERSONAL. Just behind it Sam could see a padlocked safe-deposit box.

Ginny rose, closed the safe, and tested the handle to make sure the door was tightly secured.

"Do you have anything else I should see, Sam?"

"As a matter of fact, I do." Sam set the heavy leather bag on her desk, opened it up, and extracted three plastic bags, each containing a package protected by plastic bubble wrap. He unwrapped them and set the contents gently in front of her. There was a half liter bottle of Golden Ring vodka, 250 grams of Petrossian beluga, and a full ounce of Chanel No. 5. "I picked these up at de Gaulle on my way out."

Ginny's eyes teared up.

Sam tilted the case so she could look inside. "See? Nothing else. You can report to the senator that you searched and came up dry."

He snapped the top of the case shut, then stood up. "Ginny," he said, "I'll be in touch." Then he stood, took the case in his left hand, and walked out to the sound of quiet sobbing.

11:45 A.M. Sam metroed to Rosslyn. He walked up to the Hyatt on Wilson Boulevard, turned west, and made his way two and a half long blocks, skirting Purgatory to ensure that he wouldn't run into anyone he knew. Just past a firehouse, he turned onto a narrow ribbon of concrete that skirted an elementary school, made his way across the street, and used a small electronic device on his key chain to unlock the back door of his apartment building. He passed through a second locked door, turned left, then made his way down a long, carpeted hallway to a service elevator, which he took to the ninth floor.

He made his way down the dimly illuminated corridor and stopped in front of his door. He could see a bunch of circulars had been slid under the sill. He turned the key, extracted it, pushed the door open, stepped over the flyers, set his case on the rug, closed the door behind him, and rolled the dead bolt.

He'd bought the apartment just before he'd left for his Paris tour. It was a comfortable two-bedroom apartment in a glass-fronted, fourteen-story building called the Atrium. He faced northwest, and from his living room Sam could see the spires of Georgetown University; the hulking, white, boxy Russian embassy on upper Wisconsin Avenue; and beyond it, the crocket-ornamented towers of the National Cathedral. The location was convenient, the building anonymous, and the desk manned twenty-four hours a day. He'd rented the place out during his overseas tours—and each time he came home, the apartment was swept by Agency technicians to make sure no bugs had been planted during his absence.

First, Sam checked to see that the intrusion devices he'd placed before leaving for Moscow hadn't been disturbed. He dismantled them, set his case on the foyer table, and walked to the living room windows. The vertical blinds were set at an angle that allowed him to peer down at the street. There was no sign of a media stakeout. He flipped his cell phone open and called the front desk, recited his pass code number, asked if there was anyone waiting to see him, and was gratified to hear he was not in demand. That was the way things went in Washington—the lead story on Friday is birdcage material on Monday. Thank God for the media's short attention span.

He turned on the lights, turned up the thermostat, and brewed a pot of coffee. The red message light on the wireless phone in the kitchen was blinking. Sam uncradled it and dialed his voice-mail number, punched in his code, and learned he had sixteen new messages. He queued them up and listened. Most were from reporters asking him to return their call. There were two from O'Neill. Sam listened to both. His friend's voice was high-pitched, almost panicky. The same way he'd been on the phone in Moscow. The messages were almost identical. Please, Sam, call ASAP. Sam—criticom. Must talk.

Well, O'Neill would have to wait. Sam pulled the materials he'd retrieved from the concierge at the Cosmos out of his document case, sat down at his dining table, and went to work.

The two American agents Howard had mentioned at Rand Arthur's were cryptonymed SCARAB and SCEPTRE. Sam checked his notes. Edward Lee Howard had said that SCARAB, who'd managed to get the Kiev op scrubbed, worked for NSC. And that he passed messages using a safe house. And that Primakov had seen SCARAB at a reception on the eighth floor of the State Department—the Diplomatic Reception Rooms. Primakov had watched, according to Ed Howard, as SCARAB's control officer had passed the agent a tasking.

The hidden files on the pen drive included two dozen NSC documents dating back as far as 1993. The photographs were grainy black-and-white surveillance pictures. They showed meetings between individuals Sam couldn't identify, what appeared to be signal sites and dead drops at locations that could be anywhere. Sam put the pictures aside and concentrated on the documents. All were clearance memos,[41] which were classified either CONFIDENTIAL or SENSITIVE.

That told Sam that no matter what Howard said, whoever had taken the memos probably didn't have a TS/SCI[42] clear-

---

[41] All U.S. government agency statements and policies, from a presidential speech like the State of the Union, to the words spoken by departmental spokesmen or issued in press releases, must go through a vetting process in which every one of the interested parties has a chance to amend the language, or insert something. The one single paragraph in a presidential statement about U.S.-Russian relations that dealt with U.S.-Russia trade, for example, would have to be run past the relevant bureaus at State, CIA's Russia Division, the office of the U.S. trade representative, and the Departments of Commerce and Treasury, at the very least.

[42] Top Secret/Sensitive Compartmented Information.

ance. If they'd had one, they would have had access to much
better data. The memos on Sam's screen were low-grade material. Which meant Howard's claim of a Russian intelligence network operating within the highest levels of the
American government was horse puckey.

Or was it? Obviously, someone who was not Ed Howard
had betrayed Pavel Baranov. Someone who was not SCEP-
TRE or SCARAB had access to top-secret intelligence
files—code-word stuff—at Langley. That same someone
had targeted Pavel Baranov, Irina and Ed Howard, and
Alexei Semonov.

There are no coincidences. That's the key. *Look for the
pattern. Follow the road map Ed Howard left behind.* It was
like infiltrating one of the old Soviet networks: you started
with the small fry, and worked your way up the food
chain. So, the first hurdle was identifying SCEPTRE and
SCARAB.

IT WAS TIME to go to the videotape. Sam went to his book-
case and dug out the Federal Staff Directory for 1993.
FSDs were published twice a year. Each volume listed more
than thirty thousand employees working for the Executive
Office of the President, the cabinet departments, and the in-
dependent agencies. For someone like Sam, working overseas, the FSDs were as vital as phonebooks and contact lists.
And the old volumes were helpful, too. By checking the in-
dices, he could track a federal employee's career path over a
decade or more.

He flipped to the National Security Council listings, which
ran just under three pages. All the memos dealt with Russia
or the Ukraine. That meant he could discount most of the
NSC's divisions. Sam concentrated on the offices that handled Russia/Ukraine/Eurasia, intelligence programs, and
global issues and multilateral affairs. All the senior directors

had boxes next to their names indicating they were presidential appointments—Schedule Cs in government-speak. Howard had said SCARAB was a long-term employee at NSC. So scrub the political people. That left a total of sixteen directors, assistant directors, and staff assistants in the three target offices. Sam wrote their names down on a legal pad. Then he pulled out all his FSDs and began the laborious process of cross-checking.

2:15 P.M. With the absolute certainty of the naïf, Sam was convinced SCARAB had to be one of three people. Edith Johnson had worked off and on at the NSC since the Reagan administration. She first showed up in the FSD as a special assistant in the 1982 edition. Then she was back in 1984 working in the NSC's admin office as an assistant. In 1986 she'd been the administrative assistant in the Office of Defense Policy and Arms Control. In 1989 she'd been assigned to the Situation Room as a duty officer. And in 1993 she turned up in the NSC's Office of Intelligence Programs as a special assistant.

But there was a problem with Johnson. Sam knew that Sit Room duty officers all held TS/SCI clearances. They had to, given the waves of sensitive material washing over their desks.

That left two. There was Barbara Steiner, who'd first gone to the Reagan NSC as a junior staffer seconded from DOD. Steiner had remained at NSC for twelve years in a series of dead-end positions before returning to the Pentagon in 1995. Vernon Myles had served on the NSC during the SCARAB window as well. Of those two, Myles was the most likely candidate for no-goodnik of the year. Currently he was a staff assistant in the office of the assistant secretary of state for politico-military affairs. But before that he'd worked at NSC. His first stint there was during the Carter administration—a political appointment as administrative assistant in the Public Affairs Office. But Myles hadn't resigned when Carter lost the 1980 election to Ronald Reagan. He had "burrowed,"[43] first as an anonymous exhibits officer at State's Bureau of Public Affairs. Then as a staff assistant at WorldNet, the U.S. Information Agency's moribund television arm. He reemerged at NSC during Clinton, assigned to minor slots in the information management directorate. Now he worked at State. What piqued Sam's interest was that the guy was awfully old to still be a staff assistant. Staff assistant was a job for twentysomethings—maybe even thirtysomethings. Myles had to be fifty-three, fifty-four years old. Which told Sam that either Vernon Myles was a huge underachiever, or he was working far below his capabilities on purpose.

Sam walked into the second bedroom, which he'd furnished as a library-cum-office-cum-guest-room, and turned his computer on. He checked his e-mail for the first time in almost two weeks and noted with bemusement that more than eighty individuals whom he had never met nonetheless thought they knew him well enough to tell him his penis needed enlargement. Then he checked a phone number in his address book and used his cell phone to dial the number.

3:35 P.M. Sam trudged up the escalator of the Metro Center station, crossed F Street, and headed east. At Ninth Street he walked into a coffee shop and joined a lanky man in a pinstripe suit, starched white shirt, and ancient madder tie who was stirring sugar substitute into a cup of coffee so weak that Sam could see the bottom of the cup through the steaming liquid. "Hey, Forbes."

---

[43] Burrowing takes place when a political appointee does not resign at the end of the administration, but finds a permanent slot at an agency and "burrows" in that slot until he/she becomes a permanent civil service employee. Sometimes, individuals who burrow leave their civil service slots to take another political appointment when their party regains the White House.

"Yo, Elbridge." John Forbes had been LEGATT—the attaché for legal affairs, otherwise known as the FBI embassy slot—in Paris when Sam was deputy chief. Former Marines with a fondness for Guinness stout, the two had struck up a decadelong friendship buttressed by professional interests and similar histories. Both men were expat New Yorkers—Sam had grown up in Manhattan; Forbes in Bay Ridge. Both had attended Catholic schools. Both had seen combat in Vietnam. And both had an interest in spies. Indeed, until 9/11 Forbes had worked the counterintelligence beat for almost two decades. Now, like most of the FBI's CI specialists, he'd been reassigned. These days, Forbes was the assistant deputy director of the FBI's National Security Division, where he dealt with counterterrorism.

Sam shook his friend's hand, slid into the booth, and ordered a Diet Coke. He watched as Forbes ripped open a second package of sugar substitute and dumped it into the coffee. "Careful not to get any of that stuff on your hands."

"Why?"

"I wouldn't be walking into JEH[44] showing any white powder these days."

"Nah." Forbes laughed. "Anthrax task force is working out of Buzzard Point and the people I work with wouldn't recognize anthrax if was sitting in an evidence bag." He cast an appraising glance at Sam. "You're looking better than your pictures."

"Bite me, Assistant Director Forbes."

"Just committing truth." Forbes wiggled his thin mustache and graying eyebrows. "But I tell you what, Sam."

"What?"

"If I was a Russkie, I wouldn't go within twenty blocks of you. You is baaad luck for Russkies."

[44] The J. Edgar Hoover Building, FBI headquarters.

"Is that your considered opinion?"

"Not my opinion—it's a damn fact. I'm a trained professional. An expert witness. I could testify in court that being around you is bad for a Russkie's health." Forbes stirred, then sipped gingerly. "So, what's up, Elbridge?"

"I need some help," Sam said.

Forbes blinked. "Ask and it's yours." In Paris, Sam had clandestinely tasked one of the station's agents—an Algerian national—to break into the Hotel Crillon suite of an American citizen—the CEO of a Fortune 500 company—Forbes was forbidden by American law from entering. Once inside, the Algerian was instructed to photograph certain documents in the American's briefcase that proved the corporation was illegally paying kickbacks to a certain Russian oligarch.

Normally, the G-man would have approached his liaison at the French domestic security agency and asked the French to search the suite as a personal favor. But since the American had been blackmailed into spying on the Russian oligarch by DST in the first place, that particular solution was out of the question.

Because of Sam's help, Forbes could swear to his nervous-Nellie bosses back at JEH that no FBI official had done anything untoward, and the information he'd acquired had been obtained through a third party with no affiliation whatsoever to the United States Department of Justice or any of its agencies.

Things often worked that way. When the National Security Agency wants to eavesdrop on American nationals—an act forbidden by law—NSA simply asks its friends at the Canadian, British, or Australian SIGINT[45] agencies to do the job. The deals are reciprocal, allowing ministers of each govern-

---

[45] SIGnals INTelligence.

ment to deny—under oath when necessary—that there is no illegal eavesdropping directed against the citizenry.

When Ambassador Harriman discovered what Sam had done, she wrote a letter of reprimand and dispatched it to Langley, with a copies to the White House and the secretary of state. The American businessman had been both an intimate friend and a large contributor to the Democratic National Committee. But Sam didn't care: the operation had resulted in a conviction (albeit with a suspended sentence). And over the past decade, the favor—and a few similar ones—had been returned twentyfold by a grateful John Forbes.

Sam slid an index card with three names on it under the special agent's saucer. "I need to know if any of these people ever had a security problem at the White House."

Forbes snorted derisively. "I thought this was gonna be something tough." He pocketed the card. "When?"

"ASAP—with as much as you can assemble."

"How's tomorrow—five-thirty at the Dubliner?"

"Great."

"Good—because you're buying."

"Works for me." Sam thought for a minute. "John, when we were in Paris . . ."

"Ah, the City of Light. You. Me. All those *jeunes filles*. So many women, so little time."

"Forget the *jeunes filles*. Did you ever surveil Ed Howard?"

Forbes blinked. "The defector?"

"Yup."

The G-man shook his head. "Not on my watch."

"Was it ever done? I'm talking full-court press. Video."

"Maybe by the French," Forbes said. "But definitely not us."

"Can you check?"

"Sure. There'd be a record if we asked DST." Forbes rose,

flipping a five-dollar bill onto greasy Formica. "Don't forget: Dubliner. Seventeen-thirty. Your tab."

"It will be my pleasure."

"It will indeed." Forbes rapped his knuckles on the table. "Nice to see you and all that, Elbridge old chap, but I gotta get back to the grind. We're about to ratchet up into THREATCON Orange and Director Mueller keeps sending me memos about how important it is to catch Tangos before they hit us again. Tangos, Elbridge, is LE[46] talk for bad guys, just in case you missed it."

"Remember to say hi to the guy in the dress for me, John."

---

[46] Law Enforcement.

CHAPTƎЯ 25

6:03 P.M. Both of the Dubliner's barrooms were jammed when Sam walked in, filled with a bustling crowd of congressional staffers, lobbyists, lawyers, and other assorted political hangers-on. It was not lost on Sam that every time he visited the venerable Capitol Hill hangout, the customers seemed to be getting younger.

He was more than half an hour late, but he'd felt uneasy coming up the metro escalator at Union Station. There had been a series of unmistakable pings all the way from Rosslyn. And so he'd taken a roundabout route to the saloon, trying to spot surveillance but unable to do so. Maybe, he decided, he was just on edge.

He shrugged out of his coat and elbowed his way to the back room, where the adults hung out. Forbes was sitting on a stool nursing the last inch of a pint glass of Guinness. A cigarette dangled from his lips and an attractive Alien in a black pantsuit nuzzled his ear.

The G-man saw Sam, stabbed the cigarette out, and waved

him over. "Yo, Elbridge." He swiveled and signaled for a new round of stout, then turned and shook Sam's hand. "Elbridge, this is Johanna Simeone. You don't want to get on her wrong side. She's the only female currently on our hostage rescue team and she knows eighteen different ways to kill you. Johanna, this is Elbridge. He used to be a spook. You can get on his wrong side anytime."

She had cool dark eyes that assessed Sam as he stuck his hand out. "Nice to meet you, although I feel compelled to say you have lousy taste in men."

"I'm a masochist. I'm heavily into pain and suffering. Besides, he's kind of cute and he carries handcuffs and a pistol." Her voice was as rich and smooth as Belgian chocolate. "Nice to meet you, too, Elbridge." She shook his hand firmly, then turned back to the bar and topped her glass of mineral water off.

Sam reached across the bar, took his pint, and tipped his glass toward the FBI agents. "Good health." He drank. "So, what are you doing in Washington? I thought you people were down in Quantico."

"I pulled some strings—got her assigned to the director's detail. The commuting was killing us." He lifted his own glass off the bar and swallowed. "At eighteen hundred hours tomorrow, Johanna's off to Europe with Director Mueller. They get back just before Thanksgiving. But when she does, she gets six days off." He put the glass down and brushed his forehead languidly with the back of his hand. "Y'know, I'm starting to feel a little sickly. I think I may be coming down with something."

"Lemme take your pulse." Sam reached over and took Forbes's wrist. "Hmm." He looked at Johanna. "It's serious. My diagnosis is that about a week from now he's going to be one sick puppy."

Forbes fluttered his eyelids. "What do I have?"

"Blue flu. It takes a week or so to incubate. And then six days to cure."

"Blue flu." Forbes guffawed. "That's the thing about you, Elbridge—you're insightful. Perceptive. A keen judge of human nature. You are mah bro-tha. We are bro-thas. To the end."

Johanna Simeone shook her head. "I'm going to the head—gotta get back to work," she said. "Director has a twenty-hundred dinner. Besides, all this male bonding makes me want to puke."

"That's me." Forbes beamed. "I taught her that, Sam. And she can swear like a gunny, too."

Johanna twisted Forbes's ear, then kissed it as she slid off the bar stool, displaying the briefest flash of the pistol on her hip. "Don't tempt me to discipline you in a public place, my sweet." She turned toward Sam. "Y'know, every time I cuff him and walk him out of a restaurant, he gets embarrassed. I think he's getting mellow in his old age."

"Forbes is a very sensitive human being," Sam said. "That's why we all love him so much."

She ran a hand through her hair. "I like you, Elbridge," she said. "Forbes told me you were one of the good guys. How come I haven't seen you until now?"

"I've been doing the hermit thing for a few months."

"You don't seem the hermit type."

"It was a stage." Sam hadn't really thought about it until he'd just opened his mouth. But it *had* been a stage—and he was finally over it.

"You boys stay put." She wiggled her fingers. "I'll be back."

Forbes watched self-contentedly as she sidled through the throng. "Oh, God, I love it when she talks like that." He turned to face Sam. "Best thing ever happened to me, she is."

"How long has this been going on?"

Forbes wrinkled his brow. "Haven't seen you in what—

seven, eight months. So it's been six—maybe a little over." He drank his Guinness down to the bottom. "We're talking marriage, Sam."

"Congratulations."

"Never thought I'd do that again. But Johanna—" He slapped the glass on the bar and signaled for another round. "Great lady." He paused. "And as long as she's gone . . ." Forbes slid a thickly stuffed envelope out of his pocket and handed it to Sam. "Interesting material you asked for. Mind if I ask what the story is?"

Sam opened the envelope, took a quick peek at what was inside, and was delighted. "Don't really know the story yet, John," he said. "But I'll make you a deal: when I get something concrete, you're the first person I'm going to call."

"I can live with that." Forbes's face grew serious. "In the meanwhile, you take care of what's in the envelope. They can people for mishandling stuff like that these days." He drained his Guinness. "Hell, Elbridge, I even wore rubber gloves when I pulled the files."

"What does the Bureau issue these days? Last I remember it was those elbow-length yellow rubber things that were so thick they could have doubled as Russian prophylactics."

"Very funny. You catch my drift."

"I do, I do," Sam said. "And I will." He slapped two twenties down on the bar and took his coat from the back of the bar stool. "Gotta go," he said. "Say good-bye to the lady for me."

"Christ, Elbridge, whatever happened to romance? Whatever happened to commitment? This is our first date in months. I give it up, and next thing I know you put your clothes on and run for the door."

"You know me—love 'em and leave 'em Waterman." Sam tapped the breast pocket of his sport coat. "Thanks, John."

"Nada."

* * *

THE WEATHER had turned bitter—it felt like snow in the air—and Sam was glad he'd brought a coat. He started for the Union Station metro but stopped abruptly on Massachusetts Avenue, hailed a taxi, and jumped in. Tonight, he'd splurge. Although the G-man didn't know it, Forbes had helped him break things wide open.

Sam was halfway to Rosslyn when he realized he'd forgotten to follow up with Forbes about the Howard surveillance. That was Johanna's fault—she was damn impressive. Sam peered at the lights on M Street, wondering if he'd be able to salvage his relationship with Ginny. It had been years since he'd felt so intensely about a woman. The cabdriver ran a red light, swerved around oncoming traffic, fishtailed onto Key Bridge, and sped into Rosslyn.

Up the hill and to his right, Sam could just make out the illuminated exterior elevator of his apartment building. He scrunched back in the seat so he could pull the billfold out of his rear pocket and made a mental note to call Forbes in the morning.

SAM WAS UP at five. He stretched for ten minutes, working the soreness out of his shoulders and legs. Then he climbed into his foul-weather running gear: tights, turtleneck, weatherproof nylon shell, knit cap, and Gore-Tex gloves. He locked the door behind him, secured the keys in a zippered pocket, and walked to the elevator. As he rode down, Sam saw the rain had turned to light snow overnight. He waved at the desk clerk, pushed out through the Atrium's front entrance, and headed into the darkness.

Sam's unvarying five-mile course took him out Wilson Boulevard to the DIA office building atop the Clarendon metro, then east, along Fairfax Drive to Route 50. From there, he looped around the Marine Memorial, cut through Fort Meyer, and then headed back into Rosslyn. In the summer, there were dozens of joggers out at this hour. But when the seasons changed, it was only a few hardy souls like Sam who kept up the routine. He gave his legs a final stretch on a streetlight pole just past the Atrium driveway, then headed down the hill toward Oak Street. The climb to Wilson and the following half mile uphill incline past Colonial Village got Sam's heart pumping and he liked the strain it added.

Sam turned the corner. To his left, he could see the rear of Purgatory—an ugly, late-1970s glass-and-steel Seagram's Building wannabe looming in the darkness on Nash Street. Even at this hour, there were lights on. Untouchables crafting legends. Or ruining them. It wasn't just the Agency either. A couple of years back, Forbes had told him about an FBI penetration operation into a joint Russian *Mafiya*–Cali Cartel money-laundering scheme that had gone sour when the poor son of a bitch who'd been dropped undercover was given Joe Pistone's Donny Brasco Social Security number.

Pistone was a now-retired FBI special agent who'd spent years infiltrating the New York Mob under the alias Donny Brasco. Pistone did enough damage that even now, more then twenty years after the operation had closed down, there was still an open half-million-dollar contract on his scalp. And yet, the FBI bean counters, knowing how frugal Director Freeh was when it came to funding undercover ops, hadn't retired Pistone's Donny Brasco legend—the Social Security number, the driver's license, the bank accounts—the whole bloody Brasco identity.

And so, when Unsuspecting Special Agent Schlemazel's Social Security number was checked out by the Colombian *drogista* and Russian *vor* whose money Schlemazel was allegedly about to launder, they came up with the name Donny Brasco. Hell, the Russian had even seen the movie. According to Forbes, if someone sharp hadn't caught the mistake and yanked him the hell out of Cartagena *right now,* Agent Schlemazel would have been cut into bite-size pieces and fed to the Russkie's pet tiger. And that would have been the painless part.

Sam checked behind for traffic—there was none—then turned onto Wilson, heading up the long slope to the Arlington Courthouse. God bless Forbes. The G-man had not only given Sam what he needed, he'd provided photos—copies of the trio's White House, State Department, and Pentagon IDs. Sam had compared them with the clandestinely taken pictures from Ed Howard's files, photos of two individuals meeting with an SVR officer. Pictures of money being exchanged for documents. Pictures of the individuals putting their thumbprints on the receipts.

And two of the individuals Sam had asked Forbes about— Barbara Steiner and Vernon Myles—were in the photos. So were two Russian intelligence officers whose faces Sam picked out from the FBI's SVR flash book.[47]

Could Ed Howard's photos have been doctored? Obviously the answer was yes. And so, while they gave Sam a leg up, they weren't absolute proof that the two staffers were dirty. He'd need to make that determination on his own.

Sam looked up to see the Pines of Florence, a neighborhood Italian restaurant, on his right. It was almost as if he'd gotten there by osmosis. His strides were confident and regular, his breathing easy, even with the strain of the long climb behind him. The soreness from Paris was leeching out of his

---

[47] FBI counterintelligence personnel and CIA case officers are often provided with pocket-size, spiral-bound books of portraits of their quarry so they can memorize the opposition agents' features, or quickly identify them during an operation. The pictures are assembled from surveillance photos as well as passport, visa, and driver's license photographs.

body, molecule by molecule. By next week, it would disappear completely.

A car passed him, moving slowly, its DC plates disappearing into the darkness. What wouldn't disappear was the doubt that gnawed at Sam's brain. Everything was all too simple, too neat. And there was something else: SCARAB and SCEPTRE were low-level agents. They were disposables.

If Edward Lee Howard had truly been a double—if he'd really been Bill Casey's Alec Leamas—he'd have been dispatched to uncover more important moles than SCEPTRE and SCARAB. He'd have been sent to find out who'd blown America's top Russian agents. Howard's defection had taken place three years after he'd been fired by the Agency. That had given the Soviets plenty of time to check his background; three years for Moscow Center to verify his motives. It was a hugely complex and risky operation. Still, it was also exactly the sort of high-risk, high-return op Bill Casey had grown up with in OSS. Casey had precisely the sort of personality to put Ed Howard into play to steal Moscow's crown jewels—the identities of its top American moles. But Valentin Klimov was also devious. It was altogether possible for him to leak disinformation about Howard so he could double the American defector back at the United States. Sam snorted frosty white smoke from his nostrils. Christ—no wonder they called it the Wilderness of Mirrors.

As Sam crossed the wide intersection opposite the courthouse, he could see two other foul-weather joggers coming north out of the darkness, running with the tight precision of military personnel. Sam flashed a wave as they crossed Wilson. They returned his greeting and formed up perhaps a hundred and fifty yards behind him.

Sam's breathing was regular. His stride easy. Okay: let's pursue the double-agent scenario. SCARAB and SCEPTRE were disposables. That was undeniable.

Then whom had Ed Howard locked on to? That was the question. Because Howard had been killed in order to silence him. So had Ed's Russian wife Irina. And Alexei Semonov. There was something missing here; something Sam couldn't see.

And yet . . . and yet . . . Sam was convinced that Howard's actions were somehow a message. A message intended for him—just for Sam. Just like the message concealed in the seat stub. Breaking the code of the seat stub had been easy. But what the hell else had Howard been trying to tell him?

Sam sensed the runners behind him moving up. He glanced around, saw they were within a hundred and fifty yards, and increased his pace slightly.

Sam liked this route. It was easy to gauge the distance he'd run, because just like in Washington, the street names ran alphabetically. He'd just crossed Edgewood and was on his way to Fillmore when the two runners behind him really closed the gap. It was funny how he could discern their approach—as if they were pushing energy waves ahead of themselves. He sped up slightly to keep his distance.

Sixty yards ahead, two more early-morning runners emerged from the next street. They started toward him—way too fast to be joggers. That's when all the bells and whistles went off in Sam's head. He glanced behind him. The men trailing him were a chase team—and they were within ninety yards now, and closing fast. Ten yards ahead, Sam saw an alley between a Latino grocery and a pizza joint. He sprinted for it.

He ducked into the alley. Ahead, in the orange glow of sodium security lights, the asphalt dead-ended at a ten-foot-tall chain-link fence topped by barbed wire. Parallel to the fence line, a second alley led to Fillmore Street. Sam looked around wildly. To his left were half a dozen filled-to-the-brim garbage cans. To his right was an industrial-size trash container filled with construction crap. Sam ran past the huge bin. Its top was open. As he slid on the snowy macadam, he halted just long enough to grab at a three-foot length of two-by-four sticking out of the shoulder-high bin. He snatched, missed the damn thing, slipped on ice, found his footing, and went for it again.

Sam's gloved hand closed tight on the plank—right atop an exposed nail. He screamed and pulled his impaled hand away. The lumber clattered to the ground. Sam went down on hands and knees and finally came up with it.

There was no time to think about pain. He looked up to see the second pair of joggers lurch into the alley. Except they weren't joggers. One was a big black guy in a knit cap, a red ski jacket, and sweatpants—he had some kind of sap or baton in his hand. The other was a white guy. He wore a knit cap, too. And a black-and-silver Oakland Raiders parka, and jeans. He was holding something, too.

Holy mother of God, it was a stun gun. A big, evil-looking thing with two silver prongs. Sam saw the device as the dude came in low, his face contorted in a grimace, his body exuding—bizarrely, it struck Sam at the time, given the situation—a spicy, floral odor. The guy must have bathed in cologne.

Shards of boot camp thrust through his panic, shock, and fear. Sam tried for a War Face. He screamed at the top of his lungs the primeval, throaty howl that the Gunnys had embedded in his subconscious.

"Argghhh!" From his knees, Sam swung the two-by-four as hard as he could. He connected. The big nail bit into Oakland's leg just at the knee, and he screamed and went down, the stun gun skittering under the trash container.

Down but not out—as he collapsed, Oakland took a round-house swing at Sam's head.

Sam recoiled rearward. He smashed the back of his head against the trash bin and saw stars. Everything went black and white. But he never let go of the makeshift club. He screamed obscenities again, ripped the nail out of Oakland dude's leg—"Die, motherfucker"—and swatted the downed attacker's head. Home fucking run. Oakland dropped with a thud and an "ungh."

Movement on his left. Red Jacket came at him, his right arm outstretched, something in his hand. Sam rolled out of the way, tried to put one of the garbage cans between himself and the guy, but Red Jacket was a big guy—pumped and lean. Big as a house. He kicked the garbage can out of the way and went for Sam.

Something wet caught Sam's face. Pepper spray. Sam's arm instinctively went up, protecting his eyes. But some of the hot stuff was already running down his forehead, into his eyes, blinding him.

Sam backpedaled. Then he remembered what the Gunnys had told him. Never retreat. When ambushed, counterambush. He screamed and reversed course, swinging the two-by-four wildly. Red Jacket stopped, then backed away, fumbling in his pocket with his right hand, while his left, extended, sprayed liquid at Sam.

Sam's eyes stung like hell. But he never stopped swinging the club, forcing his attacker to keep his distance.

The pepper spray ran dry. Red Jacket looked at the canister and said, "Oh, shit."

That was when Sam screamed and charged him. He swung the two-by-four like a baseball bat at Red Jacket's shoulder. The big guy caught the lumber with a bare hand, stopping Sam's swing cold. Then he screamed like a wounded animal. In the orange light Sam could see where the nail had gone clear through Red Jacket's hand.

Red Jacket looked at his bloody hand and his eyes went crazy. He jerked his other hand out of his jacket, yanked—and two-handed, pulled the two-by-four out of Sam's grasp.

Red Jacket flung the club away then turned to face Sam, fury in his eyes. From his left, Sam heard growling. He looked around to see that Oakland Raider was on all fours, scrambling to reach the stun gun under the trash bin.

Sam grabbed a garbage-can lid, whirled, and smashed the back of Oakland Raider's head with the edge of metal disk, sending him face-first into the steel wall of the trash bin. Oakland went down.

That's when Red Jacket tackled Sam. Took them both down onto the snowy alley. He was strong—and Sam was having problems seeing through the pepper spray. A fist caught the side of Sam's head and stunned him. Sam's feet weren't working properly. Red Jacket's legs were wrapping around his legs and he couldn't move. The guy was a grappler. Sam caught an elbow in his gut and all the breath went out of him.

And then, suddenly, Red Jacket was yanked off Sam and thrown into the wall. He dropped like he'd been shot. The dude just collapsed. Sam looked up and saw the other two joggers—the chase team.

But they weren't a chase team. In fact, from the white-walled, buffed-from-the-weight-pile look of them they were a pair of Soldiers from Fort Meyer—maybe Tomb of the Un-knowns guard detail—out for their daily PT. Sam focused on the closest Soldier. He was holding a collapsible baton next to his leg.

Sam rolled onto his hands and knees. And then, his teary eyes unable to make out much, he sagged to the asphalt, hy-perventilating.

The rearmost soldier came up and knelt next to him. "You okay, Pops?"

"My eyes. They used pepper spray."

The Soldier rolled Sam onto his back and cupped his head with an arm. "Open your eyes."

Sam struggled to follow the man's instructions.

"Good." A stream of cold water washed Sam's eyes.

"It's bottled water. It's clean. Don't worry. Keep blinking. Let it wash your eyes out."

Sam did as he was told. The relief was instantaneous.

"Pete—" The Soldier paused. "Gimme your water."

"You got it."

More cold water washed over Sam's forehead and eyes.

Sam's vision came back. He raised his hand to his eyes. But the Soldier caught it. "Don't rub—you'll just make everything worse, okay?"

"Okay." Sam bobbed his head up and down. He tried to catch his breath but was having a hard time. He flexed his right hand. It was sore as hell, but he'd deal with it later. He struggled to get to his feet, but the Soldier just pushed him back gently. "Give it a second or two, Pops."

Finally, Sam pulled himself up. He made his way to the Oakland Raider, rolled him over, and searched for ID. The man didn't even have a wallet. But he was carrying a roll of duct tape in his Raiders jacket pocket. And a small canister of pepper spray. Sam checked for tattoos or other identifying marks. He found nothing on Oakland's arms. But when he checked the man's legs he discovered a chunky semiautomatic pistol in an ankle holster.

Sam extracted the weapon, handling it gingerly. The taller of the two Soldiers took it from Sam's hand, pointed the muzzle in a safe direction, dropped the magazine, and then racked the slide. A loaded round popped out of the chamber. The Soldier caught it with his left hand and examined the bullet. He whistled. "Ten-mil. This guy meant business."

Sam went to Red Jacket and ran his hands over the unconscious man's clothes. He came up with a single car key—

which he palmed before anyone saw it—and a spring-loaded leather sap. Sam slapped his left palm with the weapon. Nasty. No identifying marks or jailhouse tattoos on Red Jacket either.

The attackers were sterile. No papers. No IDs. There was something maddeningly, naggingly, familiar about Red Jacket, but this was no time to try to sort it out. There was a key that was currently burning a hole in Sam's pocket.

Sam stood up. "I gotta go."

The Soldier with the baton snapped the device closed and replaced it in his anorak. He pulled a cell phone out and offered it to Sam. "What about the police?"

"No police—please," Sam said quickly.

The second Soldier hefted the pistol they'd taken from Oakland Raider. "But he had a gun." He looked at Sam imploringly. "We're MPs, Pops. We gotta call the police."

"Please." Sam looked at the confused expressions on the young Soldiers' faces. "Please," he said again. "All I can tell you is this is code-word stuff. I can't explain. But no police—not until I'm gone."

The two Soldiers looked at each other, then back at Sam. Finally, the Soldier with the baton shrugged. "Your call, Pops." He paused. "You want some help getting home?"

Sam leaned against the trash container. *Obfuscate. Leave a false trail.* "Nah—I can manage. I was on the final leg—I live a block and a half from here." He looked at the two dubious youngsters. "But thanks," he said. "I don't know what I would have done if you guys hadn't come along."

Sam backed out of the alley. He scampered to the corner of Fillmore and turned right. Red Jacket and Oakland Raider had come from this direction. That meant they'd left their car close by. They'd probably been tracking him to make sure he was taking his regular route. Then they'd driven ahead, stopped, and waited for him to show.

5:48 A.M. Sam walked in the middle of the street, careful not to leave footprints. There were no parked cars within fifty feet of the intersection. He pressed on, walking quickly through an intersection, looking at the cars down the side street. All of them were dusted with snow. But there—just past the streetlight—was one that wasn't. Sam jogged up to the car. It was a big, black four-door sedan. A Crown Vic with Washington, D.C., plates.

Sam put his hand on the Crown Vic's hood. The metal was warm to the touch. He pulled on the door. It was locked. Just above the door lock was a keypad that would unlatch the driver's side door. Sam used his teeth to pull the glove on his right hand off. He used the key he'd taken from Red Jacket and opened the door. Then he put the glove back on and wiped the key on his leg. No need to leave any telltale finger-prints or blood for anyone to track.

There was no interior light. Sam slid behind the wheel, pulled the door closed, and used his elbow to lock it. He thrust the key into the ignition. His first impulse was to drive away. But then he thought better of it. Moving the car would only confirm that he'd found his attackers' vehicle—and increase the danger quotient.

Who were these guys? Sam felt under the front seat. His fingers found a wallet, which he retrieved and dropped onto his lap. He reached again and came back with a semiauto-matic pistol in a black Kydex paddle holster.

He slid the pistol back under the seat and searched the passenger side, where he discovered a second wallet. Quickly, he opened the wallets one by one and went through their contents, squinting to read the fine print in the semidarkness. Red Jacket's driver's license identified him as Desmond Reese. He was thirty-six, and he lived in southeast Washington. Oakland Raider was Larry Johnson, thirty-four, of Bowie, Maryland. The half-dozen government-printed business cards in each wallet told Sam they were members of the U.S. Capitol police's Protective Services Bureau. Sergeant Larry Johnson, a member of the 82nd Airborne Association, was in the Protective Intelligence Division, and Sergeant Desmond Reese, who carried a VFW membership card, served in the Dignitary Protection Division.

Inside the hidden compartment of Reese's wallet was a folded piece of note paper. Sam eased it open. The letterhead read: SELECT COMMITTEE ON INTELLIGENCE.

The sheet was hand-lettered with a series of numbers and letters.

211: 42428
211-CH: 88329
211-B/S: 84-11-95-01
211-A: 92391

Sam shook his head; 211 was the suite number for the SSCI committee offices in the Hart Senate Office Building. Obviously, Reese kept a list of cipher-lock combinations to some of the offices in case of emergency. You had to wonder who taught these people about security. He reached atop the driver's side sun visor and found a ballpoint pen, which he used to copy the door-lock combinations on the back of one of Reese's business cards. He replaced the pen, refolded the sheet of paper, and slipped it back exactly where he'd found it, copied both men's vital statistics on the back of a second business card, and replaced the two wallets under the front seat where he'd found them.

5:51 A.M. He searched for the trunk release, found it, popped the Crown Vic's trunk, slipped into the cold, and checked.

There was a police radio in the trunk. But that wasn't all. A black tarp lay folded. Half a dozen clear, thin, plastic bags—

the kind you get at dry cleaners—were crumpled next to it. There was a roll of black duct tape and a coil of wire. And there were also four cinder blocks. Sam reached down and hefted one. It weighed twenty pounds at least.

It would have been so easy for them. They'd have knocked Sam out with the stun gun. They'd get the car, toss him in the trunk, duct tape his mouth and nostrils, then slip a couple of the plastic bags over his head. Then there'd be more duct tape. They'd wrap him in the tarp. They'd use more duct tape. They'd attach the cinder blocks. They'd drive to a bridge and toss him over the rail or carry him down an embankment and roll him into a canal. Sayonara, Sam—*poká.*

And then, standing there, shivering in the cold, Sam realized where he'd seen Red Jacket before.

He'd seen him in the pea-gravel driveway of Rand Arthur's house in Round Hill. Red Jacket had been one of the plainclothes Capitol police officers guarding Rand's estate.

Sam looked down at the cinder blocks and the plastic clothing bags and started to shake. Then he got control of himself. He eased the trunk shut and returned to the front of the big car. He checked the glove compartment—it was empty except for a pack of chewing gum. Then he reached around to make sure he hadn't overlooked anything. He hadn't: the rear carpet area and the backseat were bare.

5:53 A.M. Sam left the ignition key on the floor next to the brake pedal, hoping Reese and Johnson would assume they'd dropped it. He locked the car from the inside, slammed the driver's side door shut, and tested to make sure it had latched tight. As he walked away from the Crown Vic, he could hear the crescendo of approaching sirens on Wilson Boulevard.

CHAPTЭR 26

6:24 A.M. Sam sat in his living room, a cold cup of coffee at his elbow, sorting the situation out as best he could. He'd been targeted. Someone had sent two men to kill him—police officers.

Someone? Rand bloody Arthur was who. The U.S. Capitol police worked for congressmen and senators. They provided security—even in the lawmakers' home districts under certain conditions.

Obviously, they were available for other jobs, too. Still, it puzzled Sam how Rand had convinced Oakland Raider and Red Jacket to kidnap and kill him. These guys weren't goons or goodfellas. They were sworn officers.

And then Sam realized that convincing a couple of law enforcement professionals to commit murder might not have been all that hard. Christ, he'd done the same sort of thing more than once. Not to commit murder, of course. That would have been a violation of Executive Order 12333, which prohibited CIA from engaging in political assassinations as a matter of national policy. But Sam had convinced scores of loyal Germans, Turks, Frenchmen, and the occasional Russian to betray their countries and spy for the United States. He knew that spies—agents—are trolled, hooked, and landed by exploiting their vulnerabilities. That's what was behind the principle of EMSI—the tradecraft acronym for Ego, Money, Sex, and Ideology. Ninety percent of all recruitments are based on EMSI vulnerabilities.

Well, there was a new vulnerability to exploit these days— fear of terrorism. In Washington, especially in the House and the Senate, that fear was endemic and overriding, With reason: Flight 93, the plane that was brought down over Pennsylvania when its passengers overpowered its terrorist hijackers on September 11, 2001, had been heading toward Washington, D.C. It had later been surmised that the plane's target had been either the White House or the U.S. Capitol. The president had been out of town on 9/11. But Congress was in session. In fact, there had been complete panic on Capitol Hill, because there was no evacuation plan in place for the 535 members of the House and Senate. And only days later came the anthrax attacks that had killed almost half a dozen and brought Congress to a screeching halt—the Hart Senate Office Building had been shut down for months. SSCI had had to move back into its old quarters in the Russell Building.

In the fifteen months since 9/11, the Capitol police had instituted a wide-ranging array of security arrangements for their lawmaker protectees. The Hill was a fortress these days—tours had only recently been reinstituted. Surface-to-air missiles ringed the U.S. Capitol. Committee chairmen and senior members had protective details as large as any cabinet official. Christ, they rode around Washington in armored convoys.

Congress wasn't alone. In fact, from the White House down to the man in the street, the whole country was vulnerable to a level of fear that bordered on paranoia. The mood was a reaction to the constantly shifting threat levels, conflicting stories about al-Qa'ida's capabilities, and constant apprehension over another anthrax attack reinforced by a growing drumbeat about Saddam Hussein's weapons of mass destruction. That Richard Reid guy who'd tried to blow up an airplane with a bomb in his sneakers hadn't helped either. Nor had the two scumbags known as the Washington snipers, who'd taken the cops a month or so to apprehend.

Anxiety manifested itself everywhere, from alarmist newspaper editorials to bombastic speeches on the floor of the House and Senate, to the tabloid shrillness of television news broadcasts. According to the *Washington Post*'s style section, fashionable matrons gathered at chichi restaurants were as likely to discuss the daily threat matrix or the pros and cons of various brands of gas masks, or the best place to score under-the-counter Cipro as they were to talk fashion, politics, or kids. All over the city, the normally extroverted mood in the nation's capital had transmogrified into a city that suffered from a terminal case of siege mentality.

Given those realities—not to mention the fact that Rand Arthur was persuasive, a master of political manipulation, and an important, influential, senior member of the United States Senate—Sam knew an individual's natural inhibitions could be overcome. Push the right emotional and intellectual buttons and you get homicide bombers like Richard Reid.

Let me, Sam thought, *put myself in Rand's shoes. How would I play it?*

It was, Sam understood, a straightforward recruitment, which meant Rand had put it together with a lot of forethought and preparation. He'd targeted these two. It was even possible he might have been able to get his hands on their psychological profiles to help him get inside their heads. And tactics? He had Ginny. Or better, he had Michael

O'Neill to teach him. It was simply a matter of asking the case-officer-turned-lawyer.

Michael, tell me about the basics of recruiting an agent. How did they teach you to convince someone to commit treason?

The same way my older brother taught me how to talk women into bed, Senator.

Oh, yes. O'Neill, God bless him, would have been only too happy to oblige. He loved talking about his successes. He'd have told Rand about spotting potentials—explained the tricks of eliciting the verbal clues that identified weaknesses, character flaws, likes and dislikes. He'd have explained how to inventory the target's strengths and flaws and then translate that list into a psychosexual vulnerability matrix that allowed case officers to predict with tremendous accuracy the responses they could provoke. He'd have explained how to set the hook—bring the target inside, and then, abruptly, slam the door to prevent escape. He'd have explained about control and manipulation. He'd have told Rand how case officers use familiarity, friendship, and camaraderie to lure their targets into a false feeling of closeness. He'd have given Rand examples of how to play agents' emotions so well that when it becomes crunch time, an agent will feel closer to his case officer than he does to his wife or family. The case officer becomes the sole source of an agent's salvation. I am your only friend, says the godlike case officer. Rely on me and no one else, or you will surely die.

But the bottom line was that it didn't matter *how* Rand had learned how to hook the two cops up. Because he'd done it. He'd *spotted* Red Jacket and Oakland Raider, he'd *assessed* their vulnerabilities, and then he'd *recruited* them in the same cold-blooded fashion any case officer would have done. They'd been snagged and netted by a pro.

* * *

IN FACT, a similar scenario had worked before. Shortly after Sam had joined CIA, a renegade operative named Paul Allen Phillips hired almost a dozen retired Special Forces soldiers to instruct overseas classes in counterterrorism operations. He selected his targets with care—the same way Rand Arthur had no doubt singled out Reese and Johnson. He told his recruits they'd be working a clandestine assignment for the Agency. He offered them more than generous wages and hefty expenses. He produced paperwork that certified they were a part of a government-sponsored operation—papers they signed.

But Phillips was lying, and all his paperwork was bogus. And instead of training counterterrorism forces, the poor schmucks traveled to an isolated camp in the Libyan desert where they taught terrorists posing as security officials how to kill innocent people. Paul Phillips pocketed millions from Mu'ammar Qaddafi.

What would Rand Arthur pocket? Rand wanted to be president. How would killing Sam help him achieve that goal? Sam hadn't the faintest idea. Not yet. But Rand wanted him out of the way. That was undeniable.

The phone rang, startling him. Sam checked the caller-ID screen and saw Ginny Vacario's office number displayed. He let his voice mail pick up the call. Two minutes later, she called a second time. And two minutes later, again.

That was when the panic washed over him. What the hell was he doing sitting here? He was vulnerable. Rand Arthur knew where he *lived*. And who knows what Reese and Johnson were saying to the Arlington police? They could claim Sam was the target of some supersecret investigation and that he'd attacked them when they tried to detain him at the behest of a senior member of the U.S. Senate.

Sam stopped cold. Panic was what they wanted—whoever

they were. He'd first learned that in the Marines. And he'd learned it again during his DAO[48] training. "The opposition will push you, crowd you, knock you off balance," the instructors had said over and over again. "They will try to force you to make mistakes. But you must not cave. Instead, you go offensive—provocative if necessary. You hit back harder, faster, dirtier. You get inside their OODA loop and you kick their asses."

Sam had never heard the acronym before. OODA, the instructors said, stood for Observe, Orient, Decide, and Act. The term had been coined by a wartime philosopher fighter pilot named John Boyd, who argued that dogfights weren't won by the pilots with the faster reflexes, but by the pilots who *thought* faster than their opponents—who got inside their enemy's OODA loop.

That's what Sam had to do now. The opposition wanted him to panic. He had to get inside Rand Arthur's OODA loop. Stage a counterambush. Run an op.

Run an op. That was it. He had to run an op. Except it wouldn't be an op to recruit an agent at Moscow Center, or convince some poor Turkish janitor working for the Poles to slip a bug in the ambassador's office. Sam would be running a penetration operation that targeted officials of his own government.

Sam shook his head. Not officials. Official. One official.

Say the words, he told himself. *You have to say them out loud.*

Sam looked through the gauzy curtains. He could make out the indistinct glimmer of lights in the office buildings of downtown Rosslyn. The workday was commencing over there.

---

[48] Denied Area Operations.

And here as well. Sam swallowed hard, gritted his teeth, and said in a low, even voice, "Rand . . . Arthur."

7:07 A.M. He grabbed a suitcase and started stuffing it with clothes and some innocent-looking possessions he'd taken with him when he'd left Langley. He took all the Edward Lee Howard files, including his own notes and the copies he'd made of Virginia Vacario's verbatim transcripts, and stuffed them into his document case along with two cell phones, his laptop, the American-flag pen drive, and some other files.

Then he went to a two-foot-high, custom-built fireproof safe that was lag-bolted six inches into the concrete slab under the wood flooring of his bedroom closet. Kneeling, he punched an eight-number combination into the first of the two electronic locks. The thick door released with a growl. Behind it was a second door.

Sam punched a six-number combination and waited until a red light blinked half a dozen times, then turned green. He punched the six numbers in reverse, then hit the pound key, turned the handle, and eased the door open. He pulled out two thick pocket secretaries, flipped them open, and removed a number of items. He reached into the back of the safe and took out a manila envelope, from which he extracted five thousand dollars in used twenty-, fifty-, and hundred-dollar bills. Before he closed the safe door, he rearmed the automatic detonator on the small, thin Thermite charge that would incinerate the contents if the safe was broken into or moved.

CHAPTЭR 27

1:45 P.M. Sam drove out of the garage into bright tropical sunlight, peering through the windshield of his rental car until he saw the arrow leading to the airport exit. He'd never been in Tampa before and so he drove slowly, finding his way to the connector road that led to southbound Interstate 275. He'd changed his appearance and silhouette before using a side entrance to leave his apartment building. It was a three-block walk to the Rosslyn Hyatt. Sam entered the hotel through the garage, then took an elevator to the mezzanine, found a restroom, and modified his disguise, adding a mustache, changing hairpieces, and switching clothes and shoes. Then he descended to the lobby, where the doorman got him a taxi to Reagan National Airport. At Reagan, he'd paid for his tickets and reserved a rental car under an alias without receiving so much as a second glance.

In fact, Sam was carrying three separate identities with him. At the moment, he was Dale Miller of Detroit, Michigan—the only one of the three legends for which he also had a valid U.S. passport. But he had working credit cards, legitimate driver's licenses, and other assorted pocket litter under the two other names.

He accelerated onto the long Skyway Bridge and finally connected to I-75 south just east of Bradenton. There was construction from Sarasota all the way to Venice. But then the traffic picked up speed and Sam crossed the Port Charlotte Bridge just after four o'clock.

Sam exited I-75 at Route 17, pulled to the side of the road, and checked the computer-generated map he'd printed out before leaving Washington, tracing the route with his index finger. Then he slipped back into traffic, drove past a small strip mall and the twin pillars marking the entrance to a golf club. He turned into a gas station and topped off his gas tank while he checked for surveillance, and paid in cash. He pulled back onto Route 17, drove a hundred yards, then veered right, onto a pitted two-lane blacktop, which he followed for half a mile. He turned right again and followed the road as it led in a wide counter-clockwise arc at whose apex stood a neat white stucco house with green trim. An aged, sun-bleached, salt-stained Buick sat in the driveway, shaded by four tall coconut palms.

Sam parked behind the Buick, turned off the ignition, locked his car, and walked on cracked pavement past a wheezing air-conditioner compressor to the weathered, louvered-glass-and-aluminum door of the screened-in porch, setting off a battery-powered frog that croaked loudly when Sam broke the beam to ring the bell.

There was no answer. He waited a quarter of a minute and pressed the button again, peering down the screened-in porch to where a big butterscotch-colored cat lay asleep on the rim of a gurgling fishpond, its four paws in the air.

The front door finally cracked. Charlotte Wells poked her

head through the opening, squinting into the brightness behind Sam. "Who's there? Can I help you?"

"Charlotte, it's Sam. Sam Waterman."

"Sam? Sam Waterman?"

"It's me, Charlotte."

"Come closer so I can see you. I'm not wearing my
glasses. The door's open."

He twisted the handle, pushed, and stepped over the
threshold onto tile so hot he could feel it through his shoes.

She squinted as he came closer, then opened her eyes
wide. "It *is* you. In full war paint and a Joe Stalin mustache.
What on earth?" She adjusted her shift, reached up, and
touched his cheek with the back of her hand as if she were
checking his temperature. "Come in out of the hot and tell
Charlotte what you're doing in this godforsaken neck of the
woods—and shame on you, Sam, you never bothered to call
beforehand."

She'd shrunk. That was the first thing he noticed. Charlotte
had never been a big woman—maybe five feet two. Now she
was a gnome, with unkempt white hair standing straight up, a
floral-patterned housedress two sizes too large for her body,
and a pair of ridiculous fluffy pink scuffs. The house was hot.
It smelled of must, cat urine, and old age.

"Want a drink, Sam?" She pointed to a kit-cat clock with
its pendulum tail keeping time on the kitchen wall. "Sun's
over the yardarm—somewhere."

He rubbed his nose, which was already affected by the cat
dander. "That would be great."

Charlotte padded to the refrigerator and removed an almost empty 1.75-liter bottle of Beefeater and a shriveled half
lemon. She took a pair of old-fashioned glasses out of a cup-
board, wiped them with a dish towel, then carefully took the
bottle with both hands, tremoring as she poured an inch of

330 • JOHN WEISMAN

gin in each. She added thin lemon slices and two small ice cubes to each glass. "You carry, Sam. I've gone a little shaky these days."

He took the glasses from the prescription-littered counter and followed her into the semidarkness of the living room.

"Watch the cats."

"I will." He waited until she'd turned on a light before proceeding any farther. There were two of them, curled on opposite ends of an overstuffed sofa whose ragged arms bore evidence that Charlotte's cats hadn't been declawed.

"The one with the evil eye and the stub tail is Rem," she said. "The baby calico's named Svetlana." She bustled to the sofa, swept Svetlana into her arms, stroked her head, then let the cat jump to the floor. "Defect to the bedroom, my darlings. It's time for the humans to talk."

Sam watched as the black, white, and yellow kitten shook itself off, scattering fur on Sam's shoes. Then it crawled under the sofa. The big gray with the stubby tail never even moved. "Got 'em well trained I do," Charlotte cackled. She settled onto the sofa next to Rem, who rolled onto his back to get his belly rubbed. The cat cracked a green eye and regarded Sam suspiciously.

Sam set Charlotte's glass on a coaster. She picked it up immediately with both hands and raised it in his direction, "Here's to you, Sam Waterman. Welcome to Oblivion." She sipped, then clumsily returned the glass to the table. "This is the condition of my life: I've gone from Purgatory to Oblivion." She looked at him quizzically. "And you, Sam? Tell Charlotte where you are going these days."

Still holding his drink, he settled into the armchair at the end of the coffee table. "I should let you know I'm hot, Charlotte."

"Hot?" She cocked her head in his direction. "Been a bad

boy, Sam? Mischievous? Nosing around where Romanoffs don't want you nosing?"

He set the gin down. "It's worse than that," he said. "This is serious."

"Tell me, Sam," she said. "Tell Charlotte all about it."

SHE'D LOST A LOT of her edge. Sam understood that much almost at once. How far the dementia had developed, he wasn't sure. But it was there. She'd zone out; her face would go blank, then she'd look at him and smile. It was the smile of a child; guileless, innocent, wide-eyed. And then the synapses or whatever would reconnect, and she'd be back, her mind as sharp as ever.

They talked until about six. Then Charlotte grew restless. She fixed them dinner—two slices of bologna between stale white bread slathered with mayonnaise, accompanied by a glass of sweet iced tea—then retired to her bedroom. Sam removed his prosthetics, peeled the wig off, washed his face, then found the linen closet. He pulled a sheet off the shelf, spread it atop the cat-hair-covered couch, and stretched out.

He awoke at three forty-five in the morning when Charlotte flipped the kitchen lights on. The calico kitten was purring happily, asleep on his chest. He used the spare bathroom and splashed tepid water on his face.

She greeted him with a piece of buttered toast and a CIA mug of steaming coffee. "I'm at my best in the mornings, Sam, so I tend to get up early."

He sat at the green Formica kitchen table and watched her sort the prescription bottles and vials into groups, open them one by one, and count out pills. "Sixteen a day," she said. "Soon I'm going to need a chart to remember them all, and what sequence they have to be consumed. Soon after that, someone will have to feed them to me. They cost me eight thousand dollars last year." She swallowed a handful of medications. "Don't get old, Sam. Don't get useless. Even Purgatory is better than Oblivion."

"I didn't know I had a choice."

She cackled at him. Then her face grew serious. "Sam, did you bring Charlotte any paper?"

He nodded. "Yes."

"How good is it, Sam?"

"I think we've got gold, Charlotte, but you'll have to pan for it."

"Good boy." Charlotte's eyes brightened. "Charlotte likes to find pure gold. Now, you give everything to me."

Sam went to his briefcase and pulled a trio of thick files out. "Here you go."

She clasped the documents to her bosom. "Go away, Sam. Watch the telly, or read, or go jogging, or do whatever you want to do." She gave him a coy smile. "Charlotte wants to be alone. Charlotte wants to sluice for gold on her own."

11:30. Sam ran his five miles, showered, read the newspaper cover to cover, and sat in the Florida room off the kitchen staring at CNN for an hour and a half. Finally, he pulled himself out of the Barcalounger, padded to Charlotte's office, cracked the door, and stuck his nose inside.

It was an oven in there. She'd covered the windows with sheets so no one could observe her from the street. And it was chaos. A mess. The ten-by-ten-foot room was literally covered in paper. Pages from Sam's memos and Virginia Vacario's transcripts were tacked to the walls and Scotchtaped willy-nilly to the desk, the credenza, and the bookcases. Charlotte had emphasized certain paragraphs with pink, blue, yellow, and green highlighters. Specific sentences were underlined in red, green, and black ink.

Wide-eyed, she looked up from her desk. She took in Sam's befuddled expression, frowned, and said, "Go away, Sam."

Obediently, he slipped out of the house, climbed into his car, and drove north over the bridge to Port Charlotte. He found a men's clothing store where he paid cash for shorts, sandals, two short-sleeved shirts, and two sets of underwear. He changed clothes in the store's dressing room, then drove over to a small mall called Fisherman's Village, found a friendly bar with tables overlooking the water, and downed a fried grouper sandwich and two beers while he checked the *Wall Street Journal, USA Today,* and the Tampa and Miami papers to see if he could find any ripples. There were none.

He was back at Charlotte's at four. She was asleep, the door to her bedroom closed. He checked the thermostat. It read eighty-five degrees. The cats were stretched out on the sofa. A note on the kitchen table directed him to buy a paper shredder. Sam checked the phone book, called the closest Office Depot, climbed into his car, perused the maps, then drove to a mile-long mall in Punta Gorda, where he paid cash for a fifteen-sheet, crosscut model. Back at Charlotte's, he unpacked the shredder and left it like an offering in front of her office door. Then he retreated to the Florida room, turned the ceiling fan to high, switched the TV on, and flipped back and forth between CNN and the Fox News Channel for an hour, searching for news from Washington. He was relieved to hear no mention of Rand Arthur, U.S. Capitol policemen, or himself. Good: at least Rand was playing everything close to the vest.

Charlotte awoke at five-thirty. She smiled when she saw the shredder, then fixed them gin and tonics, but took hers into the cramped office and shut the door. Sam took a peek in the fridge and decided he'd eat dinner out.

It rained all night. When Sam went running at five the following morning, the humidity was so palpable he felt as if he were breathing liquid oxygen. She was already up by the time he left—he could see the light under the office door. She must have heard him tiptoeing in the hallway because she called out, loudly, "Go away, Sam."

MONDAY, NOVEMBER 25, 2002

10:00 A.M. Sam climbed into his rental car and drove sixty miles east, to the town of Moore Haven, on the shore of Lake Okeechobee. There, he used the cell phone with a New York City number and dialed his voice mailbox. There were three messages from Ginny Vacario, one from John Forbes, and two from O'Neill.

He dialed O'Neill's number, using the cell phone with the Washington, D.C., number.

"O'Neill."

"Cyrus N. PRINGLE."

"Cyrus, thank God. I've been frantic. Are you all right?"

"I'm okay, Michael. What's up?"

"Where are you?"

"I'm in the parking lot at the Cosmos."

There was a slight pause. Then: "If that's the case, get your behind over to my office immediately. We have to work things out."

"Work what out?"

"With the senator. Smooth things over. Rand Arthur is furious. He thinks you're working for the Russians—that you cooked up the whole Moscow episode so you could receive instructions from the SVR. I told him he's totally misconstrued events, but he wants to get the police involved. Issue a BOLO.[49] Have you arrested."

"He can't do that."

"Oh, yes he can under the Patriot Act, Sam. And he's fix-

---

[49] Be On the Look Out notice issued by law enforcement agencies.

ated. He wants your scalp on his tent pole. I've managed to convince him not to do anything for the moment—nasty publicity and all that might affect his presidential possibilities—but I have to tell you he's being very pigheaded and he could act unilaterally at any second."

Rand Arthur had already gotten the police involved—and not in the way Michael O'Neill was describing the situation either. But Sam said nothing.

"What's your suggestion, Michael?"

"Come clean, Sam. We both know why you met with GTREQUIRE, which was to press him about Edward Lee Howard. I'll set everything up. You'll meet face-to-face—not up at the Capitol, but in a safe venue. Private. You tell Rand what we were looking for in Moscow. I'll back you up."

The thought of a private meeting with Rand Arthur made Sam very nervous—even with O'Neill in attendance. "I'll think about it. I'll call you when I've made a decision."

"I'd prefer you come see me now so we can work this out."

"Impossible at the moment. Will you be around over the holidays?"

"I'm backed up at the office, and the senator's got me running in circles. I'm going nowhere."

Sam said, "Hmm." Then he said, "Thanks, Michael. I'll be in touch."

O'Neill's voice was taut. "Cyrus—"

"Yes?"

"You be careful out there, Cyrus. Watch your back. This is turning into a nasty game."

How right he was. "I will, SAMGRASS. Bye."

WHEN SAM RETURNED to the house just after noon, Charlotte greeted him at the door. Her face was flushed and radiant. She looked ten years younger. As she handed him a mug of coffee, he caught the whiff of perfume on her wrist.

Sam said *"Spaciba"* and took the coffee with a smile: the mug was emblazoned with the star, sword, and shield of the KGB.

Charlotte fingered the top button of her housecoat. "Look at what Charlotte has for you, Sam."

He glanced at the kitchen table. Four large sheets of paper lay on the mottled green Formica. Each sheet held a neatly drawn diagram. Sam set the coffee down, went to the linen closet, pulled a towel out, and mopped the sweat off his face, neck, arms, and legs. Then he took a sip of the coffee and sat at the table.

Charlotte set the diagrams one atop the other. She pointed to the first one, which was made up of triangles, squares, diamonds, parallelograms, and pentagons, each of them numbered separately, dated, and linked to the next symbol by an arrow.

"This is a time-event chart," she said. "We begin—that's the triangle in the upper-left-hand corner—with Edward Lee Howard's defection in 1985. We end—that's the triangle in the bottom-right-hand corner—with the attempt on your life last Wednesday morning. Each major event is depicted with either a square or another symbol. Minor transitions or shifts are depicted by circles. And tectonic transitions are triangles. The idea, Sam, is to lay out a chronological record of what's gone on. It gives us a clear picture of the order in which things happened. And the chart draws our attention to pattern shifts, changes in modus operandi, or—and this is most important—anomalies."

She slid the second chart on top of the pile. It was a grid set into a right triangle, with the right angle at the bottom-left-hand side of the sheet. "This is an association matrix. Everyone who appears in the paper you gave me is listed here. What I've done is chart their associations. The matrix allows us to see who knows whom—those are the black dots—or who we suspect knows whom, which are the black circles."

The third chart looked to Sam like a timetable, or a stock chart. It was a square grid. The left-hand side charted each of the players. At the bottom, Charlotte had annotated a series of activities, events, organizations, locations, and addresses. "This," she explained, "you've probably seen before. It's an activities matrix. Sometimes, if we can pinpoint who did what, as well as when and where they did it, we can discover an association we hadn't been able to identify before. It's also good for discerning anomalies."

"Such as?"

"Well, you told me Semonov's polygraph was done by O'Neill. Your notes said you hadn't known that fact before. If you only looked at the association matrix, you'd see that O'Neill and Semonov had a connection. They did—because O'Neill was with you when you first spotted Alexei Alexandrovich Semonov, aka GTREQUIRE. But here, you can see that O'Neill and REQUIRE intersect twice, not once." She drew her finger along the chart to show Sam where O'Neill's dots and Semonov's lined up in the column that read PARIS SAFE HOUSE 1.

Sam nodded. "And chart number four?"

"That's the one that took Charlotte the most time," she said. "It's what we used to call a link diagram. It was Jim Angleton's idea—he'd used it at OSS. Jim was an English professor at heart. He should have been an Oxford don. He used to make his counterintelligence acolytes diagram sentences so as to discern language patterns. Then he got the idea of using the same technique we used for dissecting sentences to create a diagram that analyzed relationships."

Charlotte sipped at her coffee. "I'll tell you a secret. In the early 1960s Angleton showed one of his link diagrams to J. Edgar Hoover and the little so-and-so stole it to use for his congressional briefings on Communist infiltration and organized crime. Jim was outraged because Hoover took credit for developing link diagrams. Hoover actually told President Kennedy it was his idea." Charlotte's eyes flashed angrily. "Hoover had very little style. No panache at all. Behind the three-piece suits and the fedoras he was an intensely plebeian individual." She paused, lolling her head and watching the slow-moving ceiling fan. Sam could hear the wheezing of the compressor outside. Charlotte sighed deeply. "But Jim Angleton—now, *he* was a poet, Sam. Did you know he was a friend of T. S. Eliot's?"

"I'd never heard that."

She nodded, a faraway look in her eyes. Sam thought she was drifting off. But then she focused on him. "You've got a mess on your hands, Sam. Rotten apples."

"I know."

"They've been playing you. Disinformation. Active measures. Black information, Sam."

"I know that, too. I just can't figure out how."

"You forgot about EMSI."

"Emcee?"

"*E-M-S-I:* Ego, Money, Sex, Ideology. Moscow Center's classic vulnerability recruitment acronym." She looked at him disapprovingly. "You let your ego get in the way, Sam. That's how they hooked you."

"Hooked me? Impossible. I'm waterproof, Charlotte— *imperméable.*"

"You? You were *perméable* from the very beginning. Like the way Edward Lee Howard brought up the subject of Pavel Baranov. He hooked you with the words—he was smart enough to understand the name Baranov would churn your emotions. Then he talked about SCEPTRE and SCARAB—

but he never really comprehended what the hell he was saying. Oh, Howard was a fool. A drunk—and Klimov knew that. Klimov, Sam. Klimov is behind this."

"Klimov."

"Howard was Klimov's pawn. His jack-in-the-box. Klimov made sure that Howard would pop up in Washington. But he was a diversion. And by the time you figured out what he was, your attention would have been distracted long enough for Klimov's plan to work. But Howard slipped up—badly. He told you what Primakov did at the State Department. That was a jewel, Sam, except you didn't realize it at the time. And when Howard got spooked and fled to Moscow, Klimov killed him to keep him from screwing up any more."

"Screwed up what, Charlotte?"

"You were right all along, Sam. There are traitors at the highest levels of government. We're porous, Sam. We've been porous for years." Charlotte's eyes glistened. "It's in the Russian character to think long-term. We in the West tend to have short memories. But not Moscow. This began in Paris, Sam, when Klimov was *Rezident,* and you and SAMGRASS went out trolling."

"But—"

Her expression changed. Her tone turned reproachful. "You have been manipulated, Sam. They identified your pattern."

Sam was indignant. "I have never operated by pattern, Charlotte. I know better."

But she didn't give an inch. "Fact, Sam: in Paris you fought to get out of the office so you could get back on the street. You battled the powers that be at Langley to recruit GTREQUIRE. Fact: in Moscow, you repeated the same pattern when you came upon Baranov. Fact: just a month or so ago, when you saw Edward Lee Howard at Senator Arthur's, you became so excited about being back in the game you forgot to think like a case officer." She looked at him, her arms crossed. "Well?"

He looked at her. Goddammit, she was right.

"And about Baranov—"

"Yes?" Sam wanted to hear the confirmation from someone else.

"An anomaly."

"What?" She was wrong. Baranov was the key.

"Baranov was a diversion, too. Sam. I'm convinced Klimov had him killed—Putin's way of getting you out of Moscow. You'd been effective there, Sam, and were a thorn in Putin's side. But there are other possibilities that cannot be discounted. Perhaps Baranov was in bed with the Mafiya— Russian generals don't make enough to buy Rolex President watches. Maybe it was part of a preemptive strike by Yeltsin against General Lebed. But Baranov wasn't the *point*. You were. Once you'd been yanked back to Washington, you'd been neutralized."

"Charlotte, that's not true—"

"It is, Sam," she interrupted. "You were fixated. Looking for traitors. The opposition knew that. Putin, Krassilnikov, Klimov—they all knew how you'd react."

"C'mon."

"You're not listening to me, Sam. Focus. It began in Paris. Don't you think Klimov had his eye on you when you were deputy chief? You were playing games, Sam. Out of the office. Trolling. Klimov was the KGB *Rezident*. He knew damn sure that deputy chiefs don't troll; they keep the accounts. They make the assignments. You attracted his attention, Sam. So he had a psychological profile done. He's a snake, Sam. A viper. A cobra. He was told how you'd act under certain provocations. He knew your capabilities and was able to gauge your intentions. Which means he'd made you vulnerable—*perméable*. Klimov passed all that information to

Moscow Center. You know about Moscow Center, Sam. They were never rushed. They thought long-term. Still do. And so, they waited until the opportunity arose—when you recruited Pavel Baranov in Moscow—and then, like good intelligence people do, they decided to make use of you.

"It's all here." She tapped the link diagram. "Look, Sam, despite its institutional inflexibility, KGB was a world-class service. They made good use of walk-ins. They were adept at false flag recruitments. And God knows they knew how to exploit weakness. This new Russian service is no different—except these days, they get help from the Romanoffs at Langley."

Sam peered down at the diagram. Dammit, he'd screwed things up royally. How the hell had he missed the connections?

Charlotte must have read his mind. "The key is analysis."

"I analyzed everything, Charlotte."

She shook her head. "No, Sam. You'd reached your verdict before you began your analysis."

"Charlotte—"

"Sam, you didn't do anything wrong. You just aren't an analyst. You began to analyze the evidence intuitively sensing that Edward Lee Howard had killed Baranov." She looked over at him. "Be honest, Sam."

He had to admit she was right—and he said so.

"It's a natural instinct. You focus on the substance of the problem—the evidence, the pros and the cons, the empirical conclusions—and the analysis all begins to fall into place. It makes perfect sense. It forms a logical pattern."

He thought about what she was saying and nodded. "That's right."

"You sensed a pattern from the very beginning, Sam. It was just that you couldn't figure out what the pattern was."

"Absolutely."

She shook her head. "The problem, Sam, was that there is

no pattern to these events. Some of them were meant to be utterly nonrelated, in order to confuse you. Moscow Center performed something similar to a magician's sleight-of-hand trick. Klimov drew you off in one direction—using Baranov, or Howard—then acted while your attention was diverted."

Sam thought about what she'd just said. And dammit, she was *right*. He'd been played.

"There's another side of this," Charlotte said, her tone slightly rebuking. "I don't think you read the reporting as closely as you might have."

Sam drew back. "I read it all."

"Closely, Sam? Every word? Over and over again?"

Sam bit his lower lip.

Charlotte turned away and adjusted her housedress. "I would have thought Don Kadick had taught you better."

"He did, Charlotte."

"Then he would have chastised you for forgetting the basics if you'd pulled a stunt like this. Obviously, you never read the reporting. Not closely, Sam. Because if you had, it would all have become clear. Crystal. You can't ever forget the reporting, Sam. The basics never change. It's like these matrices—the Romanoffs have computer programs that do the same thing these days. But what Romanoffs don't understand is that doing the work by hand forces us to noodle the problem out for ourselves by dealing with the human element. Computers can't factor human nature—its frailties, doubts, and passions. The ability to read human nature and manipulate it is what spying is all about. The Romanoffs don't understand that—never did. Technical, that's all they care about. Technical and liaison." She looked at him, then laid her hand atop the charts. The skin on her wrist was translucent and delicate as a cobweb. "People, Sam. People see things; people sense things that machines cannot."

She looked at him with watery eyes. "You never went through all the transcripts, did you?"

"I read most of them."

"But not all. Because of that, you missed the key, Sam." She dug in the pocket of her housecoat and pulled out a half-inch-thick stack of three-by-five index cards held together by a blue rubber band. She slipped the band over her wrist, and started to deal out the cards atop the chart one by one, as if she was playing solitaire.

Sam watched her. And then, as he realized what she had been able to glean by not making any assumptions, or allowing any biases to intervene, he began to understand what a fool he'd been. He'd screwed things up from the get-go. He'd been hooked and landed because he'd charged headlong into this mess without following the basic procedures he'd been taught at The Farm.

Charlotte was right: Don Kadick would have kicked his butt into next week if he'd pulled this sort of greenhorn blunder in Bonn. He hadn't done his homework. He hadn't read every one of the transcripts—thoroughly—because he thought he'd known what to look for.

But he hadn't known. In fact, he'd missed almost every one of the signs. Big, obvious billboards sitting right in front of his nose.

Charlotte hadn't missed anything. She'd caught them all. She'd found a pattern. She'd gone back as far as Paris—and made sense of it all.

She pulled off her glasses, set them on the kitchen table, and walked to the refrigerator. "Sun's over the yardarm, Sam."

"You better make it vodka today, Charlotte."

"Oh?" She looked at him quizzically.

Sam went to his book bag, pulled out the Order of Lenin medal he'd bought for Ginny Vacario, took it from its leather-

and-velvet case, leaned over, pinned it on the lapel of Charlotte's housedress, and kissed her on both cheeks. "For service above and beyond, Charlotte," he said in his Moscow-accented Russian. "You don't miss a trick."

"Oh, Sam." She fingered the red ribbon and beamed. "At last," she said in halting, British-tinged Russian, "I am a hero of the State. *Spaciba*, Sergei Anatolyvich."

"Whoa!" Sam went pie-eyed. Where the hell had she come up with *that* one. He'd only mentioned the alias to her once, very early on in their relationship at Purgatory. She grinned coyly at him. "My short-term memory may be on its way out, Sam—I feel as if I'm dropping my life into the shredder day to day. But I can tell you precisely what I was wearing the morning I met General Donovan and David Bruce at seventy Grosvenor."[50] Charlotte looked at him. Her eyes had teared up and her expression was almost mystical. "Thank you, Sam."

It was he who was grateful. "For what, Charlotte?"

She tapped the spidery skin of her breastbone. "For reminding me, Sam Waterman, that Delphi still lives. Delphi still lives—in here."

---

[50] By 1944, just before D-Day, OSS had more than two thousand personnel in London, occupying nine buildings. Seventy Grosvenor Street, convenient both to Claridge's Hotel and a favorite OSS pub, the Coach and Horses, was the organization's European headquarters.

СНАРТЭЯ 28

10:32 A.M. Sam called John Forbes from a pay phone at Reagan National. The phone at JEH[51] rang twice before the special agent picked up. "National Security, 6151."

Quickly, Sam said: "No names. We have to meet."

There was a three-second pause. Then: "What about the most recent venue?"

"Too public."

"Can I pick you up?"

"There are security problems."

There was a five-second pause. "Take a cab. Go where you like the soup."

Now it was Sam who had to think. Then he said "Gotcha" and hung up the receiver.

Fifty-eight minutes later, he watched as Forbes pushed through the door of Nam Viet, scanned the joint, then made

---

[51] The J. Edgar Hoover Building.

his way to the rear of the long, narrow restaurant to where Sam sat with his back against the wall.

The two men liked this place. It was convenient to the Clarendon metro stop. The tables were clean, the beer was cold, the spring rolls perfect, and the bright red orange pepper-infused Hue-style soup so spicy that they sweat when they ate it. The owners were all former South Vietnamese police and military officers. The walls were bedecked with Vietnamese art, and pictures inscribed by notable Vietnam vets and POWs. It wasn't yet noon, so the wait staff lounged in the pre-lunch-hour calm.

Forbes took note of Sam's disguise but didn't comment. "Sorry I took so long, Elbridge." The FBI man dropped into a chair, summoned a waiter, and pointed at Sam's Tsingtao. "One of those, please?" He turned back to Sam once the waiter had left. "I took a cleaning route."

"Good idea."

Forbes wrinkled his forehead. "What's up, Elbridge?"

"Remember I told you you'd be the first call I'd make when I had my ducks in a row?"

"Uh-huh."

Sam looked at his friend. "Quack-quack, John."

3:29 P.M. "Elbridge, if this doesn't come off, we're going to be sharing a cell at Leavenworth for five or six decades."

"Good," Sam said. "You can be the wife."

"Very funny." Forbes's expression was grim. "High risk, Sam. Very high risk."

"Can you think of anything better?"

Forbes scratched behind his right ear. "Not really."

They were sitting in the living room of the Falls Church town house Forbes shared with Johanna Simeone. Sam had removed the prosthetics, then showered and changed clothes.

Spread out on the low coffee table were Charlotte Wells's matrices and the notecards she'd carefully lettered.

There were other materials as well. Sam had waited at Nam Viet while Forbes drove to the Atrium. He'd used Sam's pass to enter the garage. The G-man took the elevator to Sam's apartment, carefully followed the written directions he'd been given, opened the safe, and removed the half-dozen items Sam had sent him to retrieve. Thirty-five minutes after he'd left, Forbes picked Sam up and drove him to Falls Church.

The safe house was the key. Edward Lee Howard had screwed up. Charlotte had never really picked up on it, even though Sam had. Howard had given Sam a second detail he hadn't been supposed to. He'd claimed SCARAB had been invited to the Primakov reception.

Sam had tried to check out Howard's story. He'd scanned the *Washington Post* archives for a guest list and come up dry. He'd even called the State Department, and been told that the protocol office had already turned over the documents in question to the National Archives. It was a dead end for the moment.

Howard also claimed SCARAB rented the safe house from which the two "high-level moles" met with their control officer. And the lease was under SCARAB's true name. That's where Howard had screwed up. He'd obviously confused some disposables with the high-level agents SCARAB and SCEPTRE, realized his mistake, and then he'd done what all case officers are taught to do when they're caught in a lie: deny, deny, deny. Charlotte had glossed over the anomaly. But Sam hadn't.

The photos and Forbes's research confirmed that SCARAB had to be one of the Russian disposables—Barbara Steiner or Vernon Myles. Forbes had obtained home addresses for both. All Sam had to do was check to see which one of the two had rented a second residence, and they were home free.

"Piece of cake," Forbes said. He flipped his cell phone open and speed-dialed a number. "Yo, Kramer, this is Forbes. Whassup?" The G-man listened, his head bobbing up and down. "Cool, man. Love it." He paused. "Listen—I need you to check two accounts for me. Sure I can wait while you blow the call off. This is important, Dick—hush-hush. National security and all that crap." Forbes cupped his hand over the bottom of the cell phone. "This guy is Dick Kramer. Jarhead like us. Retired Secret Service. Head of security for Dominion Power. Can't nobody have a house or an apartment that doesn't have electricity, right?"

Forbes slapped the phone back to his ear. "I'm here. You got a stick? First one is Steiner comma Barbara, Social Security 202-65-5201. Second is Myles comma Vernon, Social is 392-68-2748. No, four *eight*, numbskull." Forbes tossed Sam an upturned thumb and stage-whispered, "He's checking."

Fifty seconds later Forbes scratched some numbers on a legal pad, said "Thanks, Kramer, Semper Fi," and snapped the cell phone shut. The FBI agent scratched his head. "Doesn't make sense," he said.

"What?"

"Steiner and Myles have only one account each—at the addresses we already have for 'em."

"Did he check Maryland and the District as well as Virginia?"

"He ran it as far south as North Carolina and as far north as Pennsylvania. Nothing." Forbes looked at his old friend. "So what do we do?"

Sam pursed his lips. "Call him back."

Forbes cocked his head in Sam's direction. "Why?"

"Ask him to pull up the accounts. And check the billing over the last two years."

"But—"

"Just ask."

The FBI agent punched Kramer's speed-dial number and waited. "Me again. Pull up those accounts, will ya?" Forbes's fingers played air piano. "What's your point, Elbridge?"

"If I'm right, you'll see my point."

"Yeah—I'm still here," Forbes said. Then his eyes went wide, and he said, "Oh, really?" He turned to Sam and gave him an upturned thumb. He scribbled a list of dates and numbers on the legal pad in front of him and said "Thanks, guy. Hold on a sec."

Sam said, "So?"

"So, if Vernon Myles actually lives at 3624 Idaho Avenue Northwest, he lives in the dark most of the time. Look at these bills."

Sam peered down at the list of figures. It was just as he'd thought: the bills were incredibly low. "What about the apartments on either side of him?" The Russians sometimes liked to install audio or video surveillance from an adjacent apartment.

"I'll ask." Forbes waited while his friend checked the computer records. "Normal," he said. "No anomalies—going back five years."

"Bingo." Sam had done this once before, searching for a KGB safe house near Bonn. Don Kadick was certain that the opposition had bought a new one somewhere in a two-square-block complex of flats in Pulheim, just outside Köln. He'd assigned Sam to find the needle in the hundred-and-eighty-apartment haystack. Sam did it by recruiting an agent who worked for the Köln power department. The agent checked the apartment complex's light bills. Which, being German light bills, were annotated not just by month, but by day.

Sam crossed off all the vacant apartments—there were currently five. For all the others, the electricity bills were roughly the same—within twenty-five dollars or so. Except for one anomaly: flat number 4/08, where almost no power was consumed during most of the month. But once in a while—every second week or so—there was a spike. The KGB, being cheap, obviously didn't want to pay a kopek more for power than it needed. Don Kadick congratulated Sam on his ingenuity, then summoned a team of technicians from Langley so they could install a series of microphones in the walls of Apartment 4/08.

Forbes said, "So whaddya want to do, Elbridge?"

In response, Sam picked up the phone and dialed Vernon Myles's extension at the State Department. "Mr. Myles? This is Special Agent Forbes of the Federal Bureau of Investigation's National Security Division. Do you have a few minutes to spare me this afternoon? It's quite urgent." Sam watched as Forbes shook his head in disbelief. "No," Sam said, "of course not. This has to do with an investigation of one of your coworkers at PM. It concerns laptop computer security. If you could meet me, say, somewhere around six o'clock I'd appreciate it. Anyplace convenient for you would be just fine. Since you're at Main State, what about Dundee's, at Twenty-fourth and Penn? Great. Of course I'd like to keep everything confidential, so please don't mention this to any of your colleagues." Sam smiled devilishly. "Not at all. I'm at the J. Edgar Hoover Building. Extension 6151. Thank you for your cooperation, Mr. Myles."

Forbes pulled the corner of his mustache. "I'm so charming I can't stand myself. You even gave him my phone number."

"He's a cautious bureaucrat," Sam said. "He'll call back to make sure you work there."

"So what's next?"

Next? That was simple: *Provoke. Goad. Incite.* "It's time we shake the tree, Forbes."

"Sounds good, Elbridge. Beats the hell out of chasing down illegal Pakistanis."

"We'll need a script. I'll work on that."

"What can I do?"

Sam rapped the table. "You could make me a G-man."

"You own panty hose to go with the dress?"

"Bite me, Forbes." Like most clandestine service officers, Sam had used a number of government IDs over his career. He'd taken language courses under State Department cover. At one time or another he had carried credentials that identified him as a Department of the Army civilian employee, a U.S. Department of Commerce trade official, and a deputy vice president of the Export-Import Bank of the United States. One more forgery, he rationalized, wouldn't make any difference.

So Forbes used his digital camera to shoot a portrait of Sam in the Dale Miller disguise, and take a close-up of his own FBI credential. Then the G-man used his all-in-one color printer to scan both the photo and ID as jpg files. He altered the name and physical attributes on the duplicate then reproduced the document once more—this time on photo paper.

Sam took the glossy four-by-six sheet and examined it, frowning. "This won't fool anybody, John."

"Wanna bet?" Forbes snorted. "I badged my way onto a plane three weeks ago using my Gold's Gym photo ID card. Truth is, nobody pays attention once they see the shield."

"But we're at war, right? They just upped the threat level to ORANGE."

"What's your point?" Forbes used a pair of scissors to trim Sam's photo. "You know as well as I do how people's minds work. The subconscious finishes the sentence for them. Here's a guy with a badge, a gun, and handcuffs hanging off his belt. Therefore, he is a cop." The FBI man pasted Sam's picture atop the color copy of the FBI credential. "You are with me. I am an FBI agent. I will allow anyone to examine my credential as closely as they want to. And you, Sancho Panza, you get to follow in my footsteps. Think you're gonna get the same scrutiny as me with the two of us bitch-and-moaning like the Bickersons?"

Carefully, Forbes used a home lamination kit to seal the bogus credential behind cloudy plastic. "No way, Elbridge." He slid the ID into a black leather wallet that held a gold federal special agent's shield, examined his handiwork, then handed everything to Sam. "Welcome to the Federal Bureau of Investigation, Special Agent Miller."

Forbes swept the scraps into a pile and dropped them all into a wastebasket shredder. "Johanna's getting home about eight. No need for her to see what we're doing."

He looked at Sam, who was examining the forged FBI creds, and cocked an eyebrow. "Now, if you ever try to use this on your own, I'll bust you myself. But since I'm a willing accomplice for this particular caper . . ."

Sam blushed as he slapped the wallet shut and slid the credential into his jacket pocket. "You have any good pictures around?"

" 'Good pictures'?"

"Murders. Bodies. Lots of blood."

"Hell yes, Elbridge. Us law enforcement types actually collect 'em. The messier the better. Got this great digital last week from Los Angeles. Murder by roofing hammer."

"That one won't work. But lemme check your files," Sam said. "I'll need about a dozen, including something that could pass for suicide by shotgun."

"Pass for? Heeey, I got the real thing, Dick Tracy."

6:05 P.M. The instant Vernon Myles pushed through the frosted glass door Sam knew everything he had to know.

The stooped shoulders, the careless double Windsor slightly askew in the collar of the man's blue button-down wash-and-wear shirt, the scuffed shoes, the baggy trousers, the smudged eyeglass lenses, and the hair-sprayed comb-over told Sam volumes about Myles's character—and his vulnerabilities.

Myles's files—Edward Lee Howard's material and the FBI's sparse dossier—indicated to Sam that Myles had all the makings of a developmental. The man's physical appearance cemented the verdict. By the very way Myles acted, from the manner in which he carried himself to his physical characteristics, this middle-aged State Department civil servant was the perfect espionage target: a bureaucrat in a sensitive position who probably hated his job, resented his superiors, and wanted to get even. The man was a bloody textbook for an EMSI recruitment. It didn't even get this easy at the Farm during case-officer training, when a cadre of veteran case-officer role-players would come down to Williamsburg so the trainees could practice their novice recruiting skills.

Sam watched as the man stood, arms at his sides, peering dumbly into the semidarkness of the bar, his pallid face radiating bewilderment. Sam slid off the bar stool and ambled toward his target.

"Mr. Myles?" Sam gave the poor schlemiel a reassuring look. "I'm with John Forbes. We're over there—" He pointed. "In the rear."

Myles blinked rapidly then put his hand out. "Good to meet you, Special Agent—"

"Oh, let's dispense with titles." Sam took the man's hand. It was moist and limp. Additional manifestations of Myles's character and personality. "No need to be anything other than informal. Sun's over the yardarm, Mr. Myles."

He put his hand in the small of Myles's back and nudged

him toward the rear booth where John Forbes was waiting. "John Forbes, Mr. Myles."

Forbes let his jacket fall open so Myles could catch a glimpse of the big Glock .40-caliber pistol on his hip as he rose and extended his hand. The FBI man smiled invitingly. "Thanks for coming, Mr. Myles. I know this is an imposition."

"Not at all." Self-consciously, Myles fingered the State Department ID, which was stuffed into the breast pocket of his shirt. "Happy to help. You said something about laptop security?"

"Let's get comfortable." Forbes ushered Myles to the inside of the booth, then sat next to him, pinning the man next to the wall. "Can we buy you a drink?"

Myles loosened his tie. "You know, that sounds good." He looked up at Sam. "Rye and ginger, please."

"Gotcha." Sam headed for the bar. Three minutes later he was back, holding two pints of Guinness and a big highball glass. He'd had the bartender pour Myles a triple.

Forbes was still appearing to make nothing but small talk. But in fact, the FBI agent was eliciting information in the subtle way experienced interrogators do. He also was checking the pace and manner of Myles's responses; noting the man's breathing and eye-movement patterns; watching how Myles shifted his body in response to certain questions; listening carefully to his vocabulary and phrasing. Unlike so many of his peers at the Bureau, Forbes was a gifted interrogator: patient, incisive, and flexible; a talented role-player who was able to assume the characteristics demanded by the situation.

What he was doing now was evaluating Myles through the use of nonthreatening conversation, much in the same way a good polygraph operator asks a series of bland control questions in order to develop the baseline against which to measure all the subject's later responses. Forbes, however, didn't need to hook Myles up to any box. The graph paper was already running inside the G-man's head.

Sam set the drinks down and slid Myles's highball across the table. He watched as the man took the glass in both hands and sipped, reacted to the strength of the drink, and then took three big swallows, finishing half of it.

Sam's eyebrows flicked. Forbes's head reacted imperceptibly. They'd wait and let the alcohol do its work before they began their own.

6:14 P.M. Sam caught Forbes's expression and knew it was time to strike. He dropped a heavy brown envelope with a Department of Justice return address imprinted in the upper-left-hand corner onto the table. "Mr. Myles, we think you should look at these," Sam said. "They'll give you some idea of what we'd like to cover this evening."

He slid the envelope under Myles's nose and nonchalantly sipped his Guinness while the man opened the flap and pulled a manila folder out.

They'd war-gamed this stage of things for the greatest shock value. So, the first picture was the one of Myles accepting a wad of cash. The second was a copy of the receipt—in Cyrillic—with Myles's thumbprint clearly visible, and circled in red. The third was the FBI fingerprint card that had been taken during Myles's security check for his SE-CRET clearance. Underneath those, were half a dozen of the SECRET documents Myles had passed to his handlers, all of them annotated in Cyrillic. Under those, Forbes had inserted a dozen gruesome five-by-seven crime-scene photographs he'd pulled from his home files.

Myles started to shake. He tried to stand up but Forbes put a hand on his shoulder and pressed him back onto the leather banquette. "No-no-no-no-no," Forbes said. "We're just getting acquainted." Quickly, he slid everything but the crime-scene pictures back into the folder, slid the folder into the envelope, and passed the envelope to Sam, who dropped it out of sight.

Then Forbes put his arm around Myles's quivering shoulder. "Vern," he said, "we know you've been passing materials to the Russians. But that's not why we're here. We're here because we think you are in danger."

"Danger?"

"The photographs," Sam said. "Remember that Senate aide who committed suicide three months ago?"

Myles's eyes went wide. "John Willis?"

"That's the one."

Willis, a former CIA case officer, had been a high-ranking staffer at the House Permanent Select Committee on Intelligence. The way the *Washington Post* had told the story, he'd been accused by several congressmen of leaking derogatory stories to the press, and was abruptly fired by the committee chairman at the behest of CIA Director Nick Becker. According to the newspaper accounts, the following morning a depressed Willis had taken a shotgun from his home, checked into the Wolf Trap Motel, and blown his brains out.

Sam slid a photograph under Myles's nose. "That's Willis." He watched the man's reaction. "Or at least it was. And we know it wasn't suicide."

"How?" Myles was simultaneously repulsed and fascinated by the photograph. He couldn't take his eyes off of it. "How do you know?"

Sam slid a second crime-scene photo in front of Myles. "John Willis put the muzzle of the shotgun in his mouth, then reached down and pushed the trigger."

"Which," Forbes continued, "sent twenty-seven pellets of number four buckshot from a two-and-three-quarter-inch Federal hunting load down the thirty-inch barrel of a Browning twelve-gauge semiautomatic shotgun, blowing the back of his head clean off." He pointed at the photo Sam had just placed in front of Myles. "Messy, huh? You can see his brains all over the wall."

"Oh, my God."

"Except there was one slight discrepancy," Sam said.

Myles started to sweat. He wiped at his brow. "I think I'm going to be sick."

Forbes slid out of the booth. "C'mon," he said, taking hold of Myles's arm firmly. "We'll get some cold water on your face."

When they'd returned, some minutes later, Sam was waiting with a fresh round of drinks.

"Take a sip," he urged, looking at Myles's ashen face. "You'll feel better."

Myles smelled of vomit, bile, and sweat. He complied meekly. He put the glass back onto its cocktail napkin and swiveled toward Forbes. "How did you know it wasn't suicide?"

Forbes riffled through the crime-scene photos until he found the one he wanted. "Willis put the barrel of the shotgun in his mouth and pushed the trigger with his thumb. See?"

Myles snuck a look at the photograph, then quickly swallowed some of his drink. "Uh-huh."

"Look again. Look at the barrel."

Myles forced himself to focus on the grisly photo. "I see it."

"The barrel on this shotgun was thirty inches long. The trigger is positioned seven inches behind where the chamber—that's the end of the barrel that holds the shell—fits into the receiver."

Myles's expression told Sam he wasn't getting it, so Sam pointed to the corpse in the photo. "Willis's arms weren't long enough for him to be able to reach the trigger with the muzzle of the shotgun in his mouth. He would have had to fire the weapon with a toe."

"And as you can see"—Forbes jumped in—"he's wearing his shoes."

"But the newspapers . . ."

"The newspapers printed what we told them." Sam scooped the photos up before Myles could examine any more of them. He slid all but one into the envelope. "We're the government, Vern. We run black ops."

"We gave the press that cover story to gain us time," Forbes said. He dropped his voice to a whisper. "Because the Russians killed Willis."

"The *Russians*?" Myles's face went white.

Sam picked up the thread. "You know President Putin's allied himself with the United States in the war against terror. Russia even supported the United States in the Security Council to allow the president to use force in Iraq. Vladimir Putin doesn't want us to discover any evidence that he's been spying on us all along. So he ordered Moscow Center to temporarily close down all their American networks." Sam tapped the heavy envelope. "This is how they're doing it."

"You're in danger," Forbes said. He put his arm around Myles's shoulder. "Look, guy, we know what you've been doing. If you help us now, we'll keep you safe. If you don't want to cooperate, that's fine. We'll do the formal number. The whole nine yards. You'll be charged. You'll do the perp walk into Federal Court—orange jumpsuit, bulletproof vest, U.S. marshals, shackles round your wrists and ankles. Oh—and lots of TV cameras. Remember the chaos when Hanssen was charged? TV news loves spy cases, Vern. So people will see your face, over and over and over. How many times did you see that horsey smile of Bobby Hanssen's? A thousand times? More? You'll get the same treatment."

"Then we'll make sure you're released on bond," Sam said. "After all, you're only small fry."

Forbes picked up the cue. "Oh, the Russians will *love* that,

Vern." The G-man tapped the picture of John Willis's corpse.
"The Russians want you out on the street, where they can
reach out and touch you." He slid the picture of Willis's
corpse under Myles's nose.

"We know you run a safe house for them. We know you
pass the occasional document."

Sam looked at the pitiful bureaucrat. It was all so clear
now. SCEPTRE and SCARAB were indeed cryptonyms for
two highly placed Moscow Center agents. Ed Howard said
SCARAB had a safe house where he had his face-to-face
meetings with his Russian control agent. He also said that
SCARAB had been invited to an elite reception held at the
State Department in honor of visiting KGB Chairman Yevgeniy Primakov.

Howard had either lied—or he'd misspoke. Vern Myles
ran the safe house. But Myles wasn't SCARAB. No way. And
Sam was certain he wasn't SCEPTRE either. No: Vern Myles
was another in a long line of disposables.

Charlotte had pointed it out on the link diagram. Howard
insisted that SCARAB had shaken hands with Primakov. The
defector had even claimed that a Russian control officer
brush-passed his valuable agent something at the State Department reception. He'd tried to cover his tracks afterward
when Sam had caught him in an inconsistency.

No—that wasn't what Howard had said. Howard had said
that SCARAB's control officer had passed the American traitor something right under the nose of the secretary of state.
Sam had simply assumed the control officer was Russian—
part of Primakov's entourage. Now, sitting in the bar, he realized the assumption could have been a false one.

He turned his attention back to Myles, who was in an utter
state of panic. Good. Sam took his time, reached leisurely for
his Guinness, and sipped. He looked at his target, his expression compassionate. "We need details, Vern. Your contact

procedure. Your signal sites. Your mailbox locations. Your break-off sequences. Help us, and you'll survive. Hold back, and—" Sam used the pint glass to point to the photograph.

Myles's eyelids fluttered. He started to say something, thought better of it, then took his drink in both hands and drained it.

Forbes inclined the rim of his Guinness in Myles's direction. "Live or die, boyo. Choice is yours."

Myles, having finished his drink, began to chew the ice cubes. He'd started to sweat again. "What do you people want?"

Sam could smell the man's fear. "Everything," Sam said, his face passive. "But not here. We'll talk in the car."

"Are you taking me to jail?"

Forbes shook his head. "We're going somewhere we can talk." Using the Miller documents, Sam had already rented a motel room in Ballston. Forbes would do the questioning there.

First he'd shake Myles's equilibrium by catching him in small contradictions. Then he'd take him back over the material three, four, five times, emphasizing the dire consequences of every minuscule inconsistency. He'd tell Myles jailhouse horror stories about rape and murder. He'd play Myles's emotions like a goddamn Stradivarius. Oh, Forbes was a frigging virtuoso of interrogation. A Heifitz who would threaten, coax, and cajole until Myles was pliable as putty; a merry fiddler who'd vary the tempo and the intensity of his questions to knock Myles off balance.

He'd manipulate, control, and dominate the situation until Myles would literally beg to confess his sins. And then he'd squeeze the son of a bitch dry. He'd be spy dust.

But Forbes would do it all on his own. Sam had other work to do tonight.

CHAPTЭЯ 29

8:46 P.M. Sam pushed through the C Street staff-only door of the Hart Senate Office Building. He was, he estimated grimly, either committing or about to commit half a dozen Class-A felonies. Not that the thought made him uneasy. Committing felonies was something case officers did as a matter of course. In fact, case officers who *weren't* committing felonies weren't doing their jobs properly. Sam had broken the criminal laws of Germany, Poland, Belgium, the Netherlands, France, and Russia during his CIA career. But he'd never violated U.S. criminal statutes. Until now. Tonight he was running the same sort of B&E op against his own government that he'd conducted in Bonn, Paris, Moscow, and elsewhere.

Forbes had warned that operating alone would get him busted. Sam was about to find out whether or not the G-man was correct. There'd been no problems during his approach, even though all the Senate office buildings were ringed in Jersey barriers and traffic was rerouted. In fact, the entire Capitol complex was inside a vehicle-free cordon sanitaire, even though Congress had left for its Thanksgiving recess.

As he walked south from Union Station, Sam felt as if he were entering a ghost town.

BOGUS FBI CREDENTIAL in his hand, Sam walked up to the barricade, which was manned by a single, bored Capitol police sergeant sitting on a steel chair on the far side of the metal detector. The nameplate on his uniform said N. LATTIG and below it, PA.

Sam brandished the shield. "Busy night, Sergeant Lattig?"

The burly cop looked up from his newspaper. "As you can see, I'm turning 'em away in droves."

Sam stood an arm's length away from the barrier. He held the ID next to his face so Lattig could compare the picture and see the shield up close. "Got a meeting upstairs."

"Lucky you." The sergeant beckoned him forward, never even bothering to stand. "C'mon through."

Sam pocketed his ID as he walked through the metal detector, setting it off. The cop didn't look up from the paper.

There was a gas mask hanging from the underside of the barricade. Sam said, "I see they finally got you guys some protection against anthrax."

Lattig snorted derisively. "Yeah—right. Lotta good it'll do me, too, without the rest of the chemical suit." He refolded the newspaper so he could read the next page. "Have a good one, bud."

"Thanks. You stay safe."

Rubber soles silent on the stone floor, Sam made his way down one long corridor, turned left, and headed for the closest bank of elevators so he could go up to the Hart's huge atrium lobby and get his bearings. Frankly, he had no idea where in the huge office building he was.

There were three Capitol police officers waiting to climb on as Sam exited. He nodded at them, walked into the atrium, peered up into the balconied tiers, saw where he had to go, headed for the closest stairway, and scampered up to the second floor.

He emerged onto a carpeted walkway that overlooked the lobby, made his way to a set of double fire doors, pushed them open, and continued down a deserted, marble-floored corridor that led to the SSCI offices.

8:51 P.M. Sam stood in front of Hart 211. He put his ear to the door and listened, but could detect no sound. He tried to peer under the door. So far as he could tell, there were no lights either. He reached into his trouser pocket and retrieved the index card on which he had written the cipher-lock combinations he'd copied from Red Jacket's wallet. He squinted at his writing, punched 4-2-4-2-8 into the lock set, and turned the knurled steel handle.

The cipher lock eased open. Sam pulled on a tight-fitting pair of latex gloves, reached down, turned the big flat doorknob, and pressed inward.

The door didn't budge. The goddamn door was doublelocked. Then the cipher-lock timer expired, and the bolt shut with such a loud sound Sam grew wary. This was going to be no fun at all.

He pulled the latex gloves off and stuffed them in the breast pocket of his suit coat. From his trouser pocket, Sam extracted what appeared to be an ordinary pocketknife. But instead of blades, there were six two-and-a-quarter-inch picks. A long, thin torque wrench was concealed in the dark handle.

8:51:46. Sam tried one pick after another until he found the one that worked most easily against the lock's tumbler pins. The secret was not to apply too much pressure because the tumbler pins would bind under tension. When he had the pick up against the first of the pins, he inserted the torque wrench into the keyhole. The wrench would apply pressure to the pins and hold them in position once the pick had done its work.

8:51:55. Sam's ears pricked up at the sound of footsteps echoing off the marble corridor. They were coming from somewhere to his left. Then he heard indistinct voices. Sam pulled the pick and wrench out of the lock and dropped them into his jacket. He wheeled and moved rapidly away from the sound, going back the way he'd come, searching for someplace to hide.

8:52:09. He passed a stairwell but decided against it. Just beyond, there was a restroom. He eased the door open, listening as the footfalls grew louder behind him The lights had been turned out. Sam flipped them on and went inside, found a stall, entered it, then sat on the commode, trying to slow his heartbeat and modulate his breathing.

He forced himself to sit for a full two and a half minutes, staring at the second hand on his wristwatch. Then he stood, walked to the sink, washed his hands, dried them, cautiously eased the bathroom door open, and stuck his head into the corridor, senses keened. The corridor was empty. He heard nothing.

8:55:16. He wiped off every surface he'd touched in the restroom, pocketed the paper towel, then made his way back to 211. There, he unfolded his lock pick, extracted the torque wrench, knelt, and stared at the face of the lock. It was a Schlage—a common commercial-grade pin-tumbler lock. Pin-tumbler locks were the most basic. You insert a key in the keyway of the lock's plug. The key's indentations fit protrusions on the side of the keyway. Those protrusions are called wards, and they prevent someone from using a key that hasn't been made for a specific lock.

Once the proper key is inserted, the cuts on the bottom edge of the key lift each pair of pins until the key pin and the driver pin both reach what is known as a sheer line. When all the pins are in that sheer line, the plug rotates, the bolt retracts, and voilà, the door opens.

Sam concentrated on the face of the lock. The procedure wasn't anything he hadn't done hundreds of times before. Except those hundreds of times had been during training class, or overseas. Sam hadn't touched a lock pick in more than half a decade.

Well, it was probably like riding a bicycle. Some things you don't forget. Like sniffing the lock to see if it had been lubricated recently. He flared his nostrils and inhaled. The answer was no. He grasped the pick, holding it in his right hand like a pencil, took the torque wrench in his left, then inserted both into the keyway of the plug.

Using his right hand, Sam ran the pick over the pins in order to get some sense of how stiff the lock's pin springs were. He manipulated the pick back and forth three times, and realized he had no idea how stiff the springs were.

8:57:02. Okay—back to basics. He explored the interior of the plug to see if the pinholes were aligned. Some lock makers skewed their pinholes off center while others drilled randomly aligned holes, making picking exponentially more difficult.

Sam made contact with the first pin, and then worked his way back. There were five pins in all—the normal number for a commercial-grade lock. And they were aligned. That would make the job marginally simpler.

He applied a little pressure now, used his left hand to add torque, and then slid the lock pick back and forth quickly, in a motion that is known as scrubbing.

He felt two of the pins—three and four—set on his first stroke. That was normal. A lock's pins always tend to set in a particular order. He scrubbed once again, this time applying more torque.

Nothing happened. He added pressure to the torque wrench. The pins slipped out of position.

Dammit—he'd used too much torque. Sam lost all control.

Feverishly, he moved the pick back and forth, vainly attempting to push the pins back where they belonged with the instrument's flat side.

Sam's fingers began to get moist. This was going nowhere.

He stopped completely, withdrew both pick and torque wrench, set them down, pulled a handkerchief out of his pocket, and wiped his hands, his wrists, and his face until they were dry. His chest was heaving. He looked at the inside of his right wrist and watched his pulse race. Sam rubbed at his face with both hands. This was nothing at all like riding a damn bicycle. From off to his right he heard a sound and his head snapped back, wide-eyed, a deer caught in headlights. He remained motionless for some seconds, daring not even to breathe. It was nothing: normal nighttime office-building sounds.

8:59:10. Sam forced himself to focus on the face of the lock once more. But this time he kept his breathing under control. "Zen and the art of lock picking" was how the instructors at the Farm had referred to the craft. And that's what it was: the craft of lock picking. Lock picking was a skill that could be learned.

Shut your eyes, the instructors had told the disbelieving spy trainees, and all things will become clear. They'd been right. And that's what he'd do now. Sam closed his eyelids. It took a couple of seconds, but when he really concentrated, a three-dimensional holograph of the lock's guts streamed into his brain. He saw everything: the hull, the pins, the springs, the alignment. Then, eyes wide shut, he inserted the pick, this time making sure that he used his wrist only to apply pressure. He scrubbed the pick backward and forward by manipulating his shoulder and elbow.

8:59:16. As Sam scrubbed, he could sense the pins move. Then the number three and number four pins set—just . . . like . . . that. His mind's eye saw them do so, clearly.

8:59:19. Sam's eyelids fluttered briefly. He adjusted the

torque wrench to apply pressure and turn the plug slightly to hold the dropped pins in place. They held. Oh, goddamn, it was *working*.

8:59:21. Sam shut his eyes so he could picture the tip of the pick. He shifted the torque wrench, which held the number three and number four pins in place. Quickly now he scrubbed the pick back and forth.

8:59:25. Pin number one dropped—Sam heard the telltale rattle as the tip of the pick passed over it. He adjusted the torque wrench and rotated the plug just a hair, and scrubbed again. The other pins set. He had his sheer line.

8:59:29. Crunch time. His hands moving as delicately as a neurosurgeon's, Sam used the torque wrench to rotate the plug a hundred and eighty degrees. The plug rolled easily and the bolt retracted. Open sesame!

Sam pulled himself to his feet, only then daring to exhale. The collar of his shirt was wet. Holding the handle of the steel door down to keep the lock open, he stowed the pick and torque wrench in his pocket, pulled the latex gloves back on, wiped the door handle clean with his handkerchief, then punched 4-2-4-2-8 into the electronic cipher lock. When he heard the faint click, he opened the door to 211 and eased inside.

Sam closed the door behind him, then stood silent so his eyes would grow accustomed to the dark. He was carrying a flashlight, but wasn't about to use it yet. There was a slight gap under the door, and a flashlight—even the small one in Sam's pocket—could give him away.

Besides, Sam's night vision slowly started to kick in and he began to see faint outlines in the darkness. Moving cautiously, he made his way past the receptionist's desk across the wide space to the door of Virginia Vacario's office and the big safe inside—the safe that held Rand Arthur's secrets in their padlocked box.

He'd been able to copy down four of the five numbers Ginny had punched into her cipher lock. The sequence was 0, 8, 7, and 4. Sam ran his right hand up the outer edge of the door until his fingers touched the cool metal of the lock. Eyes closed, he touched the pad to make certain of the key placement. Then, without any hesitation, he punched a five number combination. There was an audible click. He eased the knurled handle counterclockwise, opening the bolt. Sam smiled. Piece of cake.

Most people, he knew from experience, use familiar numbers as safe combinations and computer passwords. Telephone and Social Security numbers were common, as were street-address numbers, military IDs—and children's birth dates. Ginny told him in Moscow that her daughter had been born the day Richard Nixon resigned from office. That day was August 4, 1974. So Sam had punched 4-0-8-7-4—and the sequence had worked. He was hugely satisfied with himself.

CHAPTЭЯ 30

9:01:22. Sam eased the heavy door open, slipped inside, and closed the door behind him. When the latch bolt clicked shut, he reached into his pocket to bring the small flashlight out.

That's when Sam sensed he wasn't alone. He tensed. That's when he felt the air around him shift—the same palpable change in pressure just before lightning strikes—and he caught the whiff of something vaguely familiar—a spicy, floral odor he'd smelled somewhere before.

Instinctively, he stepped backward and ducked.

Too late. "Unggh." The blow caught him on the very ridge of his clavicle and drove him onto his knees. Sam rolled away from the smell. But obviously in the wrong direction. Because his assailant connected with a second shot. Sam's arms went up reactively, but the son of a bitch caught him right on the point of his left elbow, sending a huge spasm of pain ricocheting all the way through his body.

And in that split second Sam realized that he'd been set up one more time. Just the way he'd been set up with Pavel Baranov, Irina Howard, and Alexei Semonov.

His mind working at warp speed, the last few weeks flashed before his eyes. *They were here to murder him. Get him out of the way for good. It was Rand Arthur's killers—Red Jacket and Oakland Raider. They'd been waiting for him all along. Oh, Christ, that made Virginia Vacario part of the conspiracy. Or maybe she was Moscow Center's mole—recruited in Germany, infiltrated onto Rand Arthur's staff. Maybe Red Jacket and Oakland Raider worked for her, not Rand. That was it: she'd allowed him to see her cipher combination. She knew he'd figure it out—and break in to see what was in the goddamn safe. And so they'd been waiting for him. It was another bloody ambush.*

No—this time it would be different. They were really going to kill him tonight. They had to—couldn't screw it up again.

But he was so close to the end of the maze. So damn close. Far too close to die now.

9:01:24. The latex glove on Sam's right hand got caught up in the material of his jacket pocket and he ripped the cloth pulling it out. Just in time to take a third shot, which caught him in the kidneys.

"Unh!" But he lunged forward, the pain offset by rage, tackled his assailant around the legs, and took him down onto the rug. The pistol came out of the holster on Sam's hip and skittered across the floor, out of reach.

Oh, goddamn, let there not be a second attacker. Let them not have night vision. Sam thought about going back for the gun. But he'd committed himself, and so he charged ahead.

Sam was a sizable man—six feet one, two hundred pounds, and a grappler by nature. From his throat came the primeval growl he'd learned at Parris Island. "Arrrghh!"

Like an attacking croc he wrapped his attacker up and took the son of a bitch into a death roll, right hand smacking hard upside the head, then grabbing a fistful of hair to yank his head back. Sam's left hand chopped at his attacker's face then went for the throat, his big hand squeezing the life out of the cocksucker's windpipe, crushing his larynx.

The pure, white-hot fury of his counterattack stunned his opponent. Teeth bared, Sam went in for the kill.

Which is when his rampaging animal brain finally identified the spicy, floral-tinged odor of Chanel No. 5. He rolled away, horrified. "Ginny?"

Breathing hard, Sam found his flashlight and switched it on.

She was in a fetal position. Next to her lay the NYPD nightstick. He flung it across the office, rolled her onto her back, and examined her in the narrow beam of light. Her lip was cut. A trickle of blood oozed down her chin. Her cheek was bruised. He crawled as far as her shoulders and cradled her head. "Ginny, Ginny, Ginny." He found his handkerchief and used it to wipe the blood. "Oh, my God. Hold on."

He scrambled to his feet, the flashlight probing until he found the light switch. The sudden brightness of the fluorescents made him cover his eyes for an instant.

He returned to where she lay on the carpet. "I'm so sorry—"

She shrank away from him, panic in here eyes. *"Stay away from me—"* And then, she saw past the latex gloves and the prosthetics and the mustache. *"Sam? Sam Waterman?"*

"It's me." Sam bent down and daubed at her face. "Is there a fridge? Is there any ice?"

She looked up at him blankly. "Thought you were a burglar . . . you'd come to kill me."

"Ice, Ginny," Sam said. "Ice."

She squeezed her eyes shut and dropped her head because she was having a hard time swallowing. He'd grabbed her throat pretty hard.

She coughed phlegm then gurgled something unintelligible and pointed toward the outer office. Sam pulled himself to his feet. He spotted the pistol, scooped it up, adjusted the paddle holster on his belt, jammed the Glock home, then headed for the door. Half a minute later he was back, with a handful of cubes wrapped in a paper towel.

She'd rolled onto her side, and was in the process of hauling herself into a sitting position when he came through the door. She gave him a quick glance, her hand pressed against the underside of her nose to staunch the blood.

If looks could indeed kill, Sam would have been a dead man.

He went to her side, knelt, and handed her the pitiful packet of ice cubes in their soggy wrapper. She pressed the cold bundle against her lip, wincing as she did. She looked daggers at him. "God, you sure know how to treat a girl."

"I—" Sam started to say something, then thought better of it and just shut up. He helped her to her feet, put his arm around her waist, and walked her to the couch, picking up the afghan where it had fallen onto the rug and slipping it over her pantsuit legs after she'd crumpled onto the brown leather.

"Just lie there," he said, slipping a bolster under the back of her neck. "Put the ice on your lip. Let the cold work. We'll talk later."

9:32:00. "O'Neill said you'd become unbalanced—obsessive. But I never thought you'd try to kill me."

"I wasn't. I wouldn't. I swear. I thought you were the same people who tried to kill me last week."

"What?"

He gave her the twopenny version, leaving out who Red Jacket and Oakland Raider actually were.

Her expression softened, but only marginally. "Breaking in here. Sam, how could you do it? It's a *crime*."

"I thought—" he began.

"Thinking is the one thing you obviously haven't been doing," she interrupted. "Look at you—gloves, flashlight. A gun, for chrissakes, Sam. What in God's name are you doing carrying a gun?"

"I told you—they were trying to kill me."

"And you thought carrying a gun would help. And how the hell did you get past the metal detectors?"

"I took the Houdini course at the Farm."

"Very funny. C'mon—how?"

Sam let the subject drop. Finally, he said, "Ginny, you don't know what's going on."

"I know enough." The left side of Vacario's face was puffy where Sam had smacked her. When she spoke it sounded like she had a mouthful of marbles.

"Ed Howard was a plant. His whole defection was a plant."

"I figured that out," she said. "I knew it after I read the transcript—the whole transcript. Carefully." She gave him a spiteful look. "I took the notes, after all. And I know how to read a debriefing. I picked up on his inconsistencies. Believe me, I briefed the senator. He finally understands he was being set up by Howard."

Does he, now? Sam found her response interesting.

But he didn't say so. Instead, he parried. "Does he know there really are Russian agents cryptonymed SCEPTRE and SCARAB?"

Her expression told him the answer was no. She dabbed at her cheek, then set the soggy paper towel on the rug. "Who?"

"I don't know yet."

"Then why do you believe Howard wasn't lying about SCARAB and SCEPTRE?"

"Because he was mad at his boss."

"What?"

"It was revenge—ego. That's why he came back. Klimov had ostracized him. Put him in an office so small there was no desk or telephone. Shut him out. Howard decided to pay him back by defecting. But Klimov caught on. He used Howard."

"That's ridiculous."

"No, it's not. Once Klimov realized Howard was going to redefect, he made sure Howard learned about SCEPTRE and SCARAB."

"Who are . . ."

"Who are, in reality, high-level Russian agents. That was the risky part for Klimov—embedding a tiny vein of gold in the lode of black information. But Klimov also made sure Howard got his hands on files that would focus us on disposables, not the real SCEPTRE and SCARAB."

"How do you know that, Sam?"

"Because I found Howard's files in Moscow, Ginny."

"You lied to me."

"For chrissakes, I thought you were involved. You could have been one of Klimov's targets."

"You're talking about Bonn?"

He nodded.

"Bonn was a NATO matter, Sam. It had to do with Soviet penetration of the German Foreign Ministry. I'd worked with several of the people involved on counterterrorism matters when I was at Justice. Langley asked me to take on a six-month assignment under DOJ[52] cover. I had nothing to do with Klimov, or Putin, or Edward Lee Howard. That's as much of the story as I feel obliged to tell you." She pressed the ice to her cheek. "Back to Howard, Sam."

"Klimov made sure Howard got access to files—which, of course, are filled with misinformation. Howard never caught on. So after he defects he tries to impress me by passing his precious information to me—never knowing he's a cog on Klimov's wheel. But everything was a false trail—a black

---

[52] Department of Justice.

penetration op designed by Klimov and probably Putin to protect the real SCARAB and SCEPTRE. Okay: Howard defects, and he passes the information to me, and then something spooks him."

"What?"

"Don't know." Sam scrubbed the false mustache with the edge of his gloved index finger. "But Howard gets spooked, and he goes back to Moscow—where Klimov kills him."

Her expression reflected how dubious she was. "So where does this all lead, Sam?"

"I just told you: to more disposables."

"Disposables?"

"Low-grade agents. Gofers. I have my hands on one of them."

"Who?"

"I'll tell you later." He examined her face. "Let me get you some more ice."

"I'm fine, Sam. I'll survive."

His face darkened. "Then I'll finish what I came here to do: look at Rand Arthur's stuff in that safe."

Reactively, Vacario's arms folded atop her chest. "No way."

"Have to, Ginny."

"You're making the situation worse than it already is."

"I can live with that."

"But I can't. What's in that safe is lawyer-client stuff, Sam—not to mention classified materials that you have no business poking through. I will not open the safe for you— and I'll call the police if you try to break in on your own."

"I'm not here to steal America's secrets, Ginny."

"That's not what the chairman thinks. He's convinced you're a double agent, Sam. Even Michael wasn't able to convince him otherwise."

"Rand? He's off his rocker."

"Why should I believe you're not?"

"Because I'm telling you."

"That's not enough."

"It'll have to be—for now." He watched as she wiped her nose with his bloody handkerchief. "Look—I'm here with one objective. I don't give a goddamn about any secrets in your safe—except Rand's. But I want to see what Rand stored here."

"Why?"

"Because he stored it *here*. In your office. Not in his hide-away—he has a big fireproof safe there. Or in the safe in that paneled library of his out in Round Hill. He gave these items to you, Ginny. That tells me he doesn't want anyone to know about them."

"What's your point?"

"You're not his lawyer."

"Yes, I am."

"No—you're his chief counsel. O'Neill's his lawyer. So, why the hell aren't the folder and the box in a safe in O'Neill's office?"

Ginny's head cocked like a terrier's. "I don't know."

"Well, neither do I—which is why I'm going to take a look-see."

"I still don't understand."

"You don't have to." He walked to the big black steel cabinet, punched a series of numbers into the electronic lock, waited as the bolt linkages whirred, turned the handle, and opened the door. "Voilà."

She sat on the couch, dumbfounded. "How the hell . . ."

"Trust me, Ginny. Please."

He waited to see her reaction. When she didn't reach for the telephone, Sam pulled the accordion file and the locked safe-deposit box off the top shelf, set them on Vacario's desk, then closed the safe door and rolled the lock handle closed.

He opened the accordion file and riffled through it. "Rand's wife's papers—her will, other stuff. None of my business." He closed the file and secured it with its elastic band.

"Now this . . ." Sam examined the slim shackle that went through the safe-deposit box's hasp, flipped the padlock over, pulled his lock picks out, and went to work.

9:37:30. It was a rudimentary lock, and Sam had it open in less than a minute. He looked over at Ginny. "Before I open the box—do you have any idea what we'll find?"

"No. The senator told me he wanted to keep some of his personal effects in a safe place—away from the house. He brought the folder last month—just before Howard showed up. I think he brought the box a couple of days after I got back from Moscow. I didn't question him further." She pointed at the accordion file. "And personal effects are exactly what we've found so far."

Sam flipped the lid and peered inside. "These are interesting personal effects." He tilted the box in Vacario's direction so she could see the stacks of hundred-dollar bills bound with rubber bands. "What is this, Rand's presidential campaign fund?"

He put the wads on her desk. There were twenty-five of them. He undid one and began counting. There were one hundred bills in all. He resecured the pile of hundreds. "A quarter-mil," Sam said. "Not bad." Then he tilted the box further, revealing a brown clasp envelope that sat under a black felt sack secured by a narrow band of red ribbon.

Sam took the envelope, carefully undid the clasp, and peered inside.

Vacario asked, "What's there?"

"SSCI secrecy agreements for compartmented information."

She frowned. "SSCI doesn't have its own secrecy agreements. If staffers need access to a compartment, CIA takes care of the clearance."

"Don't tell that to a couple of people named Reese and Johnson." Sam gently edged the sheets out of the envelope and showed her. She reached out for the top one but he quickly drew it back. "Fingerprints, Ginny."

"Sorry, Sam."

There were regulation orange-striped Top Secret cover sheets stapled atop two-page agreement forms. Each page was signed and initialed, and the bottom of the back page had a thumbprint below the signer's hand-printed name.

Sam's eyes scanned down the page until he found what he was looking for. He hadn't been far off. "Rand's compartment is called TALL CAVERN."

Vacario frowned. "Come again?"

"TALL CAVERN."

"There is no such compartment, Sam. Not at CIA, not at NSA. Nowhere."

He hefted the agreements. "You coulda fooled me."

Lips pursed, Vacario found her reading glasses, slipped them on, and looked over Sam's shoulder. She shook her head. "I don't get it. Why would this material be anything more than confidential? What we have here is nothing more than a receipt for an unspecified amount of money and an agreement to act on the personal orders of the chairman."

"Recognize the names of the individuals who signed the forms?"

She squinted at the bottom of the page. "No."

"They're U.S. Capitol police officers—one of them headed the security detail after Howard showed up at Rand's place. Rand sent them to kill me."

Her intake of breath was audible. "Impossible."

"Then why did Rand make sure to get their fingerprints on what you call nothing more than a receipt? Why did he create a fictitious compartment called TALL CAVERN and make two officers sign secrecy agreements?" Sam's expression was grim. He didn't wait for her to answer. "Believe me, Ginny, nothing's impossible."

Sam put the documents back in their envelope. Then he took the sack from the metal box and hefted it in his hand. He inverted the sack in the palm of his gloved hand, revealing perhaps fifty or sixty flawless diamonds in the one-and-a-half- to two-and-a-half-carat range. "I'm not up on diamonds these days, but I'd bet these would be worth a million dollars on the wholesale market—maybe more. And unlike currency, they're untraceable."

"Oh, my God!" Vacario's eyes went wide.

"Hold out your hands." Sam allowed the stones to cascade into Vacario's palms. She stared at the diamonds, and the two signed security agreements. He said nothing, allowing the eloquence of his silence to make his case.

Ten, twenty, thirty seconds passed; the only sound was Vacario's labored breathing. The look on her face told Sam everything he had to know. It revealed her feelings of disbelief, horror, shock—and betrayal. Ginny might have been a Player—even an Alien—but it was impossible to feign that complex a reaction. All of his instincts told him she was on the right side of this fight.

Finally she gazed up at him. "Take everything back, Sam. Put it all away. I don't want to look anymore."

"Will do." But first he put the envelope with the agreements on the desk.

Vacario's eyes followed his actions, but she said nothing. When he'd finished she let the stones fall back into his hands. He funneled them into the sack, then dropped the sack in the safe-deposit box. He slid the cash back and replaced the envelope with the agreements, too. Then he closed the hasp, threaded the shackle, and snapped the padlock closed. But he didn't replace the box in the safe when he locked the accordion file behind the heavy steel door.

"Does Rand have the combination to your safe?"

"Not that I know."

"Then he won't know we have this." He tapped the steel box. "Ginny, you'll have to come with me."

She blinked. "I don't understand."

"I don't want to let you out of my sight now. Things are too dicey."

"Don't be ridiculous. I'm not Faye Dunaway and this isn't *Three Days of the Condor*."

"Ginny . . ."

She pulled herself off the couch "I'm serious, Sam."

He walked to the phone and unplugged the wire. "So am I. Four people are dead—and someone has tried to kill me twice in the last ten days. There's a high-level Russian network in play. But the more I discover about it, the less I seem to know. I need some time."

"You're not making any sense." She focused on his face. "And your mustache is coming loose."

Sam adjusted the device and pressed it firmly onto his upper lip. "Better?"

She examined his face. "I guess."

"Look, Ginny—"

"No, you look. I'm going to tell you to do the same thing you told me to do just about a month ago. Call the FBI, Sam. Right now. Let the Bureau handle this mess. If you don't, I'm going to put up a hell of a fuss."

Sam didn't need a fuss. His misapprehensions about Vacario might be allayed, but in point of fact he trusted no one at this point in time except John Forbes. Rand Arthur was up to his eyeballs in something. Ginny might or might not be involved—might not was his instinct, but his instinct had been miserably wrong in the recent past.

Sam couldn't afford to screw up now. So he looked at her reassuringly. "The FBI's already been called in." The lie came easily. "I can take you to meet the special agent working the case."

She looked at him skeptically. "What's his name?"

"John Forbes."

"Plug the phone in, Sam."

He did as she asked.

"Call the DOJ twenty-four-hour locator."

"Do you have the number?"

In response, she pulled a government phone book out of her credenza, perused it, then wrote seven numbers on a pad.

Sam dialed the number. "I'm looking for FBI Deputy Assistant Director Forbes's extension. John Forbes. F-O-R-B-E-S." He handed her the receiver.

Sam watched as Ginny wrote a number down. She hung the phone up. "John Forbes is the deputy assistant director of the National Security Division." Her tone told Sam she was impressed.

Sam nodded. "He handles special projects. He's totally trustworthy."

The tenseness evaporated from her expression. "I thought you were lying to me."

"I want you to meet with Forbes and tell him what we found."

"Now?"

"Forbes is questioning the disposable I just told you about."

"Then I agree." She daubed at her face with Sam's handkerchief. "Mind if I freshen up a bit first, though? You seem to have smudged my makeup."

"Of course not." Sam paused. "Are you carrying a cell phone, Ginny?"

"Of course."

"I really like you, and I don't want to sound paranoid, but why don't you give it to me while you freshen up."

"I really like you, too, but that *is* paranoid, Sam. Who the hell would I be calling?"

He could think of a few people. Like her boss. Or her boss's lawyer. Or the U.S. Capitol police operations center. But he didn't say so. Instead, he looked at her, his expression grave. "Let's play this out my way."

She sighed and her eyes flashed angrily. But she reached down, opened her desk drawer, extracted her handbag, and rummaged in it until she came up with her cell phone, which she placed in Sam's gloved palm. "Satisfied?"

He dropped the phone in his pocket and picked up the steel box. "Absolutely. And since I'm both paranoid and in love, I'll walk you as far as the ladies' loo and loiter there while you do what you do. Then we can get the heck out of here."

CHAPTЭЯ 31

WEDNESDAY, NOVEMBER 27, 2002

1:02 A.M. "There are two locations. I pass them both on my way to the office." A wrung-dry Vern Myles was sitting in a straight-backed chair that was set up against the wall. They were in a paint-by-the-numbers-decorated room on the ninth floor of the Holiday Inn in Ballston.

"And . . ." John Forbes nodded. Myles was on track.

Myles looked at Sam, then at Virginia Vacario, who were sitting side by side on the edge of the queen-size bed. "If there's a signal on the first one, I—"

"What is the signal, Vern?"

Myles lifted a can of Coca-Cola off the floor and sipped. "It's three horizontal white chalk lines on the mailbox at the corner of California and Massachusetts."

"Okay."

"So, if there's a signal on the first one, I get off the bus at Florida Avenue and leave the same sign on a wall in an alley just off Twenty-first Street between Mass Ave. and P Street. Sometimes there's a second signal."

"Which is?"

"Vertical lines—four short ones, also white chalk—on the wall across the street from the old entrance to the Acheson Auditorium at HST."

Forbes glanced toward Virginia Vacario, who'd cocked her head, then focused on Vernon Myles. " 'HST,' Vern?"

Myles blinked. "Oh—it stands for Harry S. Truman. That's what they call Main State these days. It's where I work."

"And the wall? Where precisely is the wall?"

"You know the Navy medical installation off Twenty-third Street?"

Sam knew it all too well. It was where he'd done much of his denied area operations training course. "Yes."

"There are parking meters below it, and a concrete retaining wall." Myles paused. "The site's on that wall, just north of C Street, opposite the Acheson Auditorium. There's a double red stripe on the parking-meter stanchion directly in front of the wall where the signal appears."

"And?" Forbes raised an eyebrow.

"That's it."

Forbes's tone went pedantic. "Where do you leave your second signal, Vern—if you see a sign on the retaining wall?"

"Oh, that. Go immediately to Union Station garage. Third column to the left of the escalator. Initials *DD* in capital letters. Block letters—squared off. I use white chalk."

Forbes nodded his head in Myles's direction. "What about holidays?"

"Holidays?" Myles sipped his Coke. "I'm required to check the sites holidays, unless they fall on a weekend."

"So no weekends."

Myles smiled ingratiatingly. "They give me weekends off."

"How thoughtful." Sam caught Forbes's rapid expression change. Then the G-man's face went neutral.

"What about afterward?" Sam interjected.

Myles looked at him, confused. "Afterward?"

"At the apartment."

"Oh—the apartment. I wait thirty-six hours after I've left the signals, then I go to 3624 and scrub it down. Wipe all the surfaces. Vacuum. Tidy up."

Sam said, "Thank you, Vern."

John Forbes cast a quick glance in Sam's direction, then turned back to the cutout. "Vern, why don't you go into the bathroom for a few minutes so I can speak with these folks alone."

Myles didn't have to be asked twice. When the door was shut, Forbes walked over to the television set, turned it on, turned the volume up, and then beckoned Sam and Virginia Vacario over. "And for performing his duties he receives the maintenance fee for the apartment, plus fifteen hundred dollars a month—and a two-hundred-dollar bonus for every document he hands over."

"Generous," Sam said sarcastically. "From whom?"

"I gather from SVR. There's an envelope placed under the cushions on the couch in the living room the fifteenth of every month."

Vacario said, "Like clockwork."

"It's been going on for eight years."

Vacario said: "I wonder how many more like him there are."

Sam shook his head. "And this is just the Russians. The Chinese have dozens of operations like this one. And now—al-Qa'ida, Hezbollah, Islamic Jihad. They're all set up much the same." He looked over at Vacario. "Kinda makes you wonder how well we've checked out all those people interrogating the detainees at Guantánamo."

"It's the way things are organized that keeps the parties safe," Forbes said. "They know we build activities matrices. Same site appears for two parties, and we get interested. But the way this is set up, the cutout does the hard work. All each agent has to do is check a unilateral site. Everything's sterile." Forbes pulled on the edge of his stringy mustache. "It's cell-like, not hierarchical." He looked at Vacario. "Russians learned this from al-Qa'ida, y'know."

"Afghanistan?"

"Chechnya."

"But the compartmented structure could work in our favor," Sam interrupted. "Because the left hand doesn't know what the right hand's doing."

"Only if the opposition doesn't know we snatched their cutout."

"It's a holiday,"

"Not yet it isn't," Forbes said. "Still, Myles says once the call-out signals have been posted, everything happens within thirty-six hours." He bit his lower lip. "That works in our favor."

"We'll need a full-court press." Sam cracked his knuckles. "The opposition's probably got A/V inside the safe house. We'll need to disable it and set up our own." He looked over at Forbes. "You have a digital recorder?"

"Affirmative."

"We'll need it. And I think we need countersurveillance. That'll take some doing. And we've got to stash Vern somewhere."

"My God." Virginia Vacario looked as if she'd touched a live electric line. "You two are freelancing."

"Keep your voice down." Sam's tone was severe.

"Sam, this madness can't continue." She turned toward Forbes. "For Christ's sake, John, you're a deputy assistant director."

Forbes shrugged. "What can I say?" He turned the television volume a shade higher. "Look, Ginny, we're charting new ground here. I know it seems irregular—"

" 'Seems irregular'?" Vacario looked at Forbes bug-eyed. "What you're doing is bloody illegal." She jerked her thumb toward the bathroom. "That man is a criminal. A traitor."

Sam shook his head. "He's small fry."

"He's the one with the safe house, right?"

Forbes nodded.

"So he's whatchamacallit, SCEPTRE."

Sam said, "No, he's not."

"Then he's SCARAB. Those were the two Ed Howard told us about."

"I told you back at Hart, Vern Myles is neither one." Sam was emphatic. "The point, Ginny, is that SCARAB and SCEPTRE are high level. Remember—Howard told us SCARAB was invited to the diplomatic reception for Primakov. Myles? No way. Myles is the cutout."

"How high level would SCARAB be?"

"Way, way above your government pay grade. Someone who gets invited to the secretary of state's shindigs."

Which is when she got what he was driving at. "That's impossible."

"Nothing's impossible, Ginny."

"This is. You're talking about someone for whom I've worked for almost ten years. For Christ's sake, Sam, I'm a professional. I'd *know*."

"Right," Forbes said. "Just like I knew about Bobby Hanssen, with whom I worked for more than a decade." He dropped his voice. "Believe me," he said, "unless I thought this would turn out righteously, I wouldn't have gotten involved."

Sam said: "John, where's the laptop?"

"Right here, Elbridge." He one-handed Sam's slim computer. Sam took it, set it on his lap, turned it on, and waited until Windows booted up. It took him less than a minute to find the file he was looking for.

"Here, Ginny."

"What is it?"

"A story from the *Washington Post* style section."

Vacario's voice was adamant. "What in hell does this have to do with anything, Sam?"

He handed the computer to her. "Just read it quickly."

She squinted at the small screen. "I need my glasses." She found her half frames, slid them on, then read the material. "Okay, so? It's a story about the reception the secretary of state threw for Yevgeniy Primakov."

"Right."

"So?"

"So, whose name do you see mentioned?"

Vacario scrolled through the file again. "Okay. Warren Christopher. Primakov. DCI Woolsey. NSC adviser Tony Lake. Sam Nunn, Madeleine Albright, Larry King, yadda, yadda, yadda." She looked at Sam. "What's your point, Sam?"

"Rand Arthur was there, too. Gave the writer a lovely little quote." Sam paused. "And what did Ed Howard tell us about the Primakov party?"

Vacario sighed audibly. Sam didn't wait. "He told us that SCARAB was at the party."

"Which according to you makes Rand Arthur SCARAB? What about the other ninety-nine people?" She crossed her arms. "I'm not convinced. Besides . . ."

"Besides what?"

"You say the safe house is on Idaho Avenue."

"Right. Just off Wisconsin."

"Is it one of the new apartment houses—the high-rise condos?"

"No," Sam said. "One of the older ones. One self-service elevator, and sixty-two apartments spread over eight floors."

"Garage?"

"Negatory," Sam shook his head. "Street parking."

"No way." Vacario shook her head. "You are telling me

that a United States senator, whose face is all over the Sunday-morning talk shows, whose picture is in all the newspapers, is going to show up at an apartment building in upper Georgetown—walking? Sam, you may know spies. But I know senators. And senators don't do that kind of thing. At the very least, a nosy neighbor sees a senator slipping into an apartment, and they immediately think, 'Ah—a mistress,' and they get on the phone to the *National Inquirer*."

Sam said, "Hmm."

"Rand Arthur has a car and a driver—a U.S. Capitol police officer." She frowned. "And even then, he wouldn't risk jumping out of the limo, running across the sidewalk and into a seedy apartment house. No, Sam, it's just not in his makeup. Idaho Avenue may be a safe house. But it's nowhere Rand Arthur would show up. It just isn't the way he does things."

Sam looked at her. "Then I guess we'll have to see who shows up, won't we?"

5:24 A.M. They'd solved the Vern Myles problem with a roll of duct tape and John Forbes's handcuffs. Which allowed Forbes to head to Union Station to mark a double *D* on the appropriate column, and Sam and Ginny to leave their three-white-line call-out sign in the alley off Twenty-first and P Streets. They'd stay in touch by cell phone. The G-man had a second cell phone—another of the Bureau's latest STEs, or secure telephones—charging in his car. He ran downstairs, retrieved it, and handed it to Sam. "Okay, get outta here."

Forbes said that as soon as he'd completed marking the column, he'd call Johanna and ask her to keep an eye on Myles. Sam was nervous about involving anybody else. But Forbes said they really had no other choice, and Sam had to admit he was right.

And so now, Sam was using his tradecraft skills to break-

and-enter Apartment 6H at 3624 Idaho Avenue, Northwest.
He and Ginny had cruised the neighborhood for almost an
hour, looking for countersurveillance and finding none. So
they approached 3624 from Wisconsin Avenue arm in arm,
like a couple coming home. And Ginny swayed unsteadily as
Sam fumbled with his key outside the glass-paned double
doors.

Except he wasn't fumbling with a key, but working at the
old-fashioned electronic lock with his pick and torque
wrench. Vern Myles kept the keys to the safe house at the
Foggy Bottom apartment he sublet and Sam hadn't wanted to
risk going for them.

5:26. The elevator door opened and Sam stepped out into
the sixth-floor corridor. Ginny followed. He looked left, then
right. The place was unremarkable: built in the 1950s as low-
priced housing for federal workers, it had probably gone
condo in the late eighties or early nineties. The hallways
were linoleum, not carpeted. The steel doors had old-
fashioned peek holes. Sam counted nine apartments on the
floor. Six of them had copies of the *Washington Post,* the
Wall Street Journal, or the *New York Times* in front of their
doorways. Sam headed for the closest door without a newspaper, looked at the letter, shook his head, and pointed Ginny
in the opposite direction.

It took Sam less than a minute to get through the dead-
bolted lock. He pulled his own gloves on, looked at Ginny's
hands, then tapped the back of his wrist until she slipped hers
on, too. He put his fingers to his lips to remind her that there
was probably voice-activated audio surveillance inside, then
eased through the doorway. Ginny followed him into a tiny
foyer. The place smelled as if it had been shut up for months.
It was dark, but there was enough ambient light coming
through the gauzy curtains to their left to allow them to move
without tripping.

Sam almost let go of the front door when he realized there was a self-closing spring on the upper hinge. He caught the door before it could slam, turned the interior knob, and eased it shut. Silently, Sam made his way to the window and looked out. Six-H faced a rear courtyard and, sixty feet away, the back side of another apartment house. That was good news. When safe-house windows faced the street, the drapes, curtains, and shades were often used as go/no-go signals. That wasn't going to be the case here. It was one less factor to worry about.

Sam pulled the drapes shut. Only then did he turn his flashlight on and, using his hand to baffle the light, make his way back to a door that he assumed led to the bedroom. He cracked the door, grimacing when it creaked, looked into the room, then turned back toward Ginny to give her an upturned thumb. It was just as he'd thought. He disappeared inside, and fifteen seconds later, having drawn the blinds, was back. It was a matchbox of an apartment—probably no more than four hundred square feet.

He emptied his jacket pockets onto the dinette table that sat next to the minuscule kitchen. He'd been carrying a roll of duct tape, two of Forbes's digital recorders, and two self-powered, voice-activated microphones along with the lock picks and his flashlight. Now it was a question of finding the opposition's A/V surveillance gear. There were two closets in the minuscule foyer. One, facing the door, was a wide but shallow coat closet. The other, much smaller, was a linen closet. The four shelves held three folded towels. Sam shone the light carefully, but found no audio devices in either one.

Silently, he reentered the bedroom, eased open the narrow closet door, and beamed his flashlight inside only to discover six wire hangers on the clothes rod and a pair of empty shelves. He played the light under the double bed and saw only dust bunnies.

Opposite the bed was a low, painted chest. Sam held the light between his teeth and inch by inch slid the drawers open, working from the bottom. He found nothing.

5:36. The single bathroom was off the bedroom. Sam peered inside. The toilet seat was up. That told him that the last person to use the safe house was a male. He looked behind the shower curtain, checked the medicine cabinet, and glanced under the sink, but found nothing. Careful not to disturb anything, he backed out and closed the door.

That left the kitchen, and the two closets in the tiny foyer. Sam examined the closets first, but they, like the bedroom closet, were empty. He made his way around an oblong kitchenette set—a table and four chairs, and shone the light inside the small kitchen. Straight ahead was the fridge. To its left, a sink and a narrow gas stove were crammed side by side, ringed by old-fashioned painted metal cabinets.

Sam crossed the threshold. He pulled on the door of the refrigerator. It opened. Inside was a six-pack of St. Pauli Girl beer, with three bottles left in the cardboard carton. Sam opened the top-side freezer to discover a half-liter bottle of Golden Ring vodka next to three trays of ice cubes. Instinctively, he glanced toward where Ginny waited in the living room. He'd given her the exact same bottle, and even though he knew it wasn't hers, he was still paranoid enough to pull the vodka out and check the rear label. It bore, he was delighted to see, neither tax stamp nor price sticker—not even from the duty-free shop at Sheremetevo. This Golden Ring came from the Russian embassy commissary.

He cast another quick glance in Vacario's direction, breathed a huge sigh of relief and affection, stuck the bottle back in the freezer, closed the door, then reached up and opened up the double cabinets above the fridge. He discovered nothing except the fact that his pulse had begun to race. That was to be expected: the endgame was under way.

But he was a professional. Methodically, he opened and shut each of the cabinets, including the one below the sink, and found nothing. In a fit of inspiration, he even checked the oven, but it was empty except for a shiny broiler pan.

Sam stuck his head into the living room, gave Ginny an exaggerated shrug, and mouthed, "Nada." He returned to the front door and rolled the dead bolt closed, exactly the way he'd found it.

5:58. The apartment was clean. There were no devices anywhere. Sam had checked under the couch, inspected the light fixtures, shone his flashlight into the air registers, and even unscrewed all the electric outlets, but found nothing.

6:14. The STE in Sam's pocked vibrated. He flipped it open. "Yes?"

"Mission accomplished." Forbes's voice echoed in his ear. "You inside?"

"Affirmative. As soon as it's light, I'm going to put things back exactly the way we found them."

"Good. I'll be on-site by six-thirty to set up surveillance."

"How will you know the players?"

"I've got a current flash book."

"Ooorah."

"Hang in, there, Sam."

"I didn't know I had a choice. Semper Fi, guy." Sam snapped the phone shut. He turned toward Vacario. "Might as well make yourself comfortable, Ginny, it could be a long wait. I'm going to position the recorders."

CHAPTƎЯ 32

9:14 A.M. Sam felt the cell phone vibrate. He pulled himself into a sitting position and pulled the instrument from his shirt pocket. He and Ginny hadn't dared to disturb any of the furniture. So they'd slept on the floor, back to back on the musty wall-to-wall carpeting. Slept was an overstatement. They'd been up all night, reacting to every sound. They'd only closed their eyes for a catnap after eight.

He checked his watch and nudged Ginny with his left hand. She rolled over, rubbing her eyes.

Sam had to smile. Her hair was standing straight up. Her makeup was smudged. She had dark circles under her eyes. His verdict: she looked absolutely beautiful.

Sam cleared his throat, flipped the phone open, and said, "Yo?"

Forbes's voice singsonged in his ear. "You've got *mail . . .*"

The hair on the back of Sam's neck stood up. "Anyone we know?"

"According to the picture I'm looking at, one Nikolai S. Ostrovsky, commercial counselor. Works out of the trade representative's office on Connecticut Avenue. He's deputy *Rezident*."

Sam used his free hand to make sure his prosthesis and hairpiece were straight. "Alone?"

"Da."

He pressed the mustache firmly onto his upper lip and cocked his head in Ginny's direction. "Any countersurveillance, John?"

She caught Sam's eye and mouthed "You're okay."

"None that I can tell, Elbridge." Forbes's voice was momentarily interrupted by static. Then: "He should be arriving in about two minutes."

"We'll be ready." Sam's tone was serious. "Ring me once when the second party arrives—one ring only. I've got the phone on silent. Then get your G-man butt up here fast." Sam slapped the phone shut and looked at her, his expression grave. "It's showtime, Ginny."

She ran a hand through her hair, smoothing it down. "What do we do?"

"We wait."

"In here?"

"Of course not. We conceal ourselves."

He could feel the adrenaline starting to pump. But he forced himself to remain outwardly calm. He reached under the dinette table and turned the recorder on, went to the coffee table, knelt, and repeated the action. "You go into the bedroom—close the door behind you but leave it ajar by an inch or so. It creaks, so you'll know when someone's coming. Get inside the closet now. Make sure the door shuts firmly. Pull it tight, Ginny—tight—and don't make a sound. I'll be in the linen closet behind the front door. We have to wait until both targets have arrived, and are conducting business.

Then we seal things up until Forbes arrives." He looked down at her, waiting for a response. "Ginny—are you with me?"

Finally, she nodded.

He could see the tension in her face. Inexplicably, he drew her close and kissed her softly on the lips. She didn't protest. He kissed her once again. "Don't move until you hear me speaking. Not until you hear me loud and clear. Don't you even breathe." He took her hands in his. "Got it? We have to get them on tape. We need evidence of collusion. Conspiracy. We need unimpeachable evidence."

"I understand." She hugged him tightly, then dropped her arms to her sides and stepped back. "My God, Sam, I'm shaking all over."

He smiled at her reassuringly. "You'll be fine, Ginny. Okay—c'mon, move."

9:16:22. Sam crouched inside the cramped linen closet. He'd left the door cracked just slightly. He could just make out the luminous second hand on his watch as it swept around the dial. He counted off seconds, estimating Ostrovsky's progress. Through the outer door. Push the elevator button. Wait for the elevator. Push the scuffed black button. Wait as the coffin-size elevator creaks upward floor by floor. Exit. Down the hall to 6H.

9:17:31. Ears keened, Sam heard a key turn in the lock. His body tensed. He slowly swept his suit coat aside and he placed his right hand on the butt of John Forbes's compact Glock backup pistol riding in its Kydex paddle holster.

9:17:34. Through the fissure, Sam heard the door open, then slam shut. He waited for the sound of the dead bolt but it wasn't thrown.

Sam listened intently, his mind's eye playing the movie in his brain as the Russian provided the sound effects. *Ostrovsky shrugs out of his coat. He flings it across the back of the nearest dinette chair—the chair shifts. A second chair scratches across the parquet floor when Ostrovsky brushes against it as he moves into the living room. He slides the chair back into position. He reaches for the bedroom door and it creaks as he pushes it open.*

Sam counted eight seconds of silence—an eternity—and then he heard the faint splatter of liquid as Ostrovsky, obviously in the bathroom with the door open, took a leak. Despite the tension of the situation, the thought of Ginny's reaction brought a smile to his face. Sam's reverie was interrupted by the sudden explosion of water pressure when Ostrovsky flushed the toilet. The water pipes ran behind the linen closet.

9:22:50. The STE in Sam's shirt pocket vibrated like a pacemaker gone berserk. Instinctively he almost reached for it but caught himself in time. One ring. One ring only. But the phone kept vibrating. Three, four, five times. What the hell was Forbes up to?

Finally, the STE went quiet. Sam was perspiring now, standing in the dark closet, his whole body trembling with tension. He forced his breathing to slow, working to calm himself, although his pulse was racing and the hair on the back of his neck was standing up. *Christ, I've been out of the game far too long.* He stared down at the luminous dial on his watch. *9:24:41 . . . 42 . . . 43 . . . 44 . . . 45 . . . 46 . . . 47.*

And then. And then, he heard the second key in the front door lock. Not daring to breathe, he eased the pistol out of the holster and held it parallel to his right leg. His hand tight around the butt, his right index finger straight against the frame, just as Forbes had instructed him.

The spring-hinged front door closed itself, the latch shutting with a click so loud Sam almost jumped. He heard the scrape of leather soles on the wood flooring. And then a voice: "*Salut*, Nikolai Sergeievich. *Comment tu vas?*"

Sam's blood ran cold. His hand tightened around the pistol. His finger slipped onto the trigger. He had to force it back onto the gun's frame.

Ostrovsky's gruff voice answered, but in English. "This was your signal, not mine."

"I beg to differ. But no matter. There's enough to discuss."

"Is there a problem?"

"The senator seems to feel there is. The senator is getting nervous."

"And you?"

"When the senator gets nervous, I become very uneasy."

"You must reassure him."

"He believes the whole thing is falling apart. I'm not so sure he's wrong. Using Ed Howard was a huge mistake. So was bringing Waterman back into the game."

"That was the idea—the bull in the china shop."

"Except Waterman isn't following the script. He's dropped out of sight. I'm certain now he picked up Howard's materials in Moscow. God knows what he's done with them."

"We factored that eventuality in. That was the reason for Semonov."

"Semonov was always a loose cannon, Nikolai Sergeievich. We can't be certain what he told Waterman."

"Semonov gave Waterman exactly what he was instructed to give. Howard was Casey's man in Moscow. His Alec Leamas. Semonov even passed the confirmation signal as he left the restaurant. That is why we were able to . . . conclude the operation successfully."

"And off the poor son of a bitch before you had a chance to debrief him thoroughly? Waterman is talented, Nikolai Sergeievich. He might have gotten something out of Semonov. Something small but significant—which you wouldn't have known until the debrief."

"It is unlikely."

"You're too goddamn self-assured. I keep telling you that

intelligence is an ever-changing petri dish, and you have to keep your eyes open as events modulate. But no: you people are so damn doctrinaire. KGB, SVR—nothing changes. You somehow always manage to combine the two worst characteristics of espionage in your operations. You're inflexible, and you adore labyrinthine scenarios. It's been more than a decade since the Soviet Union imploded. Haven't you learned anything from us?"

"We have learned quite a lot from you over the past twelve years, Edward. P████. TOP HAT. VERMILLION—a dozen other programs as well. CIA considers SVR a sister service. As a part of the international war on terror we have a liaison relationship with Langley. SVR's director is invited to the seventh floor for lunch with Director Becker once a year. Putin and Klimov are geniuses. Don't lecture me on tradecraft or philosophy."

Sam couldn't wait. He exploded out of the closet, pistol in hand. "Jeezus fucking Christ."

Michael O'Neill spun around, wide-eyed. For an instant, he went ashen-faced. Then the color returned to his cheeks. "Cyrus N. PRINGLE—in what's known as light disguise, if memory serves," he said. "Fancy meeting you here on Thanksgiving Day." His gaze dropped to the weapon in Sam's hand. "And armed, no less."

The lawyer turned to Ostrovsky. "I don't believe you've been introduced. Nikolai, this is Samuel Elbridge Waterman, CIA retired. You've probably heard of Sam. He was a friend of Pavel Baranov's. Sam, this is Nikolai Sergeievich Ostrovsky of the Russian Foreign Intelligence Service."

Ostrovsky's watery gray eyes flickered in Sam's direction. He was a short, stout, bald man in a very well-tailored three-piece suit. His ears were red and his pockmarked, bulldog face resembled the Frank the Pug character in *Men in Black II*. Sam noted that both Ostrovsky and O'Neill had shed their coats but they were both wearing latex gloves. O'Neill's tradecraft certainly had improved.

"I must be going now," Ostrovsky said in accent-free English. He glared at Sam. "You know the rules, Mr. Waterman."

Sam pointed the muzzle of the pistol at the Russian's belly. "I know only Moscow Rules, Mr. Ostrovsky. Besides, I'm no government official, so you stay right where you are."

There was a "shave and a haircut" rap on the door. Sam took three steps backward, turned the knob, eased the door open, waited until John Forbes stepped inside, and was gratified by Michael O'Neill's horrified expression. "You remember Assistant Director of the FBI John Forbes, Michael. He was LEGATT in Paris. He—" Sam was interrupted by a pounding noise and muffled screams coming from the bedroom. He looked at Forbes and was reassured to see the Glock semiauto in his right hand. "You comfortable?"

"I feel right at home, Elbridge."

"Good." Sam slipped past the dinette table and disappeared into the bedroom, sidled past the bed, and yanked on the wedged closet door until it opened, revealing a red-faced, hyperventilating Ginny Vacario.

"Damn door stuck on me, Sam. I couldn't hear anything not a single word and I thought I'd put you in danger not to mention I thought I was going to have a panic attack. I'm so sorry. And then—"

"It's okay," he cut her off, "Forbes is here."

Vacario took a deep breath and exhaled audibly. She rubbed her eyes. "You got them."

"C'mon." He allowed her to precede him into the living room.

She pulled the door open. "Holy Mother of God—Michael." From behind, Sam watched Ginny's shoulders sag. Her body language said it all.

O'Neill stared at Forbes. "You've screwed up big time, John-boy," he said.

"Oh?"

"Idiot. Numbskull. This is a recruitment. Have you any idea how long we've been working this guy?"

"Probably not as long as he's been working you," Forbes said. "Tell you what—we'll straighten this all out downtown."

"I protest," Ostrovsky interrupted.

"Duly noted." Forbes looked over at Sam. "I guess it's time to switch the recorders off."

That was when Ostrovsky bolted for the door. Forbes never appeared to move. But Ostrovsky was suddenly on the living room floor, gasping for breath.

Forbes looked at O'Neill. "Michael, you want any?"

O'Neill's hands went up in surrender. "There'll be no trouble from me," he said. "We can straighten this out with a simple phone call."

Sam said, "And that would be a phone call to . . ."

"My boss."

"Vlad Putin?"

O'Neill flashed Sam a nasty look. "Easy does it, Cyrus. Things ain't what they appear to be."

"In this particular case, Michael, I think they're exactly what they appear to be."

"Which is why I'm going to call the DCI, and then Rand Arthur," O'Neill said. He dropped his arms to his sides. "When you understand how we set this operation up, you'll realize why we had to keep you"—he swiveled toward Vacario—"and you, too, Ginny, in the dark. Everything was just too damn precarious." He paused to see how the monologue was playing. When he realized it wasn't, he said, "Fact: Ostrovsky is my developmental. Fact: Rand Arthur can confirm it. Fact: retirement is just another form of cover. That's the truth. Because you can corroborate what I'm saying with the senator, or with Nick Becker. One phone call."

O'Neill was following textbook case-officer procedure: *Deny everything. Admit nothing. File countercharges.* "No phone calls, Michael."

But somehow, O'Neill already had a cell phone in his hand.

Before he could switch it on, Sam launched himself, wrestled it out of the lawyer's grip, pressed the catch on the back, and dropped the battery onto the floor.

"Huh?" Vacario looked puzzled.

"He was going to warn Rand Arthur." Sam brandished the dead phone. "These can be set up to send an emergency signal simply by turning them on in a certain way," he said.

O'Neill, wincing, shook his hand, then turned defiant. "Or by dropping the battery, Cyrus. The technology's been improved since you retired."

Forbes examined the instrument in Sam's hand. "Sorry, Michael, but you're wrong. This particular phone doesn't transmit without a battery." He turned to face Sam. "What's the call, Elbridge?"

Sam pursed his lips. "I think we go to Rand Arthur's," he said. "I've always liked the idea of Thanksgiving in the country."

"I protest," Ostrovsky said. "I'm not going anywhere."

Sam turned toward the Russian. "Then you can stay here." He ran his hand under the dinette table, wrenched the recorder and microphone free, turned the device off, and handed it to Ginny. Then he knelt by the coffee table and repeated the action. He tossed the second recorder to Forbes, who switched it off.

Sam pulled the thick roll of duct tape from where he'd hidden it under the sofa. He taped the Russian's arms tightly behind his back, checked his pockets and removed the man's cell phone, allowed Forbes to check the instrument, then, having received a curt nod, removed the battery and stuck it in his pocket. Then Sam bound Ostrovsky's legs and feet together, rolled him onto the sofa, and taped him immobile. He tore a three-inch length of tape off, then another eight-inch strip and made a gag, which he pressed over the Russian's mouth, running the ends of the strip back behind Ostrovsky's ears.

Then he switched the TV set on. "Make yourself comfortable watching the soaps, Nikolai Sergeievich. We'll send someone for you in a few hours."

CHAPTЭЯ 33

2:38 P.M. Sam felt the suspension of O'Neill's vintage Mercedes give as the car left black macadam and veered onto the three-tenths mile of rutted gravel lane that led to Rand Arthur's Round Hill estate. He lay stuffed rudely onto the rear floorboard, the driveshaft hump wedged uncomfortably against his kidneys, his long legs tucked fetal, his body hidden under a stadium blanket, his mind producing an unsettling series of memories concerning the last time he'd been in this position.

But now things were different. O'Neill was driving, not some young consular officer. And John Forbes was riding shotgun, his Glock stowed at the ready under the fed's left thigh. And Sam could feel the warmth of Ginny Vacario's legs on his rib cage as the car bounced along the washed-out road. This time Sam was in control.

They'd traveled in convoy from Washington. Forbes drove with O'Neill; Ginny and Sam followed behind in the G-man's Bureau wheels, a huge silver Mercury with concealed red and blue flashers behind the grille and five radio antennas on its trunk lid. Three miles north of Round Hill they'd stashed the big sedan and transferred into O'Neill's ride.

It all began to make sense now. O'Neill's sudden illness in Moscow—giving him time to receive instructions from an SVR officer masquerading as a room-service waiter. And the outrageous performance at the police station in the Ukrainian quarter. It was designed to make sure they'd be PNG'd.

Except Sam had managed to find Ed Howard's materials. And Howard, ever the incompetent, had provided Sam with the clues to pursue the truth—or at least a shard of the truth. Which ultimately had led them here—back to the start of the maze Sam had entered on his forty-fifth birthday in Moscow.

"We're here," O'Neill said. " 'Home is the sailor, home from the sea, and the hunter home from the hill.' " He paused. "Robert Louis Stevenson, y'know."

Sam was wary of O'Neill's puckishness. "Be smart, Michael," he growled from under the blanket.

"Don't you worry, Cyrus. I am with the program."

Forbes said: "Car ahead."

"I'll flash my lights twice, just as I always do." O'Neill's voice was calm and even.

Sam felt the Mercedes slow and felt a rush of cool air as O'Neill lowered his window and called out to the rolling roadblock. "Hi, guys—just me and a couple of friends."

Still, Sam held his breath until O'Neill picked up speed and he felt the ruts and potholes of the road give way to the scrunch of the pea gravel that covered the long, arced driveway.

As the car came round the top of the curve, it gained some speed. Then O'Neill slowed to make the tight turn that Sam remembered would take him onto a small circle in whose center stood an ancient willow. Except O'Neill applied the brakes—hard, and the vehicle came to an abrupt stop.

Sam muttered: "What's up?"

Ginny said, "Stay quiet," and shifted her position, adjusting the stadium blanket that covered her legs—and most of Sam's body.

O'Neill's voice: "Hey, Desmond, happy Thanksgiving. Whassup, guy?"

"Sorry to have to hold you up, Mr. O'Neill, but you weren't expected."

"No prob, man." There was a pause. "Just some last-minute details Ms. Vacario and I have to work out with the senator. Brought the feds with me, too—this is FBI Assistant Director John Forbes. John, this is Sergeant Desmond Reese of the U.S. Capitol *po*-lice. Nation's finest."

Forbes's voice: "Nice to meet you, Sergeant. I'll bet you'd like to be home with your family instead of standing post out here."

"Roger that, sir."

"Well, me, too. You stay safe now, Sergeant."

"Thank you, sir—you, too." Sam could hear the muffled sounds of radio transmission. Then Reese's voice: "You're clear to go ahead, Mr. O'Neill. Senator will meet you in the library. Happy Thanksgiving."

"You, too." Sam felt the vibration as O'Neill raised the window, put the car in gear, and drove ahead slowly. Forbes said, "The senator must be a little nervous these days, Elbridge. Think you have anything to do with that?"

The car slowed to a crawl. John Forbes said, "Pull around there, Michael, out of the cop's direct line of sight." The Mercedes moved what Sam figured was another fifteen feet, then stopped. Forbes's voice stage-whispered, "Michael, I'm turning the ignition off and taking the key. You open the driver's side door, then keep both hands on the steering wheel while I get out and come around to your side of the car. Got it?"

"Affirmative, John."

"Good."

Sam heard the doors open. Then he felt the front seat move forward. Ginny's legs lifted off Sam's frame. "Sam, you can get out now."

Sam went to his hands and knees and crawled from the back onto the cold gravel of the driveway. He stood up. Stretched. He reached back inside and pulled the long metal box he'd taken the previous night from the Senate Select offices and cradled it in his left arm.

Ginny said, "Disguise," and Sam reacted, straightening the mustache and adjusting the hairpiece and prosthetics.

Forbes crooked his index finger to summon O'Neill out of the car. The lawyer adjusted the chain that hung across his vest. "I'll need my briefcase, John. It's in the trunk."

"I'll get it for you." The G-man unlocked the boot, retrieved an ancient leather briefcase, opened it, peered inside, riffled the papers, poked the bottom, then closed the bag up and thrust it into O'Neill's arms. "Here."

The lawyer clutched the big case like a football and turned toward the hand-finished door adjacent to the big garage, his polished brogues scrunching on the gravel. "This way, please."

2:43. They entered a long corridor redolent of cinnamon, apples, and roasting turkey that led past the Spainsh-tiled kitchen where a trio of women in starched white chef's tunics were preparing the senator's Thanksgiving dinner. O'Neill turned into a narrow passageway. They marched through a pantry and small wet bar, then made their way to the thick, ornate library door. O'Neill punched the cipher lock, waited for it to click, turned the handle, pushed the door open, and stood aside. "After you, gents."

"No way, Michael." Forbes nudged the lawyer through the doorway first.

Rand Arthur was standing in front of the huge stone fireplace, flipping through the pages of a leather-bound book as the mournful tones of Mahler's *Kindertotenlieder* reverberated through the high-ceilinged room. He turned as the group came through the door, his left hand signaling that he was in the middle of something and he'd be with them as soon as he was finished. His eyes flickered in Sam's direction, but there was no sign of recognition, even as Sam was closing the door behind them and quietly throwing the dead bolt.

The senator slapped the covers of the book shut, then turned to face his attorney. "Michael, what was so urgent?"

O'Neill stood aside for John Forbes. "Senator Arthur," the G-man began, "I'm Assistant FBI Director John Forbes." He brandished his credential so Rand could see it. "We have some disturbing news relating to national security. I wonder if you'd join us over here." He indicated the kilim-covered sofa.

The senator gave Forbes a quizzical look. "I'd be pleased," he said warily. Then he set the book on the edge of the ornate wooden mantel, crossed the room, and dropped into the black leather wing chair facing the door.

Forbes indicated that Michael O'Neill should sit on the edge of the desk. The lawyer complied, dropping the briefcase between his feet.

The G-man turned to Virginia Vacario. "Perhaps you might take notes, counselor."

That was when Rand Arthur realized what Sam was cradling in his left arm. And that it was indeed Sam.

"You," he gasped. *"You!"*

Rand Arthur tried to push himself out of the wing char. Forbes forced him back. "You stay right there, sir, please."

Sam pulled on his latex gloves, lay the metal box on the coffee table, and flipped the lid open. "You're SCARAB, Senator. Remember SCARAB? Ed Howard told us about SCARAB—he was sitting on this sofa."

"Impossible." Rand Arthur bristled. But his face had

turned ashen. "Even if I were this SCARAB, there's very little you can actually do, my boy," he said.

"I don't see it that way, Senator."

The color returned to Rand Arthur's cheeks. "You don't get it. None of you people get it."

Sam said, "Perhaps you'd like to explain yourself, then."

"It's quite simple actually. Consider the implications of frog-marching me out of here in handcuffs. A high-ranking member of the president's party. Incoming chairman of SSCI. The Bush administration would be DOA, Sam. There'd be calls for impeachment. The war on terror would be fatally affected. Iraq? The invasion would never happen. Saddam Hussein would go on building up his weapons programs until the Israelis decided they couldn't allow things to develop further and launch a nuclear strike against him, starting a regional conflict that could go on for years. And I can tell you truthfully, Sam, that I never passed a single document. Not one. All I ever did was give Moscow a sense of what the U.S. position might be—and I emphasize the word 'might.' I provided Moscow a heads-up. Nothing more. I turned over no more information than any political officer at the Moscow embassy when they gossip with their Russian counterparts at a cocktail party."

Sam said nothing.

"Now," he continued, "the question of Michael O'Neill is something else to consider."

Sam said, "Oh?"

"I can't condone what Michael has done."

"You idiot," O'Neill exploded. *"Mudak. Zalupa."*[53]

Sam cast a quick glance at O'Neill. The lawyer's Russian was pretty good for someone who wasn't supposed to speak any.

---

[53] Dumb-ass; dickhead.

"Michael O'Neill asked me to have you killed," Rand Arthur continued. "The contents of that safe-deposit box belong to Michael, not to me. I swear it."

"Oh, Senator!" Ginny's voice was so loud she startled herself. She looked at Forbes. "It's not true, John."

"Not to worry, Ginny." Forbes looked down at Rand Arthur. "So we won't find your fingerprints on the money, Senator, or the inside of the lid?"

The expression on Rand Arthur's face told Sam the senator hadn't thought of that particular detail.

Forbes continued: "Or on the agreement form signed by the cop outside."

"That was Michael's idea, too," Rand Arthur said, his eyes imploring. "He panicked after Moscow—told me you were a double. Said everything was compromised and you had to be eliminated."

Sam looked contemptuously at Rand Arthur. "Tell me the truth, Senator. Give me something I can believe."

"You have to understand, Sam. I was telling the truth when I said I never gave them anything more than cocktail-party gossip. That's all they asked for."

"How did they hook you, Senator?"

Rand Arthur's tone grew desperate. "I was never *hooked*, Sam."

Sam's fingers rapped the metal box. "So you received what's in here for being a nice guy."

Rand Arthur's eyes swept from Sam to Forbes. "There was one thing and one thing only they ever asked me for."

"Which was?"

"When I became chairman of SSCI—"

Vacario said, "*When* you became chairman?"

"I always knew, Ginny. I always knew I'd get the chairmanship if the elections went right." Rand Arthur looked in her direction. "And even if I was only ranking member, I was still to put pressure on the White House to get rid of Nick Becker."

He swiveled toward Sam. "With justification, Sam. Believe me, I have been doing CIA oversight for six years now and the Agency is completely dysfunctional. Just look at everything that's happened on Nick's watch. CIA gave NATO the wrong coordinates, so we bombed the Chinese embassy in Belgrade. Until after we invaded Afghanistan, we had no unilateral assets there. We still have no unilateral assets in Iraq, either, Sam—not a one. They all belong to the Brits, the French, or to Ahmed Chalabi's Iraqi National Congress. The station chief in Riyadh doesn't even speak Arabic. The Moscow Station chief has two-level Russian—which means he speaks it like a four-year-old. I had no problem with that request, believe me, Sam. Nick Becker is an utter disaster."

"That was all?"

"Everything."

It didn't make sense. Sam hooked his head in Rand Arthur's direction. "Senator," he began, "the night back in 1993 you met Primakov. Did anyone from the Russian delegation speak to you?"

"Just Primakov—on the receiving line." Rand turned to Michael O'Neill. "Isn't that right, Michael?" The senator swiveled back to face Sam. "Michael was with me that night."

Which is when the ten-thousand-watt flashbulb went off in Sam's head. Rand Arthur wasn't SCARAB. Rand was another in the long list of disposables. An agent of influence. A stooge. A puppet. Michael O'Neill was SCARAB. The degree of loathing and rage Sam felt at that instant could not be quantified. And then, like the pins falling into place when he'd picked the lock on Hart 211, Sam's brain turned the plug and rolled the figurative dead bolt open. "Senator, whom would you have pushed to replace Nick Becker as DCI?"

Rand Arthur blinked. "Why, Michael, of course. For years Michael has told me he wants the job. He would have gotten it, too."

That was Klimov's goal. Charlotte had called it correctly. Everything had begun in Paris, when the Russians spotted, assessed, and recruited Michael O'Neill. Klimov's long-term operation to put Moscow's man on the seventh floor of Langley. Moscow's man. Michael O'Neill. Sam's protégé.

Sam started to hyperventilate. He was so enraged he couldn't bring himself to look at the . . . creature who'd betrayed him. Who'd lied every step of the way. Who'd blown the church mailbox op in Moscow on purpose. Who'd had Pavel Baranov murdered. And Edward Lee Howard. And Irina. And Alexei Semonov, and who knew how many others. "Senator—"

Rand Arthur cut Sam off. "Isn't that right, Michael?" The senator looked over to the desk where O'Neill had parked himself. "Michael has always said—oh, my *God!*"

Sam jerked around. O'Neill was holding Sam's suppressed Browning Hi-Power on his right thigh. The mouth of the briefcase at O'Neill's feet was open.

Sam's eyes flashed toward John Forbes, whose expression instructed Sam not to do anything rash.

"I told you never to talk about our secret handshake, Rand." As the lawyer slid off the desk he brought the pistol up in a two-handed grip. He took two steps, bringing him six feet from Rand Arthur's chair. The gun bucked in his hand as he shot the senator twice in the side of the head.

Vacario screamed.

Rand Arthur, already dead, twitched half a dozen times and then folded onto the floor.

Sam started toward the lawyer, but O'Neill had already backed around behind Virginia Vacario. He put the fat suppressor muzzle up against her head. "Don't screw with me, anybody."

He looked at John Forbes. "Take your pistol out, John, throw it on the couch, and step away to the fireplace."

Forbes did as instructed.

"Now you, Sam."

"I don't have a gun, Michael." Sam had returned the backup pistol, as well as the bogus FBI ID and shield to Forbes as soon as they'd left the Idaho Avenue apartment.

"Show me."

Sam opened his suit coat, spread the jacket wide, and turned all the way around.

"Okay—stand with him." O'Neill watched as Sam joined John Forbes by the fireplace. "Counselor, you walk with me to the door." With O'Neill holding her by her upper arm, pistol muzzle to her head, the two of them started across the room.

Action was useless of course. Sam had taken enough self-defense classes to understand that in the split second it would take to pull the Hi-Power's single-action trigger, Ginny would be dead before he'd gotten five feet closer to O'Neill.

The lawyer punched the cipher combination into the lock, opened the door, and backed out, pulling Vacario with him.

Sam didn't waste a millisecond. He dashed for the door, Forbes followed, picking up his pistol on the way and shoving it into its holster.

The damn door opened inward. There was no way to kick it off its frame.

Forbes said, "We knock the hinge pins out." Then he looked at the hinges and saw the pins were enclosed.

Sam said, "O'Neill won't be taking the Mercedes very far, John. He has an escape plan—got to. That's the tradecraft."

The G-man cocked his head. "How do you know?"

"Edward Lee Howard. He disappeared from this room.

Had a car stashed somewhere—probably in the same general area O'Neill has one stashed."

"How did Howard get away?"

Sam pointed toward the window behind Rand Arthur's desk. "He pried the lock."

The two men ran to the window. The cheap lock had been replaced with a heavy, double dead-bolt arrangement.

Forbes said, "Jeezus, Elbridge." He sprinted to the fireplace and grabbed the big brass poker from its rack. "Goddammit, Sam—time to rake and break."

Then he snatched one of the arm protectors off the big padded arm of the couch, vaulted onto the heavy credenza behind the desk, wrapped his left hand with the arm protector, held the poker in a two-handed bayonet grip, thrust its tip through the upper-right-hand corner of the window, and using the wooden stile as a guide, raked the heavy shaft down the glass, across the bottom, then up the opposite stile and across the top rail, shattering the pane and splintering the wooden sash bars.

"Follow me." Forbes lunged over the glass through the empty frame. Sam was two steps behind, and like Forbes, plunged headfirst into the ornamental hedge of thornbushes planted outside.

"Oh, goddammit to hell." Sam brought his arm up to cover his eyes as he rolled onto the ground, found his footing, scrambled to his feet, and got his bearings. He looked left, then right, then pointed toward the side of the mansion leading to the front drive. "This way."

Forbes had his pistol drawn as they came around the corner. O'Neill still had Vacario by the arm. They were heading for the Mercedes. Just beyond them, he saw Desmond Reese.

Sam shouted, "Michael—"

Just as O'Neill brought the pistol up and fired half a dozen quick shots at the Capitol police officer. Sam could hear the suppressed shots popping as the rounds missed and ricocheted off the gravel. Reese rolled to his right and ducked behind the willow in the center of the circular driveway.

Sam shouted, "Ginny—get down. Hit the deck!"

Vacario twisted out of O'Neill's grasp and fell prone. The lawyer tried to grab her arm and stand her up but she was deadweight now and not moving. He left her lying where she was and scrambled for his car.

Forbes screamed at the top of his lungs, "Reese, Reese—O'Neill shot the senator. Stop him!" He dragged Sam to cover behind a tree. "Reese?" He dropped to one knee. "Christ, I think he was hit."

Sam snuck a look. O'Neill was crouched at the rear of the Mercedes, his left hand working under the bumper, the right still clutching the pistol. "Michael's looking for a spare key."

That was when Reese emerged from behind the willow tree, his pistol in a two-handed combat grip. O'Neill looked up. But it was too late. The cop advanced, firing again and again until he'd emptied his gun into the lawyer. He stood above O'Neill's corpse, dropped the magazine from his weapon, loaded a new one, released the slide to chamber a fresh round, then holstered the Glock. He rolled O'Neill over with his foot, knelt, roughly pinioned the dead man's arms behind his back, and handcuffed the wrists together.

Forbes and Sam emerged from behind cover. "I'll deal with the police stuff, Elbridge," Forbes rasped. "This has just become one bodaciously humongous crime scene. You go grab the lady."

"Gotcha."

"And take off all the spy crap."

"Wilco." Sam ███████ the prosthetic, removed the mustache, hairpiece, and gloves, and jammed them into his pocket as he ran to where Vacario lay. Sam knelt, slipped an arm under her, rolled her onto her side, then sat her up on the gravel.

"I think I turned my ankle."

He brought her close. "Lean on me."

"I'd like that, Sam." She turned to him. She had tears in her eyes. "I'd like that very much."

Sam held her close and kissed her gently on the forehead. Then he brought her to her feet.

He glanced toward O'Neill's corpse. Sam was torn. Part of him was glad the son of a bitch was dead. But the intelligence professional in Sam wanted O'Neill alive so he could be debriefed. Sucked dry. Left desiccated. He shifted his attention to Vacario, holding her tightly as the two of them made their way across the gravel.

"It's over," she said.

Sam knew better. He looked back at O'Neill then at her. "It's never over, Ginny."

"What do you mean?"

Sam's head jerked toward the traitor's body. "SCARAB's dead."

"Precisely. So it's over."

"No. SCEPTRE's still out there."

"Christ almighty, isn't it time to let someone else worry about SCEPTRE? If there really is a SCEPTRE." She stopped in her tracks, turned to face him, clasped his hand between her palms, and brought her hands and his to eye level. "It's time to let go, Sam. You're retired."

He looked at her face and all that it promised. "Maybe," he said. "But then again . . . maybe not. You heard what they say at Moscow Center, Ginny. They say retirement's just another form of cover."

DIRECT ACTION

A Covert War Thriller
by John Weisman
Available in hardcover

An off-the-books black ops team must locate and eliminate a group of terrorists in this compulsive page-turner based on true life CIA casework and military intelligence. . . . "Nobody writes better about the dark, dirty, and dangerous world of the CIA and black ops. John Weisman's knowledge and research are phenomenal."—Joseph Wambaugh

In *Direct Action*, the celebrated author of *Jack in the Box* and *SOAR* takes readers deep into the world of highly secret CIA and DOD paramilitary operations, shadow warfare waged by special "civilian contract personnel"—former SWAT cops, SEALs, Delta operators, Rangers, and Recon Marines—against terrorists across the Middle East and southeast Asia.

Moving between Israel, Jordan, Paris, London, and Washington, these lethal specialists must target and destroy a Western-educated Islamist and a notorious Palestinian crime family with access to WMD in the West Bank and Gaza—and double agents within their own ranks. . . .

ON SEPTEMBER 21, 1995, at 11:47 AM, five senior officers from the Central Intelligence Agency's Directorate of Operations—the CIA's clandestine service—quietly gathered in Room 4D-627A, one of the sensitive compartmentalized information facilities colloquially known as bubble rooms, on the fourth floor of the headquarters building at Langley, Virginia. The Agency was still reeling from the February 1994 arrest of Aldrich Hazen Ames. Ames, an alcoholic, money-hungry wreck of a career case officer, had betrayed dozens of America's most valuable Russian agents to the KGB, resulting in their arrests and executions. He had also handed over many of CIA's technical tradecraft secrets and the identities of American undercover operatives.

Two of the clandestine officers at the meeting had been tasked with writing a Top Secret/Codeword damage assessment of the Ames debacle, a preliminary draft of which, at their peril, they were now sharing with three of their most trusted colleagues.

The assessment was grim. One had, it said, to assume that CIA had been completely penetrated because of Ames's treason. The Agency, therefore, was now transparent. Not only to the opposition, which still included Moscow, but to all of Moscow's current clients, including Libya, Syria, Sudan, and Iraq and—equally if not more critical—to the transnational terrorist organizations supported by those states. Transparency meant that the entire structure of the Directorate of Operations had to be considered as compromised; that every operation, every agent, every case officer was now known to the opposition and its allies.

The only way to ensure that the clandestine service could survive in the coming years, the seniormost of the report writers suggested to his colleagues, would be to build a whole new and totally sterile spy organization inside CIA— a *covert* clandestine service within the *overt* clandestine service. But such a Utopian solution, all five knew, would be impossible to achieve. The current Director of Central Intelligence, John M. Deutch, would never allow it. Deutch, a tall, bumbling, angular, bookish MIT professor of chemistry who served as undersecretary of defense, had been sent over from the Pentagon the previous May to clean CIA's post-Ames house. Instead of selecting savvy advisors to help ease his way into Langley's unique culture, the new director— himself a neophyte in matters of spycraft—brought with him as his closest aides two individuals neither of whom had any operational intelligence experience.

Deutch's Executive Director was Nora Slatkin, a presidential appointee assistant secretary of the Navy. His deputy and right arm was George John Tenet, an NSC staffer who'd toiled on Capitol Hill for Senator David Boren among others. It didn't take more than a few weeks for the great majority of seasoned intelligence professionals of CIA's clandestine service, the Directorate of Operations or DO, to detest all three. The situation was made even worse when Deutch appointed David Cohen, a DI (Directorate of Intelligence) reports officer, to head the DO. Cohen, the corridor gossip went, absolutely *detested* spying and those who did it.

So no one was surprised that it took only a few months for Deutch and his associates to promulgate a series of orders that, in effect, prevented CIA's clandestine service from . . . spying. Under the new rules of engagement, every agent who had a criminal record, or was suspected of human rights violations, or who might be involved in any kind of criminal or terrorist activity was to be jettisoned. Dumped. Ditched. Discarded. Their agent networks were to be disassembled.

By the September 21 meeting, more than half of CIA's foreign agents had been struck from the rolls and their names erased from BigPond, CIA's computer database run by Nora Slatkin's Administrative Division. More than 50 productive agent networks in Europe, the Middle East, South America, and Asia were summarily disbanded. Unable to recruit the sorts of unsavory but productive individuals it had targeted in the past, American intelligence quickly found itself going deaf, dumb and blind. After the BigPond debacle the old hands started referring to Slatkin as "Tora-Tora" Nora.

And voting with their feet. By summer's end of 1995, more than 240 experienced case officers—forty percent of those with more than 15 years field experience—had resigned or taken early retirement. The Agency's Counterterrorism Center (CTC) had been eviscerated, with many of its physical and technical assets either eliminated altogether, or handed over to other agencies including CIA's detested rival, the Federal Bureau of Investigation. CTC operations at Rhine-Main airport, Frankfurt, where its European crisis-management "crash team" was forward-deployed, was shut down completely.

It wasn't long before it was proudly announced during a closed-door session of the House Permanent Select Committee on Intelligence (HPSCI), that the new CIA leadership was saving more than three point six billion dollars annually by closing nine CIA stations in sub-Saharan Africa, and CIA's bases[1] in half a dozen Western European cities. The rationale was that with the Cold War over, America didn't need to keep tabs on Soviet agents anymore and the Agency outposts in such places as Düsseldorf, Barcelona, Marseille, and Milan were superfluous.

Alan Martin, CIA's Assistant Deputy Director for Collection, couldn't get an appointment with Deutch or his deputy George Tenet. So he finally corralled one of Tenet's growing army of special assistants in the cafeteria. He explained that the bases could be used to keep an eye on the growing number of Islamist radicals living in Germany, Spain, France, and Italy.

Martin was greeted with a blank stare. *Islamist radicals*? Who the hell cared about Islamist radicals living in Düsseldorf? We are into saving money here. Get with the program, Al, he was told, or get lost.

But that wasn't the worst part. The worst part was the tectonic shift taking place in the quality of the DO's people. The situation wasn't new: under previous directors William Webster and Robert M. Gates, DO had been forced to accept within its ranks analysts, reports officers, and secretaries, few of whom had either the inclination or the ability to spot, assess, and recruit agents to spy for America. The prissy Gates even had a politically correct term for it: "cross-fertilization."

Now, under Deutch, Slatkin, Tenet, and Cohen, the vacuum left by the loss of experienced case officers was being

---

[1] A CIA base is a small intelligence operation that functions as a satellite to the main intelligence gathering unit, the CIA station, which is normally quartered in an embassy or in some cases a consulate general. The CIA station in Germany, for example, is physically located within the U.S. Embassy in Berlin. There were, at one point, CIA bases in Frankfurt, Düsseldorf, Hamburg, and Munich. All were closed between 1995–2000.

filled by a growing torrent of unskilled, naïve, risk-averse individuals who had no field experience. None whatsoever. Zip. Zilch. Zero. Analysts had already been appointed as chiefs of station in Tel Aviv, Riyadh, Nairobi, and Lisbon. A reports officer was running Warsaw. A former secretary with only six months of training had been made station chief in Kiev. *Kiev*, with Ukraine's vast store of Soviet-era nuclear weapons. Geezus, it was like appointing a hospital's chief file clerk to head its neurosurgical team.

12:26 PM. The five men in 4D-627A had more than 100 years of combined intelligence work under their belts. Between them there wasn't a region anywhere on the globe that they weren't familiar with.

Until Deutch had replaced him with a reports officer, Bronco—for Bronislaw—Panitz had been CIA's Assistant Deputy Director for Operations. Panitz had served in Eastern Europe. He'd been chief in Budapest and Singapore, come back to run Agency operations in Western Europe, then gone out again, this time to Madrid. At 55, Bronco still had the imposing build of an NFL fullback. He worked out in Langley's gym four days a week, pumping iron and playing the same kind of full-contact, half-court basketball he'd first learned on the streets of Manhattan's Yorkville neighborhood as a teenager.

Antony Wyman currently ran CIA's much-reduced Counterterrorism Center. But the corridor gossip said he was about to be eased out, replaced by someone who'd be more compliant to the new director's wishes. Wyman was known as tony Tony because he was a complete and devoted Anglophile. His MA (History, honors) was from Cambridge. He wore bespoke chalk-striped London-tailored suits, loud Turnbull & Asser shirts, even louder T&A ties, and bench-made brown suede shoes from John Lobb. A gold-rimmed monocle customarily hung on a black silk ribbon around his neck, and a silk foulard square perpetually drooped from his breast pocket.

But Tony Wyman was no more a foppish dandy than the Scarlet Pimpernel. He'd served as chief in London, where he'd helped MI5 and MI6 put a dent in IRA terrorism, and in Rome, where he'd pressed SISMI, the Italian military intelligence service, to dismember the Red Brigades piece by piece. After Rome, tony Tony had been assigned by DCI William Casey to destroy the Abu Nidal Organization. The ANO had just killed five Americans during simultaneous December 27, 1985, attacks on TWA and El Al passengers at international airports in Rome and Vienna, and Casey wanted to put them out of business.

"You do what you have to, Tony," Casey bellowed, spewing tuna salad as he spoke. He dropped the half-eaten sandwich onto its plate and slapped his cluttered desk for emphasis. "I want that rotten son of a bitch's head on a pike right next to our front gate. So don't you let me down."

Tony Tony had brushed the director's food from his strié velvet vest and gone to work. By the middle of 1987, a series of Wyman-devised covert action programs had turned Abu Nidal into a paranoid psychotic. That November, he machine-gunned 160 of his own people. Two weeks later, the terrorist chief ordered 170 of ANO's Libyan-based operatives killed. By the end of the year, he'd tortured and murdered more than 400 of his closest associates because Wyman's covert action program had convinced Abu Nidal they might be leaking information to CIA. By 1988, the ANO ceased to be a serious threat.

Charles Hoskinson, the oldest officer at the meeting, was a lifelong Arabist. Short and round-faced, with longish, wispy white hair and neutral gray eyes set off by old-fashioned, tortoise shell round-framed spectacles, Hoskinson presented a lot more of Bob Cratchit than he did James Bond. But his string of achievements was nothing short of remarkable.

In 1972, as Damascus chief of station—Hoskinson's first COS posting—he managed to recruit the brother of the Syrian

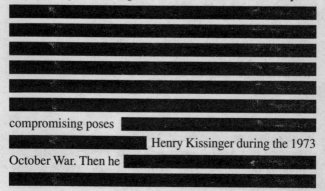

compromising poses

Henry Kissinger during the 1973 October War. Then he

As chief in Beirut during the bloody Lebanese Civil War, Hoskinson maintained a clandestine backchannel relationship with the PLO that had included chaperoning Ali Hassan Salameh, Black September's chief of operations, the architect of the Munich Olympics massacre, and a CIA developmental, on a 1977 honeymoon vacation to Hawaii with his new Lebanese wife, the former Miss Universe Georgina Rizak. Hoskinson even tried to teach Salameh how to scuba dive, but discovered that the man who'd cold-bloodedly ordered the deaths of so many hundreds got claustrophobic and panicked underwater.

In Cairo, where he'd served from 1978 through 1981, Hoskinson was not only responsible for helping to guide Egyptian president Anwar el-Sadat through the negotiations that had resulted in the Camp David peace treaty, but he also convinced Sadat that it was in Egypt's long-term interests to throw the Soviets out—something Sadat did mere weeks before his October 13, 1981, assassination.

Hoskinson, however, had been sidelined. It happened after the 32-year veteran had refused to terminate MJPLUMBER, a Palestinian agent who'd been involved in the 1987 attempted assassination of the Israeli ambassador to Spain. Sure, PLUMBER had murdered Israelis in the past, and he'd probably do so again if given the chance. But these days he was the one of the PA's highest-ranking West Bank security officials. PLUMBER, however, always had a weakness, a predilection for little boys. It was a vulnerability that had made him an ideal (and successful) candidate for recruitment by Giles T. PRENDERGAST, one of Hoskinson's case officers in the mid-1980s.

Hoskinson was convinced Arafat was going to cheat on Oslo. And PLUMBER, who didn't like the way Arafat was skimming millions without sharing the loot, would divulge how the Chairman planned to do it, since he was now a trusted member of Arafat's inner circle.

But Deutch's troika wanted no part of MJPLUMBER. "I get everything I need from the Israelis," Deutch had reportedly growled. "I don't want some senator complaining that we hire buggering pedophile assassins as agents."

Hoskinson wasn't about to tell the DCI that you don't *hire* an agent, you *recruit* him, because the distinction would have been lost. Despite his entreaties, PLUMBER was cut loose, and CIA was denied its only unilateral access to Arafat's clique. When Charlie went to CIA's Inspector General and filed a formal protest, Deutch's people went ballistic. The DCI summoned Hoskinson to his office and flat-out ordered him to retire. When Hoskinson refused, Deutch loosed his attack dogs to hasten the decision.

Ten days ago, Hoskinson had been forced to become a hall-walker after Tora-Tora Nora had him evicted from his office. Undeterred, he'd set up shop in the cafeteria and used the extension of a friendly NE desk officer to receive messages. But one of the troika's spies had ratted him out.

This very morning, Tenet's toad of an assistant had appeared in the cafeteria with a note instructing Hoskinson to appear forthwith for a psychological exam. Obviously, since Hoskinson hadn't obeyed Deutch's every command he was mentally unstable. An old friend who had access to Deutch's office suite warned Charlie the DCI was going to terminate him with cause.

Hoskinson had spent thirty-four years and three months at CIA. He loved the place and what it stood for, and he was damned if he was going to let Deutch and his people destroy it. Stan Turner, Bobby Gates and Bill Webster had been bad enough. But Deutch, *Geezus H. Keerist*. Hoskinson looked at Tony Wyman. "Goddamnit, Tony—it's time to get off our asses."

P███████,[2] the case officer who'd been tasked to write the majority of the Ames report, blinked. "I agree, Charlie. But what course do we take? I think we should sleep on it. Reconvene tomorrow with some ideas."

"Some of us already know what we have to do, STIGGINS," Hoskinson growled. Even in the bubble room he used the undercover officer's Agency pseudonym, Edward C. STIGGINS. "Ed, you made the perfect suggestion yourself an hour and a half ago. Sleeping on it won't change anything. There's only one element that has to be changed."

"Which is," Wyman continued, "that instead of building a

---

[2]This officer, who retired on ███████ 200█, spent his entire career working under cover. He was listed as a senior Foreign Service officer (rank of Career Minister) of the Department of State when he left government service. Later that same day at a private ceremony on Langley's seventh floor, ███████ was awarded CIA's Intelligence Star for Valor, the Agency's third-highest award, as well as the gold medallion signifying more than 30 years of service. Since ███████s retirement was covert, both awards currently sit in a safe at CIA headquarters.

new DO on the inside, we do it on the outside—and we make a lot of money in the process."

Alan Martin's knuckles rapped the table. "Take the DO private. Brilliant."

"A two-level organization." Wyman polished his monocle. "Level one: overt. A privately held corporation. Commercial and industrial risk and threat assessment, crisis management, and security counseling. Big market. Believe me, I've been approached." He looked at Panitz. "We're talking revenue in the mid-seven figures our first year."

Bronco Panitz caught the look between Hoskinson and Tony Tony. *They'd been plotting this for some time now.*

Wyman shot his French cuffs to display antique $5 gold piece cufflinks. "Level two: covert. We target the areas where the DO is blind—Middle East, Southwest Asia, Africa, etcetera, and then we sell our product—24-karat stuff—back to Langley. For a stiff fee, of course."

"And Langley will pay," Hoskinson said. "Because it's a Potemkin Village these days."

"He's right," Alan Martin grumbled. "There's virtually no human product coming in. It's all liaison and technical."

"Recruiting won't be a problem, believe me," Tony Wyman said. "Deutch is pushing the best people out. I've got commitments from more than a dozen of our colleagues."

Alan Martin had to admit it was brilliant. In order to save the Directorate of Operations from self-destructing, Hoskinson and Tony were suggesting they run the same sort of covert action they'd used successfully in the past against the Soviet Union, China, Iran, and dozens of other nations, political parties, and terrorist groups. But instead of providing information that would destabilize, they'd pass on the intelligence CIA was currently incapable of gathering for itself.

STIGGINS frowned. "Deutch won't like it."

"Deutch won't ever know." When STIGGINS started to object, Bronco Panitz said, "Christ, David Cohen's always contracting annuitants for odd jobs. As well as farming out work to half a dozen consultants."

It was true. Retirees currently ran one-man CIA stations in five sub-Saharan African nations on a contract basis. In the NE bureau, there were two acting branch chiefs who were actually employees of private risk-assessment firms. One had resigned from CIA in 1994, the other in 1995. But because they had current clearances and polygraphs, they'd been hired back—in their old slots no less—because CIA had so few experienced case-officers available with real street experience in the region. The two, who'd retired at the GS-14 level and earned roughly $86,000 a year, were now costing the American taxpayer $1250 per day each, plus benefits: $325,000 a year.

"You'll need a network at headquarters, Tony." Alan Martin's expression grew intense. "Access agents, penetration agents, agents of influence, and most important, *moles*. You know how it is on the seventh floor. It's all about job security. If you don't have a handle on what the seventh floor is thinking, sooner or later they'll scapegoat you."

Tony Wyman fixed the monocle into his right eye and stared first at STIGGINS, then swiveled oh . . . so . . . slowly toward Martin, then panned back again to STIGGINS. He released his facial muscles. The monocle fell. "And your point is . . ."

Alan Martin got the message. "STIGGINS and Martin. It sounds like a Vaudeville act."

Tony Wyman grinned. "It sounds more like the 4D-627 Network to me."

* * *

BY 2:30 PM they'd reached a consensus. An hour and a half later, Antony Wyman, Bronco Panitz, and Charles Hoskinson had started the paperwork for their retirements. When Tony's secretary asked what he planned to do, he said he and a couple of friends were going to open a private security firm.

"What are you going to call it? Wyman and Associates?"

"Wyman and Associates. Has a nice ring to it, m'dear, but perish the thought. Far too . . . *égoïste pour moi*. We are calling ourselves . . . the 4627 Company."